W9-AHP-917

DATE DUE

THE
BUGSPIT
CHRONICLES

THE
BUGSPIT
CHRONICLES

Doc Markin

RUTLEDGE HILL PRESS
Nashville, Tennessee

To the ones that got away
and to those who got even.

Published in Nashville, Tennessee, by Rutledge Hill Press, Inc., 513 Third
Avenue South, Nashville, Tennessee 37210.

Typography by Bailey Typography, Inc., Nashville, Tennessee.

Library of Congress Cataloging-in-Publication Data

Markin, Doc. 1947-
    The bugspit chronicles / Doc Markin.
      p.   cm.
    ISBN 1-55853-028-2
    I. Title.
PS3563.A6647B84   1989   89-34332
813'.54—dc20   CIP

Printed in the United States of America
1 2 3 4 5 6—93 92 91 90 89

THE
BUGSPIT
CHRONICLES

1

The wind was out of the west, bringing with it the distinct odor of the new sewage refinement plant a scant mile away. To Josh it smelled like the men's rooms of every redneck service station in the world had come here to die. The Turd Factory, as he called it, was one of the mayor's "small prices to pay for progress." It had lowered the resale value of Josh's place by about half.

He paused to slam a hand down on the hood of his truck before stepping around and getting in. This was a habit he had developed five years earlier when he had discovered—too late—that Thelma's cat liked to sleep between the warm engine block and the radiator. It had been a fur-blowing mess at the time, involving as it did the replacement of a radiator fan and nearly two hundred dollars for the vet to reupholster the puss, but today the reasons didn't register. He just felt like hitting something.

The engine of his '53 Chevy pickup coughed to life, revved for a couple of seconds, then settled down to a near inaudible purr. It was inaudible, in part due to the baying of several hounds that came running as soon as he'd engaged the starter, but mostly because the engine was in perfect tune. He smiled briefly as he reflected upon having overhauled the engine himself, twice. Over 130,000 miles he'd put on this rig, and it had never failed him. *Something for a man to be proud of,* he thought. *Perhaps the only thing just now.*

A scowl replaced the smile as he put the truck into reverse and honked the horn. The hounds quieted abruptly and left their position behind the truck. When he figured most of them were clear, he popped the clutch and shot backward down the drive. His dogs were renowned car-chasers, but for some reason they seemed to figure the only place to chase one was from behind. He had run over a few before he started honking prior to backing. *Compared to the dogs,* he thought, *the old patchwork cat sitting on the porch, its hide stitched up like a softball, is positively brilliant!* He wondered if perhaps his animals were somehow related by blood to his wife.

The mud-grips sang merrily as Josh ran through the gears and pointed the truck toward what passed for town: Dilbert's Forge. To keep the roar of the tires from lulling him to sleep, he switched on the ancient AM radio and twisted the knobless tuning stem until a station blared out at him. It was a radio evangelist relating how he had personally been called to preaching and telling of God's Plan for all his listeners. Within one minute Josh knew that the preacher had met Him while both were looking at Weedeaters in K-Mart and that His Plan somehow involved the listeners mailing in a few bucks each week. Annoyed, he wrung the opposite stem until the preacher went away.

"There's one born again every minute!" he yelled aloud, aware that Thelma had set the radio's preselect buttons and that each of those would be more of the same.

The countryside rolling past his windshield was beginning to shake off the drab of winter and to come alive. The box elder trees already had their early leaves, and others were beginning to show healthy buds. Here and there in the few yards he passed, brave little buttercups were lifting their heads above the muck of a recent snow. Though there was still a bit of bite to the air, he elected to keep his window rolled halfway down to drink in the rich country essence.

Josh was as close to desperation as he'd ever been, and the drive was as much away from things as toward his last remaining unemployment check. Patches of gravel and left-over road salt spattered under his floorboards in counterpoint to the nasal hum of the mud-grips. *The song of the open road,* he thought. *Maybe I should point this sucker south and hear the whole concert!* The thought was oddly appealing.

Dilbert's Forge wasn't much, just a misnomer. There was no forge anywhere, nor had there ever been. What there was was a *ford,* a shallow crossing of the tire- and trash-choked stream known as Caney Creek. In keeping with the way things were, it was neither particularly caney nor an honest creek. It was a wet weather spring branch that doubled as a storm sewer for the town of two thousand.

Some industrious ladies of the Methodist Auxiliary had re-searched the town's name and had traced it back to the early 1800s and the original settlers. Although they never discovered who Dilbert was, they did come to appreciate the misunder-standing in the name. Elijah Flick, the town's founding father who had come west (from North Carolina), had happened upon the place and taken a liking to it. Elijah had returned with tales of the new land he'd found, with few and friendly Indians and a wealth of limestone springs, at Dilbert's Forge. Elijah, unfortunately for historical accuracy, was harelipped. As a matter of little moment, save only to those who cannot bear to do without such information, Sheamus Gilbert (whose ford it had been) suffered no speech impediment beyond his being Irish.

Its name aside, Dilbert's Forge had much to commend it as towns go in this section of Middle Tennessee. It was incorpo-rated, had city water (fluoride treated), three public schools, TVA electricity, Rotary Club, Lion's Club, 4–H and Eastern Star chapters, and a brand new courthouse. And an even newer sewage refinement plant. Josh wondered about that term. It seemed to imply the human body was incapable of completing the job and that *real* sewage was something to as-pire to, something worthy of a major bond issue.

A sour look crossed his lumberjack face and knitted the bushy brown eyebrows over each dark eye under the bill of his

CAT ball cap. Dilbert's Forge was still a podunk little town where newlyweds picked out a pattern of jelly glasses along with the bride-to-be's maternity clothes and a man's success was largely judged by what model car he had sitting on blocks in his front yard. Josh disliked the place and wouldn't mind moving on. Had to, in fact, if he were to work again.

The "Ba-Da's Grill/Open All Night/Real PIT BAR-B-Q/ Worms and Minnows/Eat Here!" sign over a converted Pure Oil station slid by without notice. Normally he would pause to wonder exactly what Barbara and David Cole (Ba-Da) served that attracted such a diversity of wildlife, but today he just wanted to cruise along breathing the cool air. Past Ba-Da's was the courthouse where, even in the cold, two old men sat like gargoyles along one wide brick banister at the top of the steps, playing checkers.

One of the men, a withered old gent wearing the standard bib overalls and an Army surplus field jacket, looked up from the board long enough to wave a greeting. Josh waved back absently. It was a custom he'd grown used to, and he often initiated the greeting himself. He had to admit, folks here were uncommonly friendly.

Being from all the way down in Florida, he had been something of a celebrity when he moved to Dilbert's Forge and had enjoyed the questions and disbelief the locals expressed when informed that there were, indeed, places where a man could legally buy a beer on Sunday, stores that remained open after dark, and more than three television channels. He later discovered they expressed the same awe toward someone from a mere three counties distant and viewed anyone who had been to both Nashville and Memphis as a world traveler.

The pickup skittered to a halt next to the courthouse, sliding the last two feet in the as yet unmelted ice next to the curb. Josh leaned against the door while pulling up on the worn handle until it popped open with a loud *ca-chunk!* From under the seat he took half a brick that served as his parking brake and wedged it under a front tire. The air moved lazily, but added enough chill to coax his hands into his parka pockets. At the top of the stairs, a wisp of cigar smoke hung like a ghost above the checker players, peeked around the corner to find the wind, then flew off to chase a Sears delivery truck as it rolled past. Josh bounded up the steps two at a time.

"Cold 'un last night, wuddn't it, Jackson?" one of the men asked as Josh arrived next to them.

"It was that, Mr. Peevey. It still don't seem like checker weather, now that you mention it."

Peevey considered this carefully, his chin rising to almost even with the tip of his nose as he sucked in his lips over empty gums. Before he responded, he jammed his King Edward into the center of his mouth and took a long appreciative draw. Peevey's face collapsed in the middle from the effort like a punched pillow. His pause brought the other man, Old Bobby Calous, up from contemplating strategy to consider this meteorological observation as well. Old Bobby had been Big Bobby when his son, Little Bobby, was younger and weighed less than three hundred pounds. Now Little Bobby had a Littler Bobby of his own and had inherited Big Bobby's name. It was about all the legacy he would get.

"Might be right about that, Jackson. What do you think, Bobby?"

Josh almost groaned as Old Bobby's eyes glazed over in thought. The process was quickened by a train whistle announcing the advance of the L & N three-thirty load of lime and gravel. It would have taken at least another half hour to hear Old Bobby's words if they had to wait for the train to pass, counting the boxcars as the old men always did to see how business was coming along at the quarry. A dribble of tobacco juice escaped one corner of his mouth as his muse provided the words he wanted as the train chugged into sight.

"Maybe."

Then he went back to studying the array of rightside-up and upside-down RC Cola caps that served as checker surrogates.

The "checkers" themselves seemed to be quaking in the cold, Josh observed, as the old men's eyes focused on infinity to study the oncoming train. Touching the brim of his hat with two fingers, Josh turned and strode through the double glass doors. Old Bobby and Mr. Peevey acknowledged the farewell

11

with absent-minded waves of their own as they began counting the box cars.

The quarry had been their lives for more years than either could remember. Even time was measured by events at the place, like the flood of '37, the wildcat strike of '52, or the crusher building fire of '66. Throughout the county everyone's living came from the earth. It was scratched out one day at a time tobacco farming; carved out one minimum wage hour at a time cutting, snaking, and sawing the trees that grew in abundance; or ground out making tiny rocks out of huge ones in the Blalock Brothers' Lime and Stone Quarry.

Once inside, Josh felt light-headed from the heat. The courthouse boasted—nearly roasted—a state-of-the-art central heating system that came under the iron-fisted control of The Widow Simpson, County Court Clerk for the past thirty-eight years and a grower of orchids. Some of her finest specimens were to be found sweltering along the walls of her office, hanging there clutching preformed vine planking like they were fearful of falling off. The orchids prospered while every other living thing perspired.

Josh passed by The Widow's office, the public library, city hall, and the County Agent's office en route to a small, part-time office placarded State Gov't on its opaque glass door. Inside he filled out forms, then surrendered his three slips of paper that verified he had sought and been denied employment over the past two weeks. In exchange for his papers, he received a green check, the last of thirteen to which he was entitled. With mild amusement he noted the wet crescents beneath the armpits of the pudgy woman at the desk.

"Kinda chilly outside. Want me to have The Widow Simpson crank up the heat a little on my way out?" he asked.

"You mean it'll go higher?" A note of disbelief was in her voice.

"Sure. Last winter someone left the coffee pot unplugged, and it was three weeks before anyone noticed."

"Do it and die, Mister Jackson!" she said, emphasizing each word with a jab of a clinched fist.

Josh paused inside the big doors and listened. When he'd

determined the train had completely passed, he thought better of running the gauntlet of the checker players and went out the side door instead. *Who knows,* he thought, *the weather may have changed, and I'm not sure I have enough life left to completely discuss it.* Mr. Peevey and Old Bobby raised their hands in the obligatory wave as he tossed his brick on the floorboard and quickly fired up the truck. To his annoyance, he instinctively honked the horn before backing out. The checker players waved with more enthusiasm, thinking he'd missed their first efforts.

He realized it was foolish to drive to his next stop, a mere two blocks. Josh surveyed himself in the rearview mirror. Even with the cap on he could tell he needed a trim. From above each ear sprouted little rust-brown sprigs of hair that in the muddled reflection of the age-clouded mirror looked like knotholes filled with granddaddy long-legs.

Every chair in Carl's Barber Shop, except a recently vacated nail keg near the potbellied stove in the rear, was taken. This seat, the "amen corner," carried with it the obligation to tend the fire should it need stoking or feeding. Josh knew that few of those present were awaiting haircuts.

"Whatyasay, Jackson?" Carl greeted him while snapping his scissors idly to clear the hair from them. He was holding a young man's head at an uncomfortable angle with the other hand.

The customer flinched away from the snapping shears only to be jerked back into position by Carl's strong hand. Carl didn't brook any wrestling in his chair. Since he was the only practicing barber in town, he could get away with whatever force it took to hold his victim in place. He also had the unusual style of cutting hair from the top down, making the customer look like Friar Tuck until he'd completed the job. Most thought Carl did this merely to entertain his spectators, but it was a custom left over from his first job (which had led to his present), shearing sheep.

"Say, Carl. Gents?" Josh said, nodding to the rest who returned his greeting in like fashion.

These formalities out of the way, the conversation resumed. The topic of the moment was snakes.

"You mean to tell me, a snake can tell what a man's thinking?" one lounger inquired of the barber.

"That ain't what I'm sayin', Jim. All I say is, some snakes, and rattlers in particular, can sense when a feller's afraid of 'em. Dogs can do that, too. You ask any mailman or meter reader. They'll tell you it's true!"

"I don't know. How could they tell what you're thinkin'?"

A scrawny man with three day's stubble on his cheeks and a dip of Skoal under his lip got up and walked briskly to the stove, opened its door and spat inside, then turned. All eyes were upon him as he looked wild enough to live among snakes and could be an authority. He did and was.

"Ain't no real trick to that!" the spitter began. "S'long as a rattler can smell shit, he'll know damned well most people's afraid of him!"

His observation met with approval all around as the men slapped first their own and then their neighbor's knees while laughing. The customer in the chair joined in at first, then remembered Carl was trimming the base of his haircut with the clippers and became alarmed at the way the barber was shaking with laughter. When things had died down, Carl changed the subject.

"Speakin' of shit, how's things out your way, Jackson?"

All eyes switched from the snake wizard's wiry face to Josh's fuller one.

"About the same, I guess. Smells like Satan cut a fart."

"Ah well, it's about spring, so I reckon the wind'll shift here before long and maybe it won't be so bad." Carl said while whisking hair clippings from the young man's neck onto the floor.

All those present noted in the big mirror behind Carl that one side of the fellow's taper was somewhat lower than the other but reasoned that, so long as he held his head at the angle Carl had, it would look straight enough. The customer sat tensed in the chair as Carl removed the protective cloth and popped it, filling the air with tiny snips of hair. Assured it was

14

over, he sprang from the chair, produced two dollars from his jeans, and departed. On his way out the door, he retrieved a ball cap with *Hurst* emblazoned on the front. Josh noted how the hat sat low on the head and rocked slightly with each step as though it were suddenly far too large. The customer had gotten his money's worth of haircut.

"You here for a trim, Jackson?"

"Guess so. Am I next?"

"Sure are. Just step up and tell me how you want it."

Josh assumed the seat without comment since Carl cut hair however he felt like cutting hair and to try to influence his judgment was to invite disaster. As an afterthought, Josh lifted off his cap and tossed it toward the shelf in front of the big mirror. It missed. The sudden removal of the cap flipped Josh's hair out in all directions, except for the distinct ring above his ears where it had compressed neat indentions. Carl spun him around in the chair to face the mirror. He looked like he'd combed it with a firecracker.

"So what'll it be? A little off the sides and top, or just a trim all over?" Carl asked absently.

Josh couldn't see that there was really a choice being offered.

"Just make me look civilized enough to look for work, Carl. I gotta hit it again next week."

"Still no luck, huh?"

"Nope."

"You tried the aluminum plant?"

"First thing. They won't have an opening until somebody dies."

"Yeah, I guess that's right. No chance of the quarry opening things up again I guess."

"You'd know that better than anybody. What do you hear?"

"I hear it'll be a while. The Blalocks backed the wrong crook for governor this time around and ain't apt to get any state contracts for gravel any time soon. Silly bastards should have bought-off both sides like any self-respecting businessman would have done! You'd think their daddy would have taught 'em better."

15

"Yeah. I suppose they just don't understand politics."

A round of muttered agreements and "amens" circled the room.

"Be some hay to put up in another month or two, Jackson," one of the men volunteered.

"Not soon enough, Russell. Looks like I'm gonna have to head out to find anything I can live with."

"Ain't that what brought you here to start with, Josh?" Carl asked, referring to Thelma Lewis, a local product he'd married while serving at the army base nearby.

"Don't remind me."

The men around the room chuckled or laughed outright. Thelma had been a beauty, by their standards anyway, and had almost put Dilbert's Forge on the map twenty years earlier when she had finished third runner-up at the Catfish Festival Pageant in nearby Paris. Had she won the thing, she'd have gone on to the big time: the Miss Tennessee Pageant. Folks agreed loudly and often, even now, that she would have taken all the marbles plumb up to Miss America had she won The Catfish. As a talent she was a lock. Nobody, but *nobody*, could twirl a baton like Thelma Lewis Jackson!

In witness to this fact, she still taught twirlers at the local high school and regularly turned out a crop of dandies. That she was known to have become somewhat eccentric following her defeat did nothing to dim her star in their eyes. Josh often wondered at the range of activities that "somewhat eccentric" covered and couldn't imagine what one would have to do around these parts to be labeled an out-and-out loon. He shuddered at the thought and was rewarded by Carl firmly grasping his left ear to steady his aim.

"Looky goin' yonder, boys!" the man nearest the glass door and window pointed.

Josh fought the urge to turn his head, figuring correctly that his curiosity might cause him to be disfigured for months. It was bad enough that no one nearby was in a hiring mood when he looked his best. He didn't dare go out looking like his wife's cat! At the next remark, however, he decided to risk disfigurement and felt Carl's firm grip fall away as he, too, walked to the window. A scant twenty yards from the end of the man's pointing finger, a woman walked down the sidewalk.

No, they all would have agreed, she didn't exactly walk. It was more like a dance, the energy of which, if converted to strictly forward movement, would have resulted in an amazing pace.

"Pamalou Swift!" one of the men named her softly while eyeing appreciatively the gentle rise and fall of her ample bosom and her long, sensuous stride.

Even in a bulky sweater and thick wool slacks she managed to rekindle the primal fire in the oldest of her observers. Her hair was honey-colored and long with loose curls at the ends that bounced happily with each step. She turned abruptly and caught them red-handed and red faced. Instead of a snub, she flashed a winning smile, waved, and winked. That Josh could plainly see her wink from that distance reinforced his opinion that Pamalou Swift had the prettiest eyes and longest lashes he'd ever seen. The delicious jiggle of her breasts when she waved reinforced something else. The men waved back sheepishly, then watched in silence as she rounded the corner toward the bank and disappeared.

"She used to mow my yard when she was younger, you know," the man who had spotted her said proudly.

"Bet you'd like to see her Snapper now, wouldn't ya!" the snake man all but screamed, then burst into laughter.

"You bet your ass I would! There might be some snow on the roof, but that ain't no sign the fire's out in the furnace!" he declared.

"Otho, I'll just bet that if you checked, there's some snow piled right up next to the furnace door," Carl jibed. "Of course you boys know what it takes to catch her fancy, don't you?"

"Yep, I reckon we all do. Can't see myself in one, though," Otho said.

"Can't see myself with the payments!" the snake man observed.

"I think," Josh added while craning his head forward to allow Carl unlimited access to his neck, "the guy she'd go for wouldn't have to worry about payments. That's the whole idea, right?"

"Right," Carl agreed, then snapped the scissors menacingly.

"Well, she's held out for what now, twenty-five or twenty-six years? I doubt she'll give it up for anything less," Otho opined.

"I think she may be a tad older than that, but I don't blame her a bit. Hell, if I had her looks and body and all, I'd hightail it out of here and head for Nashville. Marry me a doctor or something and live high on the hog!" another observed.

"Don't sell her short," Josh cautioned while dismounting the chair amid a cloud of clippings. "If I had her equipment, I'd be retired by now and own Bermuda!"

Josh considered stopping at the Bide-A-Wee Cafe for a beer to steel himself for his return home, then decided against it. Instead he drove around for several hours and eventually found himself on the high banks of Kentucky Lake watching the sun go down. The air here smelled to him like freedom. To his wife it always smelled like fish, *dead* fish. That they both thought it had a smell was about as close to agreeing on anything they'd come in a long time.

The dogs were braced for the chase as he drove up the driveway and chased him from all sides the last twenty feet. He slammed on his brakes and skidded to a halt, forcing three of the back-pedaling hounds to slide under the stopped truck far enough to bounce off the spare tire. The rest sat barking insanely at the tailgate until he honked the horn. Then they quieted and walked off proudly, wishing in their little doggie minds that the truck had gone farther. Josh walked slowly up the steps to his back door, wishing to hell he'd stopped for that beer after all.

2

Thelma Jackson heard the gravel crunching even before the pack of beagles opened up. She was just adding the last of her before-bed regimen of creams, oils, emollients, astringents, and masques that, at dangerous proximity to forty, were the price of retaining one's youthful appearance. The corners of her mouth drooped into a small frown as she consulted her wristwatch and calculated the span of Josh's absence. *Probably stopped by the Bide-A-Wee to hobnob with the other heatherns!* she thought. Well, as the song went, he'd better not "come home a-drinkin' with lovin' on his mind!" As God was her witness, there'd be none of that tonight, nor any other night until he found work befitting the spouse of Dilbert's Forge's beauty queen emeritus. *And God,* she thought solemnly, *was her witness.*

Despite this devout thought, she rose from the stool to survey in her dressing mirror the treasures she would be denying her husband. Legs, still holding up well. Oh, a slight varicosity behind one knee and high up on the opposite thigh, but shapely and long. A dancer's legs. Hips full and nicely curved. She rotated at the waist to confirm the smooth roundness of her buttocks, unconsciously tensing their muscles until a dimple showed on each through her sheer shorty gown and bikini panties. Waist, still under control. She tensed those muscles, too, to heighten its flatness.

Breasts? Beginning to show some early signs of deterioration there. Still ample and full, but starting to droop even with the added support of an underwire bra. Clasping her hands together in front of her, she rotated her shoulders forward until her breasts were both facing her in the mirror. This position also brought them close together, creating a sharply defined and deep cleavage, the effect she normally achieved only with the help of her side-clutching and up-thrusting twirler outfit. She liked the look and made a mental note to carry her shoulders farther forward in the future.

Her neck made her cringe. Age was most evident there now, a leathery texture taking over despite all efforts at exercise and chemical persuasion. The face above the neck would have to wait until morning for critique as it currently was covered in goop and resembled a Haitian voodoo mask more than anything. The hair on either side of the mask was coiled tightly around oversized rollers. Her scowl deepened, causing narrow lines to run from the corners of her mouth down to her jaw line like those on a ventriloquist's dummy. The slamming door broke her evaluation at an unfavorable point. Throwing a gray housecoat over her choicest parts, she left to confront the man she deemed responsible for her beauty's wane.

Josh stepped between the random collection of Piggly-Wiggly grocery bags filled with garbage that sat just inside the door awaiting his disposal. In the kitchen two days worth of dishes tried to escape from the sink, adding their odors to those of the dinner on the stove. Even without looking he could tell the night's fare: macaroni-and-cheese casserole (purchased at five prefab boxes for a dollar), canned green beans, thin pork chops fried until they were the consistency of beef jerky, and brown-and-serve rolls. Better than usual, but then it *was* Friday. Baton-twirling cheerleaders, he reasoned, never had to take Home Ec.

In the living room FrankenKat, as was the much-stitched feline's name, sat with paws tucked under his chest watching Josh's advance with his lone remaining eye. The cat was aptly named, Josh thought for the thousandth time. His fur jutted out around a tangle of railroad track-like suture scars to the point that, when he arched his back to stretch or became angry, he resembled a commode scrubbing brush more than a cat. *FrankenKat* would do.

Above the fireplace hung a portrait of Thelma in her twirling outfit taken at the peak of her "career." It was bordered with four old batons and accented below by the silver-plated bowl awarded her at the Catfish Festival. On other walls hung Home Decorator prints of owls and old barns, along with a bizarre collection of religious prints. One of these, a winky-blinky depiction of Christ on the Water, was Thelma's favorite as it was "imported." Josh smiled thinly at the idea. Tijuana seemed hardly a cultural capital, but if she wanted to consider it imported then he'd allow her the point as being technically correct.

He rather liked the picture himself. In particular, he liked the way it moved when the door was left open and there was a wind about, the way it set the figure of Christ to running-in-place upon the water and His disciples in the boat to pointing back and forth like a choreographed number by the Ink Spots. *Simple pleasures,* he thought, leaving the phrase incomplete when he saw the apparition advancing upon him from the bedroom.

"Hi, babe," he said with uncertainty. It could be a Juju priestess instead.

She didn't answer but continued up to him and lifted her painted face toward his.

Josh was at a loss. It seemed she wanted a kiss, yet he couldn't quite locate a large enough area above her collarbone to plant one without getting a mouthful of goop. Closing his eyes, he puckered and waited for her to present whatever she wanted smooched. She sniffed at his mouth and, finding no evidence of Demon Alcohol, lowered her head in disappointment.

When it became evident there would be no kiss, he opened one eye to see what was happening. FrankenKat's eye met him, and they stared at each other in a two-way parody neither overly appreciated. Thelma was already in the kitchen. Josh unpuckered and joined her there.

"Did you go by and see the Blalocks?" she asked while agitating the macaroni, which had begun to harden on top.

"No, I didn't. We've talked that to death, babe. I'm not going down there and kiss ass to get back in their good graces, and that's final! Silly bastards should have known not to play politics half-assed to start with."

"But you know they'd take you back if you showed them where they're losing money. They may not have inherited Old Henry's gift for politics, but they for sure got his greed for money. Talk with them, Josh."

Josh reflected upon the Blalocks' decision to scale-down their operation and wait out the current administration, which included one of the brothers relieving him of his duties as production manager of the lime operation. He'd have gladly rolled back to foreman, had they asked. Instead, he was shown the door along with forty other workers on his line. Now Jim Blalock, who had been in charge of the gravel operation, which sold a substandard mixture of chirt and stone to the state highway system at top dollar, was trying to run the operation while maintaining something he'd never cared about before: quality.

It was a mess, too. Each morning the train took off sixty or so boxcars of Blalock lime and the next day brought back as many as twenty to be reprocessed due to lumps and impurities. It was only a matter of time until the number of boxcars leaving and those coming back would be equal, and then there would be none going either way. Under current management, that is.

"Screw 'em," he said with a shrug.

"I've asked you not to use that language in this house. It's not suitable for Christian ears!"

"Are they Christian again? As I recall, you had quite a bit to say about this situation when it first developed. Little of that would be suitable for Christian ears!"

"That was then, this is now."

"Don't tell, you've been saved again."

"Not yet, but my heart's back in the right place. I'll take care of the details next week at the revival."

"Is it that time again already?"

Throughout the Bible Belt, on which Dilbert's Forge occupied a position at or near the buckle he was certain, spring was celebrated with a constant deluge of rain and jack-leg preachers who descended upon the masses when they were most vulnerable. A circuit similar to that of circuses seemed to be maintained, with the erstwhile evangelists retiring to winter homes in Florida during the off-season, then firing-up their buses at the first blush of spring and saturating the South with their version of The Word.

For those sick and shut-in friends who weren't able to get out to the tents and brush arbors to receive The Word in person, it was available in cassette form ("Check or Money Order, No CODs"). Thelma had been saved and baptized so many times Josh often thought of her as a Wash and Wear Christian. It was with mixed feelings that he noticed an animated spark light her eyes as she answered.

"Yes! And do you know who's gonna be here next week to start off the season?"

"God?"

"No, and don't be blasphemous!"

"Then I give up. Who's going to throw out the first sinner this year?"

"Reverend Ray-Bob Thomas, *himself!*"

"My, my! Who the hell is Reverend Ray-Bob Thomas, and why does he have so many first names?"

"Josh!" she said, disbelief tingeing her distaste for his irreverent attitude, *"Brother Ray-Bob!* 'The True Path Gospel Hour?' You know!"

"Oh yeah. *Brother* Ray-Bob. I remember now. He's the one who sells the butane-powered burning bushes and splinters from the One True Cross. I thought he would be into Herbal Life or doing time by now."

"Josh, if you're not going to be serious, I'm not going to talk to you any more."

23

"Okay, so Brother Ray-Bob will be here next week. Are you going?"

"Of course! I can't see passing up an opportunity like this. He received this year's Golden Pulpit Award, you know. Best gospel radio and television show on the air. I listen to him all the time and, believe me, he's all they say he is. Why, just last week he touched me so deeply as I was driving home from town I had to pull over to the side of the road and pray! I couldn't see where I was going for the tears."

"Sounds like one kick-ass preacher, all right," Josh admitted grudgingly while pilfering a green bean from the pan and munching on it.

"Wouldn't hurt you to come, too. I think if you ever heard The Word as Brother Ray-Bob presents it, you'd become a better Christian, too. God knows you could use it."

"Oh, I don't know. I'm about an average Christian, I suppose."

"And what, pray tell, does that mean?"

"I cuss when I'm angry and pray when I'm scared, that's what. Like most people."

"Well, I think you're a heathern and have a long way to go before you're even close to being average."

"And Brother Ray-Bob can point my little footsies on the path to righteousness, is that it?"

"Exactly."

"I'll think about it, but I'll tell you up front: I've never seen the man in person, but I'll guarantee he'll show up wearing a white linen suit and alligator shoes. And he'll have his hair styled way back like a carnival barker's and say 'uh' at the end of each word. Furthermore, he'll have an assholier-than-thou attitude that will imply that *he's* going to heaven and, for enough money, he might take some of *us* along."

"That does it. Fix your own dinner! I'm going back in our bedroom and pray for your useless soul. I wouldn't blame God if He doesn't pay a bit of attention to me!"

"All right, all right. I'm sorry. I just get sick of all these guys putting religion on the same footing as professional wrestling, that's all. Hell! Your average gospel program has more commercials than the second half of the Super Bowl!"

"It takes money to reach out with the gospel these days, Josh. They're just bringing the ministry into the twentieth century, that's all."

"I'll bet you heard Brother Ray-Bob say that, didn't you?" he said with a smile.

As a matter of fact, she had. She figured God and Brother Ray-Bob would forgive her a small distortion of the facts in this case.

"No, I didn't. Now get washed-up and let's eat. I want to do my nails after while, and you need to take out the garbage."

After dinner they watched a couple of hours of television before Thelma retired to the bedroom to wax her legs and Josh trotted out the garbage accompanied by the six hounds. He returned while Thelma was working on the second leg and paused to admire it. A small triangle of canary yellow panties played peek-a-boo with the gown each time her hands smoothed the upper portion of her thigh. An urge was building within him that he hoped would be reciprocated in his mate. When the lights were at last extinguished, he threw caution to the winds and pulled her oily face near his own, feeling the warmth of her freshly-polished flesh against him.

"Not tonight, dear," she said, satisfied that the situation had arisen so she could refuse him. "I have an appointment with my OB-GYN tomorrow, and I don't want to be all yucky."

Josh released her and rolled onto his back. After a moment's thought, he asked a question he knew she would ignore.

"Well, when's your next dental appointment then?"

*   *   *

Big Un was content with the way the winter had gone and could see nothing but continued prosperity in the months ahead. He had found the perfect place to live, though quite by accident, and his food didn't have to be chased down; it came to him! Even now as the snow melt added its water to the already bloated stream, he could tell this would be another banner year, for everything alive that drifted past him fighting the current tended to pause and consider seeking shelter in his sturdy home. Several did come in. Very few went out again.

3

The Reverend Ray-Bob Thomas arrived in town two hours ahead of his contingent of trucks and vans bearing the tents, folding chairs, and sound equipment that were the tools of his trade. Brother Ray-Bob, as he was known to his audiences throughout a seven-state area, rode in the private office section of his Silver Eagle bus. The bus was a source of pride to him, in particular the radio-telephone on his desk and the fold-down queen-size bed that, when raised, made up one wall of his office. At present he was reading and missed the waves of the two old men who sat on the courthouse steps as the bus slid past on a cloud of diesel fumes.

The words on the page made his heart quicken. The *Wall Street Journal* held news of a stock split that would double his holdings once the stock regained its current value, which he was certain it would. Life was being very good to Brother Ray-Bob lately.

The bus slowed and hissed loudly as it turned onto a side road leading up a massive hill overlooking the small town. Atop this hill sat three splendid homes that could only be called mansions when compared with those nestled along the lower hillside and in the valley below. This affluent gathering was known to its five residents as Aerie Manor. The name 'Blalock' appeared in black wrought-iron letters atop two of the mailboxes at the crest of the hill, and the other bore 'Klotz' in hand lettering.

Typical, he thought. *Klotz would never part with hard cash for anything so nonproductive as a mailbox.* Klotz wasn't the type man who would rob Peter to pay Paul, either. He'd rob Peter, all right, but then he'd arrange it to where Paul got the blame. Brother Ray-Bob admired that in a man.

Air brakes spat as the bus pulled to a halt in front of the middle house. Brother Ray-Bob continued to read for a time, content to let one and all wait on him. It was a power play and he knew it, but one that worked. For the same reason he had his pulpit elevated to the point that everyone had to look up to him. Years earlier a psychologist had told him this particular flaw in his character was a reaction to insecurity on account of his diminutive height. At a mere five foot four he'd had to concede the point at the time, but now?

"Horse biscuits!" he said aloud. "Us psychotics might build castles in the air and neurotics might live in them, but it's the shrinks who collect the rent!"

He rose from the specially designed leather chair that allowed his feet to rest firmly on the floor yet was still higher than the matching sofa across from the desk. Smoothing his silk tie, he strode to the door of his compartment, checked teeth and hair, then put on his best Brother Ray-Bob smile and went out to meet one of his many silent partners.

Rolly Klotz was getting slightly chilled waiting outside the door and becoming irritated because of it. His mood wasn't elevated by the sudden appearance of Brother Ray-Bob in the bus door, but he did manage a semblance of a smile in greeting.

"Rolly! So good to see you my friend. My you're looking well, I take it God is *smiling* on your business endeavors." The preacher spoke in an overly loud voice, as though he wanted the entire neighborhood to hear.

"Can't complain. I've had better, of course. Lots of unemployment about since the election. Yourself?"

"Oh, you know how it goes. I pick up a morsel here, a crust

27

of bread there. With His help I manage to make ends meet. Hallelujah!" he said from the top step of the bus, which allowed him to remain above the heavy-set banker.

"And how do you think this session will go?"

"You've said it yourself, Rolly. Lots of unemployment, rotten weather that's beginning to lighten up, folks have been cooped-up all winter. A whole lot of angst there and folks will be wantin' to come out and air their sins, to offer thanks for being delivered from the clutches of foul weather, or to ask divine intervention on their behalf in finding work. All the earmarks of a glorious debut, I'd say."

Klotz scowled a heavy-jowled scowl that reminded Ray-Bob of the bulldog on the Marine Corps recruiting posters.

"Can you put that into terms I can appreciate?"

The preacher toyed with his tie as he considered his projection. He wasn't kidding. The harder times became, the better his business. Like the numbers game, tent evangelists fed off the lower end of the economic scale, and the more there were, the better his take.

"I don't think five grand is unreasonable for the opening night. Say seven to nine the second and third. Then, once we get rolling and word of mouth gets out, I think ten-to-fifteen each night until closing. I look for twenty grand or more the last night, plus some follow-on contributions come the next payday. That's Wednesday around here, isn't it?"

Klotz had raised one bushy eyebrow over a smallish, pig-like eye as the smaller man recited his numbers. Klotz also knew damned well that Ray-Bob knew exactly when the paydays of each major employer fell in every city on his tour, that he planned his stops meticulously to coincide with them to beef-up his take.

"Same arrangement as last year?" Klotz asked, knowing it wouldn't be.

A pained look came over Brother Ray-Bob, and he turned his soft, dead fish white palms upward as he began to speak.

"Brother Klotz, being a man of the economic world as you are, I'm sure you realize that my overhead has gone up considerably since last year. In fact, keeping last year's arrangement the same as the previous year's proved something of a strain monetarily. But I did GIVE YOU MY WORD *(uh!)* on that and a man's only as good as his word, right?"

Klotz nodded slowly in agreement, then again for Ray-Bob to continue.

"Well sir, I figure things have inflated to the point that I'm gonna have to ask for a slight bump, say five points? I know, inflation has been far higher than that and, what with so many of us on the roads these days, the class acts are getting more and more expensive to line up and all. But I think I might could eke by with just that little bump."

"I appreciate your situation, Brother Ray-Bob, but I must ask that you consider mine as well. Five points represents a fifty percent jump over last year and is a bit more than I can in good conscience pay."

"Now, now, Rolly," Ray-Bob said in a soothing voice, while reaching out to lay a perfectly manicured hand on the big man's shoulder. "I don't think conscience has a whole lot to do with it. Do you?" Then he laughed a high-pitched cackle that would never do from the pulpit.

Klotz considered this and laughed along with him before returning to the subject at hand.

"I can go one point, Ray-Bob. Maybe two on the overage if you pull in, say, fifty thousand total?"

"Twelve it is and thirteen on all over fifty grand, deal?" Ray-Bob stated, as though that was what Klotz had proposed, then released the shoulder and offered the hand for a shake.

Klotz looked at Ray-Bob's hand and considered it for a moment before taking it into his own meaty grasp. He had been prepared to go as high as thirteen base and fifteen on the overage, so he felt he'd struck a bargain of which he could be proud. *Hell,* he thought, *if Ray-Bob does bring in fifty grand, the six it'll cost me will be worth twenty-seven five on my taxes.*

Ray-Bob smiled a blessing as they parted the shake. He would have easily gone eleven and twelve, so he was satisfied too. At that, each man had to fight the urge to wipe the other's sweat from his palms until the bus was headed off the hill. It was a symbiotic relationship, one that offered one partner a little bit more of the pie immediately and the other a larger slice to horde at the end of the year.

Brother Ray-Bob was pleased with this transaction and considered pouring himself a few fingers of celebration. It was good to be back on the circuit again, back among the people, following the back roads without the searing heat of Klieg lights on his face and the nervous gestures of his director from the wings. He was about to allow himself a moment of sheer satisfaction when the voice interrupted.

"Well, here we are again!"

"Why do you always say *we*?" Ray-Bob asked in a voice torn between anger and anguish.

"First, you answer me this one: Why are you starting off like this? I thought you agreed to play it straight this year. Didn't you promise?"

"Well, I. . . ."

"Lied! That's what. You promised to play it like the old days if I'd leave you alone, didn't you?"

"I reckon I did at that, but . . . ."

"But you're not keeping your word! You already broke your promise. Know what?"

"What?" Ray-Bob asked in a tiny, childlike voice that was near tears, though tears were as much a part of his profession as folding chairs.

"I plan to keep mine!"

4

Josh rose early Monday and reflected on what had been an interesting, if unproductive, weekend. There had been the obligatory visit to his in-laws, a tradition he and Thelma had maintained for years without it ever growing beyond the "Hi Herman, Hi Ethel" stage where he was concerned. To them he was still the no-account soldier who had deflowered their darling girl. They would never admit that following her crushing defeat at the hands of the Catfish mavens, Thelma had taken to sleeping with anything that would hold still long enough, to bolster her flagging confidence and to prove—to herself at least—that she was still desirable.

He had tried not to believe it, too. But as their first year together closed, she began toting up her score of previous lovers in such a loud and insistent fashion that he'd come to understand the extent of her promiscuity. It was just his luck she had found in him a mixture of physical attraction and naiveté that appealed to her.

She had come to him with her tiny kitten voice and informed him she was carrying his child. They were married the next day, and that was it . . . for three weeks. Then she reported a miscarriage. He'd often wondered about that, especially since she had adamantly refused to bear him children since, citing the unsightly stretch marks that would no doubt show when she wore her twirling outfit. Their sexual encounters had also dwindled in frequency and intensity since then. Not that they had been that much to begin with, for Thelma never gave anything of herself, despite her considerable equipment.

Herman and Josh watched the football double-header in relative silence while Ethel and Thelma prepared dinner and gossiped. Ethel again bemoaned the fact that she had no grandchildren, and Thelma again cautioned her not to mention it to Josh as he was self-conscious about his "deficiency." The incongruity of this never registered on Ethel, and neither she nor Herman had ever broached the subject with Josh.

Following dinner, Herman went to bed and Josh retired to Thelma's old bedroom, which was maintained just as it was when she left, right down to the pom-pons on the walls and stuffed animals on the bed. There he read and reread the help wanted ads in the Sunday paper. With what amounted to relief, he came to realize there was no work beyond donkey labor available nearby unless he could luck into something in Nashville. If not, it was time he moved on, perhaps back to Florida where he'd longed to return since leaving the service—a move Thelma had fought against and won with his appointment as management trainee at Blalock Brothers some years earlier. It was time, he realized, that he got back in charge of his life or leave it. Either way seemed preferable to the existence he was saddled with at present.

On the way back to their house on the outskirts of town, they passed the fairgrounds where Brother Ray-Bob's band of converted carnies were setting up camp for the week's festivities. At Thelma's insistence, he slowed while she drank in the sight like a circus-hungry child watching the Big Top go up at the efforts of a dozen elephants. The elephants in this case were a rag-tag collection of ex-alcoholics and Halfway House alumni who sported the white shirts and dark slacks that were the uniform of Brother Ray-Bob's minions.

The Silver Eagle, with lights glowing gently behind the frosted glass of Ray-Bob's office, occupied a place of honor next to the main tent. Smaller tents were already erected nearby where coffee, sandwiches, tape cassettes, photos, and True Path Gospel Hour hymnals would go on sale the next day. To Thelma's eyes there was an air of impending festivity to the scene, and she could hardly wait for Monday night. The sight of sawdust being scattered to form a floor for the main tent made Josh thirsty and want a beer. He said as much, and the rest of the drive was spent in silence.

Josh made his own breakfast, then changed into his job-hunting clothes. His selection was the result of much thought, an attempt to look respectable while not too prosperous. An L.L. Bean rag wool sweater pulled on over a cotton shirt, tan slacks and rough-out boots seemed a logical choice. He did not wear a tie. He never did. Josh was fond of saying, "If God had meant for man to wear ties, He'd have just made our tongues a lot longer," and firmly believed it.

Pumping all the optimism he could into his heart, he thumped the hood, honked the horn, and headed out for Nashville. When he returned nine hours later, he had a promise of employment at the new Japanese auto plant there, to commence with their next training cycle in six weeks, and a ravenous thirst. Thus, he found himself pulling into the gravel parking lot of the Bide-A-Wee Cafe.

Your typical southern honky-tonk is a place typical southern gentlemen go when they have the urge for a few cold beers, feel the need for some meaningful conversation, or haven't had the hell beat out of them recently. The Bide-A-Wee was typical. It boasted sturdy cinderblock construction with a concrete floor that could be hosed down on odd Sundays or whenever it got so sticky that the skinnier patrons found it hard to move around. It also had the requisite number of pool tables (two), pinball machines (three), juke boxes (one), and windows (none). The restrooms were labeled with wooden silhouettes of bird dogs, a *pointer* for the men and a *setter* for the ladies, which supplied many moments of entertainment when some visiting Yankee failed to recognize their implications.

Josh paused inside the door to give his eyes a chance to adjust to the dim light before negotiating his way between the pool tables and to the bar. Failure to do this had once resulted in his walking into the back-thrust of a pool cue, costing him a severely bruised testicle and the pool shooter a nine-ball shot worth five dollars. A fight had been avoided when Josh threw up on the pool table, thereby canceling the rest of the game.

The sparse crowd today was representative of the Bide-A-Wee's customers. At a table near the bar sat a foursome of retirees who were each present at both Pearl Harbor and D-Day, or so they claimed. Three of these claimed to be actively involved in the fighting, while the other's job was so hush-hush that he couldn't talk about it even after forty years. Truth be known, his job *had* been hush-hush; he'd been post librarian at Camp Shelby, Mississippi, for the duration.

Seated at one end of the bar was a frumpy bottle blonde with huge breasts and a week's worth of makeup, wearing plastic go-go boots and a leather miniskirt that was at least two axe-handles wide across the rear. *Honky-tonk chic,* he thought as he nodded a hello to her. At the other end of the bar, engaged in a one-sided debate with Clyde, the bartender-bouncer-cook-owner, sat Slats Spivey, the resident snake expert from Carl's Barber Shop. Slats patted the stool next to his own as an invitation. Clyde welcomed his release from Spivey's attentions and waddled off to fetch Josh a cold Blue Ribbon on the house as payment.

"Glad you stopped by, Jackson," Slats began, then paused as Clyde wiped the area immediately in front of Josh and set down the beer.

"Something up?" Josh asked while surveying the chipped top of his beer bottle and wondering if perhaps the missing piece had found its way into the brew.

"I think I've finally got it! That up enough for ye?"

When a cursory inspection of the bottle failed to locate the missing shard, Josh turned the bottle up and drained a third of its contents. A belch fought its way up through his chilled esophagus and exited as he answered.

"*Ga-AHT!* what?" he said.

"The recipe for bugspit, that's what! You know . . . the ree-search I been doin' for the past coupla years?"

34

"Bugspit?"

"Yeah. Grasshopper spit, to be per-cise about it. Don't tell me you forgot! We talked about it right over yonder by the door that night Gib Stewart and The Skillet Lickers was playin' here. Remember?"

Josh did remember the band and had vague recollections of Slats blabbering on about grasshoppers, but such snatches of their conversation as he'd heard over the blare of the bass guitar were incoherent when strung together.

"Refresh my memory, Slats. I want to make sure I got it all."

Slats warmed to the subject, another on which he was the lone authority, and leaned forward to educate his younger friend in a low conspiratorial voice.

"Well-sir, here's the way I see it. Now you do some fishin', right?"

Josh nodded while taking another pull on his brew.

"Awright then. Now, what bait can you use that you know damned well something will take no matter what? I mean, when the signs are all wrong, the water's too hot and slow. All that's wrong. What will they still bite, hmmmm?"

"Worms?"

"Worms!? Hah! Worms ain't shit ridin' or walkin' when the water gets too hot. Hell, you can't even get a carp to take a worm then. I'm talkin' about *grasshoppers,* Jackson!"

"Grasshoppers. Right"

"Damned right grasshoppers. Ain't a fish in the world can refuse a grasshopper when it's presented right. They might turn up their noses at nightcrawlers, chicken guts, baby mice, or even crickets, but by damn they'll gobble the shit outa grasshoppers! And I know why."

"Why?" Josh wondered aloud while motioning to Clyde for two more beers.

Slats caught the signal and quickly drained the rest of his present beer to make room for the fresh one. He resumed in an even lower voice once Clyde had collected his two dollars and retreated.

"They spit, that's why."

"How do you figure that makes them special?"

"Glad you asked, Well-sir, you know these highfalutin' bait companies what sell catfish bait?"

Josh winced at the mere mention of catfish, a conditioned response developed after hearing Thelma's rendition of her betrayal at the beauty pageant about three hundred times, then nodded agreement.

"Well, they always advertise that their bait 'bleeds.' That is, it's got some oil base or t'other that floats off'n the ball of bait and leaves a smell trail the fish can follow right up to the hook. That's where the grasshopper has it over other bait critters, 'cause it carries its own 'bleed'!"

"You mean the spit, right? The fish is attracted to the spit."

"Damned straight! I done 'sperimented with it, too. Took me a whole passel of grasshoppers and whacked their heads off, see? Put them bastards in a blender and whupped 'em up into a gritty paste that's mostly spit. Then I soak different things in that paste and try 'em out on fish direct-like."

"And?" Josh asked absently, his mind busy at the moment making a promise to never, *ever* accept a margarita at Slats's place.

"And the fish loved it! No matter what I threw out, they snapped it right up."

"What kind of stuff did you try?"

"Hell, everything. Pieces of mop string, paper sack, tobacco sack, even a wad of cotton outa a aspirin bottle. Just a dab of spit and them fish went batshit. I'm tellin' ye, there's a million bucks to be made right here if'n a feller's got the right backin'."

"Where did you try this stuff, Slats?"

"Well, I didn't want to go public with it right off, you know? Might be them industrial spies out there and all, so I took it to the sloughs over at Yellow Creek and around to some ponds. I know, they's only punkinseeds and bass there, but dammit, what one fish'll take you know t'others will too. 'Specially since the bass gobbled it right up, and they's the finickiest feeders of the bunch!"

Josh considered this over another slug of Blue Ribbon.

Spivey's wild ideas were legend, as was his somewhat bent logic. Some things did work out, though, like Slats's suggestion that he honk the truck horn as soon as the dogs stopped barking when he got home. The dogs began to associate the horn with their own silence, thereby giving him some measure of control over them. His choice of test sites in the present case, though, was unfortunate. Josh and everyone else who fished knew that, given the concentration of fish in a slough or pond and the corresponding limited food supply, fish there would bite at anything from BBs to bowling balls. He wondered if Slats had considered this.

"Have you tried it out in open water yet?"

"Nope. But I plan to this weekend if the weather's decent. You a mind to come along?"

"Might. Where you going to get enough grasshoppers this time of year?"

"That there's the beauty of the whole thing. I done found a way to what you call *sympathize* the spit!"

"Synthesize?"

"Whatever. I got to studyin' them bugs, see? I'm talkin' all them suckers too, from them little pointy-headed shits that's all legs, right up to katydids. Anyway, I watched them eat and found out which plants put out the most spit per bug. Know what it was?"

"No idea."

"Pigweed. Plain ole everyday pigweed! Here I been tryin' to get rid of that shit for years, and all along it was tryin' to tell me somethin'. '*Slats*', it was a-sayin', '*jerk my butt up and bile me down! Here's your fortune, son!*'"

"And that's what you did, huh?"

"Yep. At least that's where I started. I ended up with a green slimy mess at first, so I had to back up and start over. Come to find out I had to ferment the stuff first, let it sit in a lardstand full of water for a few weeks until it turned the right color, *then* bile it down. Got a lot of skeeter wigglers in the water, of course, but I figure a few extra bugs more-or-less don't make no difference, right?"

"Right," Josh agreed while trying to imagine how synthetic bugspit would look, let alone smell.

"Worked like a charm. Come out the right color and all. 'Course I had to add a mite of cornstarch to get it sticky, but you can't tell it from real spit!"

"Sounds like a winner, Slats."

"Wait, it gets even better. I was out for an all-day test one day, so I packed along a nickel package of crackers and a can of sardines, right? Well-sir, I had some juice left over from them there sardines and said, 'What the hell, I'll pour it into that bugspit,' and you know what?"

"The fish liked it better?"

"Liked it? Hell, they almost come outa the water and took it away from me! 'Specially them bass, they was poppin' and snappin' along on top the water like flies after shit."

"Sounds like you might have something there all right. I'd be careful who all I told about it, though. If you don't have a patent, somebody might come along and steal the idea from you."

"A patent, eh? Yeah, that's right. I need to get me a patent. Where do you buy them patents, Jackson?"

"I think you have to write off to D.C. for some forms or something first. Might have to get a lawyer to help you fill them out, too."

Spivey's weathered face screwed up in distaste at the thought. A deep slug of beer seemed to lessen his discomfort, though, and after a moment of contemplation he resumed.

"A lawyer, you say. I don't cotton to lawyers a whole lot, like I've said often enough, I reckon. Them bastards are just a piece of paper away from the crooks what hires 'em, in my book. Sit around gettin' fat off other men's bad luck. You ever know anybody what went to see a lawyer over a happy occasion? Nope. Them and undertakers both just lay in wait for somethin' to go to shit so's they can cash in. You're educated, Jackson. How about you fill out the papers for me? I'll give you a cut, and you can help me sell it."

"I don't know a damned thing about patent law, Slats. And I don't have a degree, either. Just a couple of years of business courses, that's all. Tell you what, though. You get the forms, and I'll help you fill them out. How's that?"

"Shake on it, partner!" Slats said happily, then presented a sinewy hand for a shake.

Josh wondered about gripping a hand that routinely beheaded grasshoppers and held sardines, but reasoned that not many germs could survive in such an environment and took the shake. Slats Spivey felt as though he'd just embarked upon one of the greatest business ventures of all time. He'd not planned on going much farther with the bugspit project until young Jackson reinforced his confidence in the theory.

Josh Jackson was an out-of-stater, admittedly, and as such his judgment might be flawed on matters of a more local nature. But Florida was recognized as the bass fishing capital of North America, with the fattest, sassiest lunkers, and Slats figured any man who hailed from there ought to know shit from Shinola about fishbait. He ordered up another round of beers, then another, and another. When the painted lady opposite them began to look good, Josh knew it was time to go home. Slats, somewhat in his cups by this time, swore undying allegiance to Josh and their partnership with the sincerity unknown to teetotalers.

Due to the traffic lined up to enter the fairgrounds, the trip home took longer than normal. For an instant Josh thought he recognized Thelma's red Mustang in the lot. It turned out to be a Firebird instead, just another of the roughly five hundred cars parked in the field. The carnival, Josh realized, was about to start.

5

Like any good showman, Reverend Ray-Bob Thomas had a
warm-up act. Several acts, in fact. Even as the set-up men
were unfolding and lining up the last of the chairs under the big
tent, Mr. Leon Chalmers began with the organ stylings that
had made him a fixture at revivals and all-night singings, not to
mention horse shows, for the past thirty years. Behind Mr.
Chalmers and his gigantic Hammond hung the heavy crimson-
with-gold-fringe curtains that had until recently hung across
the movie screen at the now-defunct Loew's Vendome Theater
in Nashville. Behind the curtains another group of musicians
were warming up. They, too, had an organ.

Their organ was much smaller than Mr. Chalmers' and far
more versatile. It was a state-of-the-art synthesizer with the
audio output of several Hammonds and could almost talk at
the hands of its operator, one Gerald "Foo-Foo" McCool, late
of the rock group Down's Syndrome. Foo-Foo was working off
his public service time as dictated by the judge in Atlanta who
heard his most recent drug possession case.

Like the other musicians around him, some of whom were
working off their own sentences, Foo-Foo wore white and
black. His sole mark of individuality was his hairdo, a frizzed-
out attempt at a pony tail that looked remarkably like an elec-
trocuted squirrel. He toyed with his distortion unit and hooked

up his Leslie while hungrily eyeing the luscious collection of satin-robed lovelies in Brother Ray-Bob's Hallelujah Choir. The lead guitarist leaned in to get a *G* chord for tune-up and to inquire whether or not Foo-Foo was "holding." The Foo made a quick mental calculation and determined that he would need each of his three remaining lines of cocaine to weather this gig, so he didn't turn the axe man on. The dying strains of Mr. Chalmers' final number blared through the thick curtains, Foo-Foo's cue to crank up.

Thelma and Ethel were just getting seated near the rear of the huge tent when the Hammond died amid a rousing round of applause that sounded louder than possible from the group seated within the tent. It was. Brother Ray-Bob had taken the precaution of having the tent posts miked, thereby enabling him to electronically enhance his reception and to let the people know they were part of the show. He also had two video cameras panning the audience and stage, one of which actually had film in it. As the applause died down, the audience became aware of another sound, a throaty warble that seemed to rise up from the earth itself.

The crowd hushed as the sound took on a more animated quality and rose steadily in volume until it occupied every cubic inch of the tent's interior and spilled out into the night. The curtains parted slowly, revealing a purple-lighted pyramid of stage that stair-stepped up to a darkened pulpit at its apex. The musicians were on the first tier of the stage, set well back from the front. The choir occupied the second and third tiers.

As the players were becoming discernable to the audience, the synthesizer rose to a crescendo and was joined by the amplified flail of sonic drums running around the clock before settling in on a driving beat that brought a tingle to every scalp in the crowd. Bass, lead, and rhythm guitars joined in as the band struck the opening eight bars of a maddeningly up-tempo gospel number. Lights from high above the stage throbbed and flashed in a rainbow of colors as they ran through the frenzied introduction, then abruptly stabilized on a bright blue as the soloist ran onto stage followed by a yellow spotlight.

"Once more, boys!" she shouted into her microphone, then tucked it under one oversized sleeve and began clapping along with the beat. She jerked out the mike and shouted happily, "Come on brothers and sisters! You know the words and, even if you don't, you'll catch on. So let's *hear you!*"

The drummer rolled around the clock again as the crowd picked up the clapping, then the soloist uncorked her first verse. Her voice was clear as she alternately shouted and sang the words, augmented initially by the Hallelujah Choir and then by the audience. By the end of the number everyone was singing, clapping, and stomping the floor, actively getting into the spirit of the occasion. A slower hymn, an old standard, was next and was brought off in sterling three-part harmony by the choir. Thelma remarked to Ethel that the young women looked like angels, and Ethel chanced an opinion that if they were angels their wings would be hanging out since their robes were cut low in the front and even lower in back.

Next the soloist did a number *a cappella* that was so beautifully rendered it brought tears to several eyes in the crowd. Then the group went back up-tempo for the finale. This spirited number ended abruptly and, before the audience could start to applaud, phased smoothly into the theme song of Brother Ray-Bob's television show. The music was drowned out by applause, whistles, and shouts as first one, then another, recognized the tune and its portent. For those who were slow on the up-take, a bright white spotlight cut the night like a laser beam, illuminating the pulpit atop the stage.

Backstage, Brother Ray-Bob mounted the steps up to the platform behind his pulpit. A sound engineer nearby monitored a Vu meter on his panel that measured the output of noise from the audience. As the needle dropped slightly, he pointed to the evangelist first, then drew his forefinger across his throat in the direction of the lighting engineer. On the opposite side of the curtain the audience saw the blinding white spotlight blink out for a second, then relight as a soft, magenta-tinted ray that terminated on the upturned face of Brother Ray-Bob Thomas who now had magically appeared at his pulpit. The effect was stunning and, after a collective gasp, warranted an even louder and longer round of applause. Thelma's hands were beaten sore by the time Brother Ray-Bob raised his arms again to ask for the silence his sound engineer had signaled him was inevitable.

"Thank you kindly brothers and sisters, and HAS JESUS TOUCHED . . . yourhearttoday?" he asked in his herky-jerky fashion that played the words of each sentence like sheet music, rising here, falling there, and slurring the last several words together.

A few of the audience claimed to have been touched. Others denied it. Most sat expectantly silent.

"Well, HE WILL! Iguaranteeit. HE STANDS READY totoucheach-and every-oneofyou. STANDS READY AND WILLING! That's what I'M here to tell YOU tonight. NOW, here's a QUESTION . . . I have . . . for YOU!"

He pointed at them to emphasize beyond any doubt which *you* he meant. Starting with the four touts who were placed there for this purpose, members of the audience began saying in low voices, "Hallelujah!" "Praise the Lord!," "Amen!," and "Ask it!"

"My question EE-YUZ *(uh)*! . . . WHO AMONG YOU is-READYtobetouched?"

He paused to let them look at one another as if some of them were already designated to answer and might be visibly marked in some way. Ray-Bob kicked off again before anyone could answer.

"Now NEIGHBORS . . . I think I can call y'all neighbors, can't I?" he said with a small smile and a slowly closed hand to signify he was finished with that thought.

Several assured him loudly that he could.

"Neighbors, are YOU ready to be TOUCHED? Are you PREPARED? Are you PURE ENOUGH AT HEART *(uh!)*? But most importantly, neighbors, have you ASKED HIM to touch you? That'swhatIwanttoknowtonight." He put both hands on the edges of his pulpit and pulled himself forward to study the group, the spotlight fading to a golden color that accented the silver highlights in his hair. Then he began anew in a less-demanding tone. "He'll do it if you ask him to, you know. Let me tell you a little story. When I was a young boy, it was the end of the thirties and we ALL KNOW *(uh!)* what that was like, don't we folks?"

More "Hallelujahs" and "Amens," along with one male voice accidentally shouting "HELL YES!," followed by the sound of a hand being slapped.

Brother Ray-Bob chuckled along with the audience at this and then said, "I can't blame you for that one, brother! Times was HARD, weren't they brother? YOU DON'T HAVE TO ANSWER ALOUD, SIR, JUST NOD!"

The crowd enjoyed his jest with the man and warmed to his obvious sense of humor.

"But I digress. Anyway, one day when I was a young boy back in the thirties, I went into town with my daddy to sell some chickens. We were DIRT POOR, 'bout like everybody else back then, but we did have a few fryers and such that we could spare, so we went into town to sell 'em. While we were there, Daddy let me walk around and window shop whilst he tried to work out his best deal for them chickens, don't you know.

"WELL, I happened into the general store and there on the counter was THIS BIG OLE JAR OF PEPPERMINT PIL-LOWS! Do you remember the kind I'm talkin' about? I don't mean that hard ole ROCK CANDY stuff that sticks to your teeth, NO-SIR! I'm a-talkin' about that soft, sugary type that would MELT IN YOUR MOUTH! And I WANTED SOME! Yes, I did, friends. I dearly wanted some of that candy. It went for two pieces, BIG OLE PIECES mind you! Two pieces for a PENNY! ButIdidn'thaveone. No-sir. Why, in those days a penny to a six-year-old looked as big as the LID OFF A COOK-STOVE! And I didn't have even ONE.

"Well, I went outside and I looked up and down that gravel street in hopes I'd find me a penny. I found myself a FLAT-TENED FROG, two Model T LUGNUTS, and A WORLD of what we called HORSE BISCUITS, but no penny."

He waited until a mild titter of laughter at his description of horse manure had died down, then with a sad little smile re-sumed.

"I went back to where my daddy had just sold them chickens and I said 'Daddy, just HOW MUCH did them chickens bring?' He said 'Bobby'—he called me Bobby in those days—'I could only get a DIME a piece for 'em, but that's still better than the SEVEN CENTS I got a chicken last week. So I think God may be about to smile on us!' Well, I knew better than to ask for a penny when money was so scarce, so I just tucked my head and stood there.

"Later on, just before we loaded up in our wagon and headed back to the house, I saw two other children comin' outa that general store with a peppermint pillow in each hand AND I WAS SO JEALOUS *(uh!)*. I WAS ENVIOUS *(uh!)*. I WANTED TO DENY MY OWN NAME AND PARENTS AND BE ONE OF THEM CHILDREN *(uh)!* And the TEARS began to well up in my EYES, and I had to LOOK A-WAY frommydaddy. It didn't work, though. Daddy's are smarter than that. He looked over and he said 'SON? What on EARTH isthematter?' And I DIDN'T WANT TO TELL HIM! He wouldn't let it go though, and when at last I told him that I was cryin' because I couldn't have some CAN-DY, HE SAID . . ."

He let it hang there for a moment, then finished in a stern but loving voice that could have been any caring father's.

"He said, 'SON, if a thing MEANS THAT MUCH to you, then YOU'VE GOT TO STEP UP AND ASK FOR IT! Chances are, YOU CAN HAVE ANYTHING IN THIS WORLD YOU WANT . . . so long as YOU ASK FOR IT! Providing you ask the RIGHT FELLOW FOR IT!' That's what MY FATHER said. AND, we often refer to GOD HIM-SELF as the FATHER, don't we? Don't you think there's a REASON for that?"

The crowd enthusiastically assured him they did think there was a reason.

"I think you see my point, brothers and sisters. We can have ANYTHING wewant. SO LONG as we ASK . . . therightfellerforit. WHO DO YOU THINK WE'D ASK, if wewantsalvation? WHO do you think we'd ASK, if we want peaceofmind? WHO are YOU gonna ASK, to REACH OUT,

and to TOUCH YOU tonight and each night theREST-
ofthisWEEK? I think you know the answer. Join hands, one
with another now, REACH OUT and grasp your neighbor's
hand, and let's ASK HIM, together. Let us pray."

The organ began softly as Brother Ray-Bob, his face and
hands soaked from his vehement gesturing, led the group in
prayer. He asked that each member of the crowd be PERSON-
ALLY TOUCHED, as he had been. Prayed that each would
come to enjoy the RICHNESS OF HEART, that he currently
enjoyed. And, near the end, he put in a plug for the collection
plate along with the many sick and shut-in friends who
couldn't be with them tonight, but who also longed to hear
THE WORD.

He neglected to mention the cassette tapes outright at this
point, but this was remedied by an assistant preceding a short
intermission during which the band played and the Hallelujah
Choir girls made their bodice-bouncing ways around for the
first of three eventual cycles of the collection plate. The main
message of the night followed, with Brother Ray-Bob reap-
pearing in a solid white three-piece linen suit with matching
alligator shoes and belt.

Thelma was too touched by the man to acknowledge Josh's
accuracy in predicting the evangelist's wardrobe. By the end of
the night, she was certain she would return the next evening to
make that long journey down the aisle that would assure her
salvation. She wanted more than anything to tell the world of
her sin, her lone one to her notion, but one of those listed
among the ten Deadly's: vanity. She wanted Brother Ray-Bob
to lay his soft, manicured hand upon her brow and tell her God
understood and forgave her. Then, she thought, her heart
would be free of its burden. She also hoped, though not aloud,
that HE would halt time's march on her and let her be beautiful again. She figured in her little cheerleader brain that it
was worth a shot.

By the time Ethel and Thelma left the main tent, cars were
already lined up to exit. Another line of people formed in front
of the tent where cassettes, hymnals, and other goodies were
available for purchase.

Reverend Ray-Bob Thomas retired to his bus-*cum*-office, poured three fingers of Maker's Mark into a silver-rimmed tumbler, and then sat back on his sofa. It was a good start, he figured. Perhaps a tad better than he'd expected. He wondered if he should have followed his program director's advice and done a little healing to kick things off, but he was glad he stayed with his original game plan. *You can't let them eat all the icing before they've finished the cake!* he reminded himself.

He took an appreciative swig of the fiery-sweet liquid and felt it sting, then soothe, his throat as it went down. A knock on the door roused him from his woolgathering and spurred him to action. Quickly he arose and set the tumbler and bottle in the side drawer of his desk, then smoothed his sprayed-stiff hair in the mirror before putting on his smile and answering the door.

"Brother Klotz!" he said amiably, then looked around his guest to assure no others were with him. "Do come in. You're a mite early, I'm afraid, but I think once the tally is in we'll have some good numbers for you. Would you, uh, fancy a small drink of whiskey?"

"Never touch the stuff myself. You go ahead though if you're a mind to," the banker said in a sour tone, overly critical of his reflection in the large mirror.

"'All things in moderation,' so sayeth the Lord!" Ray-Bob sing-songed in his preacher voice while retrieving his drink.

"And where does He say that?" Klotz wanted to know, though he was more interested in trying to finger-weave his few remaining hairs across his skull in such a manner that they would cover most of his sweaty scalp.

"Why, in the Book of Thomas, of course!" Ray-Bob shot back, then giggled in a shrill voice that Klotz found annoying but joined with anyway.

Then Klotz took out his checkbook.

Josh was sleeping soundly when Thelma's Mustang pulled into the drive, and he heard neither its approach nor the demented hounds barking during the last ten yards of its journey. They kept barking until they tired of it, for Thelma refused to honk her horn to make them stop. She'd rather berate them than give in.

Humming a hymn, Thelma sat down at her dressing table to undergo her nightly ritual. Then, halfway through the second layer of goop, she leaned forward toward the mirror. Was the light of righteousness there in her eyes yet? She decided it was, a bit. Not enough to really notice, and nothing compared to what would be there tomorrow night, but with just the right amount of lavender eye shadow she felt sure she could highlight it. Josh let go a snorkling snore at this moment, then rolled over and resumed sleeping. Thelma scowled, bringing the dummy lines into sharp focus beneath the lights of righteousness.

6

Slats Spivey arose with a head full of anticipation and aching remembrance. The beer had flowed freely, even past the point when he had exhausted the twenty-dollar bill he'd taken with him, and he was paying twice the price this morning. Hands shaking, he first broke, then ignored, two eggs for breakfast before deciding on a ration of stale cornbread crumbled into a wide-mouthed glass with buttermilk poured over it. The mixture coated his stomach, filling the void there and giving him hope enough to continue the day. Grabbing a hand scythe from a nail on the side of his two-room tarpaper shack, he headed up the steep slope to where a slick bald spot marked his earlier pigweed harvests.

When he first bent low to the ground to cut a clump of pigweed, all the blood in his body seemed to rush into his brain, causing his balance to fail. A halting step forward brought him back under control enough to straighten up and shake his head to clear it. Gradually, he again sought a suitable posture to bring the curved blade down against the stand of pigweed. It worked. Within minutes he had an armful of the weed and was ready for the return trip.

Unable to see over his leafy load, Slats' feet became tangled in surviving members of the pigweed colony just as he was gaining momentum down the slope. He had the presence of mind to toss the scythe away, lest he land on it and skewer himself, but he never thought to release the load of pigweed. At the instant before impact, he instinctively put out his right hand to brace himself against the fall. He recognized the audible crack as both bones above his wrist snapped under his weight.

Slats Spivey was a man who could no more admit defeat than a fish could shrug its shoulders, so he gathered up the pigweed in his good arm and continued to slide and walk down the hill to his house. The arm was throbbing painfully by the time he reached the picnic table out back where he routinely cleaned fish and chopped the pigweed into small sections. A great cloud of flies had gathered on the table, drawn by the ghosts of fishes past and the occasional morsel of squirrel, raccoon, 'possum, rabbit, and deer that had also been cleaned there. A pained cry split the quiet air as Slats unthinkingly waved the flies away with his broken arm before depositing his load on the table. He was certain this was serious now and wasn't sure he'd be able to keep his buttermilk and cornbread down much longer. He decided he would think about what to do next after he'd put the arm in a sling, so he went inside.

A blue bandana served well as a sling and, once the arm was immobilized, he felt much better. Well enough, in fact, to finish breakfast before contemplating the trip to the doctor. The eggs stared up at him from the skillet where they'd sat for the past hour, an impudent gesture toward one in so much pain he figured, so he turned up the heat, poured in a little buttermilk, then gouged out the eggs' eyes and scrambled the whole mess. He'd grown to like buttermilk a lot for cooking lately. Before, he'd always used evaporated milk for such chores, mainly because he'd won a ten-year supply and one hundred dollars cash in a Pet Milk Jingle Contest.

The letter notifying him of his winning entry, its edges yellowing in the sun, now hung affixed to a nearby wall with the red-headed packing pins from a new shirt. As the eggs began to fluff up into nice pastel yellow lumps, he again read the words.

Dear Mr. Spivey,

Thank you so much for your entry! After reading several thousand others, we deem this the most refreshing and original of the lot. We sincerely regret that we'll not be able to use it in our advertising campaign, but feel you will understand this. Enclosed is our check for $100.00 and a certificate you can present to your local grocer entitling you to a ten-years' supply of our products.
Sincerely,
Mortimer Ptacek
Vice President

Appended beneath it was a photocopy of his winning entry. The jingle he was to complete went:

Pet Evaporated Milk, the best in the land;
It comes to you in a blue-and-white can.

Spivey's final couplet was;

No teats to pull, no hay to pitch,
You just poke a little hole in the son-of-a-bitch!

Slats Spivey, inventor, naturalist, budding entrepreneur, and acknowledged poet laureate of Dilbert's Forge, sat down to his breakfast after making a second trip to fetch a pot of piping hot coffee. He tilted his cup to spill some of the coffee into his saucer to cool, then drained it. He ate the eggs right out of the skillet, then wiped his mouth on the ragged red-checked curtain over the sink. The wrist had swollen quite large now and urged him to town. He reluctantly gave in and departed down the deeply grooved road. After lawyers and insurance salesmen, physicians were *personna non worthashit* in Spivey's book.

*   *   *

Spivey's route took him within two miles of where Big Un lived, though his lair was not visible from the road. Big Un was full to the gills and almost uncomfortable. His abode, a natural lean-to formed when a massive slab of

51

rock had fallen from the limestone bluff above to land more-or-less intact atop another large boulder, was ideal for him at this point in his life. The past several years he had found it progressively harder on him when he tried to adjust to depths. Not that he feared them, mind you. Big Un had nothing to fear, save maybe a bear, and they were too scarce to think about and he was still too fast to get caught by a mere bear. The other predators that had haunted his youth and had made him shed pounds avoiding them were no longer a factor. He had outgrown them all. He was the largest around. In fact, he was possibly the largest of his species ever.

*   *   *

Josh slept until almost noon, an unusual occurrence. It was unusual because he normally liked to be up no later than six to plan out his day, back when he had things to plan that is, and unusual because the sight of him sleeping infuriated Thelma to such a degree that she took pains to make as much noise as possible. Today, however, she was in the kitchen rattling pots and pans in a most casual fashion while humming a tune made unrecognizable to Josh by the two walls that separated them and the fact that Thelma couldn't carry a tune in a bucket.

The distinct odor of fried chicken wafted through the house to reach Josh's nose as he was stretching expansively. *She's in a* fowl *mood!* he thought, snickering. *This could be good or bad. Either she is trying to butter me up because she's destroyed something or, worse yet, Ethel and Herman are coming over.* In either event, he felt he should rise to the occasion and proceeded to do so.

"Babe? Where's the mouthwash? I've got a taste in my mouth like a family of Iranians just moved out!" he shouted from the bathroom.

"I can't hear you when I'm fryin' stuff! I've told you that a hundred times!" she yelled back.

He found the mouthwash in the linen closet behind a clutch of L'Eggs eggs. Why she kept the empty hose containers, he never knew. *Perhaps she thinks one day we'll have a pet ostrich and the eggs will make it feel at home or something.*

Next to the mouthwash was an industrial-size box of douche powder that claimed on the label to be "pH-Balanced" and "Pine Forest"-scented. *Stood to reason,* he figured, *that the stuff would be very popular among lumberjack's wives.* He wondered idly what scent the wife of a seal trainer would use, if any? A tiny spoon came with each box, a little douche scoop—*wasn't that by the Beach Boys?* Here he noticed his mind was not yet functioning properly.

Once he had finished his morning ablutions, he made his way into the kitchen cautiously. When Thelma had The Word upon her, she had to be approached with extreme caution.

"Good morning," he said in as pleasant a voice as he could muster with his head pounding like a trip hammer and his tongue furred-up as though he'd spent the night licking pool tables.

"Good morning!" she fairly sang, but still too loudly for her mood to be appreciated. "What would you like for breakfast, or would you rather wait for lunch?"

"How about a complete blood transfusion and a salt lick of aspirin?"

"Oh dear, you went out and got large last night, didn't you? Well, when you play, you pay! It's God's way of telling you you're doing wrong, that's all."

"He could have just left a note."

"I'm serious, Josh. Look at you. You have a biblical name, and what do you do? You go out carousing like some old tomcat to all hours, then feel like the mischief all the next day!"

FrankenKat looked up from his nap at her reference to old tomcats, yawned, then went back to sleep.

"There's probably something to what you say, babe. Not sure this is the time to discuss it though. How about some breakfast. I'm not sure I'm up to yard bird just yet."

"Here," she said, fetching a box from a cabinet above the stove and tossing it to him. "Try some of this."

He fielded the box cleanly and turned it over to read the label. Instant French Toast Mix. Josh had been making French Toast the conventional way since he was eight and marveled at the fact that some folks needed a mix. *Perhaps it's for camping or hiking,* he thought, then read the ingredients on the side aloud.

"Powdered eggs, powdered milk, powdered sugar. . . . Are you supposed to eat this stuff or snort it?" he asked.

"You just add water and stir, silly. Do you have to complain about *everything?*"

"Sorry. Okay, I'll try it. How was the shindig last night?"

"Oh Josh, it was just *wonderful!* I cried. I shouted. My chest ached, it was so full!"

"Sounds like a description of angina pectoris to me."

"You *know* what I mean! Brother Ray-Bob is everything they say he is. I mean, the man just reaches right out there and touches you in such a way you *know* God is with him. I wish you'd come with us tonight. You'd see what I mean. Besides, you need some spiritual contact in your life."

"I pulled up behind a guy with 'Honk If You Love Jesus' on his bumper yesterday in Nashville and honked. Does that qualify?"

"Don't be silly. All that tells me is that you came within a few feet of a true Christian, that's all."

"Some true Christian. He stuck his head out the window and called me a colorblind sonofabitch because I was honking and the light hadn't changed. Have you tried this instant shit?"

"No, I haven't, and if you're not going to be serious . . . ."

"Why should I be serious about instant French toast?"

"I mean about the revival. You should come with us tonight. But no, you'll probably be out with some of your buddies doing God knows what. Aren't you the least bit curious about what goes on at the revival?"

"I think I have a pretty good idea, babe. I went to these things with you during your first couple dozen conversions, remember? I doubt they've changed that much, unless of course they've added a tag-team chicken-wire grudge match between rival evangelists or a battle of the bands or something I haven't heard about. Maybe they should start broadcasting the confession of the week to spur interest," he retorted, then dunked a slice of bread in the thin mixture and flopped it into a buttered skillet to cook.

"You wouldn't pay a nickel to see a piss ant eat a bale of hay, you know that Josh Jackson?"

"Yes, I would. You tell Brother Ray-Bob that as soon as he finds such an ant, he can count on me being in the front row. I do wish you'd stick to one of the standard churches instead of jumping on every wild-eyed zealot's bandwagon that travels through here. Some of these guys make the Moonies look positively stable. I mean the snake-handlers and fire-eaters and all that."

"They're just demonstrating their faith!"

"I'd think they'd realize that God is demonstrating his by keeping the damned snakes back in the woods where they won't get out among society. Can't they take His judgment on that at face value? Seems like they're tempting Him more than anything, and a lot of them get bit for all their faith."

"Ah, but very few of them die. Don't you see what God's saying there?"

"Yeah, I think he's saying 'If you're going to be dumb, you've gotta be tough.'"

He extracted the toast, taking care to dodge the popping grease of the chicken, and carried it to the table.

"You're a heathern, you know that?"

"There's no *R* in *heathen*, babe. You've been listening to too many radio preachers."

"Heathen then. That's what you are. And a blasphemer, too!"

"Sticks and stones may break my bones, but whips and chains excite me," he replied through a mouthful of French toast. "Call me what you will. I figure there will be about as many of my type in heaven as there are hype-crazed hypocrites. To be honest with you, being locked up for eternity with a bunch of sweaty, yelling, holier-than-thou weirdo preachers would be more my idea of hell than heaven."

"Not to worry, you won't be anywhere near Brother Ray-Bob and myself when judgment day comes!"

"Hallelujah!" he said with a smile, then bit into another piece of reconstituted French toast and wondered if perhaps he should have eaten the box instead.

Thelma snarled menacingly, then shrugged a dismissal and went back to flipping chicken. He wasn't going to spoil her mood with his scoffing.

"Some special occasion?"

"Not particularly. I just felt like cooking today and thought it'd be nice to fix a picnic-type dinner for Mama and me to take with us tonight. And you, are you going to get out and put in some applications today or are you content to sit around on your rusty doing nothing?"

"No and no. I've got a job, but it won't start for another month or so. This afternoon I guess I'd better go down to the bank and see if I can draw enough out of escrow to see us through 'til then. Oh yeah, I'm thinking about going fishing Saturday. So if there's something you need done around here, let me know now, and I'll get on it."

"Hmmm," she said while thinking, then her lips pursed in anger as she realized that Saturday was the wrap-up of the revival and she had expected him to at least attend that with her. "No, I can't think of a *thing* I need you for, now that you mention it!"

He caught the acid-tinged ferocity of her words and knew better.

"Let's have it."

"Have what?" she said with feigned innocence.

"Let's have whatever it is that's pissing you off."

"I'm not p . . . upset. What makes you think I am?"

"'Cause you made your pissed-off face, that's why."

"Josh! I don't know what you mean."

"When you get angry, you always pucker up your lips until they look like a chapped dog's ass, that's what."

In reaction to his words, she did it again.

"Like that! Now, what's the matter?"

"Nothing! Except your attitude! I don't know why I even bother to talk to you anymore. You don't care what I think or feel about anything. You're rude to my parents, scoff at my religious beliefs, and now you're making fun of the way I *look!*"

The last of her accusations received the bulk of her emphasis, as he expected.

"How can I be rude to your parents? Since when is 'Hi!' considered rude? I've tried talking to Herman, but there just isn't anything he wants to talk about. Ethel still thinks I broke in and raped you in the middle of the night, then spirited you off. How do you talk to someone like that?"

"I *was* young, of course, but surely she's forgiven you that," Thelma answered while patting her hair back from her face with one floury hand.

"Forgiven what? Thelma! You're two friggin' years *older* than me. How the hell can she say I robbed her cradle?"

The dog's ass was prominent on Thelma's mouth now. She had thought it might be a mistake marrying someone younger than herself, but it was the ultimate compliment at the time. Now he was throwing it back in her face, and she wasn't sure how to strike back. When a fresh strategy didn't present itself immediately, she fell back on the tried-and-true tactic that had served her and womankind in general so well for so long: silence.

Throughout the draining of the chicken on paper towels and placing it in the Tupperware container, she said nothing and didn't acknowledge anything Josh said. At last he gave up, got dressed, and made ready to leave for town. Her eyes danced with the light of victory when she heard his hand come down on the truck's hood, then flew open in surprise when the back door sprang open and he stuck his head in.

"Better to remain silent and be thought a fool, than to speak up and remove all doubt!" he shouted, then slammed the door before she could reply.

Thelma did a slow burn and thought most unchristian thoughts as she heard him honk and back out of the driveway. Then she noticed she had a stranglehold on the drumstick she was blotting and that chicken grease was running out at a stream onto her housecoat. In a fit of rage she hurled the chicken leg across the house where it splattered against her Catfish Festival portrait, the bone dropping neatly into the runner-up dish. With tears of fear in her eyes she sprinted into the living room to repair the damage, then sat in the recliner and cried tears of regret that she could not turn back the years and reorder her life.

After repairing her makeup, she tucked her wounded heart into a steel underwire and whalebone up-thrust bra, donned her Erin Green dress, the one cut the most like those of the Hallelujah Choir, grabbed her chicken, and repaired to her mother's. Herman met her at the door wearing the Sunday-go-to-meeting clothes he normally reserved for funerals. Herman's basset hound features, suspended as they were above a neck made pencil-thin by his too tight collar, made her smile. Perhaps it was the zootsuit-width crimson tie that hung like a pound of calf's liver from a knot the size of an artichoke. Then the preposterous tie reminded her of Josh and fouled her mood anew.

7

Pamalou Swift looked up from counting change at her teller cage when Josh Jackson strode through the double glass doors. She liked the square cut of his jaw, the muscular frame that seemed only just contained by his flannel shirt, and the wealth of reddish-brown hair that filled in the V where the top two buttons were left undone. A popular ploy, she was certain, a kind of mindless macho stunt she deplored in most men, but on Jackson she felt certain it was unintentional. She licked her lips to moisten the light film of lipstick in preparation for a smile, then noted the serious look about him.

Was it anger? Concern? Unlike most men, who seemed almost too shallow to occupy three dimensions, Josh Jackson was largely unreadable. Perhaps this mystery was the reason she found him attractive, though she had made every effort not to show it. Or perhaps it was the seeming indifference he displayed toward her that she found a challenge after having to fend off advances from every ball-bearing cretin she'd met since high school. With relief and then alarm, she saw him pivot on one foot and head toward her.

"Your boss in, Pamalou?"

"Yes, but I think he's on the phone at the moment, Josh," she said with a flurry of long eyelashes that would have done Scarlett O'Hara proud. "What is the nature of your business?"

"Pardon?" he said dimly, still mesmerized by her eyes.

"I mean, do you need to see him in his capacity as mayor or as banker?"

"I need to see him as a banker. I still want to strangle him in his capacity as mayor!" he answered, returning a broad smile she thought had a lot of mischievous little boy left in it.

"I'll see if he's off the line yet."

He watched appreciatively as she walked the short distance, taking in each detail from the golden hair pulled back into a loosely plaited French braid, to her over-sized loop earrings, longish neck, and down to the hem of her skirt, which swished back and forth as she walked, revealing the two-inch heels of her soft leather boots. For all that he enjoyed her going away, he found himself swallowing to find his voice as she strode gracefully back toward him.

"Mr. Klotz will see you now, Josh."

He nodded and shook her from his mind as he walked into Klotz's office. He didn't like Klotz, but then that didn't exactly put him in a minority. Klotz was a tyrant in his own way, using his stewardship of the bank as a hammer to drive his own political and business ambitions. The Turd Factory was but the latest of his projects, most of which ended up being built on a plot of scrub brush owned by either himself or one of the Blalocks. The land suddenly became quite valuable when the bond issue was floated to build these projects, but as the land was the last part of each contract to be let, the cost was usually known only after it was too late to be altered.

Josh tapped lightly on the facing of the open door and stared in at the top of Rolly Klotz's head. Had it not been for the serious nature of his visit, Josh would have been hard-pressed not to laugh. Klotz was going bald on the top, yet he still tried to stretch a couple dozen long hairs from just above one ear plumb across his gleaming skull. The result made his head look like an autoharp that badly needed re-stringing. To make matters worse, Klotz had no sense of style in selecting his wardrobe. He often wore plaids with stripes and gave no thought at all to what color anything was. The sports jacket he wore this day caused Josh to wonder if somewhere there was a Maverick with its seatcovers missing.

"Mr. Jackson? Come on in. Sit down. What can we do for you today?" Klotz said in a monotone as though he were reading the words.

"Mr. Klotz, as you no doubt know, Blalock's shut down my line last fall, and since that time I've been seeking employment elsewhere."

Klotz nodded and tapped the eraser end of an unsharpened pencil on his teeth, making a plastic sound.

"Well, I've found another position beginning the first of May. What I need to do, sir, is draw down my escrow to see me through until I have a salary coming in and, to be on the safe side, borrow an additional thousand dollars on a ninety-day note."

"I see. Well, I have your mortgage figures here, and I suppose you could draw, oh, let's say three or four hundred dollars. We could go more were it not so close to tax time, but with May just around the corner I don't think we want to go scraping the account bare, now do we?"

"In that case I'll definitely need the loan. Could we make it fifteen hundred?"

Klotz fiddled with his papers some more, sighed heavily, then rose to pace the floor for a moment.

"I'll be up-front with you, Jackson. Without collateral, I can't go risking the bank's funds on a short-term loan. Now, after you've been employed awhile—let's say ninety days or so—perhaps I could see my way clear . . . ."

"What kind of collateral? You hold my mortgage already. Do you want a second mortgage just for fifteen hundred?"

"No. I don't think that would do, either. You see, that place of yours probably wouldn't bring your outstanding balance today, I mean with the market being what it is and . . . ."

"And your precious shit plant right up on the hill in front of it, is that what you mean?" Josh snapped.

Klotz let a satisfied smile part his oily features and smoothed the strands across his head nervously.

"Well, that is unfortunate, I agree. But it had to go somewhere, didn't it? I guess you probably think I'm an out-and-out asshole, don't you?" Klotz asked with another sickly smile.

"I wouldn't say that," Josh said with conviction.

Klotz was surprised. The smile died and was replaced with a little *O* formed by his blubbery lips.

"Well, that *is* most charitable and understanding of you, Mr. Jackson! I guess I got the wrong impression when you were appearing before the council against the sewage plant."

"That's not what I meant. I mean, I wouldn't say *probably*! Good day, Mr. Klotz."

Josh stomped out of the office before he gave in to a growing desire to snatch Klotz's head off his shoulders. Pamalou was at the front door turning the Open/Closed sign around as she left for lunch. Seeing the fire in Josh's eyes, she stepped back to clear his path through the door. He stopped, smiled tentatively, and motioned her through after pulling the heavy door open. Once outside, she walked alongside him for a way in silence.

"Am I following you?" he asked after they'd made two corners together.

"I'm not sure. I'm heading to Ba-Da's for lunch. Where are you going?"

"To Ba-Da's for coffee," he lied. His truck was parked behind the courthouse.

"Then we're following each other it seems. I'm, uh, sorry about Mr. Klotz's, well, I'm sorry about the loan and all."

"Don't worry about it. I didn't really expect it anyway. I just wanted to give him one more opportunity to prove I'm not being unreasonable by hating his guts, that's all. You can tell him that if you like."

"No thanks. I don't talk to him either unless I have to."

"Then why on earth do you work for him?"

"Because he pays better than anything else I could get around here, that's why."

"Which brings us to the next logical question: Why haven't you migrated somewhere more . . . well . . . in keeping with your style?"

She smiled prettily. He *had* noticed her, after all. He smiled, too, but his was directed at a trio of flat noses pressed against the barber shop window nearby.

"At first I had to stay here to take care of my aunt, who raised me, by the way. Then, after she passed on, I guess I kept hoping some day my prince would come and whisk me away from all this. Take me off to a land of warmth and palm trees where all we had to do was gaze out over the water and sip champagne on the veranda."

"Someone on a white charger, eh? Don't get many of those through here these days."

They were almost there now. The odors of the Tuesday Special filled the air as they approached. Both knew the weekly menu by heart, as did everyone else in the county. It hadn't changed in over ten years, and Tuesday was Meatloaf Surprise day. The surprise was extra onion in the mix, so most people had something else.

"Speaking of migrating, I'd have thought you'd have moved back to Florida by now. Don't you miss the beaches and stuff?"

"Sometimes. I'm from the panhandle area we call L.A., for Lower Alabama. But I spent a lot of time down in Pensacola during my misguided youth. It looks like I may be headed back there sooner than I'd planned."

"I thought I overheard you say something about finding a job?"

"Oh, I did. It's south of Nashville building rice-burner automobiles. But I think as soon as I can find a buyer for my place, I'm gonna head back south. Maybe get on with an offshore drill rig or something."

"Sounds interesting. Wish I could go with you. This humidity and cold are taking their toll on my good humor. Buy you a cup of coffee?" she asked as he held the door open for her.

The crowd didn't fall to a complete hush, but several inside paused with a bite of Meatloaf Surprise halfway to their mouth for a second, then resumed eating.

"Thanks," he said immediately, surprising them both.

* * *

Slats was sitting at his customary stool at the Bide-A-Wee when Josh walked in, paused to become acclimated, then strode past the pool tables to join him. Slats's new cast stood out in the half-lit gloom like a glowworm on a cow pattie. A dozen discolored pickled eggs stared out at them both from a gallon jug on the bar where they swam in vile-looking liquid. Spiced sausages occupied a similar jug behind them, giving that end of the bar the appearance of a forgotten science project.

"Say, Slats, what happened?" Josh asked while nodding to Clyde for a Blue Ribbon.

"Busted my ass comin' off the hill behind the house, that's what. Snapped like kindlin' wood, too!" he said with a wince as he remembered.

Josh eyed the smallish ferret face that peered out from under the bill of a Bass angler's hat. Slats would always look younger than his years, he thought. Something about the innocence of youth in his eyes, the careless disregard for fashion, the way the man could get so excited about the things that mattered to him while largely ignoring those that would rankle others. He made Slats to be about forty, give or take a decade.

"Looks like you busted more than your ass, huh? Guess our fishing trip on Saturday is off then."

"Nope. I can still scull a boat with one wing, thank ye. Might need a little hand loadin' the boat though. Four-thirty too early for ye?"

"Depends. If I've had my coffee, four-thirty's fine. You sure you ought to be out on that so soon?"

"This ain't shit! I've had worse and still went about my business. What say I put on the coffee a little after four, slide by and pick you up, and we come back to my place to drink our coffee and load the boat?"

"Sounds like a plan to me. Remember the dogs, though."

"I 'member the silly bastards awright. Jackson, why don't you take them hounds a-huntin'? Let 'em chase a rabbit or two, and they'll bark themselves out."

"I've tried that. Every time I pass a car they start barking after it until I honk. Every time I honk and there's another car in front of me, it pulls over thinking I want to pass, or the driver gets pissed-off and slows down. They even bark at the cars in driveways! It's just too much of a pain in the ass to take them anywhere, and they seem to know all the rabbits around the house so when we go out there, they think it's just a walk."

"Yeah, you got a messed-up pack o' hounds there awright."

Mavis, the buxom, pear-bottomed bottle blonde, walked through the doors and up to the bar with the gait of one accustomed to lifting motors in a foundry. She nodded in the men's direction to acknowledge their existence, then summoned Clyde from the back room by slamming one meaty fist on the bar.

"Afternoon, Mavis. What'll it be?" Clyde asked while wiping the area before her with a moist industrial shop cloth.

"Gimme a light beer," she ordered, then snatched a clawlike handful of stale popcorn from a bowl in front of her and jammed it in her mouth.

"Light beer, huh? You watchin' your weight are you, Mavis?" Clyde asked.

"Might as well. I damned sure got it out far enough to keep an eye on it!" she bellowed, then collapsed in a heaving mass of cackling blubber.

As another peal of laughter shook her considerable frame, she wiped a tear from her eye and reached over to emphasize her punch line with a jab to Josh's shoulder. The impact nearly unseated him, which seemed to add to her merriment and brought Clyde and Slats in on the joke too. Josh grabbed Slats's new cast to right himself, bringing a keen squeal of pain from the smaller man. This tickled Mavis to the point she lost her breath mid-cackle and stood before them with eyes protruding and mouth working like a goldfish out of water. Clyde was first to notice something was awry.

"Mavis? You all right?"

Mavis rotated her head from side to side briefly, a task made more novel due to her noticeable lack of a proper neck.

"Somebody *do* something!" Clyde shouted, then started back through the storeroom, thought better of it, and returned to climb over the bar.

Josh stepped in behind the gasping woman and whacked her between the shoulder blades with the edge of his hand, judo-style. His hand bounced back like he'd struck a radial tire.

"Step aside, Jackson!" Slats ordered from behind him.

Josh noticed with alarm what he intended to do.

"Slats!" Clyde cried out.

It was too late. Slats already had taken a false swing to gauge his range, then brought the snowy plaster cast down across Mavis's back with the sound of a mop handle slapped against a whisky barrel. A soggy wad of popcorn shot out of Mavis's mouth, caromed off the cash register, then landed among a case of empty long-necks under the bar. Mavis took in a massive breath, which encompassed enough air to fill a tire on a front-end loader, held it while she batted more tears from her eyes, then released it in an explosive sigh. Slowly she turned to Slats.

Josh started to step between them, knowing that Slats would have been no match for her in a fair fight, let alone with a broken arm. Slats was massaging the fractured cast and wincing in pain when she grabbed him.

"Spivey! Honey, you saved my life! Don't think Mavis Wills is somebody as would forget somethin' like that, no-siree Bob."

With that, she wrapped him in a bear hug. Owing to her superior height, Slats found himself buried between her massive breasts and in danger of smothering. To free his nose for a breath, he raised his face as far as she'd allow in her passion and found himself staring up through the gap of her cleavage. *It's like looking at the world through the rear sight of a big rifle,* he thought, then she kissed him.

"Mmmfffff!" Slats managed to say while flailing both good arm and cast like a wounded bird trying to take off.

Clyde and Josh thoroughly enjoyed his discomfort and, as he reflected later, Slats didn't find it altogether disagreeable either.

8

Brother Ray-Bob was still in his bus office preening when
Thelma and her parents joined the line of cars waiting to get
into the fairgrounds parking lot. Even from the road they could
tell the crowd would be considerably larger than the opening
night's, and the rear flaps of the main tent were rolled up to
allow an unobstructed view of the elevated stage from another
three hundred folding chairs set out in the open air. Additional
loud speakers sat atop metal posts alongside these seats, and
electricians worked frantically to get everything connected
prior to the eight o'clock opening time. In the parking lot clus-
ters of people gathered around picnic lunches spread on
pickup truck tailgates, adding a "Homecoming Game" atmosphere to the affair.

The weather promised a perfect evening. The sky was crys-
tal clear, with no sign of wind and an unseasonable warmth to
the air. *It's as though the Supreme Being Himself has sanc-
tioned the meeting,* Thelma thought, then stated it aloud to
Ethel, who grunted a noncommittal reply. Ethel was still of the
opinion that the Hallelujah Choir could do with T-shirts beneath their outfits. She'd noticed how the men seated near the
center of the rows had dug deeply into their pockets when the
plates were passed the second and third times. She had also
noticed how they held their contributions just out of reach of

the young women, forcing them to lean forward to collect, revealing an unholy amount of bosom in the process. Brother Ray-Bob had noticed this years earlier, along with the marked increase in offerings the gowns produced.

Brother Ray-Bob sprayed a final coat of Final Net over his hair, giving it the texture and sheen of a batting helmet. Then he tugged at the gold chain that swagged across his silver silk mohair vest producing a pair of keys that swung hypnotically before him. With the larger of the two keys he locked his office door; he applied the smaller to a drop-down door beneath the sofa. From this compartment he extracted a ledger with *Number Four* crudely emblazoned across its cover.

He sat at the desk and reviewed entries from the previous night, taking care to check off each item: rent paid on the vans, lease payments on the sound equipment, amounts taken in offerings, souvenirs, and so-forth, the personal check received from Rolly Klotz. This was his private set of books, and all entries were accurate.

In another ledger, also under the sofa, he'd entered somewhat edited figures that included amounts for fairground rent (there was no charge for his use of the fairgrounds), and names of temporary help for setting up and the amounts paid to each (all temporary help was provided by local religious groups, gratis). The check from Rolly Klotz was not mentioned, let alone the additional twelve percent over the amount collected that Rolly had paid Ray-Bob for his pile of change and bills. The latter of these books would be sent to the accountants who serviced his non-profit corporation. With a steady hand he penned a heading at the top of tonight's page: Dilbert's Forge Revival—Night Two.

A hush of whispers hissed through the crowd as neighbor elbowed neighbor when Foo-Foo struck the growling first note of his opening number. The resultant silence sharpened the contrast when the drummer opened up with his staccato rift. The night was electric, Foo-Foo had to admit. The Hallelujah Choir looked ravishing in their silver gowns with floppy sleeves and daring necklines.

His attention tonight was divided between the bevy of war-bling beauties upstage from him and a foxy number seated dead-center of the front row dressed, more or less, in a mossy-hued dress. Of particular interest was the way the woman's breasts peeked up above her neckline and the tight crease of cleavage between them that made the whole look like she had a baby's butt tucked between the cups of her bra. *Her cups runneth over!* he thought happily, paraphrasing one of his boss's favorite lines. Then a wave of chemical euphoria swept over him, which he allowed to flow down his fingers and out through his keyboard. The sound attracted the object of his attention, and she beamed a smile his way in appreciation.

"What are you grinning at?" Ethel asked under her breath.

"I'm just happy, that's all. Isn't it all wonderful? Can you believe this music?"

"No, I can't. And I can barely hear you over it, as a matter of fact. I tell you, it don't seem right for a church meetin', Thelma. Next thing you know, they'll have go-go girls up there in cages, for cryin' out loud!"

"Relax, Mama. Daddy's enjoying it. Look."

Indeed, Herman did appear to be enjoying himself. His face had flushed to a rich purple, partially due to the constriction of his tie but largely the result of his perusal of the Hallelujah Choir. His foot patted counterrhythm to the music.

"The old maggot's eyeing the women, that's all. I guar-an-tee it ain't the music, 'cause he's so deef he ain't heard hisself *fart* in ten years!"

"Mama! Remember where you *are*!" Thelma cautioned.

"Hmph! I wish to God I'd brought my cushion. You know how these hard seats hurt me, Thelma. And you had to sit right down front where I can't even massage nothing to get the circulation going. I tell you one thing, young lady, if I start getting the itch, I'm goin' back out to the truck where I can scratch!"

The opening ended and the soloist launched into her number, the clarity of her voice ringing true in the night air. Then came the upbeat finale to which the Hallelujah Choir undulated in syncopated choreography until the final note, leading into Brother Ray-Bob's theme. When the song was over, Thelma felt her chest tighten in anticipation, Ethel took advantage of the diversion of applause to tug her dress free and to scratch a buttock, and Herman had lost interest. All present felt immensely relieved as Brother Ray-Bob's flawlessly coiffed head appeared, rising above his pulpit.

Brother Ray-Bob stepped from the ersatz platform on the forklift tines that had replaced his stairway, then pulled the curtains closed behind him. As they closed, the lighting engineer began bringing up the voltage on two small quartz lights situated behind the opaque curtain until, some seconds later, a sort of aura encircled the diminutive preacher, as though he radiated it. The crowd was loud and appreciative.

Following his opening spiel and the first orbit of the collection plates, Brother Ray-Bob returned to do some healing. Thelma didn't recognize any of the people, but she was close enough to see the miracles as they unfolded. An elderly man advanced using an aluminum walker so feebly she was tempted to rise and assist him. Moments later, he did three minutes of respectable soft-shoe to the accompaniment of "When the Saints Go Marching In" by the band.

Hunchbacks walked out six inches taller than they'd walked in, the deaf heard Brother Ray-Bob even when his back was turned and he whispered, and arthritics magically became jugglers—all under the minister's loving, yet firm, supplications. The one that caught Thelma's attention most, however, bringing tears to her eyes and making her mascara run until she had to retire to the pickup and fix it, was a young blind girl.

The girl walked the distance from the rear of the tent to the stage assisted by a wolfish German Shepherd and her white cane. Brother Ray-Bob read from an index card that the girl had lost her vision at age three due to an accident and was deemed inoperable by doctors from Mobile to Boston. The girl stared straight ahead during this and never batted an eye, not even in response to the titter of laughter that slithered through the audience when the dog decided to lick himself. Brother Ray-Bob asked her if she would like to see, to which she replied in a small voice, and to no one's surprise, that she would.

He told her that was a tall order and that he wasn't sure he could bring it off alone, then suggested that she ask the audience to pray along with him. In the same small voice she begged the crowd for their prayers, bringing a few sniffs and sobs from them as they agreed. Then Brother Ray-Bob went into his work with vigor. He clasped a hand so firmly over her eyes that her neck jerked backward, then began to ask God's intervention on the girl's behalf. It didn't work. He tried again without results, then badgered the audience for their help in this matter. The third time he was certain they were praying as hard as they could, and the girl uttered a startled little yelp that brought everyone's eyes up from prayer and onto the stage.

"What was that, honey?" Ray-Bob asked into his microphone, then held it for her feeble reply.

"I said . . . this dawg ain't *white*!"

"THIS DAWG*(uh!)* . . . AIN'T WHITE, shesays! GLORY! You can SEE thedogthen, is that right?"

"Yes, but he was supposed to be white," she said in a disappointed tone.

"Are your parents present in the audience tonight, honey?" Ray-Bob asked, tears flowing bountifully from his own eyes now.

She nodded affirmatively, and he asked for them to stand, which they did.

"She says her dawg(uh!) ISN'T WHITE, brother and sister! She can SEE the DAWG! Can you tell us what she means?"

A middle-aged woman, tears flowing profusely down her cheeks, honked loudly into a handkerchief in one hand while her equally distraught husband held her other hand until the microphone was placed under her chin.

"When she got her seeing-eye dog, she wanted a white one . . . but . . . *(Honk!)* the white ones were *(sniff!)* a hundred dollars more and what with the doctor bills and all . . . *(honk! sniff)*. Besides, we never thought she would know the difference, but now . . . Oh, thank you Brother Ray-Bob!"

"Praise the *Lord*!" her husband added.

Applause exploded like thunder.

Thelma was shivering with emotion now. Ethel tugged her skirt out of her cheeks again, and Herman was asleep. When the meeting wound to a close, Thelma sought someone who might know if Brother Ray-Bob would be doing confirmations and soul-cleansing later in the week. She found Foo-Foo Mc-Cool.

*   *   *

Big Un had a lot to be thankful for, too. As a youngster he had had a vicious scrape with death, one that had brought him to this part of the country. He and a few thousand others were being transferred from their birthplace near Ocala, Florida, to a new home in Missouri when the truck transporting them suffered mechanical failure. While the driver was walking into town to get help, the batteries that powered their artificial environment gave out, resulting in the death of most his traveling companions. Big Un and a mere dozen more were alive when the driver returned in a tow truck, a fact the driver bemoaned loudly.

As the wounded vehicle was being hooked up, the driver noticed a suitable area nearby and released the survivors, three of whom perished the first day. Three more succumbed to snakes, raccoons, and such, and another four had met their ends from their only natural enemies as adults: men and lampreys. Big Un didn't know these facts about his counterparts (such thoughts were beyond his limited mental capacity), but he did have a lot to be thankful for anyway. A one-pound sauger pike had been caught up in the swift current just upstream and had decided to duck into the dark haven that was Big Un's lair. With one spasmotic flinch Big Un opened his massive mouth, creating a suction that drew the smaller fish inside with the speed of a switchblade opening. He swallowed and was again thankful.

9

Josh awoke from a discomforting dream to see Thelma at her dressing mirror. *What a bitch!* he thought, then reviewed his dream.

The setting was Dauphin Island near his home in Florida. Scattered along the sands were graying beach houses built of a type of wood that would fade within two seasons to the point no one could tell how long they had been there. He stood surveying what looked to be a prefab ghost town while gulls wheeled overhead. It would have been a peaceful place, were it not for its reminders of Mother Nature's bad side.

Naked foundation piers jutted from the sand in the few vacant lots, tombstones of the beach houses that had come and then gone with the wind. Harriet had been the wind's name, and she had cleared this beach of buildings one afternoon in August two years earlier, then sent a storm surge ashore to blot out the driveways and mailboxes, all signs of man. Now these flimsy replacements faded in the sun among their predecessors' bones.

He was crabbing in the surf near where the old fishing pier had stood. He'd throw out a chicken neck on a string, wait until he felt the tickle of greedy crabs, then slowly pull the neck to him until they were within reach of his net. It was as he was emptying his net into a styrofoam cooler that he first noticed the purple and pink clouds rolling off the sea toward him. At this same moment, he noticed that the beach houses nearest him had their windows and doors covered with plywood or tape.

Onward the cloud came, pushing a wall of water before it. In panic he dropped his net and ran inland and up a sand dune. Halfway up, his feet began to churn the loose sand and his forward progress stalled. The sound of the advancing wave brought the hairs up on the back of his neck and caused his scalp to tighten in fear. A scream worked its way into his throat as the first heavy drops of wind-tossed water hit him. Then he woke up, wondering what it all meant.

It means, he thought to himself while watching Thelma watching herself, *that my existence on this planet thus far has amounted to but a plop of seagull poop in the sea of life. Nothing I've done, nor likely will do, will last any longer than those flimsy beach houses the ignorant rich toss onto the beach as hurricane fodder, generation after generation.* It troubled him. He'd never thought of himself in such insignificant terms. In fact, he spent little time thinking of himself at all.

Thelma was thinking of herself a lot. The rag-tag musician had informed her that Brother Ray-Bob would, in fact, be having an altar call during his last service. Beyond this, he mentioned Reverend (had he actually pronounced it Rev-*Runt*?) Ray-Bob also did one-on-one sessions for those who contributed a generous "love offering." The duration and intensity of these sessions were directly in proportion to the size of the contribution. After much consideration, he reckoned she could have a fifteen-minute personal encounter with God for about two hundred dollars, slightly higher during the peak hours immediately preceding and following the services. Having personally witnessed the man cure blindness inside five minutes, she reasoned fifteen minutes should be adequate to restore her soul to like-new condition, with perhaps a little left over to take care of her sagging boobs and leathery neck.

"Morning, glory," she said as his image filled her mirror.

74

"Morning. What time is it?"

"About half-past eight. Why? I mean, are you catching a train or taking medicine or something?"

"Gotta go by the bank, that's all. I need to transfer some bucks out of escrow into our checking account."

Thelma's keenly penciled and brutally plucked eyebrows shot up at this.

"How . . . how much are you thinking of transferring?"

"Four, five hundred I suppose. Klotz won't let me touch the tax reserve, the asshole."

"Josh! You should be more understanding. I'm sure that if you reasoned with Mr. Klotz, he'd let you have that money, too. Then when our tax refund comes next month, you could repay it."

"I tried reasoning with him. We were one reasonable person short. Well, time to wake up and smell the . . . shit."

The air was heavily laden with the sewage refinement odor this morning. A wind shift, he reckoned correctly, and this time of year that would mean rain. As though to confirm his suspicion, a sound like a bowling ball rolling down its lane issued from the sky above the house and terminated with a muffled crump. It was strangely comforting to him, but the opposite to Thelma who pursed her lips in disapproving fashion. Josh neglected to mention what the lips resembled.

"Gonna rain like a cow pissing on a flat rock!" he announced with a smile.

"Maybe not. It might blow over you know."

"Uh-uh. That sounds like the real thing all right," he said with assurance, then wondered if distant thunder had brought on his dream.

"No matter. That's what tents are put up for. I'm still going again tonight, and that's final!"

"Who's arguing? By all means go."

"And tomorrow night there's an all-night singing with a prayer breakfast the next morning. I'll be going to that, too."

"Great. What then, a sanctimonious slumber party followed by a taffy pull?"

"Smart ass."

"Yes ma'am. I guess I am at that. See ya whenever you get through with all this. We'll go out and have a drink or two, then come home and make wacky-wacky 'til the sun comes up."

"That'll be the day, Josh Jackson!"

"Now *that*, I believe." He smiled while pulling on his shoes.

The youngest dog of his bunch, scarcely more than a pup, was at the front of his vintage pickup wagging and smiling when Josh came out of the house. After soliciting a pat on the head, the pup sat staring at the grill of the truck expectantly. *Maybe,* Josh thought, *this one will have some sense. At least he's at the right end of things.* His illusion faded when he slapped the hood. The puppy dashed to the rear of the truck and started yipping at the top of his lungs. Just to be aggravating, Josh held the horn down for over a minute. With satisfaction, he noted Thelma's face pressed against the kitchen window, her lips pursed accusingly. Then he roared off toward town.

The rain started just as he passed the sewer plant, coming in such a torrent that he had to roll up his window. By the time he passed the fairgrounds, the entire countryside was drenched and water was standing in large puddles between the tents. He smiled on seeing Brother Ray-Bob's engineers and gaffers chasing through the growing puddles dismantling loudspeakers. Thelma, it seemed, was in for a major disappointment. Since he was in an expansive mood, he decided to stop at the Ba-Da for coffee and breakfast. The face framed by the door window made him happy he did.

"Hope you're not walking, Pamalou. I think that'd knock the curl out of your hair for sure!" he said while indicating the rain with a thumb over his shoulder.

"Just the opposite with me, Josh," she said with a concerned look as a gust of wind threw several fat drops through the door before he could close it completely. "My curls are natural, such as they are, and rain just makes them tighten up into a frizz."

"Well, I'll bet you're still cute with a frizzy do. Want some coffee?"

"No thanks. Just had some."

"Then you can watch me drink a cup, and then I'll give you a lift to the bank. I'm told I drink coffee with the best of 'em."

She looked at her watch, clucked her tongue softly, then shrugged.

"Why not. Not often one gets an opportunity to watch a Floridian drink coffee. Why are you going to the bank, if I might ask?"

"Need to transfer some bucks from escrow. I should have done it last time, but I was afraid if I stuck around any longer your boss and I might have gotten unpleasant, if you know what I mean."

Pamalou slid gracefully into the opposite seat of his booth and shook off Ba's offer of a menu.

"I think I know what you mean. I must say, though, that I wouldn't mind seeing that myself."

"Ah well, if Klotz wasn't an ass, he'd have no personality at all. Excuse me, Pamalou."

"For what? It's the truth!" she exclaimed, then leaned across the table and whispered. "My aunt used to say that when she found things like Rolly Klotz on her lawn, she poured salt on 'em!"

She allowed herself a small giggle, and Josh smiled happily. Her nearness brought the smell of her into his nostrils and set his mind to reeling with ideas. It seemed the most natural thing in the world to lean forward and plant a kiss on her full mouth, a thought that retained much of its appeal even after he'd calculated its consequences. He thought with alarm that she'd read his mind, for she leaned back abruptly. Then Barbara set a steaming cup of coffee between them and flipped open her order pad.

"Coffee'll do for right now, thanks. I'll be back in a bit for breakfast. Or lunch. Whichever."

Josh stirred his coffee absently.

"Why are you doing that?" Pamalou asked.

"Doing what?"

"Stirring your coffee. You didn't put anything in it, you know."

"Oh! I don't know. Habit, I guess."

"Do you normally take something in it? I could get you some sugar or the creamer."

"No, thanks. And no, I don't usually take anything in it. Except sometimes I like a shot of Grand Marinier."

Pamalou perked up at this.

"Do you now? That seems oddly cosmopolitan coming from someone who drives a pickup truck."

"Ah yes, but a red, *classic* pickup truck. And one without bumper stickers or a gunrack, at that."

"Oh, I see. Yes, I suppose you're right about that. I like Kalhua in mine."

"*You* have a pickup truck?"

"Don't be silly. I mean in my coffee. I like Kalhua and cream, the real stuff though, none of that nondairy crap."

"Sounds nice. I'll have to try that sometime."

"Wait until winter. It's better when it's cold outside, especially after skiing or sledding."

"Do you ski?"

"No, but I wear a set of bibs pretty well."

"I'll just bet you do," he said picturing her in a tight ski outfit, never getting past the sweater.

"Do you ski?"

"Water. Never tried snow. Not much call for it in Florida, and this is as far north as I've lived."

"You should try it. You look like a skier. Bet you could wear a set of bibs well, too."

"I'll think about it. Do you go often?"

"Twice. Once last year, once this. Same guy both times."

"Your boyfriend?"

"Not really, but that's about as close to anything steady I've had lately."

He wondered about this. Couldn't believe it.

"I can't believe that. Surely the guys are beating down your door."

"*Were* is the operable term here. I think they gave up on me. Guess I'm too hard on them."

He wondered if she meant sexually, hoped maybe she did, knew probably she didn't.

"Oh?" was the best he could do.

"Too demanding. They tend to try and be super smooth, super rich. *Gentlemen's Quarterly* kind of guys. I'd rather they just be themselves."

"Even if they drive pickup trucks?"

"Especially if they drive pickup trucks!" she answered with another small giggle. "But then I haven't dated anyone who does."

"Yeah, I've heard that about you. It takes a red Porsche, right?"

"Well, it did, I suppose. That was just a put-off line I used on one of the Blalocks' nephews, then damned if he didn't get one and I had to go out with him. Can you believe that?"

He thought for a moment and decided he could believe it. Might be worth the price of a sports car at that.

"I guess you need to raise your sights somewhat, Pamalou. By the way, I find your name kinda bulky for such a trim lady. Can I call you Pam?"

"Please do, and it's not my name. My real name is Pamela Lynn. Lynn was my mother's maiden name. When I came to live with my aunt after my parents' accident, the kids in school called me everything—Pam the Spam, Pamalee, Pamela-dee-da—you name it. They settled on Pamalou because I hated it the most."

"Boys can be cruel at that age. They were probably trying to flirt and didn't know how."

"Forget it! It was the girls that did most of the name calling. I was something of an . . . uh . . . early bloomer, I suppose you'd say, and I think they were jealous."

Josh drained his coffee and dropped a dollar on the table, then stood to leave.

"I bet they still are, Pam."

"Thanks, I think," she said with a slight blush. "Ready?"

"I don't think it's gonna let up, so we might as well make a

79

run for it. Tell you what. You wait here, and I'll pull around to the door."

Pam's dash through the rain didn't take into account his opening the door for her or the narrow width of the slick leather seats in the truck. She dove inside and slid right up next to him. He initially recoiled at feeling her against him, then fought the urge to take her in his arms and. . . . Before he could act upon or dismiss his urge, she leaned away and slammed her door shut.

The drive was all too brief. When he arrived at the bank and she had reentered her world behind the teller window, she handled his transaction with cool efficiency and without a trace of the warmth and friendliness he'd come to expect. Her reason for this became evident as he turned to leave, for there standing in his office door, looking like he'd dressed with Ray Charles as his batman, was Klotz puffing on one of the thin, black cigars he affected. Before Josh could leave, Klotz walked over to where Pam sat, placed a hand on her shoulder in a possessive way, and took the cigar from his mouth.

"I hope you have good luck with your financial problems, Jackson!" he said in an overly loud voice Josh took as an attempt to belittle him in front of Pam.

Through the rage that flew into his eyes, he noticed the grimace on Pam's face and that she had wiggled out from under Klotz's hand.

"And I hope when you get home tonight, Klotz, your mother runs out from under the porch and bites you on your big, flabby ass! Now go back to sucking on your whippet turd, and leave me the hell alone."

Klotz's mouth fell open in shock, as did Pam's. Then hers drew itself up to a pucker and fired a kiss at him silently before breaking into a grin she had to cough to remove from her face. She couldn't shake it from her eyes, though, he noticed. There was something else there, too. Something lying behind the rich green and gold of the iris that he couldn't quite quantify, but it looked like respect or admiration. Before Klotz could regain his composure and order him to do so, Josh turned and walked out into the rain.

"A great day for burning your bridges," he said aloud. "No danger of the fires spreading in this."

Then he drove back to the Ba-Da and ate a hearty breakfast. For the first time in a long time, he felt good about himself.

10

So. It starts again, he thought to himself. *What next time, hmm? Will it be more of the same, or will you feel it again— like the lady in Mobile? Can you really, really help some of these people? Or is it all just part of the show?*

"I don't know that!" Brother Ray-Bob countered aloud. "Anymore I'm not so sure about that one."

But you are *sure, aren't you? Isn't she the reason you stayed on the road? Don't you still think, deep down, that He sent her to keep you going?*

"Maybe I just wanted to believe that. Maybe I just psyched myself into it that night. Besides, where would I have gone?"

Back to Monroe, back to your family, his mind answered him.

"No family there to return to, we know that right enough, don't we?" he said.

You still haven't forgiven her, have you? It was the war, you know. Lots of other girls did it—the boyfriend's last night before he ships out to combat, emotions are high, why hold it against her? You could forgive and understand in any other case, even your own. Especially your own!

"All right, but what about him?"

He died, Raymond. Don't you think he'd have made an honest woman of your mother had he lived? He's still your father.

82

"No, he's not! He's *dead,* you just said so! He's always been dead, even before I was born he was dead! I never had a father. That's why . . . ."

That's why your mother's father threw her out, and her great with child. And a great child you turned out to be, too! Preaching love and hope and forgiveness night-after-night, yet you won't let go that little string of hurt and hate, will you?

"No."

You'd forgive her if she was the old woman in Mobile, wouldn't you?

"Well . . . ."

Of course you would. She was special. She made you feel special! Isn't that right, Raymond?

"She made me feel His *power.* She made me feel He had really called me to this, that He had real plans for me. She made me feel I was all the things I wanted to be . . . to do His work. She made me feel loved."

By Him?

"Of course."

And you thought He gave you that feeling, is that it?

"Yes, that's it. He gave it to me, and it felt soooo wonderful!"

Here's a thought for you, Raymond. If you really believe that it was Him that gave you the good feeling when you cured that old woman, then you have to believe He is the one who has structured your life from the beginning. Now ain't that right?

"He is in charge of our lives all the way. From the cradle to the grave! From the womb to the tomb!"

You don't have to preach to me, Raymond. I'm your conscience, remember? I'm just here to remind you of things, to let you bounce things around until they settle out in a way you can deal with them. Like that good feeling of yours.

"What's to rationalize about that? It was good, a gift from Him."

Then if you really believe He gives and controls and determines who will have what, then . . . .

"Then what?"

Then it was He who took your Daddy! He who made your poor mother a fallen woman who had to take in washing to make a living and to feed you!

"I'm sure He had a good reason."

Are you? Is that what you told your mother before you left? Maybe He just put you both down there in shanty town so you could learn all them old spirituals from Miss Hattie and Gert. Is that what you're thinking?

"Well, I *did* learn a lot of scriptures from them, and there's no denying I loved singing those old songs. I was pretty good at it, too."

Damned good! That's what got your little feet pointed this way, remember? Silver-voiced little angel you were, brought tears to all the old women's eyes when they heard you on the soft ones and set all them hobnail boots to stomping on the quick ones. That's why old Brother Clay took you along, re-member?

"I remember. He took me, all right."

Ah, but was it him? Or was it Him?

"Whoever, whichever, whatever. . . . I didn't ask for it to be like this. It just happened, that's all. Gert and Hattie said I could sing, claimed it was a gift. Then Brother Clay came along and said so, too. You hear a thing often enough, you start to believe it yourself."

So you went along. I remember. I was there, too. And then?

"And then he died. Then the old bus died, and we needed the money to keep going. Even if we were going to pack it in, we still needed enough to get the bus going again so . . . ."

So here we are. He left you quite a bit of baggage, didn't he? I mean, he made you wonder what you really are, didn't he?

"I was just a kid of a boy! Mama entrusted me to him, who'd have thought that underneath all those platitudes he was a . . . ."

"Pervert? Pederast? Child abuser? There's lots of names for it now. Made you ashamed, didn't it? Makes you wonder still if you are a man or doomed to become what he was, doesn't it? Made you want to leave the business, huh?

"Yes, yes to all that! Why bring it up?"

Just making sure we are both singing from the same sheet of music, that's all. The shrink said you had to understand all that before you could understand what you are and what you have to do to get back where you were originally headed.

"I'm not going to jail, if that's what you mean."

Beneath you, is it? I wonder if anything is any more. Lots of precedence for preachers being in jail, Raymond. John the Baptist laid that foundation.

"Yes, but . . . ."

I know. John didn't have to worry about getting raped in jail, did he? Well, you pays your money and you takes your chances, Raymond. Now, you need to do something to boost that sagging ego before you start thinking of swallowing all those pills again. We nearly did it last time, didn't we? Have a drink instead, bed one of your songbirds.

"Thanks for the latitude. You're a bastard, you know that?"

Look who's talking.

11

Josh had been right about the rain keeping people away, Thelma grudgingly admitted as she pulled into the series of small lakes that was now the fairgrounds parking lot. The few vehicles present bore out-of-state license plates and belonged to the troop of gaffers, sound engineers, concessions operators, and general flunkies who traveled with Brother Ray-Bob. She was entertaining thoughts of returning home and trying the next day when a ray of light beamed down from between thunderheads to illuminate the fairgrounds. As quickly as it had come, it was swallowed up by a tall, anvil-shaped cloud and the area was again plunged into the rainy gloom of early evening. The electric eye-operated street lights on nearby utility poles blinked in confusion, then sputtered back to full intensity. Thelma took the ray as a sign from above and, holding a shawl over her head to stave off the rain, slogged and plodded toward the main tent.

Brother Ray-Bob was in a sour mood. The rain had cost him an estimated five grand in collections for this night and, more importantly, it had broken the orderly progression of his services. Now many who had attended the previous night would be hard-pressed to attend tomorrow or would lose the inclination to do so. He also had to decide whether to use his planned third night's show or to skip directly to the fourth.

Right now he was considering opening an hour or two early for his final service on Saturday and perhaps staying over for an early afternoon session on Sunday. It went against convention for him to perform on Sunday, against business ethics, too. The local clergy generally enjoyed his visits because it helped their attendance long after he'd departed, but a Sunday service would put him in direct competition with them and could leave a bad taste in their mouths. God knows he'd had enough friction in the past from those who self-righteously referred to themselves as legitimate clergy.

No, he decided, Saturday would be it. Tonight he'd relax, rest his throat, and maybe go visit some sickos at the local hospital as a goodwill gesture. For an instant he thought he heard the voice reminding him of his early days, back when he routinely visited the hospitals and old folks homes while the tents were being erected. Those visits had made him feel good. The sick and shut-ins were so grateful for someone to talk to now that society had elected to move on without them, to know that someone out there cared they still existed. Now, of course, he'd take a photographer along to cover his visits. The local paper would probably welcome a story, and every inch of ink translated to operating capital in the long haul.

He shook the thought from his mind and pulled the bottle of whiskey from its drawer, pouring three fingers into his tumbler. He smiled as he did so, remembering the time in Natchez (or was it Tupelo?) when he'd almost said something about folks "being prepared to meet their Maker's Mark" from the pulpit! He'd switched brands for a while after that, certain that he'd never stumble into evoking Jack Daniel's name during a sermon.

Beside the tumbler, two pink pills stared up at him like the eyes of an albino Barbie Doll. *Godspeed,* he called them. *Won't need them tonight, either,* he thought, then scraped them into the drawer with the whiskey.

The liquor went down smoothly, leaving a trail of fire along his tender throat, then a numbing sensation he found particularly pleasant. Pouring another shot, he flipped the pages of his personal ledger and did some quick calculations. If things went well the rest of the month, he stood to take in close to two hundred thousand dollars above overhead, most of which was already earmarked for other commitments. This didn't include the ten to twelve percent "vigorish" he'd pull in from the greedy businessmen along his route for "selling" the cash offering to them for the tax deduction. That the money came largely from low income farmers, sawmill workers, pensioners, and the like didn't bother him a bit. He'd come up as poor as any of them and had come to consider it mere coincidence that a fool and his money ever got together in the first place.

Foo-Foo was nowhere to be found when Thelma hesitantly poked her head inside the big tent, but the Hallelujah Choir was gathered around the stage running through some hymns. They looked a random collection of females without their makeup and sleek gowns, she thought, and didn't sound much better. Not only were they practicing without music, but there didn't seem to be anyone in charge. Brother Ray-Bob probably leads them himself, she assumed, then felt a wave of disappointment wash over her as she considered that he must be absent from the premises. With the members of the choir now reduced to mere human females in her eyes, she felt more comfortable approaching them. The nearer she got, the better she felt since the "girls" were not particularly young, nor were any of them more attractive than herself.

"Excuse me," she said to the back of a shortish brunette who turned suddenly, startled.

"Shit!" the brunette blurted out, then covered her mouth with a hand while the other girls giggled openly. "I'm sorry. You scared me. I'm a little goosey, I guess. Can I help you?"

"Yes, I would like to speak with Reverend Thomas. Is he around?"

The girls looked back and forth at each other, then studied Thelma closely.

"I think he's in his bus, but he doesn't like to be disturbed. Are you with the press or something?"

"No, I'm not." Thelma said slowly, thinking. "But I have some money for him, an offering."

"Oh! Well, in that case, I imagine he'll want to see you straight away, right girls?"

Some laughed curtly while others agreed that he would.

"Tell you what. You wait here, and I'll go see if he's in. Who shall I say is calling?"

"Thelma Jackson."

"Right. And who do you represent?"

"Thelma Jackson!" she said, holding her chin out defiantly.
"Right."

Brother Ray-Bob took his time putting things away when the knock came at his door. If asked, he invariably let his visitors know they had interrupted him in meditation, then good-naturedly refuse their apologies. When he opened the door, however, he realized his ruse wouldn't be necessary. Nor would it have been believed.

"Paula! You're a might early, honey, but I'm in a generous mood, so . . . ."

"So you'd better snap out of it, R.B. There's a woman here to see you, and she comes bearing gifts."

"Oh?" he said while slicking his hair back on both side, with his hands. "From what source?"

"Personal, she said. Didn't mention an amount, but the name is Jackson. Thelma Jackson. Do you know her?"

"Can't say as I do. Jackson, eh?"

Paula's eyes narrowed perceptively, looking for signs of recognition in Ray-Bob's. She knew better than to expect anything. The man could lie as smoothly as he could preach, perhaps better, and in some cases they were the same thing.

"Yeah, Jackson. Attractive, tall, reddish hair. She looks familiar, but I can't place her."

"Well, show her in. Probably from a local congregation or maybe the newspaper."

"She says she's not press, R.B., and she don't act pushy enough to be, either."

"Has it occurred to you she might be lying about that?"

You should know about lying better than I, big boy, she thought. Aloud she said, "She don't look the type. You want to see her?"

"Give me ten minutes, then show her in."

Paula nodded and departed. In the interim Brother Ray-Bob changed into his evangelical lounging clothes: navy blue slacks, a pale blue Givenchy shirt with a gray cardigan sweater worn unbuttoned with the sleeves pushed up to the suede patches on the elbows. To complete his outfit, he wore half-lens glasses tilted well down on his nose. He opened a worn Bible on his desk and scratched hasty notes onto a yellow legal pad. As an afterthought, he crunched two breath mints in his mouth to mask the whiskey. They burned away the anesthetic effect of the Maker's Mark and left a wintergreen chill in their wake. He was ready when the knock came on his door again.

"Yes? It's open!" Thelma heard the celebrated voice call through the thin door, then felt a flush of heady anticipation as the brunette turned the knob and eased the door open.

"Well! Miss Jackson, is it?" Ray-Bob said through a beaming smile in the ventriloquist fashion he'd learned from his mentor.

"*Missus* Jackson, actually, Rev . . . Brother Thomas," Thelma replied airily.

"Please! Brother *Ray-Bob*. Everybody calls me Brother Ray-Bob. Won't you come in and have a seat, Mrs. Jackson?"

Thelma walked stiffly inside, eyeing the tidy office and its equally tidy occupant. Ray-Bob nodded a dismissal to Paula who nodded back and closed the door behind her. He stepped up to Thelma's side and took her by the elbow to speed her pace to the sofa, while with his other hand he reached back and silently turned the lock on the door.

He was impressed by the tall woman, but then he was always smitten by stately females. Another function of his ego, the distant shrink had said. *They're all the same height, when lying down,* he remembered having replied. This one, though, she had something woefully absent in his harem of singers: she still had at least a modicum of innocence. He could sense it and knew from experience he could use it against her. *Inno-*

cence, after all, he thought, *is more often a weakness than a virtue.*

"Now, what is it I can do for you today, Mrs. Jackson?" he asked while rubbing his small hands together briskly as though before a fireplace.

The only heat in the office came from Thelma's blush as she sank backward into the soft sofa, lost her balance, and flashed a glimpse of white panties in the process of regaining it. Ray-Bob registered the peek from his vantage point in the chair, and his smile broadened momentarily before sinking into feigned concern.

"Oh dear! I should have warned you about that. I've tried to get it replaced, but once you've paid for one of these custom jobs the dealers don't seem to care about you. Would you rather sit here?"

"No, thank you. This is fine," she answered while trying unsuccessfully to press her legs together, the soft material of the sofa constantly insinuating itself between her thighs to prevent this. Finally, she managed to maneuver to the front edge and leaned forward slightly in a pose that allowed her more modesty. "And you can call me Thelma, if you like."

"All right. Thelma it is then," he said while adjusting his reading glasses to cover his stare down the low neck of her green dress. "Now, I understand you have something for me, is that right?"

"Well, yes. I've attended your last couple of services here, and I listen to you on radio all the time, and I think I'd . . . that is, I feel I'm ready to . . . ."

"Yes? Ready to what, Thelma?"

"I want you to pray for my soul, Brother Ray-Bob. I've not been the person I'm capable of being. My husband is a *heathern* who makes fun of me, *and you,* and lately I've had a heavy heart because of my feelings toward him and my own . . . well, *shortcomings,* . . ." she blurted out in a gush. Not the speech she'd planned, but she felt certain she'd covered everything.

Brother Ray-Bob pulled the glasses from his face and nibbled on one of their earpieces while he considered her words. *Lots and lots of possibilities,* he thought. The remark about the husband's attitude alone could be the hinge point around which he could build his case. Along with the desire he felt welling up within him as he again eyed the rounded mounds of breast that rose from the dainty lace at the top of her slip, he felt something else he enjoyed even more: power.

This woman had just placed her entire life in his hands and at his disposal. He could attack the husband and perhaps break the marriage, or he could play the forgiving angle and come off as a modern-day saint, perhaps even convince her to bring the husband to a service and recognize him in front of the crowd. Judging by Thelma's stature, her husband would likely be a tall man, and he did so enjoy humbling tall men. He was almost decided on defending the husband when Thelma burst into tears and broke his concentration.

"Now, now! Thelma, God heals all wounds, you know that? Whatever it is, however you've strayed, HE willunderstand. Now talk to me, honey."

He didn't go to her immediately, preferring instead to watch the delightful way her breasts rose and fell with each sob and particularly enjoying how each breast was revealed beyond the suntan line when she took in a deep breath between bouts of crying. She put her face in her hands denying him his view, but replaced it with an unobstructed view of creamy thighs. He felt a throb in his groin, which spurred him into movement. Bending low beside her, he placed an arm across her shivering shoulders and began to gently pat her on the back. She responded by grabbing him around the waist and laying her head against his hip. Soon she had recovered enough to speak through jerky sniffs and snubs.

She poured out her heart to him. She covered her life as a little girl, with particular emphasis on her perfect Sunday school attendance through junior high. Then she continued right up to the point she perceived as her downfall—her disappointment at the hands of the Catfish Committee. She went on to voice her opinion that the contest had been rigged all along before encapsulating her behavior immediately afterward.

She used phrases like *wanton disregard for her parents' wishes, God's punishment for her vanity,* and *engaged in ca-*

sual and unnatural sex. She even confessed to having trapped Josh with her pretended pregnancy. He liked the sex part and was tempted to press her for details; the whiskey was playing havoc with his objectivity.

"Thelma, there's nothing you've told me that HE can't understand and forgive. You say you pretended to be pregnant in order to get your husband to marry you? Well, I can't say that wasn't a sin, but I think I understand why you did it and I'm sure the Lord does too. You KNEW, deepinyourheart-ofhearts, that the BE-HAV-IOR you'dlapsedinto, wasn't right. So you duped this man into marryin' you, Thelma, NOT BE-CAUSE YOU LOVED HIM, no sir. But because YOU wanted to CHANGE your wicked ways. And you DID! Didn't you, Thelma?"

She nodded that she had, disappointing him slightly.

"And you never loved him, did you?"

"Oh, I don't know. He's OK most of the time. But he can be so aggravating sometimes!"

"And he's a HEATH-ERN! Right?" he used her word, which was originally his own anyway.

"Well, his heart is probably in the right place, but he don't understand why I need to . . . ."

"Need to FEEL THE TOUCH, oftheLord! Is that it?"

He was on a roll now, working the subject back into his arena.

"Well, yes. I suppose so."

"Well, Thelma. I'll tell you what I'm a-gonna do. I'm gonna PRAY for YOU, right now. I'm gonna ASK JAY-ZUS, to come-intoyourheart! Do you want me to do that for you, honey?"

Thelma was mesmerized by his voice to the point she couldn't speak. She nodded affirmatively and took his hand as he leaned back to help her from the sofa. Ray-Bob became even more physically excited as she stood to her full height, a whole head above his own. He reached up and placed both hands upon her shoulders and closed his eyes. Thelma shut hers tightly as he did this, then he began.

"Lord? We ask that you look down upon us here tonight."

She recognized this as the opening line he'd used leading

into his healing session the night before. She gasped as she felt his hands tighten on her shoulders and fought an urge to pull up a sleeve that had slipped off her shoulder under his grasp. Then she focused within herself and concentrated on his words. Tears flowed in a steady stream down her cheeks.

"Look down especially on your loving servant THELMA JACKSON, here, and bring the light of YOUR LOVE into-herheart. For her HEART is HEAVY!" His hands slid down from her shoulders to a position over her heart and lingered there, touching her with the softness of a butterfly with sore feet. Then he pressed down firmly as he began again.

"Yes it is, Lord! HER HEART IS HEAVY BECAUSE *(uh!)* she feels the weightofsin. And she is SORROWFUL, oh Lord, YEA, she is RE-PENT-ENT *(uh!)* and she wants to put her-burdendown."

With each heavily accented word, he gathered her flesh into his hands until both breasts were in danger of escaping their confinement. When she didn't react to this, he proceeded to get bolder.

"We ask that you REACH DEEP DOWN, Lord!"

He reached deep down, juggling the fullness of her breasts in his hands as though they were mushmelons he was considering buying.

"REACH DEEP DOWN and let your spirit FLOW THROUGH THESE HANDS and intoThelma'sheart!"

He paused to catch his breath. Thelma could feel her heart racing and knew for certain that Brother Ray-Bob could feel it too. She didn't care. Sweat was beginning to form a shiny glow upon her face, and she truly *did* feel something! She felt a tingle flowing through her that she attributed to divine stimulation. When she cracked one eye open, she noticed Brother Ray-Bob was sweating profusely, yet had a beatific smile on his face, so she assumed he was feeling it too. She gasped as he resumed.

"We ask that you TAKE SISTER THELMA in YOUR HANDS (he responded accordingly and squeezed) and show her the TRUE PATH torighteousness. We ask this in JAY-ZUS' NAME, amen."

He released her, tucked the boobs back pretty much as he'd found them, then collapsed into his chair in an attempt to hide the bulging erection pressing its little wet nose against his dark trousers. Nervously, he crossed his legs and looked up at her. She still had her eyes closed.

"Thelma? Honey, do you feel it?"

"I . . . why yes! I think I *do*!" she said. "I DO!"

"HALLELUJAH!" he shouted, then stood and embraced her.

Thelma gratefully wrapped her arms around him and squeezed. In her ardor she failed to recognize the jab of his manhood as it pressed against the inside of her thigh, well below its intended target. After a time she released her hold and held him at arm's length. A troubled look knitted the evangelist's face, a look Thelma took as disapproval. It frightened her and robbed her of much of the elation she was feeling.

"Brother Ray-Bob? Is something the matter?"

He reached into the small refrigerator beside his desk and fetched out two Nehi Grape sodas, opened both and handed her one. He paused for effect, then spoke in halting, humble tones as though he didn't quite know how to verbalize what he felt.

"Thelma? God has a message for you."

"He does?"

"Yes, He *has*!" he said emphatically, tears escaping his eyes to run down his nose and drop off.

"Well . . . what is it? Am I forgiven? Is he going to . . . ."

"He wants YOU, Thelma."

"Me?" she whispered. She wanted to go to Heaven, sure, but this sounded like she was being rounded up to leave right now!

"Yes, YOU! When I went to him at your BE-HEST, a moment ago. When I LAID HANDS on you, in the fashion prescribed for healers. When I asked HIM, to come into YOUR HEART. I felt HIS HAND on MY shoulder! Yes I did. And he whispered to me, Thelma. Do you want to know what He said?"

Thelma was staring, wide-eyed. She nodded, not sure what might be coming next.

"HE said, 'RAY-BOB'—remember, I said EVERYBODY calls me Ray-Bob!" he said with a wink that released another pair of tears. "He said 'Ray-Bob, this is a FINE woman, who to her most GRIEVOUS ERR-OR, is married to a HEATH-ERN who doesn't deserve her!' He said that, Thelma. Then He said, 'I have DELIVERED HER unto YOU this day *(uh!)*, so that your FLESHES MIGHT TOUCH, and that THROUGH YOU . . . HER SOUL maybesaved!' "

Thelma nodded at each pronouncement, tears flowing down her cheeks again leaving a trail of mascara. She wiped at them with the back of her hand, smearing the mess under each eye.

" 'TAKE-HER-WITH-YOU!' He said. 'Take her with you so SHE might join YOU in spreading MY word!' "

He watched carefully as she absorbed this, measuring her for a response. When none came immediately, he turned his bottle up and drained half of the cold liquid. When he resumed, it was with a tongue that, while not visibly forked, was distractingly purple.

"He said that, Thelma. As surely as we're here tonight enjoying HIS bounty," he stated matter-of-factly, while hoisting the Nehi. "He wants YOU to come with ME. Now what do you say?"

"I'll have to think about this. I'm . . . I *am* married, after all, and . . . ."

"Let me ask you this, Thelma. Were you married in a church? I mean a REAL church! One whose minister was CALLED PERSONALLY to preach *THE WORD*?"

"Well no, I . . . *we* . . . were married by a Justice of the Peace in Springfield. I'm afraid I lied about my age, you see. I told Josh I was just seventeen so we had to go to Springfield because . . . ."

"That's IT, then! Don't you SEE?"

She didn't.

"Think about the CER-E-MO-NY, Thelma. It say-uz, '. . . those whom GOD . . .' not some nig-nog petty function-ary like a judge or Justice of the Peace!" he said with obvious distaste, then paused to let her savor his displeasure with elected officials. "But 'Those whom GOD has joined together, let NO MAN put asunder!' Don't you see what God is saying here, Thelma? Your marriage to that DO-NOTHING, BEER-SWILLING HEATHERN, is null and void in the eyes of the Lord! HE didn't bring you together, SATAN did! During your period of disillusion."

Brother Ray-Bob smiled and spread his hands palms up before himself as if to say "What could be more evident?" Thelma looked from his hands to his face and back again.

"Are you sure?" she asked in her kitten voice.

"I am. He wants you on the bus to GLO-RY! HE wants US together as a TEAM! HIS team, Thelma. Can you deny Him that?"

She shook her head from side to side, then a small smile of hope broke through the rain of her tears.

"Could I . . . ?"

"Could you what, honey?"

"Could I sing with the Hallelujah Choir?"

Ray-Bob felt the warm flush of victory spread through his frame, dimming both the whiskey and his sexual glow in comparison.

"We'll get you fitted for some gowns tomorrow. Now, you'll want to shed that millstone back at your house. You don't . . . no, that's right, you told me you had no children. Believe me, Thelma, you were very smart in that regard. Too many women jump in and have children thinking God will smile on their pitiful unions because of it. Then, when HE offers THEM a new life, and that's what He's offering you, Thelma, THEY'RE too tied-down to take Him up on it! Can you meet with an attorney tomorrow? Say noon? At the courthouse?"

She nodded, still thinking of how she'd look in the gowns and remembering his comment about her having been smart. No one, not even her doting parents, had ever credited her with more than token intelligence. The idea of a new life appealed to her, too, but there was still a nagging sense of obligation to Josh.

"Fine. I'll phone our attorney, and he'll take care of all that

97

for you. You go on home and get some rest. I'd like you to be here tomorrow, backstage. You'll want to talk to Paula and the rest of the choir, of course. And you can start packing, too. We can only allow what you can put into two suitcases, and a makeup kit, of course. The rest of your wardrobe travels under the bus. Oh yeah, you'll need a place to stay. Tell you what. You can stay here in my bus until there's an opening in the choir trailer. That okay with you?"

"Well, it doesn't seem . . . ."

"Right? GOD HIMSELF has brought us together. Now what could be more right than that?"

"I guess you're right about that."

"He MOVES in mysterious ways, His MIRACLES to perform! Goodnight, Thelma. See you tomorrow."

Ray-Bob stood on tiptoes to kiss her lightly on the cheek. Thelma kissed the air idly at the same time, making a smacking sound like a perch taking an insect off the surface of a pond. Without further words, he accepted her envelope with the "love offering" inside, then led her to the door of the bus and shooed her out into the rain. Paula appeared in the door of the main tent and cast an evil look his way. Brother Ray-Bob smiled at her, then lifted the middle finger of one hand in the familiar salute and retired to his office for the night thoroughly satisfied.

A new high in lows, Raymond, the voice taunted him, then said no more.

Thelma drove around aimlessly for over an hour trying to sort out what had happened to her. On the one hand, she felt renewed and saw the chance for a new life, a starting over. She also felt the glow of Brother Ray-Bob's comments on her intelligence. But there was convention to contend with, and Ethel. To marry in haste, and for all the wrong reasons, was one thing. But to actually get a divorce? It was scandalous, a stigma the Lewis family had managed to avoid for as long as anyone could remember.

She knew she had to talk to Josh. Scoffer that he was, she still respected his levelheadedness. She thought with a shudder, if this was the best thing for her he would probably tell her so even if it meant giving her up. This thought brought on more tears. Not only had she lost the beauty pageant, but now it looked like she'd lose the man she'd taken to wear in place of the crown.

Josh was in the living room watching the Johnny Carson show when Thelma arrived at home. A fresh flood of tears was working its way into her makeup-blackened eyes as she approached him from behind. How could she phrase this? Should she sit down and lay it out line by line as it had unfolded, or should she just give him the gist of it? The clack of her high heels caught his attention.

"Hi, babe. Must have been some wingding of a service. You look like a raccoon!" he said with a grin, then turned to catch Johnny's next line.

Thelma froze in her tracks, all questions answered, all decisions made.

12

Josh awoke Friday morning to the sound of someone pounding on his door. At first he thought it was just a dream, but the accompanying din of beagles barking reinforced its reality. After waiting what he considered a decent interval for Thelma to answer it, he rose, stretched, pulled on a faded pair of blue-jeans, and padded barefoot to the door. Something about the living room didn't look quite right as he walked through, but exactly what didn't register. He pulled back the curtain on the door window and stared into the emaciated face of Deputy Sheriff Darnell Poston. Darnell had his eyes open wide, staring at the noisy pack of baying hounds surrounding his patrol car.

"Morning, Darnell. What brings you out here?" Josh asked while running his fingers through his hair and yawning.

"Do they bite?" Poston asked with a nod over his shoulder.

"Nope. Not even the mailman. They just like to chase cars, that's all."

"But mine's not movin'."

"Yeah, well, they're smart that way, see? A parked car's a lot easier to catch! What can I do for you? Don't tell me you're hitting the campaign trail this early. You running against Grady next fall?"

"Maybe. Depends on whether or not he gets his disability, I

reckon. Well, anyway, that ain't why I'm here, Josh. I gotta serve you with some papers, I'm afraid."

"Papers?"

"Yeah, let me read this like I'm supposed-ta, else Grady'll have my hide."

Thus, Josh learned of Thelma's plans to divorce him. Since speed of execution seemed as important to her as the deed itself, she was asking nothing in the way of support, alimony, or a cash settlement. *I guess she's not so dumb that she don't know that half of nothing is still nothing!* he thought as he read the document for the third time. He wondered if perhaps this was a ruse to get his attention. *God knows she has pulled weirder stunts.* As he raised his coffee cup to his lips and allowed his gaze to leave the page, however, he found confirmation that she was serious. Over the fireplace in the living room an unfaded rectangle of wall stared back at him in place of her twirler portrait.

Thelma awoke facing the wall of Brother Ray-Bob's office. It took her a moment to understand where she was and why she found herself there, to replay the events of the previous evening. Brother Ray-Bob had been magnificent at the Thursday night service, had healed several hard-core cases, and prayed for people from the audience with varying degrees of success. Then he'd launched into a plea for conversions and, just as some others were getting fidgety in their seats like they were ready to walk down the aisle to salvation themselves, he'd pointed at HER! He told the audience that God Himself had guided his finger, had signified unto him that THIS LOVELY LADY, is READY to give herselftoJAY-ZUS! *(Ain't that right, Miss?)*

Before the entire congregation she had taken his hand, stood, and received a loud and convincing, if somewhat less physical, rerun of his previous night's plea for her soul. Her tears had flowed anew, and she'd heard something then that she'd not heard the night before. It was a sound she'd almost buried in her past, but one that warmed her inside and made her decision to join this man on the road seem divinely inspired, indeed. The crowd had *applauded* her!

It was a simple step from redemption to seduction. Ray-Bob repeated his notion that God had willed them to meet, touch, and travel together. Then he averred that it was a natural progression that they should enjoy one another as any couple whom "God hath brought together!" might do. The act itself was over quickly enough, and any guilt she might have felt was overcome by the wonder she felt at what happened afterward. While she lay near dozing, there came a knock on the door that Ray-Bob stepped out into the hallway to answer. Through the thin door she could clearly make out the voice of none other than Rolly Klotz! Wonder changed to complete awe as she heard their words.

"Evening, Rolly."

"Brother Ray-Bob. How was it?"

"Marvelous! I wish you'd been there to see it."

"Yeah, well, maybe next time. What'll it be?"

"Rolly, I need a personal check from you to the tune of seventeen thousand dollars."

Klotz issued a low whistle upon hearing the figure. So did Thelma. The unmistakable sound of a fountain pen scratching on paper came next, followed by the crisp rip of perforated paper as the check came free from its pad. Thelma closed her eyes and feigned sleep when Ray-Bob stepped inside, grabbed two cloth bags, and a book from underneath the bed, then stepped outside again.

"Much obliged, Rolly. And God bless you."

"Hmmp. Think you'll make your goal by Saturday?"

"If God's willin'."

"Well, let's hope He is. See you tomorrow."

"G'night Rolly, and it's a pleasure doin' business with ya!"

Thelma fought the temptation to roll over and say something for as long as she could, then compromised. Anyone who could get a nickel out of Rolly Klotz would have become an instant legend in Dilbert's Forge. But seventeen *thousand* dollars? She had to look for herself, expecting to see a halo perched at a rakish angle above Brother Ray-Bob's head. Instead, she rolled over to see him scratching an entry into the book as though it were an everyday occurrence. The whole affair made what she'd done pale by comparison. After all, all she'd given up was a somewhat-used "pearl of great price." Rolly Klotz, a man who could have calculated the price of that pearl to within a farthing, had given up something far more dear to him—*money!*

Josh lounged around the house until the silence drove him out. Thelma would be at her mother's, he reasoned, and probably expecting him to come by and plead with her to come home. The thought of having to face the stern countenance of Ethel on an empty stomach helped reinforce his basic aversion toward doing this. Truth be known, Ethel would have been on his side for a change. She and Herman had once discussed splitting the sheets themselves but had decided to wait until their children were dead before taking any action on it. What he needed at the moment was a bite to eat and some manly companionship, so he headed to town.

On the way he had time to ponder how long it would be before word got out. The early lunch crowd at Ba-Da's undercut his most pessimistic estimate by two days. Every face turned toward his, numerous forkfuls of Friday's Spaghetti Creole suspended midair as though E. F. Hutton had just shouted. He nodded toward a table of acquaintances, one of whom had a three-inch noodle hanging out of his mouth, and walked slowly to a booth. His appetite now depleted, he settled for coffee.

Pamalou Swift was not among the early eaters, he noticed. Then a chill ran through him as he realized what some people were probably saying about them, especially here in the cafe. He wondered if his brief chats with Pamalou had prompted Thelma's actions and realized, much to his displeasure, that he should confront Thelma and at least clear up that issue. Ba refused to give him a check, stating the coffee was "on the house," and making him feel more estranged than he did already.

He also saw it as pity and, while he didn't particularly like the idea, was relieved that at least there was no animosity. Pale faces again turned his way as he backed from his parking spot, making him even more self-conscious. He never made the association between their final stares and the fact that he had walloped the truck hood and honked the horn prior to leaving.

The route to Herman and Ethel's took him past the fairgrounds. He was lost in thought about how he would approach Thelma and what to say about what, but not so preoccupied that he didn't notice her red Mustang in the fairgrounds parking lot. He slowed as he went by, considered turning around and confronting her there, and was almost grateful that he wouldn't have to tangle with Ethel, also. Then he noticed the car's windshield; it still had a full covering of dew!

The scarcity of other vehicles confirmed that there was no Prayer Breakfast in progress, unless it was a very exclusive affair. And he was relatively certain that Thelma had said something to the effect that the all-night singing had been canceled due to the rain. This left him with but one conclusion, and he reacted to it in what most would consider a most inappropriate way—he laughed. Then, following more acceptable custom, he stopped by the Bide-A-Wee to have a beer.

Clyde materialized before him as his eyes adjusted to the dim lights.

"Goin' down to Hall's for some sandwiches, Jackson. Want anything?" Clyde asked while cramming a pork pie hat down on his meaty, close-cropped head.

"Yeah, thanks," he answered, then dug into his jeans pocket and fetched out a five-dollar bill. "How about two? Extra hot sauce, no pickle or onion."

Clyde took the five, scribbled the order on the back of a piece of pork rind box, then waddled off in his heavy, shambling gait.

More faces greeted Josh, all *not* saying the same thing. A nod of recognition here, a tip of a beer bottle there, just "Jackson" from a few, and "Lo, Josh" from another rose as greetings, all in the hushed voices normally heard in funeral parlors. A notable exception came from the bar.

"'Bout time you got here! I wuz about to haul my ass out to your place and see if you's still breathin'." Slats Spivey spoke from his throne at the bar.

"Say, Slats. Mavis. How's the arm?"

"Won't be wrestlin' no bears any time soon, but it'll do I reckon. Sorry to hear about your 'ree-vorce, by the way."

"That's all right. I guess it was inevitable. Seems we just weren't all that compatible."

Mavis delivered two fresh beers, winked at Slats, then retired to the storage room and started stacking cases of bottles noisily. She knew when men wanted to be left to man talk and had read the arch of Slats's brow as she'd set the beers down. She especially wanted to stay on Spivey's good side, though she had to admit he was so thin he scarcely had more than one. At one hundred forty pounds, Slats was easily the least man in the building. He was accustomed to this, of course, as he had always been small of stature. In fact, he'd been fifteen before he could go to the movies; the spring-loaded seats kept threatening to toss him into the balcony.

"I could've tole you that aforehand!" Jim Kendall of Kendall's Garage averred. "Trouble is, Thelma Jean is too *citified*! You'd-a done better marryin' yourself a country gal."

Josh couldn't recall ever thinking of Thelma as being particularly cosmopolitan. That she could pinch the head off a tick without losing her place in a telephone conversation seemed to indicate she was country enough. She *was* from within the city limits, though, so he supposed Kendall was technically correct. Beside, Jim was at least six beers up on him and therefore entitled to an opinion.

"Might be something to what you say, Kendall."

"'Course I'm right!" he bellowed, then tucked his thumbs under his suspenders, leaned back in his chair, and leveled a steely eye on Josh. "You ought to get yourself a big, strappin' country gal. I mean one from way outchonder that'll appreciate a feller, cut kindlin', chop wood, dig him a bucket of worms, and send him fishin' from time to time."

"Jim's right about that now, Josh," Rupert Tubelville, the local auctioneer, said in atypically few words. "These hills are chock full of good-lookin', corn-fed gals that'd lay down their lives for a man what'll provide 'em with runnin' water and indoor plumbin'. Go to the ends of the earth for him, too! S'long as it didn't interfere with "All My Children," of course."

"Healthy gals, you mean?" Josh joined the fervor, enjoying the departure from the original topic.

Slats decided to get on the bandwagon, though from experience he'd learned it was not wise to get in the middle of domestic troubles. As soon as you'd let fly an opinion that the woman, or man, was useless baggage, well that's when they'd get back together and neither would speak to him again. Strong women, though, this was something he knew about.

"I hope to kiss a pig they're healthy! Why, my own mama used to carry papa over her shoulder like a sack of flour all the way from the spring branch at the foot of the hill, where he generally passed out, to the top and didn't think a thing about it! Sometimes she'd pick us a mess o' poke sallet on her way up and never even put him down."

"Yore mama was some woman, all right," Kendall allowed with reverence. Rupert nodded agreement.

"Strong as a ox!" Spivey continued with a slap on the bar for emphasis. "Hell, she milked six head of Jerseys mornin' and night for nigh onto fifty years, I reckon. Had a grip so strong she could squeeze open a hick'ry nut with her bare hand, and that was when she was seventy!"

"They get that way from milkin', awright," Rupert agreed, then took a slug of Sterling. "From wringin' chicken necks, too."

Everyone paused for a swig and to consider the relative strength of the garden-variety country girl's hands. An odd thought struck Josh.

"Guess it'd be real dangerous to ask a country girl for a hand-job, huh?"

"Damned right!" several of the men answered at once, alternating between chuckling and grimacing. Jim Kendall was the first to get his memory straight enough to relate. He looked

106

back toward the store room and lowered his voice in deference to Mavis.

"Had a gal from over to Peezee Ridge damned near pound my jewels into my bung hole once, now that you mention it. Yes-sir, that was in the rumble seat of a '32 Ford Roadster, as I recall. Son, she latched onto that thing like it had rattlers on one end and fangs on t'other, then gave it such a pounding I almost passed out! Well sir, I couldn't catch my breath to tell her better, so I had to get her in a headlock to make her quit. That was in '37, and my balls ain't been the same since."

Nine beers and half a dozen hours later, Josh was feeling no pain. He'd passed the critical "bullet-proof" point two hours earlier and was now about as tanked as he ever got. A mental alarm clock sounded in his head, urging him homeward. The truck swayed ever so slightly as he headed back through town, drawing no untoward attention but forcing him to concentrate on his driving. Thus, it was a surprise to him when he pulled up at one of Dilbert's Forge's two traffic lights and found Pamalou Swift leaning over, staring into his windshield. He slid across the seat and rolled down the passenger window.

"Evening, Pam!"

"Hi, Josh."

"Can I offer you a lift somewhere?"

"I'm just going up to the Ba-Da to meet Judy Hendricks. We're going to Dickson to catch a movie. Would you like to come along?"

"No thanks. I only go to movies for comedy or sex. Everything else I can get at home."

"You've had a few, haven't you Josh?" she said, smiling easily and pulling the fur collar of her coat up around her face.

"You could say that. Can I get a raincheck on the movie? In case you haven't heard, I'm about to be among the living again soon."

"So I've heard. I'll think about the raincheck."

"Are you playing hard to get, Pam?" he said with a smile that didn't quite come out straight.

"No, I'm not playing hard to get. I *am* hard to get!" she stated truthfully, then giggled. "Are you going to be okay?"

Despite the mild rebuke, Josh detected sincere concern in her voice.

"Hey! I've got a classic red pick-um-up truck, six retarded beagles, and the ugliest cat in seven states. What else could a man ask for?"

"I'm serious. Are you okay to drive?"

"Yeah, I'll take it easy. Thanks for asking though."

"Everybody needs somebody at times, Josh. As a friend. You know how the song goes, 'A man without a woman is like . . . .'"

"A fish without a yo-yo," Josh finished the verse, then noted the light had changed and was about to go red again. "Well, thanks for the concern. Enjoy the movie."

"You be careful," she said, then straightened up to allow him to depart.

As he approached the driveway to his house, Josh considered how empty the place looked without lights on or the Mustang in the drive. Then he wondered if there really was something to the lyrics to that song. Even the dogs seemed lackluster in their efforts as he pulled into the drive and honked. *It's just the alcohol,* he told himself. To counter its effects, he fixed himself a thick bologna sandwich and ate it while leaning over the sink to catch the crumbs and tomato drippings. Then he sat down to a cup of acidic, warmed-up coffee and thought. It finally occurred to him he was alone in the world.

The realization caused a sinking feeling that was part remorse, part fear. Hearing what sounded at first like a motorbike climbing a hill in the distance, he felt the soft pad of a paw in his lap and looked down to see FrankenKat's one eye staring at him, then closing as he arched his back and rubbed up against Josh's chest. Josh placed his hand atop the mat of mangled fur on the cat's back and followed the curve of the arch out to the end of its tail. FrankenKat purred even louder. It was the first time since the morning he'd pulled the cat out of the radiator fan that it had been friendly, and he took that to be a confirmation that things had changed, or were about to.

*   *   *

A small storm centered itself over the Grice's Creek area of Lake Barkley just as Josh and FrankenKat were going to bed. A lone cell with fairly localized effects, it managed to whip the waters of the lake into a frenzy and press down with its heavy air so that the amount of soluble oxygen in the water increased significantly. This was important to Big Un, as was the increase in atmospheric pressure. At his age, the walls of his swim bladder were beginning to lose their elasticity, making it difficult for him to change depths as readily as he'd like. It was downright uncomfortable, too. For this and other reasons, his current home was ideal.

The water level in this hole seldom varied more than a couple of feet. More importantly, the original creek channel dropped fifteen feet just upstream from him, then ran between his lair and the undercut base of the cliff. This rush of clearer, highly oxygenated water brought with it a bounty of food. His stone roof's proximity to the cliff added its force to the already deep water and kept the pressure fairly constant. In short, it was ideal for a fish that needed a lot of food, yet lacked the mobility to run it down.

The storm passed after midnight, leaving Big Un to the baritone rumble of stones rolling along the limestone bottom of the creek bed. It was a peaceful sound, one he'd become accustomed to and wanted to remain near for the rest of his life.

He'd learned the most difficult lessons along the way: never get into shallows unless there's a certain way out, stay away from mud bottoms where the huge snapping turtles and tiny lampreys liked to hang out, and—most importantly—if it doesn't look like something you've eaten before, don't! He still bore a gap out of the left corner of his mouth where he'd attacked a large worm some years earlier. The force exerted on the worm's hook had ripped right through his lip, enabling him to escape; and he remembered that vividly. He had not taken anything since unless he had seen it moving along under its own power. Nor would he ever.

109

13

Saturday was but four hours old when Josh and FrankenKat both opened an eye apiece. *Again?* Josh thought. Waking to the sound of knocking was getting to be a regular thing. The silence of his beagles told him who he'd find there before he opened the door.

"Mornin' Jackson!" Slats greeted him loudly.

Josh recoiled from the shrill bark of Spivey's voice and pulled the door open wide. Slats looked inside warily.

"She ain't back, Slats," Josh said with a weary smile that conveyed more hurt than humor. "She's off preaching the Gospel According to Saint Bubba, or some such shit."

"I'm sorry about that, Jackson. Really, I am."

"So you said. Not to worry. I'll make it. Come on in."

"We ain't got long, you know. I got coffee a-brewin' over at my place, and there's the boat to load up. You want to follow me in your truck? I figure we leave one truck downstream, then put the boat in upstream and drive back when we's finished."

"Sounds okay to me. Let me grab some duds and see if I can round up some fishing tackle. Just be a minute."

"Forget the tackle. I got all we'll need. Plenty of rods and reels, too. You just grab yourself a shirt and some shoes, and we're gone."

FrankenKat watched from his modified crouch atop a pillow on the bed. *Thelma's pillow!* Josh thought. *Is that appropriate? No,* he decided. *Thelma is just the opposite of a cat; no matter how you toss her up, she'll always come down flat on her back.* He felt a twinge of jealousy and wondered again if he should send Slats on his way, then slide by the tent meeting and brad Reverend Ray-Bob's beak. Again he decided against it. If Brother Ray-Bob wanted Thelma, then it'd serve him right to get her. As Josh left the bedroom, the cat leaped up, stretched in a tonsil-baring yawn, then jogged out with the slightly catty-cornered gait he'd adopted following his injuries.

"I swan, that cat looks like he's fightin' a heavy wind, don't he?" Slats asked as the two arrived simultaneously.

"Yeah. He's looking for his morning feed, I guess. Hang on a second."

The kitchen cupboard revealed nothing remotely resembling cat food, and neither did the refrigerator. Desperate, Josh peered into the freezer section. Nothing there but three packages of frozen Brussels sprouts. His mouth screwed up in a frown at this. He hated the "baby cabbages," as Thelma had always called them. No real point in keeping the damned things now, he thought, then looked down at FrankenKat who was voicing his concern. With a shrug, Josh closed the heavily frosted door, then shivered as a chill ran down his spine from the crisp scrunching sound the ice crystals made.

"Ne-ooow?" the cat seemed to ask.

"Nope, not *now*," Josh replied, then rummaged around in the refrigerator drawers in search of something the cat might eat until he could get to the store.

The nearest thing he could find was half a package of sliced bologna that was beginning to discolor and harden at the edges. It would have to do. FrankenKat nosed the pink meat in disapproval at first, then looked at Josh. Josh responded by peeling the skin and part of the darker edges off the meat, then tore it into bite-sized strips before placing it in the cat's bowl. It was satisfactory, but only just.

"Well, he may be one ugly scutter, but seems like he's about got you trained," Slats observed.

"I'll be amazed if there's not a custody fight," Josh said smiling. "The cat's got lots of sense, though, now that you mention it."

"I wouldn't have said that when he first came outa that radiator fan, you know? That was one homely critter."

"He was that. Lots of personality, though. I guess I'll keep him."

"You don't keep a cat, Jackson. They decide whether to stay or not, and it don't make one helluva lot of difference what you might think."

"Yeah, I can believe that. Ready to go?"

Their departure put the dogs into a fit of confusion as first one and then the other truck started, honked, and backed out of the narrow drive. Half a dozen quivering beagles sat watching as they left, trying to figure out why it was there was nothing to chase when there had been so much potential just moments earlier. A short drive later, Josh hefted the aluminum jon boat into the back of Slats' truck while the smaller man scurried about his kitchen cooking breakfast. The smells of eggs frying and bacon sizzling came out through an open window, making Josh hurry. Once the boat was tethered with lengths of grass baling twine, Josh stepped up onto the rickety porch and went inside.

Spivey's house had an amenity that was rapidly disappearing from the local culture: it *smelled* like an old house. It smelled like Josh's grandparents' house where he'd been brought up after his mother had died. A broken heart was what they'd said. His father had been among the Marines on Porkchop Hill in Korea, among those that didn't come back. The house held memories for him, and not all of them were unpleasant.

There was the distinct odor of wood smoke that had cured the lumber, leaving its tangy smell impregnated in its very fibers. Overlaying it all, like the facing on an olfactory quilt, was the smokehouse flavor of salt pork, the ghosts of hams past that swam unseen through the fresh essence of today's fare. The bacon sang its tenor song from the cast iron skillet until all the sizzle was sazzled-out and it turned golden brown and crisp.

"Biscuits'll be a minute. How do you like your coffee?"

"Same way I like my women, blonde and sweet."

Slats shrugged, then reached into a small refrigerator and fetched out a quart of milk from among a collection of buttermilk cartons.

"Sugar's right there in the peanut can. Help yourself. Eggs over?"

"Over's fine. Why the peanut can?"

"Keeps the piss-ants out. Pismires, you know?"

"Right, makes sense."

"Biscuits'll be burnt on the bottom, by the way."

"Oh?"

"Yup. They always do. Can't figure it out, either. I even tried puttin' 'em in upside-down, and it still didn't make any difference."

Josh wondered, but didn't ask, how a piece of dough would know which way was up. It didn't do to address such things around Slats Spivey, not if you were in a hurry to get somewhere. While Slats did battle with popping bacon grease and eggs that wanted to stick to the skillet, Josh surveyed the small house.

There was a sink in front of the window, which itself was so covered with fly specks on the outside that the view was like looking through a gin bottle. Behind the stove were cupboards of sorts stocked with a variety of canned goods, boxes of baking soda, sacks of flour and cornmeal, sardines, and several pounds of coffee. Through the open door was the combination bedroom/living room with its wood stove, which would be taken down soon in celebration of spring. The bed was an ancient affair and swaybacked as a two-dollar mule, but made up nice and tidy. Atop the bed, to Josh's surprise, lay a thick book of poetry.

"Is that a book of verse I see in yonder, Slats?"

Slats looked back toward the bedroom as though trying to read the spine of the book through the wall, then shrugged and went back to poking at an egg with menacing little jabs of his spatula.

"Yep."

"Didn't know you went in for classic literature."

"So? Lots of stuff folks don't know 'bout me. Ain't nothin' wrong with readin' a little Longfeller now and then, is there?"

"Not at all! Is that who it is? Longfellow?"

"Yep. Get ready for your eggs 'cause this skillet is hot!"

Josh leaned away from the table as Slats paced over and paused long enough to dump a pair of brownish-tinged eggs with traffic cone-orange yolks still intact onto his plate. A second low pass by Spivey, and three thick strips of country bacon cozied up next to the eggs. Longfellow now forgotten, they dug in while the yolks were still hot and runny. Slats dumped some coffee into his saucer, picked it up and blew, then slurped loudly before sopping up the remainder of his eggs with a fluffy biscuit which, true to his word, was slightly overdone on bottom. When he was finished, Slats snatched up a broom and wrenched a straw from its top, then sat back down to pick his teeth while another saucer of coffee cooled before him.

"You ready to hit it?" Slats asked around his straw when it seemed Josh was finished.

"Whenever you are."

Slats nodded, stood, then disappeared out the back door with his cast moving in rhythm with his steps like the bar on a locomotive's drive wheel. When he hadn't returned in several minutes, Josh went outside to join him. Slats was loading the last of his gear into the truck, a hodgepodge of off-brand reels, rods, and a Craftsman tool box that apparently held his tackle. Serious scientists were rarely known for aesthetics in their equipment, Josh reasoned. A final item, however, Slats carried with the reverence afforded human eyes and other donor organs. It was an olive jar filled with synthesized bugspit, more valuable in Spivey's eyes than an equal amount of ambergris.

"I take it that's . . . *it*?"

Spivey looked up solemnly and nodded, then placed the

small jar of vile looking liquid in the truck's seat where it would ride beside him to its proving grounds. Without further words, the men mounted their vehicles and headed off down Spivey's drive.

Josh felt he was taking advantage of his friend's injury when they'd launched the boat and Slats insisted on sculling the craft along with his good hand while Josh fished the banks. Fine wisps of morning mist still clung to the water's surface as though reluctant to rise up and join the atmosphere. The air was still and the water glassy as they cut their zig-zagging path across the flooded creek bottom toward the main lake. A perfect morning, they had to admit. Once out from the dock far enough to satisfy Slats that no prying eyes could determine what he was doing, he let the boat drift while he tried to open the olive jar. The cap was on too tight, however. He couldn't budge it.

"Gimme a hand here, Jackson. The damned thing's jammed on there tighter'n a gnat's ass stretched over a cannonball."

Josh grabbed the slender bottle and gripped it firmly with both hands. When he gave it a twist, the cap came off, releasing an odor beyond description.

"Damn, Slats!"

"I done told you I put that sardine juice in it! Musta fermented a mite. Might make it even better, huh?"

"Might just make 'em throw up their fins and die!"

"You'll see. Here, take yourself one of these and dip him in there," Slats said while producing a fluorescent chartreuse spinner bait from the top drawer of his tool chest.

"What is it?" Josh wondered while studying the bait closely.

"That there's a Hoosier HawgHunter! Feller up in southern Indiana makes 'em by hand. I get 'em through a chewin' tobacco salesman what runs outa Louisville. Tie it on, then dip the skirt in the bugspit and let's get on with it."

Josh did so, then dropped the lure into the water beside the boat to study it some more. A rainbow patina of sardine oil rose in the lure's wake, reflected the rising sun, then floated off to wherever rainbows go. Slats leaned back and began swishing his short paddle back and forth silently, pulling the little boat along at a crawl. As he neared a pile of brush, Josh tossed the lure out to drag it past. Nothing.

"Wait 'til we're nearer a bank or some weed beds, Jackson. Fish is smarter than to think a grasshopper flew all the way out here! You need to work it right up under the bushes and weeds like it just fell offa somethin'."

"Makes sense. How often do I dip it in the bugspit?"

"I don't know. Smell it. When it starts dyin' down, dip it again."

Josh didn't like the idea much initially and liked it even less by the time they reached the main body of the lake, for he'd re-spit the plug three times by then. The sun was climbing over the bluffs and beginning to warm the still air, and all signs of the mist were gone. Slats was beginning to tire of sculling and took short breaks to work the kinks out of his good shoulder. Josh was about to suggest they just troll the lure behind them while he spelled Slats on the paddle when the current picked up and began sweeping them downstream toward one of the bluff holes.

"You gonna be able to steer this thing once it gets moving?" Josh asked.

"I'll keep it off the banks, if that's what you mean. Looky yonder! See that outcroppin' there with the weeds sticking out from it?"

Josh eyed the grassy rock, noting the way the high water from recent rains had drooped the taller weeds into the water.

"Yeah, I see it."

"Well, drop your plug right in there. If there's ever a place a grasshopper might fall off, that's it right there!"

Josh aimed the lure for the clump of weeds trailing in the water. It went long, the lure bouncing off the rocks and half-way back to the boat. Ignoring Slats' scowl, which said, "I could have hit them weeds!" he reeled in and cast out again. The clump was almost even with them now, and their speed had increased to a quick pace, causing the line to appear to curve as it played out from the reel.

With satisfaction Josh noted the muted *ker-plunk* as the Hoosier HawgHunter splashed down among the weeds where they joined the water. He gave the lure a second to sink, then wondered if it would snag in the weeds as they drifted past and, if it did, would he be able to get it free before they were too far beyond to go back against the brisk current. With this thought in mind, he cranked the reel's handle gently a couple of times, then brought the rod tip up sharply to set the lure's spoon to spinning. Halfway up he met resistance.

"Hey!" Josh shouted happily, then snapped the rod tip up to set the hook.

"Shit!" Slats hollered back, but there was something other than joy in his voice.

Josh half-turned to see the cause of Spivey's chagrin. There directly before them was a rippling eddy skirting around either side of a sharp slab of rock that rose just above the surface. The fish on his line, a smallmouth bass of about twelve ounces, chose this moment to take to the air. The rod danced in Josh's hand as the bass broke the water's surface, skittered along for a few feet, then plowed back under in a wild spurt of energy. Josh looked from the jerking rod and singing reel to the upcoming impact, trying to decide upon a course of action.

The fish would be too small to keep, yet had enough fight in it to pull the rod overboard should he lay it down. But then, they could well be overboard themselves soon enough, so the point was moot. In desperation, Slats stabbed out with his sculling paddle and pushed off against the rock. It slowed them but an instant, then the light boat crunched upon the lip of rock with a sound like a car being crushed in a junkyard. Josh held onto the rod with one hand and the boat gunnel with the other, hoping Slats didn't go over the side with his broken arm. Come to think of it, he wasn't sure Slats could swim. Come to think about it, he noticed they had no lifejackets!

*   *   *

Big Un was taking what passed for a nap in fishdom when it happened. First, there was a gentle tap against the roof/wall of his lair that startled him into making a single circuit around his nap area. This was common enough. The heavy rains lately had washed lots of limbs and logs into the lake, and they all congregated at the

117

center of the current as the water level went down. This flotsam was forever bashing against the rock, making strange vibrations that his sophisticated lateral-line system picked up as keenly as sonar.

The next sound, however, startled him into a fin-raised defense posture. It was a metallic clang and scream that threatened and angered him at once. Then he saw the other fish coming at him through the gloomy depths, jerking from side to side provokingly, as though openly challenging him for his lair! In reflex and confusion, he did what he always did when approached by some young upstart. He ate him.

*　　*　　*

The boat hung upon the rock, a pair of creases rising up through the floor for three feet past Slats' seat, then erupting in thin spurts of water where they cut through. Slats sat on the elevated bow, whirling his cast in midair to maintain his balance while flailing at the distant water with his paddle. Josh only half felt the added weight at the end of his rod and even then subconsciously credited it to the line becoming fouled on the rocks below.

The boat balanced precariously for an instant before dropping bow-first back into the water. Josh flinched as his end of the boat went up in the air, shuddered, then slid off the rocks sideways. In an effort to remain in the boat, he brought the rod up sharply and felt what seemed to be a sack of sand on the other end of the line.

*　　*　　*

Big Un felt an odd discomfort as the two bared ends of the treble hooks hanging from the smallmouth's jaw plunged into a bony corner of his own. A shrill vibration went down his lateral-line system as the fine monofilament line stretched taut and sang in the air above like a banjo string. It tugged him upward and out of his lair with such rapidity that he was already in the swift current before he could react. Instinctively, he headed for the bottom and downstream. The line proved only a minor obstacle to his movement.

*   *   *

Spivey dropped his paddle into the boat as it came free to start heading sidewinder-fashion downstream and right at the boiling water next to the cliff. He grabbed the long-handled dip net and held it out before him to push off against the rock wall. He barely heard Josh when he spoke.

"Slats? I think I've *got something!*"

Spivey felt this was a stupid thing to say at the time. He'd heard the small bass as it did its water walk and, judging from the hundreds of others he'd caught, figured what Jackson had on his line wouldn't be enough to make a seal bark, let alone be worth getting slammed up against a rock wall in an already leaking boat! He was about to say so, too.

"*Gawd-damn!*" Josh let out at the top of his lungs as the rod bent double and the last foot of its tip disappeared into the water.

Spivey had the net up against the wall now, and the boat was beginning to swing stern-first downstream. The way the rod was arched and Jackson's stout forearms twitching in effort caused Slats to rethink his opinion.

*   *   *

Big Un didn't care for the strain he felt that kept tugging him sideways and causing him to swim right for the base of the cliff and the strongest part of the current, so he reversed directions. Immediately, the strange force relented and the strong sweeps of his broad tail propelled him upstream at a respectable clip. Despite his aversion toward doing so, and the uncomfortable fullness he felt as his sclerotic swim bladder inflated under reduced pressure, he started up. Once on the surface, he was certain he could dislodge the thing in his mouth. In the near distance he could make out a wavering silvery form like a waterfall entering the stream from above. He headed for it at full speed.

*   *   *

"What the hell was *that?*" Slats cried out in wonder as a solid thump reverberated up through the boat's bottom.

119

"I don't know, but I think I lost whatever I had. The line went slack." Josh cranked rapidly on the reel, the disappointment heavy in his voice.

"Probably just a catfish, anyways. They sometimes take a line with a small fish on it. Had it happen once over to Hurricane Creek, let's see, that was . . . ."

Josh's mouth was already starting to droop into its conditioned frown at the mention of *catfish* when his eyes shot open in wonder.

"Gawd-damn!" Josh yelled with such force that Spivey lost his grip on the dip net he was leaning on and almost went in the water.

As he steadied himself, he saw the reason for his partner's excitement. There, swimming in addled circles next to the boat, its dorsal fin sticking up a full three inches above his thick green-black back, was Big Un—the largest largemouth bass ever witnessed by human eyes!

Spivey slipped the net over the fish's head then scooped as much of its length as he could into it and thence into the boat. Big Un's twenty four-plus pounds felt more like a hundred at the end of the net's five-foot handle, but Slats had enough adrenaline coursing through his veins that he could have—as he was to claim repeatedly later—lifted a D-9 Caterpillar! The three stared at each other throughout the brief trip downstream, two of them smiling profusely.

14

Sunday morning found Josh on a rise near his house doing something he'd longed to for a long time. Seated around him like disciples were the beagles, looking on curiously and wondering if anything was required of them. FrankenKat was crouched in the shade nearby ready to spring at a bird perched near the top of a tree. The cat's depth perception had pretty much disappeared along with his other eye, but he reasoned it was only a matter of time until something would be on the other end of one of his pounces. FrankenKat had patience, so did Josh.

Josh's early efforts were major disappointments. For a while he even considered giving up as his shots continued to skitter and hop along the ground rather than rise in the majestic flights he'd pictured in his mind. Another worm-burner slithered along the knoll before bounding into the air briefly and crashing back to earth. Undaunted, Josh reached into the bag with the club head of his 7-iron and rolled out another Brussels sprout.

He improved his lie and went through his check list. Head down, wrists stiff, left arm straight, bring the club back smoothly, now down in an arc and follow through. A crisp *click* rent the still, dung-laden air as the club face lifted the frozen vegetable from the grass and into the heavens. A pent-up sigh of relief escaped Josh's throat as his eyes followed the sphere on its knuckleball flight until it disappeared in the high sky like a marshmallow in a snow storm, then he rolled out another and teed it up. The dogs watched in silence, wanting to chase the things, yet remembering an early shot that had sent a sprout winging and whizzing past their heads, nearly decimating their number.

From his vantage point at the base of FrankenKat's tree, Slats watched in equal silence. He'd only just arrived, but he knew enough from watching golf on television to know you didn't interrupt a man's backswing. The next Brussels sprout split in half, sending its hemispheres spinning and tumbling a short distance and making a whirring sound that the beagles couldn't resist chasing.

"Well, you got some good altitude on the last 'un, anyways," Slats spoke as Josh was exchanging his iron for a 3-wood.

"Say, Slats. Yeah, I was hoping the bastards would burn up on reentry! How's it going?"

"It's official!" Slats stated with authority, then cleared his lip of tobacco juice and spat past FrankenKat's head.

The cat wasted a perfectly good pounce pursuing the tobacco, but managed to miss it in spite of his efforts. The bird was too far away to notice.

"It is?"

"Yep. Them Fish and Wildlife boys are tickled shitless, too. Don't you want to know what he weighed in at?"

"Sure!"

Josh braced himself. They'd both realized the fish was far beyond anything they'd ever seen as soon as he appeared on the surface after ramming the boat like some miniature Moby Dick. The swamped jon boat managed to stay afloat and provided a natural live well during the trip back. Though the fish spent the entire trip in the dip net, it had been very energetic when they got to McDougal's Bait Farm and tried to weigh it. McDougal's minnow scale only went up to twenty pounds, and their hearts had taken a sudden leap when the fish bottomed out the scale even without flopping around.

They stowed the fish in one of the aerated minnow wells while they went off on a search for larger scales.

Their hunt took them to Hall's Barbecue across the tracks in the black section of town. Old Man Hall, which was his name as far as anyone could remember, was not present when they arrived, but the place was teeming with second generation Halls. There were thirteen in all, and seven of these were busy boiling pork shoulders, slicing the cooked meat, stoking the long bed of charcoals, or fighting flies off with swatters made from innertubes. Slats approached one of the older daughters, Ruth, mainly because hers was the only name he could remember or pronounce.

Mama Hall had named the first nine children and, being a religious woman, she had picked names from the tops of pages of the Bible for each. Since she was illiterate, she always had a neighbor identify whether the name was masculine or feminine. It was after she'd inadvertently named a son Psalms CIV that Old Man Hall had assumed responsibility for naming the children. Old Man Hall didn't care whether a name was particularly masculine or feminine, so long as it rolled off the tongue nicely and he didn't know anyone else with it. This fact could have been attested to by the two youngest Hall children, Paraphernalia and Sizzlean.

Even allowing for some optimism on behalf of Hall's scales, the fish was within range of the record, so they called in the local game warden. The game warden ooohed and aaahed, then took measurements of girth and length before phoning his home office in Nashville. When he got home, he made another call and announced to the first outsider that the fish weighed . . . .

"Twenty-by God-four pounds, seven ounces! That's what! You know what that is?"

"Dinner for eight?"

"Hell, no! That's a new world record, that's what! *And* it proves that bugspit works!"

Josh knew just how much luck was involved in his catching the fish. But he also knew that were it not for Spivey's insistence and hare-brained scheme, he'd never have gone fishing in the first place.

"Did you tell them about the bugspit?"

Slats jerked in his tracks, his eyes protruding off to one side as though he had an insect spotted and was about to flick out his tongue and nail it.

"Do I look like a total *id-jit?*" Slats barked, almost losing the oily ballcap that sat on his head sideways.

Josh didn't even consider the question.

"Well, what do we tell them then?"

"I say we tell 'em, or *you* do that is, that you's usin' a bait dressin' but that you'll have to get back to 'em on the brand cause you borried it! That way, once we get that patent and start producin' the stuff, we can use the fish for advertisin'!"

"Sounds reasonable. When do you think you'll be in business?"

"*We!* We'll be in business as soon as I get the formula protected. You're in this thing for half, you know."

"Slats, it was your idea. You made the stuff and all that. Hell, you even provided all the gear and everything."

"*I* made it, *you* proved it! I know you could have told me to go piss up a rope, Jackson. And I know that lots of guys would have, too. But you stuck by me on this and helped me prove it works. So you're in and I don't want to hear no more about it!"

"All right. And thanks, Slats. So what do we do now?"

"Well, for now I'd recommend you go answer your phone. The damned thing's been ringin' since I got here."

"Yeah, probably reporters. I was waiting until I heard something before I talked to them. I guess I've heard it now, huh?"

"You bet your ass!"

"Ready for a beer?"

Slats spat the last of his tobacco juice along with the cud into the bushes nearby sending FrankenKat bounding off in hot pursuit. The cat scampered back out a second later with a distraught look on his face and tobacco juice on his chin.

"Thought you'd never ask!"

* * *

The voice on the other end of the phone was not a reporter. It was "Major" Mike Balleau, talent scout and agent. Mike had laid around Nashville for years looking for the next Elvis Presley, with an eye toward becoming the next Colonel Tom Parker. The times had not been kind, though. Major Mike's only current act that was getting any bookings was a bluegrass band called The Knotholes.

Major Mike had tenacity, a thick skin, and that main driving force that makes an agent go: a nose for money. He also had a sister who was married to a man whose sister was married to a Tennessee state game warden, and he had the good sense to offer a sizable finder's fee for just such instances as this.

"Mister Jackson? This here's Mike Balleau, and I'm an agent. I'd like to make you a mess of money, son!"

"Mister Blue?"

"Ba-loo. That's right. Anyway, I think I can help you out, son. I can get you more money, residuals, follow-on contracts, spin-offs, personal appearances . . . whatever. You name it, I can get it. What do you say?"

"I say you're a little premature. I haven't been offered anything so far, except your services that is, and I don't anticipate anything so big that I'd require an agent. But thanks."

"Wait a minute! You say you ain't been offered *nothing*? Well, you just stand by! I'll get you more than you can imagine. Tell you what. You write down my number, then whenever somebody calls, and they will, you ask for their best offer. Don't agree to nothin'! You just tell 'em you need to talk with your agent and call me with the info. If I can't get you a better deal, you don't owe me a penny!"

"I'll have to think about this, of course."

Major Mike was near panic. Coming up as a door-to-door salesman, he'd come to hear "I'll think about it," in the same light as most people hear "Kiss my ass!" Then he decided on a rash offer.

"Well, I'll tell you what I'll do. You give me twenty-four hours, that's all. You call me with any offers you get in the next twenty-four hours, and I'll sweeten 'em for you! Now, how would you like to get some up-front money for starters?"

125

Josh was suddenly interested. During their scales hunt the day before, he'd stopped at the bank for some cash and had made an interesting discovery. In addition to the "love offering" she'd given Brother Ray-Bob in exchange for her freshly cleaned and pressed soul, Thelma had returned and drained the account down to a mere ten bucks.

"How much, uh, up-front money are we talking about?"

Major Mike heard the curtain of his sale about to drop and smiled. Much of the desperation was out of his voice when he spoke again, but there was still some bravado. Major Mike's checking account was approaching the elastic zone, too.

"I'll get you five grand by close of business tomorrow if I have to pay it myself! Now how's that? You willing to give me a shot for twenty-four hours?"

"You got it. Give me your number."

No sooner had Josh hung up the phone than it rang again. This time it was a bait company with an offer of ten thousand dollars for a still photo of Josh and the fish to use as a background for one of their ads. Josh managed to put off accepting their offer until he could phone his agent and give him the details. Not an hour later, Major Mike called back, stating he had ten grand being wired to Josh's personal account in Dilbert's Forge, another forty grand to follow, residual payments for any future use of the photo beyond the current campaign, and a lifetime supply of their products. Josh was elated, Slats swallowed his tobacco, and Major Mike was hired for six months. Slats and Josh opened fresh beers and clinked their bottles together in a toast.

"To two assholes who went out in a boat broke and came back rich and famous!" Josh offered.

"To the *three* assholes who came back! Can't forget old Big Un over there at the bait farm."

"Right. To *three assholes!*"

"To Bugspit!" Slats shouted.

"Amen!" Josh said happily.

"Amen," Thelma said demurely, after waiting for the other amens to die down so her humble offering would be heard.

126

They were about to dine on a meal of Wendy's hamburgers during a break in the erection of their tents outside Camden. Thelma felt overdressed in her light sweater and skirt outfit. All the others wore jeans and sweatshirts. Foo-Foo sat at a folding card table nearby munching away on a burger while he and Mellow Man hummed tunes back and forth. The tunes were muffled by the food and came out a full octave flat, but each knew what the other was humming.

Foo-Foo had a few months left on his "goodwill" tour, and Mellow Man Marshall would be free a couple of weeks later, so they were thinking about a collaboration, perhaps even an album. Foo-Foo ignored the G7-diminished chord as it struggled through Mellow Man's all-beef patty, choosing instead to focus his attentions on the latest addition to the Hallalujah Choir.

Thelma registered his gaze. She found the musician a bit bizarre, but at least he was someone she could talk to and that was something rare here. For a reputed gospel outfit, the people didn't seem very friendly. When Brother Ray-Bob had introduced her to the other members of the Hallelujah Choir, for instance, some of them had seemed downright snooty.

Paula was especially rude, and since she was apparently the leader, though no one ever stood before the group when they were performing, it carried over to the rest. Her case with the girls wasn't helped when Paula and Brother Ray-Bob got into a screaming argument in the bus, and Paula had stalked off. Paula's gowns were a tad short but fit Thelma everywhere else just fine. *So,* she thought, *I'll just have a little more of my best feature showing, that's all.* She knew how men liked a little leg.

"Yo! Foo-man? You in there?" the guitarist asked while passing his hand back and forth before Foo-Foo's glassy eyes.

"Yeah! I was just . . . thinking."

"Right. And I bet I know what you was thinkin', too! You be thinkin' how you'd like to get in the new bitch's britches. Am I right, or am I wrong?"

Foo-Foo grinned sheepishly.

"Yeah, you're right."

"Well, you can forget that old shit, my man, for two big

reasons. One, she's the Preach's main squeeze, and you don't want to go pissin' him off when he could send your ass to the slammer, right? And two, she's too tall for you!"

"She might be worth the climb though. I hear you about the little dude, though. Don't trust that joker at all, man. Something about his eyes, you know?"

"Yeah, I get that too. Wouldn't put nothin' past the little shit. My daddy, he say, 'How come it is, ever time you see a preacher comin' outa another man's house, he's either wipin' chicken grease off his lips or zippin' up his pants?' That's what my daddy say!"

"Right on!" Foo-Foo agreed, then exchanged a series of hand slaps and clasps with Mellow Man. "The man does put on a good show, though. You gotta give him that much."

"Yeah, you right there. Dude's got him a pack of groupies, too. Have you noticed that?"

"Yeah, I've seen 'em. Wonder how many of them are on the payroll?"

Mellow Man watched appreciatively as Thelma stood, smoothed her skirt and sweater, then walked off in her long-legged stride. The musicians went back to humming, and Thelma visited one of the portable outhouses to throw up. Her debut as a singer was but hours away, and she was nervous. "As nervous as a whore in church!" she remembered Josh was fond of saying, then she threw up again.

*   *   *

Big Un was miserable. The small area of his confinement helped equalize the pressure in his swim bladder, but with the exceptions of the few times he'd been taken out and weighed he'd been in the dark since the day he was caught. Without the sunlight to regulate his day, he had not developed a feeding urge and hadn't eaten since before he was yanked from his lair. The aerator pumps hissed constant streams of bubbles providing him with oxygen and monotony.

It was dark when the door of the tank swung open, so he didn't fully appreciate the change. Had he been able to see and read, he might have noticed the University of

Florida crest emblazoned on the truck's door and might have taken this as a sign of better things to come. As it was, he only felt the vibration of the truck beneath another tank and remembered the last time he'd felt it, and the disastrous results that had ensued.

15

By noon Monday Josh was sick of answering the phone and had taken to giving Major Mike's number instead of even saying hello. What had started as a trickle turned into a deluge of offers from some of the most far-fetched sources he could imagine. A cereal company wondered if the fish could be cajoled, or starved, into gobbling up their product on camera to emphasize that "Champions from *all walks of life*" began their days with Fruity Whangers!

A men's underwear outfit wanted him to pose for a still session and had the audacity to ask if he were "sufficiently endowed, physically" to stand up to a close-up! They went on to offer the use of a dancer's belt or Idaho potato if he thought himself deficient. He was tempted to take their offer, then stick the potato down the *back* of his briefs. The rest ran a broad range from deodorants to Derby parades. Most expected his curt reply and rang off instantly to contact Balleau, so it came as a pleasant surprise when he recognized a voice on the line.

"Now who's playing hard to get, Josh?" Pamalou asked in her husky voice.

"Pam? Hi! I'm sorry, it's getting hectic out here. How are you?"

"Not as harassed as yourself, it seems. I can call back later if you're busy."

"No! I mean, please don't hang up. I could do with talking to someone who doesn't want me to dip their snuff, eat their freeze-dried beans, or wear their undies."

"Wear their . . . *undies*? Sounds kinky. Can't give any guarantees on that one, but I think you're safe on the other counts. I take it you'll be pretty busy before long, huh?"

"Seems that way. We sent the fish to Florida, and we'll be shooting down there I suppose."

"Sent the fish to Florida? Must be nice. One day maybe I'll get out of here and go off to some sunny place with orange blossoms and a beach and . . . ."

"And three million retired Jewish grandmothers with blue hair! Yeah, you'd fit right in there, all right."

"Josh! I hope you're being sarcastic about that. You'll bring me a bag of oranges, won't you?"

"Oh yes, I think it's law down there that you are required to carry at least one bag of citrus fruit before you're allowed to board an airplane. That's unless you're a native, of course. Natives are just expected to sneer at the tourists."

"And do you?"

"I don't remember," he said truthfully. His last relative had died years earlier, and he hadn't been back since.

"Well, if I ever make it to the land of sun and fun, you'd best not sneer at me, Josh Jackson. Now, how would you like a home cooked meal before you hit the road?"

"You mean you can cook, too?"

"What do you mean, too?"

"Nothing. You're not planning on having Brussels sprouts by any chance, are you?"

"Well, I normally don't, but if they're a favorite of yours, I suppose . . ."

"No! No thanks. Sure, I'd love dinner. But wouldn't you rather go out somewhere? Maybe go to a movie afterward or something?"

"I remember what you said about movies and doubt that anything showing would fill the bill. Can I have a raincheck on that?"

Josh paused before answering, a vague recollection trying to fight its way through the cobwebs of memory.

"That sounds familiar. *Déjà vu?*"

"As you recall, you were drunk and broke that night, Josh. I might could have overlooked either of those by itself, but both?"

"Deal. I'll give you a raincheck if you'll give me one. How about it?"

"Hmmm. What'll be next, show you mine if you show me yours?" she said, then giggled.

"Maybe you'd better consider what the underwear people had to say about me, before we get that far. I'll tell you about that sometime. What time do you want me there?"

"Well, let's see. I get off at four or four-thirty, then I need to get fresh veggies and rolls. Let's say six or so. That okay with you?"

"Sure. Can I bring anything?"

"Perhaps a gas mask. I plan to grill steaks, and no matter where I stand I always end up in a cloud, so *you* get to tend the meat."

"Smoke follows beauty, they say," he said, then considered the wisdom of this saying in this case. "If you've breathed the air out this way since your boss put in the Tur. . . facility out here, you'd realize that smoke will probably be an improvement."

"I know what you mean. He's full of little fun things like that. You should have to work around him."

Josh wondered about that. Wondered if Klotz had tried to get into Pam's pants, shook off an urge to wonder further if he'd been successful.

"I suppose he's always hittin' on you, huh?"

"No, that's not it at all. But he looks like he dresses in the dark and delights in screwing people over, foreclosures and all that. I'll bet he's highly ticked that you won't default now."

A shudder ran through him at the thought.

"You mean he thought I would?"

"I mean he hoped you would. He's had your file on his desk for weeks now. He figured he could buy your property for a song, now that the refinement plant has lowered its value, then turn around and sell it to the county for some trumped-up project. That's enough shop talk, and I'm talking out of school anyway. See you at six. Come hungry!"

Josh stared at the phone after he'd hung up and counted aloud to fifteen before it rang. He hoped it would be Pam again, that maybe she'd forgotten to tell him something. It was Major Mike with an early total. Josh was booked solid for several weeks at a total take of over one-half million dollars. Josh was flabbergasted.

Balleau also informed him that the phone company would be by the next day to install several additional lines and call-forwarding so that he, Josh, would no longer have to field the calls personally. Josh was delighted. Major Mike was, too. He'd made almost as much as his client, though he'd been honest about taking only his ten percent on deals involving Josh. Mike felt no remorse about this, feeling that *caveat emptor* applied to services rendered as well as to goods. If Josh Jackson hadn't the business savvy to take care of himself, then he deserved whatever hiding he got.

Pamalou hurried about her small house picking up things, fluffing throw pillows, and rinsing her lunch dishes in the sink. As a final step in returning to work from her noon break, she paused before her bedroom mirror and took inventory. The miles spent pedaling her old Western Flyer bicycle along country roads was reflected in her tight buttocks and trim legs, but had done nothing to scale down her bosom. While not enough to threaten her balance, she still saw them as overly large and a major flaw. Her lips, too, were too large for her liking. *Yuck!* she thought, *I could play a trombone from either end!* Her eyes met with approval, however, and were large enough to compensate for the full mouth. Overall, not bad for someone closing in fast on thirty.

"So why *hasn't* Klotz tried to get into my pants?" she asked aloud, then looked around the room.

None of her stuffed animals knew why, and neither did the bronzed bathing beauties who smiled down from the travel posters depicting Nassau, Jamaica, and the Virgin Islands. She turned to view herself in profile, frowned in puzzlement, then shrugged it off as one of the world's many mysteries. So big deal.

Josh fielded a few more phone calls, noting with mounting disbelief that some of them were from truly large corporations. Several automobile manufacturers wondered what type of four-wheel drive truck he preferred, others what sort of car. The makers of jeans, jackets, and cowboy hats all asked his sizes and if he'd ever, *ever* worn their products. Jimmy Houston and Bill Dance, two of the leading television bass fishermen, called offering their congratulations along with fishing trips to be filmed and aired nationwide.

His favorite, though, was from a major brewer who just happened to bottle his brand. The beer people were more than pleased and gave him a number he could use for a bottomless stein anywhere their products were sold. This sounded like a much better deal than Slats had gotten for his poem, so he decided to try out this latest perk immediately. On the way out, FrankenKat reminded him they were out of cat food. He made a note to stop by the store en route.

The Bide-A-Wee was filled to capacity when he arrived. It was just after quitting time for Blalocks, and many of those present had merely stopped by for a cold one to tide them over until traffic died down. So many Blalocks' employees did this, in fact, that an airplane could land safely between cars going through town at this hour of the day. A hush fell over the crowd as Josh entered and paused his customary minute to adjust.

The air inside was heavy with cigarette smoke and the usual honky-tonk odors of popcorn and piss. From the battered juke box in one corner (no less than three cue balls had been through its multicolored front) came strains of a particularly heartfelt country song entitled, as near as he could tell, "Get Your Tongue Out of My Mouth, Woman, 'Cause I'm Kissin' You Good-bye!" The crowd came to life as he walked between the tables and up to the bar.

"Afternoon, Jackson! How you doin'?" one asked.

134

"Dandy-fine, thanks. Yourself?"

"Can't complain. That was some fish you caught!"

"Yeah, it was. Thanks again."

"Was it as big as they say it was?"

Josh didn't have to answer this because Slats beat him to it.

"Foley, a *photograph* of that loud-mouthed bass weighed nearly *three pounds!*"

A chorus of laughter went up from those who were listening, causing those who weren't to look up from their conversations and hands of Rook in wonder. Wonder didn't last long in the Bide-A-Wee, though, so things were quickly back in order.

Foley pressed in close and asked in an exaggerated whisper, "Come on, Jackson. What do you catch a world record bass on, huh?"

"A two-pound grasshopper," he replied with a wink, then nodded to Clyde for a beer.

The conversation returned to what it had been before Josh arrived: what to get Clyde's daughter and her new husband for a wedding gift. The bride herself sat at a table nearby talking in an animated fashion with Mavis and another female he didn't recognize. Had he not known already, he'd have never made the connection between Clyde and his daughter, Prissy, because they were nothing alike. Prissy was thin to the point of almost disappearing when she turned sideways, while Clyde was built, and weighed, about the same as a refrigerator.

"So, what do you think we ought to get 'em?" Slats asked through a mouthful of popcorn.

"Heck, I don't know. What do you normally give as gifts around here?" Josh answered.

Clyde wiped at his bar, took the cigar from his mouth and looked over at his offspring while he considered whether or not he should mention that she was three months pregnant. He decided he shouldn't and restored the stogie.

"How 'bout you, Bill?" Slats asked an overalled customer sitting nearby. "What kind of gifts do you get for anniversaries and such?"

Bill pushed his cap back to allow his brain breathing room as he remembered, the effort plainly etched on his face.

Before Bill could answer, Mavis walked over to the counter and stood behind Slats's stool. She nodded a greeting to Josh, then placed her hand gently on Slats's shoulder to attract his attention.

"And what are you peckerwoods jawin' about over here that's got your giggle boxes all turned over?" she asked, then smiled through fire engine-red lips.

"Say, Mavis," Josh said. "We were just trying to come up with a suitable gift for Prissy and Duck. Got any ideas?"

"No, they're living with Clyde 'til Duck finishes his electrician apprenticeship down at the steam plant, so they won't need household stuff for a while. Slats here is good at gifts, why don't you let him pick out something? He surely found the right thing for my little nephew for his birthday, and you know how hard it is to choose stuff for teenagers," she concluded, then reached over Spivey's shoulder to retrieve the three beers Clyde held toward her.

She leaned all over Slats as she did this, causing him to blush. When she'd hustled off to deliver the brews, Josh turned to him and winked.

"Seems Mavis has taken a shine to you, partner."

"Aw, she's just still feelin' grateful for me knockin' that wad of popcorn from her goozle, that's all," Slats said, then blushed even deeper.

"Well, she seems to have a lot of faith in your choice of gifts, and you *did* help her out with her nephew, right?"

"Yeah, well that weren't nothin'. She just couldn't think like a teenage boy, that's all. So I made a suggestion."

"And?"

"Well-sir, she was tryin' to decide whether to get him something to play with or something to wear, see?"

Josh took the final swig from his Blue Ribbon, then remembered he'd not mentioned his "Magic Number" to Clyde. He also noticed the time on the big Miller's High Life clock on the wall behind the pickled eggs. Even allowing for the fifteen minutes fast that Clyde normally kept it, to give him time to shoo out the last few drunks before legal closing time, it was crowding four and he had things to do before he met Pam for dinner.

"So, what did you suggest?"

"A compromise. Got him a pair of pants and cut out the front pockets!"

Slats was duly appointed to select the gift and, to no one's surprise, Mavis volunteered to go along and help. Josh made his move to leave, which Mavis welcomed as it freed up the seat next to Slats. Spivey sought to delay his departure for the same reason.

"Where you runnin' off to, Jackson?"

"I've got a . . . an appointment."

"At this time of day? Does it concern . . . uh . . . what we was talkin' about earlier today?"

"No. It's, well, private."

"He's havin' dinner with little Miss Swift, I'll betcha!" Mavis sang out as she nestled herself onto the stool like a hen warming its eggs. "I saw her over at the Piggly Wiggley about noon, buyin' up some stuff, and she seemed to be pickin' two of everything."

It was Josh's turn to blush and Spivey's to smile.

"She's right, ain't she? You're tryin' to rob that cradle, ain't you son?"

"Nope," Josh said as he turned to leave. Then he shot a grin of his own over his shoulder and added, "But I'm willing to let her rob the grave, if she's a mind to!"

16

Josh couldn't help but notice the empty fairgrounds on his way out of town and felt a slight tug at his heart. Did he really miss her? He did and was as surprised as he was annoyed. Despite her narcissistic ways and unsavory habits, Thelma had been someone to come home to, and he felt awkward without her. Not heartsick, he was pleased to note, but the feeling that a part of him was gone forever.

At the crossroads he remembered the cat food and started to turn around. Instead, he pointed the truck toward the nearest "wet" county, which loomed thirty miles to the north. Once there, he purchased a huge bag of dry cat food and two dozen cans of assorted brands. At the checkout counter he saw himself smiling from the front page of the Nashville *Tennessean*. With chagrin, he noticed the huge fish he was holding in the photo, remembering it strangling and gasping for air.

He decided against buying a copy. An odd sense of shame came over him, a feeling that he was reaping enormous benefits at the expense of a dumb animal. Animal? Were fish considered animals, really? If so, then why had Catholics been allowed to eat them on meatless Fridays for centuries? No, he decided, fish were animals all right and, as such, were entitled to man's benevolence. He decided then to check on Big Un's welfare and to make certain he was being properly cared for. He also decided to stop by a liquor store.

At the liquor store manager's suggestion, Josh selected two bottles of a tangy rosé, Chateau D'Anjou. During the drive back he wondered what people would think of his purchases, which looked like a pussy cat picnic in the making. Indeed, he wondered what they would think of French wine in a pickup truck! Such wine drinkers as there were in this part of the country had no need for corkscrews as they tended to drink the generic brands with twist-off caps. French wine in Dilbert's Forge was a rarity on a par with finding an angel perched on a telephone wire.

With a frown he tried to remember if he had a corkscrew at home, or if he could assume Pam would have one. Opening a twenty-dollar bottle of wine with a Swiss Army Knife would likely knock the culture out of the vintage and perhaps make him seem even more of a redneck than he already felt. Then he realized he *was* driving around in a pickup truck, not the legendary red Porsche, and decided to act like he felt and to hell with trying to impress anyone. He was tempted to toss the wine out and bring a six-pack instead, but for the life of him he couldn't picture Pam with a can of beer in her hand.

When he arrived at home, as a treat, he slowed the pickup early and let the dogs chase it a little before honking the horn. They wagged their gratitude and panted happily as they escorted him to the door. FrankenKat sat in stoic silence at the top of the steps eyeing the bags coldly, like some disinterested cyclops. The cat dug in once a can was opened and its malodorous contents jettisoned into his bowl. The smell reminded Josh of Spivey's concoction and brought another thought to mind: was Pam being openly friendly just because he had money now? No, she'd been just as amiable before he'd caught the fish.

"That damned fish!" he said aloud, distracting FrankenKat.

"Neeow?" asked the cat.

"Yeah, now!" Josh answered, then tried to put the fish out of his mind and concentrate on what to wear.

The fish wouldn't leave his mind, though. Would he go on questioning the motives of everyone who was nice to him in the future? Was that the price to be paid for accidental wealth?

Was it worth the price? No, he decided, it wouldn't be. Before, he'd had friends who had absolutely nothing to gain by befriending him, and he would maintain those friendships, regardless of what fortunes came his way. It would, however, be harder to make new friends now that he had that indefinable thing called status. No, not indefinable at all, he thought. Status is merely spending money you don't have to impress people you don't like! He'd have none of that.

The phone was ringing plaintively as he stepped from the shower, and he decided to answer it on the off chance it might be Pam. It wasn't. It was another bait company to be referred to Major Mike. He wondered idly what the total was now and took a guess that missed by a mile. FrankenKat watched as Josh walked by in his underwear, sans potato, and quickly dressed in khaki slacks, cotton shirt, and ragwool sweater. He even considered, for the briefest instant, putting on a tie.

That'll be the day! he thought, then dragged a comb through his wavy brown hair and slapped on some aftershave as his lone concession to Miss Swift. The dogs were ready when he fired up the truck to leave and were severely disappointed when he shut it off again to go back in to get the wine from the freezer where he'd put it to chill. In their confusion they almost missed out on chasing the pickup at all. He honked as his fender pulled even with his mailbox at the end of the driveway and watched them in his rearview mirror as they screeched to a halt.

When Pam met him at the door, he put all thoughts of pretension out of his mind. She was wearing denim cut-offs and an overly large man's shirt, the tail of which bracketed her lightly-tanned thighs. Her hair was piled atop her head, with several rogue wisps escaping at the back of her neck to stick out in defiance. She wore virtually no make-up, and a light glow of perspiration lit her face. In all, a picture of casual. Her smile made him feel at home.

"Your timing is perfect, Josh. If you'd been here a minute sooner I'd have had *you* light the charcoal. Come in, I'm just about to grease the potatoes, and I know you'll want to watch that!"

"Wouldn't miss it for the world. Here's a couple of jugs of wine, I . . . hope you have a corkscrew."

"Oh yeah, there's one here somewhere. If not, I've got an old Cub Scout knife with one on it, if the cork's not too long. Right now I'm having a beer, care for one?"

Josh stood just inside the door with his mouth hanging open in surprise. She pulled the bottles from his hands and ignored his slack-jawed expression.

"Well? Come along. I want the potatoes slimed and zapped before the coals are ready for the mesquite, or we'll end up eating things one at a time."

"Right," he said, the spell broken. "Mesquite?"

"Sure. It gives the meat that Texas trail taste that's all the rage now."

Between sips of her beer, which he noticed was not a light variety but a no-fooling, industrial strength brew, she coated the potatoes with shortening. Once they were slicked to her satisfaction, she rolled them in rock salt and set them into a small microwave. They chatted about the relative merit of different brands of charcoal, and she heard the tale of the big fish and an encapsulated version of what had transpired since. He did not mention any monetary figures, and she requested none.

While she scrubbed away at getting the grease off her hands, which she felt was probably beneficial since they always felt softer afterward, he tore fresh leaves of spinach into a salad, along with tiny chunks of cucumber, mushrooms, and bean sprouts. They covered their early life histories and found several hitherto unknown similarities. Both were the single offspring of deceased parents, and both wanted to see the world.

Josh had made an effort in joining the Army but was stationed a mere five hundred miles north of his childhood home and never got any farther. He almost cited his marriage as a major factor in this, then recalled that he *was* still married, for the time being anyway, and felt it would be impolite to bring it up. Here Pam surprised him again.

"Thelma brought you here, right? That should have been a tip-off that it wasn't going to work out. Don't you think?" she opined while stirring the marinade in which two thick steaks swam, then dipped a forefinger into the liquid and tasted it.

Her eyes, those marvelously lush lashes framing twin emerald orbs, went to him as she licked the marinade from her finger, and he felt a stirring in his blood. Whether the act was conscious or not, he perceived it as sensual and found himself confused by the divergence of her words and actions.

"I suppose I should have fought that at the time, but coming right out of the service and walking into a good job, it just seemed a logical move. As for my . . . our . . . marriage, it was never what you'd call stormy. I never struck her or anything like that, and she pretty much let me go my own way. Looking back, I can't think of a single thing we had in common. I guess we just stayed together for convenience more than anything."

"I knew it was just a matter of time, you know. I think you did, too."

"Oh? Not saying you're wrong, but just how did you know?"

She smiled with full mouth and sparkling eyes and fixed him with a stare that said, *A woman has a way of knowing things about men.* Then she articulated the thought aloud. "We women have our ways."

"Oh, ho! I'd best be careful what I think around you then, huh?"

"Not especially. I said we have ways. I didn't say we use them all the time. Besides, some things are better left unknown. Now, there's an apron in the top drawer over there. Would you get it, please? The coals should be about ready, so I'll nuke the potatoes in the microwave and put the bread on to brown later."

He handed her the apron, a large affair with an enormous sunflower emblazoned across the bib. She shook her head and smiled again.

"It's for you, remember?" she said, then twisted the knob of a pepper mill large enough to have come off a four-poster bed over the salad.

Pam placed the microwaved potatoes on the grill along with the steaks to soak up some of the smoke, and Josh wiped tears from his eyes as the smoke followed him around the kettle-shaped grill. He also kept an eye peeled for any acquaintance who might walk past and catch him in the flowery apron. As the meat sizzled and dripped, adding its odors to the smoke, he forgot all about the apron.

Pam brought him out a fresh brew, then used the remainder of her beer to extinguish a small blaze that sprang up under the meat. When the steaks were finished, they were ready for them. True to Pam's word, they were reduced to opening the wine with a Cub Scout knife.

Pam endeared herself by snapping the cork off in the neck of the second bottle, becoming more fallible, more real, in Josh's eyes. With a shrug she simply pressed the rest of the cork down the neck and they fished the crumbles out of their glasses. The wine lost none of its character for this. Over dinner they spoke of places they'd like to visit, which ran the gamut from the surface of the moon to Bali. Pam preferred the sunnier spots and confessed to belonging to a tanning club in Clarksville where she touched up her pigmentation from time to time so she could at least *look* the part of a beach bum.

"Tanning booths take some getting used to, you know," she said with a little giggle. "I stayed in too long my first visit and sunburned my bottom!"

"Pity. If it happens again I'd be happy to kiss it and make it well," he said, meaning it.

"The wine makes you bold, eh? I'll remember that, but I'll still keep my *Aloe vera* plants in case you're not handy. Ready to help with the dishes?"

"Sure. I'll dry."

"You'll wash, mister. Everyone who eats in this house washes their own."

"Then let's get to it. I can't go getting dishpan hands, you know. I've some serious fishing to do before long."

"I'm not surprised. Do you enjoy fishing a lot?"

143

"Oh yes, I *like* getting up mornings before sunrise and driving several miles so I can drown a few worms. I'm not very conversant in it, though, and that might be embarrassing before long."

"Ah, but you knew enough to catch the big one, now didn't you? That should be enough I'd think."

"For now, perhaps," he said while suds rose in the ancient enamel sink. "But it's gotten to be a real science, with all sorts of gadgetry and gear, some of which I may have to endorse. It'd be real embarrassing if I didn't know how to turn something on or what it was supposed to do after I did."

"You'll do fine, Josh. You don't impress me as a guy who'd panic over some far-fetched gizmo. You'll make a fine talking head, too."

"Talking head?"

"Sure. I did the news on our college station for a while before I decided on accounting as a major. A talking head is just a camera shot from the shoulders up. They'll put a jumpsuit on you, or a lumberjack shirt, and you'll look like Mister Outdoors himself. The women will swoon, and the good ol' boys will rush right out and buy whatever you're selling."

That would make an interesting picture, he thought.

"I doubt that you'd swoon, Pam."

"You media stars are all alike!" she said, then flicked a fingerful of suds into his face. "So insecure!"

Before she could move away from him, he had an arm around her waist and had deposited a handful of suds on her nose. She giggled and squirmed, trying initially to free herself then, failing that, began splashing wildly in the soapy water until they were both soaked and laughing. A sharp pivot within his grasp brought them face-to-face.

The suds were now spread in little bubbles around her face and her hair tumbled down around it. Their eyes continued to laugh even after their voices fell silent. Then, just as Josh was trying to will himself to step away, her lashes slowly lowered and her face tilted up to his, inviting the kiss he so wanted to give her. He didn't mind that she tasted of Lemon-scented Joy, and when their embrace ended he stepped back, not knowing what to say next.

"It's difficult, isn't it?" she asked softly.

"What's difficult?"

"Getting accustomed to 'dating' again. I should imagine that would be difficult for someone who's . . . ."

"Oh, yes. I suppose so. I hadn't really thought about it. Does it show that much?"

"There was some . . . reluctance . . . I guess you'd say. Not that I didn't enjoy it, mind you! But you *are* still somewhat married in your mind at least."

"And on paper, now that you mention it. I hope you . . . we . . . aren't going to give you a bad name with your neighbors. You know how people like to talk and all, and they might put two and two together and come up with five, if you know what I mean."

"Screw 'em!" she said with a toss of her head that sent a spray of sudsy water across the kitchen. "If they're talking about me, they're giving some other poor soul a rest. I don't care either way. If you feel uncomfortable, I can understand that, but don't stay away for my reputation's sake."

"I doubt that I would. I'm not much into chivalry and I . . . ."

"Yes?"

"I'd like to see more of you."

"Oh? And exactly how do you mean that, Josh?" she said, teasing again.

"Poor choice of words."

"Or perhaps it was a Freudian slip, hmmm?"

"Maybe, but you know what I meant."

"Well, either way, I think that can be arranged, in due time. And largely up to you. When do you start your travels?"

"I'm not sure. Soon, I'd imagine. Photo sessions with the fish, of course, and maybe some television spots. I don't know how much time it'll all take, or when it begins. Major Mike Balleau is handling all that."

"And when do you unveil your mysterious Secret Added Ingredient? I read the papers you know."

"That'll come later. It's going to sound pretty silly once it's out, but it really did play a big part in catching the fish. Was directly responsible for it, if the truth be known."

"Oh? I thought it would be some rustic ritual from these parts. Like spitting on your bait maybe?"

Josh's eyes flew open wide and he took a step backward. *Can she really read my mind?* he thought.

"Spit? On the bait?"

"Sure. I remember my father doing it every time he baited his hook, for luck."

"Oh, I see. I thought for a minute there you were testing your feminine wiles on me again."

"Oh, I don't use womanly skills for anything so mundane as ferreting out a fishing lure, Josh Jackson," she said, stepping up and posing for another kiss before he left. "That's not what being a woman is about."

The nearness of her, her smell, the electricity sparking in her eyes, all contrived to rid his mind of any thoughts of fishing, breathing, or anything other than her. He took her into his arms and pulled her gently to him, then asked in a husky whisper, "And what *is* being a woman all about, then?"

"The art of being a woman," she began, then punctuated the first phrase with a light peck on his chin, "is knowing when *not* to be too much of a lady."

When Josh left Pam's house, he could not fathom a force great enough to keep him away from her for long. That was before he'd run the gauntlet of barking hounds and stepped up on his porch to find FrankenKat rubbing his arched back against a large floral arrangement. Major Mike, being a logical thinker, had sent the flowers via a local florist after he'd not been able to reach Josh by phone. Flowers arrive much faster in the country than do telegrams.

The card on the bouquet read:

"J. Jackson—Meet me at airport, Nashville, tomorrow morning at 7 A.M. Pack bags for Florida and points west.
Yours,
M. Balleau"

Josh considered driving over to Spivey's, but opted instead for calling Pam. She sounded even more wonderful than he'd remembered, her voice sleepy yet excited for him. She agreed to come out once a day in his absence and feed FrankenKat and the hounds, providing that he remembered to bring her back a bag of fresh oranges. He would, he promised, bring her a veritable grove.

He rang off after promises of future dinners, then tossed a few items into a suitcase while the shower water warmed. He then wondered if maybe a *cold* shower might not be more appropriate.

17

Brother Ray-Bob knew he had to do something. Even with all the efforts of the sound engineers, the best tone that could be squeezed, rounded, filtered, and deamplified from Thelma's throat still sounded like someone was maltreating a walrus. It put him in an awkward position for, while Thelma was a bust as a singer, her bust was a boon for collections! Now he pondered a way he could break the news to her without putting her into the dumps so deeply that she'd leave. He was sitting at his desk watching himself in the mirror, tapping his teeth with a letter opener when an idea formed in his flinty little mind. Smiling his famous smile, he made a tentative stroke in the air with the letter opener and mentally exchanged an image of Thelma in her abbreviated robes for his own. It would work!

When Brother Ray-Bob first told Thelma he wanted her to get herself a baton, she very nearly fainted. Slowly she realized the type of baton he meant, and some of the blush fell from her rose, but the thought that she'd be out in front as leader of the Hallelujah Choir far outweighed any remorse she might have felt at not lending her voice to the harmony. The other girls were so relieved they'd not have to drown her out in the future, they wouldn't have cared if she led them or popped out of a cake.

Some did express concern that Thelma would be running

148

around wielding a sharp pointy object, but these fears soon died away as they saw how well developed her dexterity was in this regard. After just an hour's practice, she could roll the thin baton through her fingers until it was but a blur and could smoothly toss it spinning into the air a short distance, pirouette to face the audience, then catch it without looking! In all, she was a stunning visual addition to the show, and they were happy with the change. The audiences were vocally appreciative to the point that after a few shows, Brother Ray-Bob had Thelma do a brief introduction for him. This made Brother Ray-Bob's entrance oddly reminiscent of a game show but, since he well knew the ratings such shows routinely registered, it worried him not at all.

Josh didn't think until he was almost to the airport that he didn't know where to meet Major Mike, that he didn't even know what the man looked like. His worry was unfounded, however, for Major Mike Balleau was a man who knew how to stand out in a crowd. As Josh was leaving the long-term parking area, he saw a pair of men standing outside the main terminal who were drawing a lot of attention. One was a shortish fellow dressed in a magenta shirt and pants outfit, gray glove leather shoes, a sweater tied loosely around his neck, and a pair of glasses suspended from a rhinestone chain. Standing next to him was what looked like an Indian sidekick left over from an old Gene Autry movie. He walked up to them, hoping they weren't who he thought they were, yet knowing better.

"I take it one of you is Major Mike?" Josh asked hesitantly.

The sidekick jerked a thumb toward the dandy. It was as though the silent partner had pressed the button on a spring-loaded stiletto. Major Mike's shaking hand flew out in front of him in a blur, grasped Josh's, and began to pump while Mike's jaw flapped at ninety miles an hour.

"Josh Jackson, I presume? Well, it is indeed a pleasure to finally meet you, partner! I've got some sweet, sweet deals cookin' for us and some others already in the can, as we say in the business. Let's see now, yes, yes, you'll do just fine! High cheek bones, yes, yes. The hair could do with a touch of gray at the temples. You know what I'm saying, Josh? Just a touch to make you more of an authority figure, right? The rest though, lots of potential. Gobs and gobs of potential, yes, yes. I think we'll do just fine, yes I do. I really do. Have you had breakfast? Well of course you haven't! I had you up at the crack of dawn, now didn't I? Silly me, well, let's go into the lounge and have a cuppa. Oh! You'll want to check your baggage first, won't you? Yes, yes, that's what wants doing first, right? Canebrake? What say you check Mister Jackson's luggage for him, can you do that? Sure you can."

Then Major Mike took what Josh was certain was his first breath since he started talking. To his astonishment, he realized that not only had Major Mike covered a variety of topics, opinions, and directions, but he'd not left anything required in the way of an answer. Major Mike was one of those rare humans who can conduct a completely self-contained conversation. Now the sidekick, who on closer inspection didn't seem to be an Indian at all but was definitely of some obscure ethnic origin, picked up Jackson's luggage and began waddling off toward the Delta counter.

Canebrake Prudhomme was a leathery-faced man of probably forty years, thin and sinewy with eyes like washed coal. He wore an odd combination of clothes that included cowboy boots, fringed jeans, and a camouflage fatigue shirt that seemed to have been through several wars. He topped his garb with a straight-brimmed hat from which a hawk feather stuck out of the snakeskin band and something like a clump of coarse hair hung down from the brim. Josh felt conspicuously normal.

"What say we have a little bite to eat? Hmmm? Yes, I think a morsel would go down well at this point, don't you? Of course you do. Continental? Two continental breakfasts, please, and one tea with lemon on the side and . . . coffee is it? Yes, I thought as much, two coffees. That'll be all, thank you!" Major Mike sang off to waiter and client, leaving both wondering.

But not for long. Major Mike never allowed the subjects of his conversations to wonder for long, lest they ask something that he might have to answer.

150

"Now. I'll give you a rundown on where we are, where we're going . . . of course this morning we're going to Florida, but I mean down the road fiscally . . . what you'll need to do and say, and then Canebrake can have you on the plane, okay?"

Josh saw a crack in the conversation and dove through it.

"Who is Canebrake, and what does he do in all this?" he blurted out.

His haste seemed unnecessary as the waiter arrived with their tea and coffee. Major Mike seemed lost in thought as he dipped his tea bag in and out of the hot water until it had taken on enough color to suit him, then lightly traced around the rim of his cup with the lemon. Without so much as a brief blow to cool it, he lifted the cup and drained it in one swallow. A vein in the side of his neck inflated and pulsed, then his entire neck turned a violent red.

"Whew! I'm ready now!" the agent exclaimed, then launched into another tirade.

"Well! This afternoon we have wardrobe call. We'll pick you some good woodsy duds from a couple of lines and, should we find what we want from Lee's and/or Bean's, we can knock two birds in the head by getting a floater contract to wear them in other campaigns, right? Of course we'll want a tag-in, tag-out clause for some items, more bucks if the product is clearly identifiable. Then tomorrow when the fish arrives, we'll go right into the sessions. That'll take about three days on this set-up and we'll get Ray-Ban, Daiwa, Wright-McGill, Berkeley, Champion, Pabst, Coleman, Shasta, Rapala, and *Field & Stream* knocked out before we move on to the water shots.

"You'll do interviews between takes, of course, and we'll have our guy do the action follow-ups this weekend at Eufala. I figure two, three days there at the outside, if it doesn't rain of course, then we'll sky to the coast. He's here to teach you about fishing."

Josh was still wondering what Shasta was and what he'd be doing for them.

"Who's here for what?"

Major Mike nodded at his oddly dressed companion who had seemingly materialized in a chair next to Josh.

"Canebrake Prudhomme, Josh Jackson. Canebrake's here to teach you all you'll need to know about bass fishing. He's a guide on Bedageaux Creek in Louisiana. Knows his stuff, too, or so I'm told."

"You're an Indian?" Josh asked the top of the dusky man's hat as he bowed over his coffee, sniffed loudly, then grimaced.

"Be un Caj-un! The Mouth Man heah done brought myself on over to talk dem big-mouth basses to ya. He say, you don't maybe know poo about dem fishes, no matter anyhow dat you done up an' caught dat biggest mo-fo of em all. I done told you, you wanna cotch a mess to eat, you gonna go wif dem night crawly worms or dem shrimps! Ain't dat right?"

Major Mike and Josh both nodded in agreement, unsure which of them he'd "done tol'."

"Okay, we know dat's fer dam-sure, but! Mouth Man here, he say don't give no good damn what you gonna cotch dem fishes on mostly, 'cause dem shrimps and crawly worms don't be bringin' in no revenoo, now ain't dat de trufe? I done told ya, it is a fack. He be right as rain on dat nail-head, so what I gonna show you, be tellin' you some of it 'cause ain't much to show on de rest, is dem fancy thing-a-majigs what dem slick-headed Yankees be bringin' wif dem to try an cotch dem basses wit'out havin' to go gettin' worm poo on they froggy-feelin' little hands. Dat's what."

Canebrake was satisfied that he'd justified his existence sufficiently to stop abruptly and slurp his coffee.

"Needs three maybe two pinches chick-o-ree!" the Cajun opined, then slurped again.

When they boarded the plane, Major Mike produced a blindfold that matched his outfit, replaced his glasses with it and went to sleep as rapidly as he appeared to do everything else. Canebrake and Josh watched in wonder as the man's chest heaved up and down like a dog having a nightmare, amazed that anyone could actually sleep that quickly.

Canebrake took his employer's sudden silence as a cue to begin his instruction. He covered various aspects of bass fishing, but mostly he covered cover. Cover, it seems, is the most important aspect of finding the finicky fish. Available cover varied from deep stumps to weeds to cypress knees and fallen logs, and a bass's preference for any of these was subject to further matters of prejudice. The depth of the cover and time of year played a big part, as did available food, the pH of the water, current, and temperature. Josh came to appreciate Canebrake's expertise and to appreciate even more his own lack of it.

Canebrake was interrupted by a large woman seated behind them who wanted him to remove his hat. Josh winced in anticipation and was genuinely surprised when the Cajun complied meekly and offered an apology. Prudhomme's hair was crow feather black and as stiff as a robot's toothbrush all the way down to the full sideburns that terminated at the line of his jaw. Josh took the opportunity to ask about the unusual decoration hanging in a bristle from the back of the hat's brim.

"Dat dare be a wile turkey wattle, dat's what! De Ju-Ju Lady done give me dat to keep off dem bad spirits, don't you know. Works, too. Keeps dem haints and *par mon faits* away 'n' makes dem ol' cotton-mouf snakes hightail they scaly asses de other way too. Can't be leavin' no bayou lessin' I take dis ole hat, an' dat's a nachul fack! Now, you gonna be wonnerin' about how you gonna know dem Pee-ayches an' shit, ain'tcha?"

Josh agreed that he was wondering and felt Canebrake was about the last guy in the world he'd expect to know bugger-all about chemistry.

"Well-sir, I gonna told ya. Dem pee-ayches, dat's P-H, don't know rightly what it stands for, but I speck it's the feller what discovered its initials. Anyhow, dem pee-ayches they come from leaves and bark, dey surely do. Around the swamp you allus got dem leaves fallin' in and such and the bark be right dare a-settin' in the water alla time so that ain't no nevermind, right? Other places you got leaves what fall in the cricks, oak leaves mostly, then dey run down dem cricks until dey come to de ribber and on down to the lakes, right?

"Den dem leaves *rot*! And dat leaf rot, dat dare's where dem pee-ayches come from and you want about six point somebody of 'em. Yankees got a doo-dad they hang down in the water what ciphers up dem pee-ayches and reads it right out like a speedometer or sumpthin'. Don't matter much whuther you know how many of dem pee-ayches you got, so long as you know it's supposed to be important!"

Josh agreed it was important, and Canebrake went on.

"Anyhow, the mainest t'ing what you gonna need ta know is how to look like you already know ever-t'ing. An' dat's so plumb easy I hate to take this little shit's money just fer the tellin', but o' course I will. You ever watch them boys what sell fishin' shit on television, Jackson?"

"Sometimes, but I've never paid a great deal of attention to them."

"Well, it's just plumb damned easy, 'cause dey be sayin' de same shit alla time. Don't be makin' no nevermind what dey's tryin' to sell, nuther! Here's what you be sayin', furstest you say, 'It's a fine piece of gear, if you know how to use it.' You got that?"

"I think so. It's a fine piece of gear."

"Ifn you know how to *use* it! Gotta say dem words an' it don't make any diff'rent what it is, nuther. Could be a motor, could be a googly-eyed poppin' bug lure, could be a gosh-damn cookstove! You just say . . . ."

"It's a fine piece of gear, if you know how to use it."

"Right! Next, you say, 'It can help you locate, catch, attract, cook, or whatever, fish and is a big part of your fishing system. Gotta be sayin' *system* so they t'ink it's all compul-catied an' all, right? Lets 'em know you don't just stick a hook up a toadfrog's ass and t'row his butt out next to a tree-lap, no suh! You got a *sys-tem!*"

"It can help you locate, or whatever, fish and is a big part in the fishing system. Right?"

"Right! Now, dis part is where dey git all poor-mouth on ya. Nex' dey say, 'Now, dis thang ain't gonna cotch you no fish by itself, no. *But*, it goes a long ways in your *overall approach* to bass fishin'!' See dat right dare, Jackson? You done tol' 'em you ain't only got a *system*, but now you got yourself a *ap-proach*, too! Sound like you flat know your shit, don' it?"

Josh smiled, liking the Cajun's outlook on the whole business and the way he seemed to take none of it, least of all himself, seriously. He felt he could work with Canebrake and resolved to keep him near until he at least had his feet on the ground in this business. Canebrake made him repeat each item until he was satisfied that he could poor mouth with a proper amount of modesty.

Prudhomme's heavy accent aside, he apparently did know quite a bit about bass, their habits and peculiarities. That he made his living showing others where to find and how to catch them encouraged Josh to stay near him while these talents might come in handy. One item dug at Josh's mind though, tugging at him like a cat at a mouse until he had to ask.

"Canebrake, when *you* go out to catch a mess of fish, what sort of bait do you use?"

The Cajun looked around warily, then smiled a crooked smile and said, "I take myself out de night before, see. An' I cotch myself a big mess of frogs, big uns, little uns, all kinds. Den, I don't put myself in bed, no-sir. I stays up until ole man sun is peekin' down t'rough dem cypress trees. I pole my pirogue over to some big ole log, and I takes one of dem frogs, a little un, and I pokes a hook up his ass, see, and I t'row him out next to dat log and let him try to clum up it! Only I don't let 'im, see? Well-sir, if dey's a bass anywhere in dat bayou, he gonna hear dat an' come runnin'! If dey ain't, I go home an' eat dem big frogs myself. Hell, I like frogs better'n fish anyhow, 'cept catfishes maybe."

"I think that'd be heresy where we'll be goin', Canebrake."

"You prob'ly right on dat one. I be keepin' my flap shut lessin' you got sumpthin' you want me sayin' then. You want a drink o' whiskey? Them women walkin' around tellin' ever'body dey gots to woke up or put they seats up an' shit, they meaner dan hell, but they'll bring you a drink of whiskey if'n you ask 'em."

"I think I'll pass for now, Canebrake. You go ahead if you want one, though."

"Naw. Ain't the same without some hot boo-dang to gnaw on anyhow. Guess I'll get me some sleep. You wake me up afore dis t'ing starts down, you hear? Scairt shit outa me las' time. I tell you for true!"

"Takes some getting used to, I guess. I'll wake you up when they say to buckle up."

"T'anks Jackson," Canebrake said, then lowered his voice to a hoarse whisper. "You work for dis feller, do ya?"

"You mean . . . him?" Josh asked, indicating Major Mike and lowering his voice as well. "I think he works for me, at least that's how I understand it."

"Jes' wonderin', the boy talks too much, you know? Sounds like a tree full of blackbirds once he gits goin', an' I don't hear half what he be sayin', but I don't like some o' dat little I does hear. One of dese days the boy gonna let dat mockin'bird mouth overload his hummin'bird ass! I done tol' you dat, done tol' him, too!"

Josh nodded his understanding and proposed to keep an eye on both in the future. Canebrake slid forward in his seat until his head was well below the headrest, placed his hat over his face, and was soon sound asleep. Josh looked out the window at Alabama rolling past five miles below and wondered what he'd gotten into and where it would lead him.

18

The first day's activities blended into the next and soon merged into a routine Josh found interesting, profitable, yet very uncomfortable. At dawn he'd be up staring into bright white Klieg lights mouthing insensibilities off cue cards while staring at the bloody red eye of a camera. It took several days before he had mastered the intricacies of looking at ease while on camera. At first he watched the cameraman more than the red light and reacted to whatever happened on set and off.

During one such session, he was to speak a line in total seriousness beseeching those sportsmen present in the viewing audience to rush right out and buy a certain product. Unfortunately, the cameraman chose that moment to scratch at his crotch and Josh came off sounding like the very thought of anyone buying the product was absurd. They reshot this take five times before he could get past the line, "take matters into your own hands today!" without breaking up.

The fish arrived the second day of shooting and spent many long moments being hoisted aloft in Josh's hand while he held various products up in the other. The ichthyologists from the university were on hand to insure Big Un got enough time in his tank between takes, so he didn't dry out or suffer from oxygen deficiency. The tank was an ingenious affair of some five hundred gallons mounted on the back of a large truck. It had numerous aerator pumps and featured a soft fabric net wall that could be pushed from one side of the tank to the other to facilitate capturing and recapturing the fish without hassle.

Big Un looked somewhat smaller than Josh remembered but was still a monster of a bass. The photographer went wild, swore his camera "loved" the beast, and filled the air with the shrill scraping screams of his automatic film advance. Major Mike had the photographer shoot the fish with Josh, the fish by itself, Josh by himself, and himself by himself, repeatedly for "file shots" and "promos." The bright Kliegs and galaxy of strobes took their toll on Josh's eyes before long, and he began to get a headache, so Major Mike moved in on a follow-on contract with Ray-Ban in return for Josh wearing their products in other photo sessions.

The days ended well after dark when Josh and Canebrake retired to their hotel for a few beers and more of the Cajun's "edgi-cayshun," and Major Mike laid out the next day's schedule. Canebrake proved a veritable storehouse of useful information beyond mere fishing. He knew, for instance, that dogs hike their legs before taking a leak in order to "kick they asses out of gear, so they won't shit!," something Josh had always wondered about. He also felt that the reason the hotel televisions received X-rated movies and his back in the bayou didn't was because his was an older set and resolved to get a new one as soon as Major Mike came across with his pay.

After three days of local shooting, they moved north to Lake Eufala in Alabama for some on location shots. Big Un arrived beforehand and was installed in a huge tank belonging to a major bait manufacturer that simulated a more natural environment. The gentleman who owned the bait company, which also bore his name, threw a gala party . . . for the fish! For the first time since Josh and Spivey's brief interview with the local paper, the media was allowed in for questions, photos, and a general round of probing. This exclusion from the press had heightened the prices paid by major magazines and endorsing agencies, as Major Mike explained, by keeping Big Un and Josh from saturating the media for free.

Josh had rehearsed his answers well, yet found himself being called an out-and-out liar by some of the more pushy journalists who were trying to provoke him into something they could claim as an exclusive. Some alluded to the ichthyologist's report that the fish was a Florida variety, citing this as proof positive that the fish was not caught in Tennessee as Josh claimed. To this Josh merely stated that he, too, was a transplanted Floridian and didn't see any reason a bass couldn't make the trip if he was a mind to.

As to the equipment he had used to catch the monster fish, he was more generic in his approach. Major Mike had anticipated this, as had some of the companies whose products he now endorsed.

"What kind of boat were you using?"

"I don't go fishing without my Ranger 6000. I've found it to be a good piece of equipment and an integral part of my overall fishing system," Josh answered truthfully, well, kind of. . . . He *did* have a new Ranger and had used it in most of his recent photo sessions.

"And the bait. It was a Headhunter I believe?"

"Hoosier HawgHunter. Yes, they're rare right now, as each is handmade by a gent in Indiana. But I'm happy to announce that the HawgHunter will soon be in mass production." He neglected to mention that he would also be endorsing it at a healthy chunk of the gross.

"Do you intend to keep the fish alive, or do you anticipate it not adjusting to captivity?"

"Haven't decided yet. As long as he remains healthy, he'll stay in captivity to be studied. That's for the immediate future. The professors at Florida tell us he'll do just fine for a while, though bass really don't take well to feeding in captivity. Should he develop some problems, I don't know. Maybe we'll release him or something . . . give someone else a shot."

Major Mike's eyebrows shot up above his designer sunglasses at this, a totally unrehearsed, remark.

"Gentlemen, gentleman!" Mike said, throwing his hands up

like he was surrendering. "We've lots more to do while we're here, and we really need to get on with it. I have an info packet for each of you along with some file shots of Mister Jackson and the fish that are already released. We'll try to work in something for you tomorrow before we leave. Thank you."

While speaking, Major Mike was busily herding Josh out of the cluster of reporters and into the corridor of their hotel. Once clear, he turned to and on Josh.

"Don't *ever* say anything about that again! There's no way in hell we can turn that fish loose and no way anyone expects us to, either!"

"And why not?" Josh wondered, somewhat irritated at Balleau's tone.

"Because, if we was to, it'd cause havoc! That's why. Big Un, as you call him, is an integral part of our package, and without him you're just another hillbilly fisherman. I promise we'll take damned fine care of the fish, hire only the best professionals to monitor his health, and all that shit. But he's ours until the day he dies, and then he'll be stuffed like he probably should've been to begin with!"

Josh took on a stoic pose, looking down on Major Mike from his superior height while considering whether to punch his lights out. Mike had come through with a wealth of contracts, though, and had netted Josh more money in the process than he'd ever expected. More than he'd ever dare think of!

"It appears to me the boys like having the fish alive, Mike. What makes you think it'd be better with him stuffed? Would *that* make me more than just 'another hillbilly fisherman'?" he asked, letting his distaste show as he used Major Mike's own words.

The smaller man smiled weakly, attempting to put a hand on Josh's shoulder which was easily shrugged off.

"Now, now. Let's not get testy with each other, Josh. No, no. That's the kind of thing the press does best, you know? If they were to sense a rift between us, they'd start manufacturing things I allegedly said about you and you allegedly said about me and so forth until we were at each other's throats. All I meant was, the fish would have been much easier to transport were he. . . . Dammit! As it is, we've got to provide a tank and air pumps and that funky-smelling fish paste the egg-heads feed him . . . feed him! Someone even has to take the fish out and dribble that crap down his throat until he swallows!

"Josh, it's a lot of trouble. But I know how you feel and I've developed a soft spot in my heart for Big Un, whether you believe it or not, and have contracted to have a portable cage . . . uh . . . environment built for him so we can take him by plane if we need to. For now, though, the professors have the say, and they think he needs a stable environment until he starts feeding on his own. So we'll leave him with them for a while. Happy?"

"I suppose so. Just don't lose track of who's working for who here, and don't grab me by the sleeve again and lead me off like I'd been smacked away from the dinner table for farting, understood?"

Mike's smile now was brighter, though still too ingratiating in Josh's estimation.

"You got it, babe! Now, what say we get on over to the lake and let you practice with the new equipment? Hmmm? You can go by yourself if you like, or Canebrake will be happy to go with you, I'm sure. Maybe he can give you some pointers."

"Fine. Tell him I'll be in the bar."

Major Mike's smile faded at this, but he nodded assent and went off to coddle the press and locate the Cajun. To channel his supressed anger at having been chided by Josh, he led off his apology to the press by citing Josh's pending divorce action as reason for his short temper and vacillating moods. He took delight in the way the writers broke into a flurry of questions and began scribbling in their pads. Mike enjoyed being the center of attention, almost as much as the man he thought of naming as correspondent in Jackson's divorce: Brother Ray-Bob Thomas.

At a strategic moment, when the questions had reached a fever pitch, he began working his way through their clutching hands and extended microphones. He paused beside the door and smiled in friendly fashion.

"That's about it for today, boys. I'll speak with Mister Jackson and perhaps he'll be more willing to answer questions day after tomorrow, when we're in Ocala. Hope to see you there and the name is Balleau, B-A-L-L-E-A-U. See ya!"

Once safely in the elevator, Major Mike reached into his jacket pocket, pulled out the small tape recorder he kept there, and rewound the tape to the beginning of his recent session. Using a small earplug, he reviewed his comments and answers, smiling all the time. No, he'd not actually said the word *correspondent,* nor had he identified the man by name. That could come later. What he had done, though, was start them to thinking and allowed them to arrive at the right answers. Right as far as he was concerned, anyway.

Jackson, he reasoned, would be a dead issue within six months. Since his contract expired at that time, he would need to bleed every nickel he could get before then. Controversy sold papers far better than a big fish. Ah yes, the fish. How very stupid of Jackson not to set himself up as a corporation and claim the fish as an asset! With very few strokes of the pen and dials of the phone, he, Mike Balleau, had assumed the role as guardian for the scaly giant, and it was he who would draw the handsome fees Big Un would soon draw for personal appearances. The fairs, symposiums, and bass tournaments all would want the fish on display and would pay ridiculous amounts for the privilege. Particularly so if they were in competition with one another for the same dates!

Satisfied with himself, Major Mike stepped out of the elevator and strode to the door of Canebrake's room. His face twisted in distaste at the thought of having to face the semi-wild man, having those beetlelike eyes stare at him as though they could see right through him and didn't like what they saw. It was eerie! The man himself was eerie. He was of no determined age, had no formal education that he knew of, yet there was something about him he dreaded. No, something that he honestly feared.

Mike resolved to be rid of this nuisance as soon as this first round of interviews and filming was over. His feelings were

162

reinforced when the door opened as he was about to knock on it. There stood Canebrake, eyes fixed upon him as though watching something odious in the distance.

"Jackson wants you to meet him in the bar. I think he wants to go fishing," Major Mike said into the eyes.

The feather in the Cajun's hat gave a slight twitch in response, and the turkey wattle swung hypnotically for an instant. It was close enough to a nod that the agent took it for an answer.

Prudhomme watched the agent walk off in his mincing little steps that seemed so inefficient to him. *Never do in the bayou,* he thought. *The boy would be sunk up in the soft mud before he could get fifty yards with that walk and them pointy toed shoes. For damned sure Major Mike had never walked behind no mules, either, not like that he hadn't or he must have had a sure enough slow team.*

Mules were something else Canebrake knew about. He figured he could just about smell a mule fart and tell you what size collar it wore. By conservative estimate, he had surveyed the better part of ten thousand acres before he was twenty-five using a mule's rear as a transit. But that was before *they* came. Before he had to leave his family farm and head off into the bayou for good. *Now look at me,* he thought. *I done run away all that time and for what? So I can get jerked out of the bayou by some oily haired slicker and paraded around getting my picture in the papers! Only a matter of time until someone sees me and remembers, only a matter of time.*

Canebrake closed the door silently and went to the chest of drawers to fetch the croaker sack that held his professional goods. As a concession to the flashy world of big time bass fishing that existed outside his room, he grabbed a plastic laundry bag from the shelf in the closet and put the croaker sack in it, then paused to look up and down the corridor before entering the hallway. He ignored the elevator, chosing instead to walk the eight flights of stairs to the ground level. Elevators seemed unnatural, unsafe. More importantly, they were so confining that they reminded him of . . . .

"Don't go thinkin' on that one, old son!" he said aloud. "We done come a long ways since then and, soon's this here's over wit', we can plumb sure take on down dat road some further, too! I guar-an-tee."

19

Pam licked her thumb instinctively, then reached into her drawer for the rubber thumb she used when counting money. The twenties were crisp, newly minted, and probably far more sterile than the average restaurant silverware, but some precautions were in order even if one did know where the money had been. A black man stood on the opposite side of her window watching the money mount into piles as she counted, but he did not display the joy one would expect from one about to take possession of a goodly sum, and for good reason.

Glover Sampson, as was his name, had found himself forced to do something he'd sworn faithfully to his late father that he'd never do, and he was feeling the weight of the past hundred-odd years fall upon his shoulders. He'd had to take out a mortgage on the family home, the home that had seen five generations of Sampsons born and the better part of three die within its walls. Glover hefted the total in one cracked, calloused hand after Pam pushed the stacks toward him.

The weight of the money didn't begin to equal what he felt pressing down on his heart. It felt so insignificant. *But then,* he thought, *it's probably about as much as thirty pieces of silver would weigh.* The thought was not comforting, nor was the analogy. The pretty lady smiled at him sadly, apparently understanding at least part of what he felt, and he was grateful enough for that to return the smile.

She'd probably gone to college somewhere, he thought, then wondered that he didn't remember anything about that. Seems she came here late in school to live with the old Swift woman and maybe left for a time after that. He wondered if perhaps he could ask her about colleges or have his son Thurman come speak with her about it.

"How's things at school, Mister Sampson?" Pam asked, breaking his chain of thought.

"Right fine, I reckon, ma'am. 'Bout through with another'n, looks like."

"Well, I suppose you're looking forward to a vacation then, huh?"

Glover Sampson looked from the money back to her still-smiling face and wondered what a vacation would be like.

"Yassum, them young'uns will be gone sure enough, but that ain't no vacation for me, ma'am. I'll jest go right on, sweepin' and moppin', puttin' on some new paint where them boys wrote on the walls and sech. Ah got lockers to fix up, o'course, and the yard to keep mowed an' all. Usual stuff," Glover finished. He seemed tired for having just named the tasks the summer held.

"You've been at it for quite a while, haven't you? I remember the time you helped me get my books back off the gym roof and that's been . . . well, it's been more years ago than I care to think!"

He remembered now. She was a pretty little thing, even then. And some of the girls had resented her to the point of siccing their boyfriends on her. He smiled as he remembered how this had nearly backfired several times when Miss Swift had turned her charms on the boys and scared their girlfriends! The time she was speaking of, though, a bunch of roughnecks had tossed her books atop the gymnasium to spite her and to keep her from studying for finals. He'd been in his early fifties then, still spry enough to mount the extension ladder and retrieve the books.

She'd thanked him sincerely, and he especially remembered that. He remembered the others, too. The ones who'd let the words *nigger* and *coon* slide out of their whitebread-eating mouths with the same inflection as they would *shit*. Yes, he remembered them. It was his plight to do so, and no more. But not his son's!

"That weren't long ago atall, ma'am! Lord, that was jest yestiddy th' way I'm a-countin'. In fact, my oldes' was done finished up wit' school afore then."

Finished up and gone to the army, he thought. *Still there, too.*

"Don't you have another about to graduate, Mister Sampson? I thought I saw his picture in the paper last week."

"Yassum! That there's my baby, but don't you go tellin' him I called him that." He allowed himself a hearty chuckle at the thought. "Thurman'll be walkin' 'cross that stage come th' end o' May, for a fact. Then it'll be off to college for him after summer. That's what all this . . . ."

He didn't go on. He didn't need to. Pam knew why he'd borrowed the money and felt it the most noble of the many charitable acts she'd known him to perform and possibly the most difficult. She also knew he was taking a big chance. Thurman delivered papers, helped put up hay, delivered the washing his mother had taken in up until her death, and was generally as industrious as his father. The money would be well spent on his education. What she also realized, and what she would desperately like to tell Glover Sampson, was that his credit history had never left the bank. As was his wont with mortgages on black family dwellings, Klotz had gone the loan cold, without so much as verifying the payment history on the applicant's car! Klotz was an arrogant bigot, so this anomaly confused her.

"Well, I'm sure he'll do well in college. You have a good day, Mister Sampson."

"Thank ye, ma'am. And you have a dandy yourself."

Klotz heard the bell tinkle announcing Glover Sampson's departure and smiled to himself. Old Sampson was as good as his word, all right, and would make his payments on time if he had to stand in the rain waiting for the bank to open to do it! A nice safe loan that not a soul in Dilbert's Forge, let alone anyone with the banking commission, would ever question, even after he'd defaulted on the loan a year or two down the road, as had so many other blacks in the recent past. *Then I'll have me another Coon Cottage!* Klotz thought gleefully, *and this one was almost too easy.*

Sampson is pushing sixty-four, so he'll be eligible for retirement next year and a minimum of Social Security. Certainly not enough to keep up the payments on his mortgage should he be forced to retire. Klotz had no children of his own, but he was a member of the local school board in addition to being mayor. It would be simple enough to call for a new school custodian, and he held enough paper on the remaining members of the board to make certain it passed. Then he could buy the mortgage for pennies on the dollar and rent the place back to Sampson under a federal grant for housing the poor. He was happy.

Klotz was even more pleased with his latest deposit statement from the Atlanta Federal Reserve Bank. The addition of over one-half million dollars in Jackson's account had swollen Klotz's coffers to the point he could make—legally—at least four times that amount in loans, and he had an idea where a major source of those funds should go.

The town was being besieged with fishermen since word of the big bass got out, and there were daily applications for business loans to add bait stands and boat docks along the lake, as well as to expand existing businesses. Clearly, the town was in for a boom era and, as such, could anticipate a rise in new construction. An improved water system was in order! Luckily, he just happened to own a plot of clay and sawbriars near a major creek that would serve this purpose admirably. It was time the city council held a meeting and decided on this, he felt, then rang up two of the other four members to say as much.

"Blalock," the voice on the other end of the phone answered flatly.

Josh, Canebrake, and Major Mike found themselves staring out over a majestic south Florida lake that hummed with activity. In the shallows, long-legged birds with needle sharp beaks probed the mud for grubs while being eyed malevolently by a brace of seemingly smiling alligators nearby. Kingfishers earned their names by swooping along the surface and snatching unwary minnows into their beaks with no loss of altitude. While they watched, one of the blue and gray speedsters plucked a fish almost his own length from the water, seemed to stop in mid-air, then dropped it and went on.

"I'm surprised that didn't give him whiplash!" Josh observed as he followed the bird's flight.

"Dem birds do alright for demselves, an' dat's a fack," Canebrake averred. "Saw one of 'em pick up a snake once. Reckon he thunk it was an eel, or somethin', but *boy*! You shoulda seen dat rascal fly after that! I done tole you, he was all over dat sky, man! Nevah did drop dat snake, though, no-sir. He done took dat snake way de hell up dare in them tree-tops, then *pow*! Dropped dat sombitch like a bad habit. Splattered snake all over de damned place, I mean. Den he come on down real easy like, 'n' eat himself all dat snake he wanted."

"Quaint," Major Mike commented in a dry tone, then paused to slap at a mosquito that seemed large enough to haul him away like the snake. "Damn! What say we change our plans slightly and go up into Canada for some filming? Hmmmm? Lots of nice water up there I'm told, and it's still cool enough that there shouldn't be all these damned bugs!"

Canebrake flinched at the mention of Canada, then looked around to see if anyone had noticed. They hadn't.

"I doubt you could fool enough people that way, Mike. Might get some northern pike this time of year and I'd dearly love to catch some, too. But that wouldn't go far in selling bass stuff. Besides, there's mosquitos there, too."

"Not as bad as here, I'll wager!" Major Mike exclaimed, then slapped at another to emphasize his point.

"Worser!" Canebrake chimed in. "They's got skeeters up dare what eat-up on bears! Swear to God! Call 'em *moose-skeeters* dey so damn big. Yeah, go on up dare, Mike. You get so many wheps on yore ass, you come back here a-lookin' like a ear of corn!"

Canebrake found this thought singularly funny and laughed until he had to clutch his chest in pain. "Moose-skeeters," he said as he regained control of himself.

"Well, you two can do what you will, but I'm going back to the hotel. The photographer will be here at the dock at three, and he want to get some sunset shots, too. So you'd better get something to eat before then. Try to catch something, if you can . . ." he paused to eye Canebrake with insolence and to let him fully absorb his verbalized lack of confidence, ". . . and if you do, keep it lively so they can film you in action later. I'll leave word with the manager to buy anything nice anyone else catches, and we can work them in, too."

"That be the day, *Ma-jor!*" Canebrake spat out along with a dribble of tobacco juice. "*We* cotch some fish or dey ain't no damned pictures, ain't dat right, Jackson?"

"Right. That's not necessary, Mike. No one expects us to catch fish on command! If they do, they're sillier than I already think they are. If we catch something worth filming, we'll keep it alive for the photos and then release it."

"What's with all this 'release the fish' bullshit?" Major Mike exploded, sending several would-be insect diners humming off in search of another target. "I thought you people *ate* fish! Now all I hear is 'turn 'em loose, turn 'em loose!'"

"I eat a mess of fish from time to time, everybody does. But that's not why you go fishing, Mike. If you were after a meal, you sure wouldn't count on catching a bass for it! They're too fickle, too smart. Better off going after catfish or perch. You catch bass for the sport of it and release what you're not going to eat so they can be caught again later."

"Still sounds stupid if you ask me. Well, I'm out of here. Three o'clock at the dock, right?"

Canebrake and Josh agreed, then hurriedly unloaded the boat. The Cajun felt right at home upon the lake, especially so around the edges where a jumble of cypress knees tangled along the surface. Josh marveled at the placid water, as dark among the trees as crude oil and as smooth. Soon they had left the lake proper and were cautiously working their way up a narrow inlet.

"Dem dare are your bald cypress, Jackson," Canebrake intoned with obvious pride. "They a member of the plywood family, don't you know."

"The *plywood* family?"

"Yeah, plywood. Not dat ole crumbly particle board mess, naw. Dat stuff is made from pressed beaver shit, I t'ink. Look like beaver shit, anyway. Did you know dat beaver shit floats? I done tole you it do! Dey eat up all them trees, see. Sycamore mostly, but dey eat 'em a gum ever now and den. Anyhow, dey eat up dem trees and shit out dat stuff while dey swimmin' along and it just floats right off! I seen 'em do it, *mon ami.*"

"Fascinating. I'd never have thought of that myself. Have you met anyone else that knew that?"

"Not outside de bayou, no. I did see somethin' like it, though. Took two Yankees out one day, from Memphis I t'ink dey was. Anyway, we's out dare fishin' up a storm and dese boys don't know shit 'bout no fishin'! One of 'em gets holt of a big-assed ole 'gator gar, see? He's rasslin' wit' dat ole fish and de gar he's dancin' up on his tailfeathers an' all, an' dis Yankee, I t'ink he's gonna blow hisself a spell or somethin' 'cause his veins is all standin' out on de head an' all.

"Well-sir, he git dat fish up to da boat—an' I don't say nothin', see. I mean dey pay me to fin' fish, right? Dey wanna fart away some time messin' wit' dat damn ol' gator gar, dat's one less fish I gotta fin' 'em!—He git dat fish up to de boat an' he goes to reach down an' pick him up by de *mouth!* Ole gar, he snap dem big teefs up at dat Yankee, an' de boy up an' *pissed like a tied coon!* Ole strong ammonia piss, too! Hahaaa!

"He look at me an' say 'Hey boy!'—I thunk about feedin' his ass to dem gator gars then, call *me* boy when *he* jus' pissed his britches!—he say, 'Hey boy! What de hell is dis t'ing here?' I say, 'Dat's a gator gar, ain't no good ta eat though.' He say, 'How big do dese t'ings get aroun' here no-how?' I say, 'Seben, eight feets, 'bout two hunert pounds or so.' Den he say, 'Shit!'—I look at his pants an' wonder if maybe he jus' tellin' me somet'in' else he done, right?—he say, 'Shit! Are dey maneaters?' Den I say, 'Naw, not mos' times. But dat

171

don't mean dey won't take 'em a big bite an' den spit it out!'
You know he up an' t'row 'bout two hunert dollars worth of
reel an' rod in dat swamp at dat gator gar? Sure 'nuff did."

Canebrake broke into a smile that crinkled his eyes with
numerous lines, mute testimony to years of squinting into sunlight reflecting off water.

"What does that have to do with particle board, or whatever
it was we were talking about?"

"Oh yeah! Dat's right. It was somethin' dat other Yankee
took outta his tackle box later on. I see the t'ing an' right away
I start lookin' aroun' for me some pelts, see?" he paused to
push the boat away from a fallen log that protruded into the
stream and served as a platform for five basking turtles. A
glaze of memory came over his eyes along with more crinkles
and another smile, "You 'mind me to tell you 'bout dis boy
back home we talked into tryin' to buy hisself some 'Naugha'
traps. We tol' him he'd git top dollar for some Naugha-hides!
Ha-haaa! ahem.

"Anyway, de feller take out what look to me for de world
like a stepped-on beaver turd and den . . . swear I ain't makin'
dis up now . . . he commenced to *eat* de damn t'ing! Say it
some kind of 'gladiola bar' or somet'in' like dat. Well-sir, dem
fellers don't cotch boo-shit in de way of fish, but I had me a
good ol' time, sho 'nuff! One of 'em pissin' his pants and
t'other eatin' flat beaver shit! Yankees, dey some kind o' fun
sometimes."

Josh wondered if he could ever eat a granola bar again. He
also wondered if, since Canebrake considered people from
Memphis as Yankees, he would have anything to do with him
once he knew he hailed from over a hundred miles farther
north! He didn't have time to bring the subject up because just
then they were interrupted by the sound of a massive tail slap-
ping against the water ahead. A cloud of mud boiled out from
beside a cypress stump where the bass had just surprised a
lazy shad, and the depth of the little whirlpool left in the fish's
wake attested to its size and vigor. Canebrake, it seemed,
knew his swamps.

172

20

Foo-Foo watched in silence as Thelma went through her routine alone. The sun was low in the sky and cast her silhouette high onto the canvas backdrop as she "led" the absent choir through their repertoire. He marveled at the way she could twirl the light baton between her long fingers yet still bring it down in a blurred arc at just the right moment to accentuate a silent passage. Her humming, however, needed all the help it could get.

Thelma still couldn't carry a tune, but she was beginning to learn the basics of the music business, largely thanks to him. Under his tutelage she'd mastered the balancing of microphone and speaker along with the variety of augmentation units that could be added to enhance their sound. Already she'd hit Brother Ray-Bob up for a doubler unit that would make their eleven voices sound more like thirty and electronically slur the voices into a mellow flow. Throw in a little reverb and push the volume just so, and the results were spectacular.

She'd also learned the hazards inherent to highly electrified music and the wisdom of taking off one's microphone before approaching a musician whose instrument is on a different ground. This fact had revealed itself during practice and left her with a handful of burnt fingers, three drops of urine down each leg, and a head full of respect for electricity. A crisp crunching of woodshavings on the tent floor announced the hasty arrival of his employer, so Foo-Foo elected to duck out.

"Thel-Ma!" Brother Ray-Bob announced in the preachy voice she was beginning to become annoyed with during the day, yet still admired during the services.

She turned in mid-twirl, caught the baton behind her back and looked down on him. He was aquiver about something, a string of fine beads of perspiration lining his unshaven upper lip. The lip itself was trembling as though he were about to break down into tears, though the set of his jaw said otherwise.

"Yes, Ray?" she asked evenly.

"What have I TOLD YOU aboutthese?" he asked in a voice so loud they both looked around expecting to see a crowd gathering.

In his smallish hand he held a pink plastic case, its hinged halves popped open like a dead clam.

"My birth control pills? Where did . . . ."

"On MY DESK! That's where. And just as I was about to RECEIVE Judge Cater to discuss . . . for a personal counseling session. WHAT, Iaskyou, if it had been ONE OF THE LOCAL MINISTERS? Hmmm? You'd have ME look like a HYPOCRITIC FOOL intheireyes? Is that what you want, Thelma? After ALL I've done for ya? Is THIS how you'llrepayme?"

Thelma felt bad about it, though not as bad as she felt about sneaking into his trailer now that she'd moved in with three of the choir members. And not nearly as bad as she felt when he summoned her, like she was a slave or something. But not bad enough to want to leave, though, heavens no!

Things were beginning to really move now that they were working some of the larger cities, and the Hallelujah Choir had even been called back for an encore at their latest service. Pocketing her pills and porking the preacher seemed a reasonable price for the fulfillment she felt when she heard the audience applaud. As she eyed the damning evidence with its spiral of white and pink pills hovering over their little tinfoil pop-throughs like so many bombs in an airplane, she could imagine the discomfort they could cause Ray. She'd stopped calling him Brother Ray-Bob some time before and had to catch herself to avoid referring to him as "Preach" as did Foo-Foo and Mellow Man.

"I'll be more careful, Ray. Sorry."

"SOR-RY! Sor-ry? I'll tell you something to be sorry about, dear. If those things get my butt in a pickle, just guess whose butt will be on a bus? And I don't mean a customized Silver Eagle, either! Now, take the damned things out of that silly case, for starters. I assume you can tell the difference between pink and white, can't you? Well, you'll know to take the pink ones when the white ones run out, right? Also, God has provided a way for you to tell when the pink ones are due, now hasn't he? Assuming, of course, you haven't gone through the change of life!"

Thelma's eyes narrowed at this reference to her age, and she entertained the thought of digging her claws into his pasty face and ripping his lips off. Instead she just nodded and took the pill case. It was still paramount on her mind to tell him off, but he wasn't finished.

"Oh yeah, we got an offer for you girls to do an album, so how's about working up a few extra numbers."

Anger fled Thelma's heart, pushed out by a flutter of joy that robbed her of her breath momentarily.

"An . . . album? Who?"

"Acuff-Rose, but I think we'll do it ourselves and push it at the services. We'll make a demo next time we're near Nashville, and if it sounds good enough or can be prepped in the studio, we'll go for a limited press. If they move well we can always sell the distribution rights later. Interested?"

Thelma nodded affirmatively, still dazed. In her glazed eyes she was seeing herself on the album cover, standing in front of her choir. Beyond that, she was seeing herself signing autographs! Doing talk shows! She was in ecstasy and glad she'd held her tongue. Ray-Bob smiled and departed in his quick-footed gait. She happily pressed all the little pills out their tinfoil bomb chutes and into her purse. Maybe someday, and with enough of a push, she could rise to the point where she wouldn't need Brother Ray-Bob any longer. That thought made her even happier and all but oblivious to the sounds of the band beginning to set up around her.

Brother Ray-Bob met the judge at the bus door and, after the usual banter about health and weather, ushered him into his office for their meeting. He went through his poor-mouth speech as he had with Klotz and secured about the same percentages. Then the two men had a drink to close the deal. Unlike bankers, southern judges are prone to taking a drink from time to time and, in the case of north Tennessee judges, it sometimes seems that they are appointed solely for their liquor capacity. The subject turned to the upcoming tax revision. Neither was overly fond of the impact it would have on their personal fortunes, but both found in it a handy rationale for their actions. As the judge was about to depart, he paused at the door and did some mental calculations.

"Brother Ray-Bob? This is some scam you've got here, you know that, son?"

Ray-Bob smiled expansively while rubbing his hands together before him.

"It's not a scam, Judge. It's an *art*! You know what Lincoln said about foolin' the people, right?"

"Yeah, I know. You don't think I've stayed on the bench all these years without knowing that, do you? You stop to consider it, our professions are really quite similar. We both must maintain at least a facade of righteousness, while selectively trotting out such passages from our respective texts as will best further our purposes. Right?"

"As far as it goes, you've got a point there. You surely do. But your brand of justice costs a damned sight more than mine, now don't it?"

"Oh, not really. I just exact my tithes all at once whereas you spread yours over a time, that's all. Well, a pleasure doing business with you, and I hope for both our sakes the weather holds and you have a good turnout."

"God willing, Judge. God willing!"

With the judge safely escorted out of the trailer, Ray-Bob returned to the office, had himself another short drink of Maker's, then broke out the ledgers and neatly penned fresh headings. In one column of the private ledger he listed concessions, offerings, and so forth. At the bottom he penned "Total" and under it the agreed upon percentage. Beside this he wrote the judge's name with a line after for the total of his check. Satisfied with his efforts, he returned the books to their cubbyhole beneath the sofa.

Back at his desk he used the last of his whiskey to wash down two of the little pink hits of Godspeed and began to put on makeup. He felt good and would give a spirited performance this night—the Godspeed and liquid spirits moving him even if the Spirit didn't.

After the service, as rousing a one as he'd given this season, he lay alone in bed feeling the Godspeed fading and looking forward to sleep. Then . . .

You really shined out there tonight, old son!

"Not tonight, please."

Why Ray-Mond! Don't you want to Hear, *justhowgoodyou-sounded?*

"No. I just want to sleep."

No introspection? Didn't we hear you tell the good folks not an hour ago how they had to look *deep* withinthemselves?

"Well, yes, I suppose I did."

And now you *don'twantto! I'm disappointed in you, Raymond. That's no way for the great Brother Ray-Bob to conduct himself. 'Practice what you . . . .'*"

"Shut-up! I'm tired and want to go to sleep."

You didn't feel it again tonight, did you?

"No. I didn't feel it."

And you're beginning to despair of ever feeling it again, aren't you?

"You know that."

Did you ever think that maybe it's up to you? That, if you ever stop letting this monster tail you've created stop wagging the dog long enough to be completely honest . . . with them

177

. . . with yourself *. . . that maybe, just maybe, you'd feel it again?*

"I can't think of that, not now. There's. . . ."

Bills *to pay! Gas, tires, and licenses for the buses, to be sure. The musicians, advertising, carnies, vendors, and, of course,* lawyers! *Yes, Raymond, you've got lots of folks depending on you to bring home the bacon. Is that what brought out the ham in you?*

"I'm not thinking about Mobile again tonight. Once everything is straight and there's enough ahead to carry us, well. . . ."

You'll go back to the old ways *and do it like you meant to all along, right? Don't you know by now that there will never be enough ahead? Or that there's always been enough?*

"Meaning?"

Meaning, just how much capital would it have taken to build that small church? I mean, even if you put in air-conditioning and an organ, how much would it have cost?

"Not much, I reckon."

Less than you spent on suits last season! You're all platitudes and polyester nowadays, Raymond. If you ever want to get that feeling back, you'll have to chuck all this glitz.

"And go to jail."

Probably. John did some of his best work in jail, remember?

"Yeah, I remember. Remember they cut off his *head!*"

I wouldn't suggest anything so radical as that. I mean, if they whack off your noggin', then where would I live?

"You almost make it sound worthwhile. Is this going to be a late night?"

Depends. You want to feel sorry for yourself some more?

"No."

Well, just in case, how about we recall your first unselfish act. Or was it your last?

"The Shepherd's Acres, right? About time you dredged that out again. Can't we wrap that one up for once and for all? It's been fifteen years!"

Yeah, it's been a while. But that lady and her kids, Raymond. I mean, even after all this time, they're still dead!

178

21

Spanish moss is neither. What it is is a saprophyte, like mistletoe, that sponges its living off another organism. This Josh picked up from the flora and fauna display at the Kasachi Park ranger building while waiting for Canebrake to get the boat in the water. There was a carnival atmosphere to the sleepy bayou this week as the year's first major bass tournament kicked off the pro circuit. Who would pull out the first lunker remained to be seen, but Josh was relatively certain it wouldn't be him. To emphasize his doubt, there came a squabble of shrill voices from the waterfront as the advertising types tried to get their camera boat into the water unassisted.

The movie cameras gravitated to the shoulders of invariably obese men who could support the added bulk, along with their own. A trio of these sumo wrestler types watched as their dainty brethren jackknifed the boat trailer, sending it hopping along the ramp erratically. The trailer tires left black cut-along-the-dotted lines on the concrete right up to the point where algae took over, then the whole rig slid ungracefully into the lake.

A chorus of laughter came from a point nearby causing Josh to leave the fiasco below and seek out this new source of noise that was marring an otherwise peaceful dawn. It emanated from a pair of men standing near a multicolored tent that was

179

large enough to house an entire boy scout troop. Though not fat enough to provide an adequate base for video work, one of them held a camera on his shoulder anyway. He was filming the other filmers launching their boat, their trailer, and nearly their rental car.

"We'll need to get releases, of course. Hope they'll go along with it 'cause we couldn't have staged anything near that good!" one of the men was saying as Josh walked up.

"Hello," Josh said.

"Hi! Did you watch that mess down there?"

He nodded that he had.

"Well, if you'd like to see it again we caught it all on film! It'll be perfect, too!"

"Perfect? Are you working on a bloopers film or something? Those guys looked like a monkey humpin' a football down there."

"Precisely! Allow me to explain. We're with TechnoTrek and here to get some footage for our new campaign. Have you, ah, heard of TechnoTrek, sir?"

"Can't say as I have. The name is Josh, by the way."

"Well . . . Josh . . . step right over here and let me introduce you. You're a fisherman I take it. Do you have a boat?"

Josh smiled at this. As the result of his several endorsements of boating lines, he was now the owner of an even half-dozen bass boats. Instead of pointing this out, he nodded and followed the spokesman.

"What you just witnessed is, I think you'll agree, an all too common occurrence, right? Well, here's the answer!"

With a flourish the man whipped open the drawn flaps of the tent to reveal a shiny trailer. It looked much different from any boat trailer Josh had encountered before as it had wheels fore and aft and a rectangular body that was enclosed with two-foot walls. While he watched, the spokesman walked over to the trailer and began to lower the side walls.

"Now, this is our latest model. It's stainless steel, so there'll be no rust . . . *ever*! Also, you'll note the walls, which can either be folded up or removed for hauling a multitude of loads. The bed is of perforated stainless grating, and the universal boat dolly detaches for general hauling. You'll notice the air-ride shocks, Josh. With them you can adjust your load height to accommodate any outboard motor on the market today. For ease of loading and unloading, there's a hydraulically operated tilt mechanism that elevates the forward portion of the trailer allowing drive-on/drive-off capability. And here, Josh, is the *pièce de résistance!*"

With this the spokesman stepped to the front of the trailer and lifted its tongue. Effortlessly he pushed the trailer back and positioned it to go out the door. To Josh's amazement, the trailer tires tracked each gentle tug of the tongue.

"Swiss ballbearings with lifetime races and seals make it the smoothest rolling trailer on the road and cuts your maintenance down to nothing. You no doubt noted the steering? Well, it's activated for the launch and recovery evolutions when you throw that little lever there on the side. Here, you take it and let's walk it around a bit."

Josh felt somewhat foolish leading the trailer around the parking lot but was so amazed at its lightness and ease of movement that he soon felt comfortable.

"How do the wheels know which way to turn?"

"Glad you asked. See that plug there? Well, that's your universal hookup for lights, brakes. Did I mention it has electric skid-proof brakes? Anyway, when you throw the lever, it activates a sensor right under the tongue joint that senses pressure as the car or truck attempts to turn and translates it to the trailer steering. It's rated at five thousand pounds of useful load, and—now get this—the tongue loading is a phenomenal twenty-seven pounds! You could pull an eighteen-foot ski boat with a Volkswagen! What do you think?"

"Fascinating. Pretty expensive, I guess."

"Well, they are rather dear at the moment, but you get what you pay for, Josh. For the serious fisherman who uses his trailer a lot, and particularly for one who drives long distances, it'd pay for itself in gas and maintenance within a few seasons. And you get the benefit of using it as a general hauling trailer besides. Once we get our campaign rolling and our name better known, I think we'll find our market."

"And what would it take to get one of these today? I mean, just like this one."

"Well, I'll tell you, Josh. We'll look to sell this particular one after we're through filming, rather than drag it back to Wisconsin. So I might could make you a real deal on it if you're interested."

"Do you have a contract with this fellow Jackson for an endorsement, by any chance?"

"Well, no. We tried, of course, but his agent was on the road and we couldn't meet the prices his girl was quoting over the phone. Perhaps later on . . . ."

"Perhaps sooner than you think. We can reach a deal that'll be, as they say, mutually beneficial?" Josh said, then smiled at the spokesman's realization.

Canebrake seemed preoccupied much of the morning and kept glancing around wildly as though he expected some monster to be close by. Josh found himself getting nervous, too, and began to question the wisdom of coming to this swamp to film the live segments of their latest commercials. The swamp looked a lot like every other swamp they'd been around for the past month, and Josh was at a loss to explain Canebrake's actions. Between takes, specifically while he was trying to rinse his mouth of the foul smokeless tobacco Major Mike had conned him into plugging, he asked the Cajun about it.

"You ever use this shit 'Brake?"

"Nope. Stuff look too much like dat worm dirt what dey sells night crawlems in fo' me, tell you dat! Chaw dat 'bacco, though. 'Course you know dat, huh?"

Canebrake punctuated his statement with a hark and spit that Josh found himself emulating. The Cajun pulled the hat from his head and wiped a sweaty brow on the arm of his shirt. Canebrake's hair was pasted straight back with a combination of sweat and Four Roses tonic. With his Indianesque nose and sleek hairdo, he struck a profile not dissimilar to the hood ornament on a '55 Pontiac, with the exception of the worried look on his face.

"What's up? You seem nervous today."

"Yeah, well I don't kere much fo' dis bayou, dat's all. Too many peoples around, too. Can't 'spect somebody to cotch no fish wit' so many peoples fartin' aroun'. An' . . . ."

"And what, 'Brake? Do you know this place? Been here before?"

Canebrake's eyes scanned the area around them, taking in each swollen trunk of cypress and each ragged curtain of Spanish moss. When he spoke again, it was without much of the cocksuredness Josh had come to expect.

"Yeah, I be here befo' awright. I live hereabouts for mos' of my life. Right up yonder at de head of de swamp, on a farm. We raisin' dem cows, dem pigs, lots of dem chickens, don't you know. I still brought myself down here to de swamp, though. Cotch them basses, punkinseeds, an' in de spring I sometime bring out a whole stringer of *sac au lait*! Dem's fine eatin' right dare. You like dem *sac au lait,* Josh?"

"I don't even know what they are."

"Means 'sack of milk' in Acadian, dat's where 'Cajun' come from, don't you know. From Yankees what say Acadian too damn fast like dey say ever't'ing else! Anyway, *sac au lait* is what you call crappie, only down here we don't like dat name, no. Sound like you be eatin' poo!"

"I see. But why are you so nervous? You're beginning to give me the jitters, and so far we've just gone farther and farther up this branch. Even I know there's no fish here. The water's too stagnant for anything but turtles."

"Yeah, you right dare, *mon ami*. I 'pologize for dat, too. I want . . . I got to stay away from peoples here 'cause they's a sheriff here what would love to fin' my coon-ass, don't you know, and put it on away for a spell."

"Why didn't you say something, 'Brake! We could film this crap anywhere. I'm sure I could turn green and throw up from a mouthful of snuff at Bedageaux Creek just as easily as I could here. You want me to say something to Mike?"

Canebrake's eyes shot open wide at the suggestion.

"Lawd shit, naw! Don't be told ole fancy-pants none o' dis here, Josh. He'd put dat man on my ass right now. You know we don't git along an' he be lookin' to drop my ass soon as he can anyhow. Don't trust dat boy, Jackson. He lie so damn much I bet he got to get somebody else to call his dog! Be too easy fo' him ta ring dat sheriff 'n say, 'Y'all lookin' fo' dat Prudhomme Boy what run off from Fort Polk? Well-sir, I done got him stayin' right here in yo' own tater patch! Brought yo'self on down here to da motel an' haul his coon-ass away!' Dat's what he'd say, an' den he wouldn't ever have to pay me nuther."

"You ran off from the army?"

"Dat's a fack, I did. Lots of other peoples did, too, an' mos' of 'em went way up north to keep fum goin' ta Veetnumb, but it was diff'ernt wit' me. I had me a sick mama back up the swamp a piece an' couldn't be goin' off nowheres, least of all overseas.

"That draft board, it made up of all dese rich-bitch assholes what got them oil wells poked all down in de swamp, see, and when one of der boys flunk his ass outa LSU, dey fin' out he gonna be drafted, see? Well, dey look aroun' an' say, 'Scare us up a nigra or a coon-ass to sen' 'stead of my boy here.' An' I'm de coon-ass dey fount. Mama, she all down sick wit' de mullygrubs an' de rhumetiz, so she can't even make a fist let alone haul no water or nothin'. So I come on back here on weekends, and one day she real bad, so I stay."

"Didn't they come after you?"

"Hooo-yeah! Dey come two-tree times. Fust time I was over to Jean LaTraub's garage, see. He come on down here from Thibadeaux, but dat's another story. Anyhow, we's sittin' dare woikin' on an' ol' truck when dese MPs pull up in a jeep. Dey walk over to us real slow like, an' I figure my ass is out, right? Anyhow, dey look us over like we was somethin' dey don't want to step in, den one of 'em look right at me an' say, 'Say, son. Kin you tell me where Fillipe Prudhomme live at?' Jean, he jes' smile real big an' look at me, don't you know. I look back at 'em an' say, 'Yes suh! Dat Prudhomme Boy he live right up dat road yonder, but I hear tell he done gone to Canada somewheres.'

"You know dey head right out dare! I head de other way and sneak back at night. Dat sheriff come a few days later, an' he don't like me none already on accounta he t'ink I been foolin' 'roun' wit' his girl, see. I *was,* too, but so was ever'body else, so I don't rightly know whose kid it was. Shit, tryin' to figger out whose kid dat belongs to'd be like jumpin' in a blackberry thicket then crawlin' out an' tryin' to point out which prick gotcha! Mama died little while after dat, an' I hightailed it over to Bedageaux Crick."

"Well, what say we get the hell out of here tomorrow then? Don't look like I'm gonna catch any fish out here anyway, so we'll go somewhere else."

"You wanta cotch some fishes where dey can make pictures of 'em gettin' caught, dat it?" Canebrake asked with a sudden smile.

"Yep. You thinkin' about your new home?"

"Nope, someplace better. I put it to you, den you put it to Major Mike and the rest. Guar-an-teed lots of fish, damned near one every cast or I'll kiss yo' ass in front of de courthouse here an' give you two days to draw a crowd!"

"Now that's confidence! Where is it?"

"Texas," the Cajun said with pure reverence in his voice and then, liking the way the word struck the thick bayou air, he said it again. "Texas."

"Any particular place in Texas?"

"Yep. Only been dare once my ownself, but I 'member it well. It's damned near out of Texas, an' if you ain't drove it you don't know jest how far dat is! It's right down on de Mexican border, and where we want to go is on the Mexico side. Folks dare are right poorly, ain't got a pot to piss in or a winder to t'row it out of nuther. But dey got somet'in what keeps 'em from starvin', an' dat's Lake Guerrero. If you gonna cotch some fishes while dem lard-assed camera boys watch, dat's de place to took yo'self."

"Lake Guerrero, huh? Okay, I'll see what I can do. Meanwhile, where are you gonna stay so the sheriff won't get you?"

Canebrake stepped out of the boat and reached back in to grab his potato sack.

"Right-chere! Got me my croaker sack an' a head full of swamp sense, so I be jes' fine. Y'all brought yo'self on back here tomorrow an' pick me up, you hear? I got mama's rhumatics so I can't stay out here long or I get all stove up, don't you know."

"Are you sure about this? I mean, what are you going to do with the sack, sleep in it?"

"No, man! I do some noodlin' wit' dis sack right here. I ritch up under dem stumps and knees and cotch ole man catfish a-sleepin', then *whap*! I snatch his young ass outa dare an' pop him in my sack! I eat good tonight, fo' sure."

"What about gators and turtles?"

"Yeah, got dem gators an' turtles, too. Dey fry up right tasty."

"Canebrake, what about other things? You ever grab a snake?"

"Ooooh-yah, I grab up some o' dem cotton-mouf moccasin snakes sometime. Don't put him in de sack, though. See you tomorrow!"

While Josh watched, the swamp swallowed up the Cajun like he was cotton candy. He just disappeared. Josh didn't envy the sheriff his work if he ever tried to come after Canebrake, but he had a better feeling for the Cajun now that he knew he hadn't just spawned in the swamp like a crawfish. Canebrake was a real person and, as he heard a lisping request from the camera boat on the other side of the stream for him to face the light and smile, real people were at a premium in the world he now lived and worked in. The camera crews would probably welcome a chance to get out of the swamp and go to Texas for a few days, but Major Mike would pitch a royal bitch. Josh smiled and wondered if Mike's reaction alone might not be reason enough to go.

Without thinking, he lifted a sponsor's beer to his lips and took a swig that set the movie crew to howling in anguish. Belatedly, he remembered that he had to actually use his sponsor's products to endorse them, yet could not be filmed actually drinking an alcoholic beverage. Okay to eat dirt, walk around in your drawers, or talk about your hemorrhoids, but not to drink beer on camera.

It didn't make sense. But it did make money. Lots of it.

Major Mike kept the exact figures in his head, but even allowing for exaggeration Josh realized he was now a wealthy man. How to invest and save some of it was beginning to be a concern, one he'd need to take up with a lawyer and an accountant when he got off the road. *Pam is an accountant!* his mind shouted at him. Lots of things he'd like to take up with her, but first he'd better swing back by Florida. He'd forgotten her oranges.

22

Slats Spivey spat out the window of his truck, then reset his jaw into a show of disgust as he waited for the traffic light to change for the third time since he'd joined the queue of cars, trucks, and boats trying to get through greater downtown Dilbert's Forge. The last time he'd seen this many vehicles in town at once had been seven years earlier when the Dilbert's Forge Demons football team had a shot at the state championship going into their last game with the Holyoak Holsteins.

The new attraction was none other than Josh's Fish, as the big bass had come to be known locally, and the town was filled daily with fishermen seeking out the place it had been caught. Virtually everyone who'd ever so much as drowned a worm on the end of a safety pin had suddenly become a guide and purveyor of hot tips on big bass, though just he and Jackson knew the actual site. The light changed to green, bringing a cacophony of horns blaring to spur those ahead into motion.

A grand total of six cars and four boats made it through the light before it changed again. Slats managed to draw even with the courthouse before having to halt again and noticed with mild interest that the two old men who normally played checkers on the steps were absent. They, too, had taken to guiding fishermen to augment their retirement checks.

The day was fresh and beginning to warm, the air having been cleansed thoroughly by an early morning shower. A good day, Slats decided. A pity he had to spend it in the bank and then the library digging up more facts about patents, state business statutes, and such. Gone were the days when a man with a product to sell merely pulled his truck up to the shoulder of the road and wrote a sign on the back of a banana box to advertise. The lawyers had seen to that.

He screwed his ferret face into another scowl at the thought of lawyers, spat again, then shifted around in his seat to aid circulation. The patent lawyer he'd contacted in Nashville had cited patent searches, submission requirements, rebuttals, and all manner of mumbo-jumbo required before the patent would even gain a pending status that would protect it. He'd also named some hefty fees to be paid up-front before he'd so much as read the application. Slats figured he'd have to see Josh Jackson about all that once he came off the road, if he came off the road. The light changed again and threatened to catch him at the last second, but Slats floored the accelerator and slid under just as the amber was changing to pink.

He eyed himself in the rearview mirror, then decided a haircut might be in order before going to the bank to face Klotz. Not, he realized, that hair meant a tinker's dam to the oily banker, but Slats was going to ask for a business loan using his house as collateral and reasoned he should look as businesslike as possible. Mavis had pressed his shirt and pants for the occasion. In return, he'd read her some Robert Service verse from an old book passed down to him from an aunt. A strange bond had formed between them since he'd whacked her in the back with his cast, and he was at a loss to explain it. She'd all but adopted him now and, oddly enough, he found he enjoyed her company.

The topic at the barber shop was marriages past and present. Slats nodded a hello to Carl and the others present, then marched over to his nail keg beside the now-cold stove. Mister Peevey was present, which explained his absence from the courthouse steps, and there was something about him that didn't look right to Slats. Try as he might, he couldn't really put his finger on it, but the old man seemed younger somehow. Jim Poston had the floor.

"Yeah, my first wife was a pretty good looker as women go. I met her during the war when I was going through training out at San Antonio. She was a-workin' over at the USO, and every night I could I'd slide by there and eat a stale donut and watch her. Directly she started noticin' me and afore long we was takin' in a picture show or goin' on long walks around the river and such.

"Then I got my orders out to Fort Ord and was gonna leave in a few weeks, so she suggested we go ahead and get hitched. Well-sir, I was sure lookin' forward to that, don't you know, 'cause there weren't no free love society back then and a feller had to learn to do without most of the time. I was doin' tongue-ups on my bunk to get ready for her and all that, then the big day comes, see. We get hitched by the post chaplain and then haul off to a little two room place we'd rented, and we got after it. The next mornin' I come in to breakfast, and there's some ragged eggs, couple of pieces of burnt toast, and some coffee you could have floated a horseshoe in with the hoss still in it! I said, 'Damn, babe. Can't you cook . . . *either*?' She got all pissed off and started warpin' me on the noggin with a side of bacon.

"Things went downhill pretty quick after that there, I can tell you. Then she started messin' around with some of the other guys in the unit, see. We's sittin' at lunch one day over to the USO, and one of the guys is sittin' right across from us, right? Well sir, she was all giggles and all, and actin' real strange, kinda gruntin' ever now and then and sweatin' a lot so I thought maybe she was sick or somethin'. Then I dropped my napkin and bent down to pick it up and looked under the table, see? That feller on t'other side of the table's got his foot in her lap!

"Well, I marched my ass outa there, and she come along directly. That night she knew I was madder'n hell so she says, 'Jimbo? You ain't thinkin' of leavin' me are you, honey?' and I said, 'No, babe, I wouldn't leave you fer nothin.' The next day it'd have took a dollar and a half to send me a penny post-card!"

"Don't blame you for that, Jim," Carl said as he adjusted his grip on his current victim's head in preparation for shearing around his ears. "Just out of curiosity, how many times did you and your bride do it that first night?"

Jim put his thumbs under the bib of his overalls and puffed himself up in thought then said, "I recollect it was three, four times, probably. It'd been more if'n she'd been any good at it!"

"Yeah, well me an' the missus hit the hay six times our first night," another of the men put in with bravado. "Next mornin' she brought me my breakfast in bed, too!"

"Eight times, by Gaw!" old Peevey put in suddenly, then grinned in porcelain-toothed splendor, which told Slats what was different about him. "How many times did you an' the missus do it, Carl?"

Carl paused and looked off in remembrance while maintaining a grip on the customer's scalp, which pulled his eyes up on both sides to the point he looked Chinese. "Just once, Mister Peevey. My wife wasn't used to it, you see."

The men looked at the floor and blushed slightly at this, except for Slats who was still fascinated with Peevey's new teeth and the way he whistled as he pronounced his *S*'s.

"When did you get your new choppers, Mister Peevey?" he asked.

"Took some boys from Nashville over to the river a few weeks ago, Slats. They got into a run of little buck bass and thought they'd done real well, so they gave me a big ole tip. I took that money and bought myself some sensible teeth." The word *sensible* set off such a flurry of whistles that the old dog sleeping outside the door perked up its ears.

"Bet they set you back a bundle, huh?"

Peevey leaned back in his chair and smiled brilliantly.

"Well, son, when I went to the feller over at McEwen he wanted an arm and a leg, I'll tell you that fer sure. Last uns I got from the VA didn't fit worth a shit, always got cornbread underneath 'em and all, so I decided to go somewheres else this time. Got these teeth right here for five dollars!"

191

"Five dollars? What, did you order 'em out of a seed catalog or somethin'?"

"No sir. I went over to that big funeral home over at Sylvia City, see. Old boy what runs it's got a whole big box full of teeth at two-fifty a plate. I tried on a bunch until I found a set that fit, but damned if I didn't have two uppers! Made me look like a mule what just shed for a two-year-old, but they sure felt good, so I bought them, too. You ought to see me eat a ear of corn with them things! These lowers (he stopped and popped them from his mouth to the further disgust of everyone present) had a turnip green stain right here, but a little Comet and a scourin' pad took care of that just fine."

All were silent. Jim Poston quaked as he fought off a wave of nausea, and Carl beamed happily at the looks of shock around the room. He winked at old Peevey, who returned it then re-seated the teeth into his mouth. After a test clack of his choppers, Mister Peevey rose unsteadily from his seat and bid farewell to the rest, then stalked out the door looking very pleased with himself.

"Sure glad you brought that up, Spivey!" Poston declared facetiously.

Carl released his customer and popped the hair from his cloth with vigor, smiling all the time.

"Sorry, Jim. I had no ideer he'd . . . I mean, who'da thought. . . ?"

Carl could take it no longer. Eyeing Slats with a glint dancing in his eyes, he indicated the vacant chair with a pat and then let them off the hook.

"You boys are so gullible! Old Peevey got them teeth last week, all right. But he got 'em from that dentist over at McEwen. His daughter paid for 'em as a birthday present!"

The room filled with relieved laughter as they shook off their embarrassment. Several claimed to know all along that Peevey was putting them on.

Pam felt silly buying the magazines. After all, who'd really believe she wanted to know "100 Ways To Make Money Using Sol-Lunar Tables" or "Camper Care For The 80's." She didn't.

On the cover, however, was a smiling likeness of Josh Jackson seated in the high rise seat of a boat somewhere in the middle of a swamp. He looked the part of rugged outdoorsman and, given the veritable flood of juicy checks that had been arriving at the bank for his account, outdoors was where it's at these days. At least that's where he was, and where she longed to be.

Klotz was becoming unbearable, though lately he'd been in a rare good mood as he contemplated his latest step forward for the county. Fully three million dollars had been earmarked for the new water system and road leading to it. The road would apparently take a circuitous route since it had to wind its way through the properties of the several council members. With elections due in a few months, it seemed Klotz was wringing everything he could from his office, just in case. Perhaps he had taken a lesson on politics from the Blalocks.

The magazine contained no less than seventeen pictures of Josh advertising everything from lures to tents. To her dismay there was a buxom young woman wearing short khaki walking shorts and a T-shirt she'd apparently put on with a spray gun stooping invitingly over a Coleman stove in front of a tent, while Josh beamed in the foreground and offered a thumbs-up. With her scissors she relegated the big breasted bimbo to the kitchen garbage can.

There was also an interview of him, espousing the benefit of something called a SonarChart that drew a picture of the bottom beneath one's boat with uncanny accuracy. "It's a great piece of equipment," Josh averred, then added the caveat, "if you know how to use it!" She cut the article out, too, and appended each piece of paper to the wall of her bedroom between the travel posters.

"Who am I foolin'?" she wondered aloud, then looked to her stuffed animals for an answer. None of them knew. "He'd be a fool to come back here, and I know he's covered up with good-looking young women out there. Models with tiny waists and perfectly rounded butts and shredded wheat for brains who'd be only too happy to . . . ." The thought made her ill. "Dammit. If only he hadn't caught that friggin' fish!"

Oh really? the stuffed panda seemed to ask. *And then he wouldn't be rich, would he? Would you still want him then?*

"Yes! I would. He wasn't rich when he left here was he? There's something about him that I've always found attractive, you know?"

Ah, but that might have been because he was married, right? The panda continued, *and therefore, safe! No way he could get next to you if he was otherwise taken, hmmm? Admit it, the fact that he was unattainable made him seem more desirable.*

"Okay, I'll admit that. But now I *want* him to get close to me. I'm ready for a long-term relationship, to have someone of my own."

I couldn't help but notice, a careworn giraffe put in, *that you didn't say anything about giving yourself to the relationship, Pammy. How about that part? Still think you should just take, that anyone you love will just die and go away like your parents did, and then your aunt? Still hung-up on that old chestnut?*

"Yes. I am, I suppose. But Josh could be different if only we had a chance. He's been through all that, too, and now his wife has left him as well so, maybe . . . ."

So maybe you should tell him about it. Maybe you two would be good for each other, if . . . if . . . you put yourself into it and don't just sit back and soak up his admiration, the panda declared in her imagination.

"Well, I'm sure all that is purely academic anyway. I doubt it'll go any further here, and I'm about ready to move on. South, I think, or maybe west. I still have a standing offer to deal blackjack out in Vegas. Might be fun for a while."

And warm! a stuffed frog who'd been silently listening put in. *Not the kind of job one would associate with a college education, of course, but then you do have your looks and that nice body and . . . .*

"I know!" she said abruptly. "It's a fine piece of equipment."

"If you know how to use it!" Josh's words glared out at her from beneath a screen of Scotch tape.

A small pout formed on her full lips as she went through a few minutes of introspection, weighing the pros and cons of deserting Dilbert's Forge for a life among the bright lights in Nevada. Of course, that offer was several years old now and might well have been offered with the same insincerity as most promises of movie contracts. She was so deep in thought that she barely heard the phone ringing in the kitchen. She shook the gossamer cobwebs of thought from her mind and reluctantly went to answer it. At first she didn't recognize the voice.

"Hi! I'm in Mexico just across the border from McAllen, Texas. The citrus groves are in bloom here, so naturally I thought of you. It's eighty-five degrees and sunny, so I thought of you again! How've you been?"

"Josh?" she managed, then suppressed a sniff as a tear of joy crept from the corner of each moss green eye. "I'm fine, how are you?"

"Fine as frog hair! Can you hear that chopping sound? Maybe not. Anyway, I'm calling from an outdoor booth in Reynosa and there's some guys chopping up mesquite behind me, and that was the third thing that reminded me of you. I took it as an omen that I should call. I'll be home next week and was wondering if you could work me into your schedule for dinner?"

"Sure. And Mexico sounds wonderful. I'd love to smell the citrus groves. Is it as lovely as they say?"

"You wouldn't believe it! It's gonna be hard to go back to breathin' shi . . . the air out at my place after this."

Go for it! the panda, giraffe, and frog yelled in unison from the bedroom.

"To hell with that, Josh. You'll stay here with me. We've got . . . we've got a lot to talk about! I want to hear all about your travels, too."

The voice on the other end was silent for a time, and she began to bite her lower lip, to brace herself for the rejection she so feared would be coming.

"Okay . . . but can I bring the cat? I mean, you're not allergic to them or anything are you? He can sleep out on the porch if necessary, but I think I owe him some attention."

"FrankenKat?" she laughed, then looked over to where the feline slept regally upon a satin throw pillow. "He's taken up residence here already! I was only inviting you along to complete the set. How about I make us reservations at the Surf & Turf in Clarksville for the night after you get home?"

"Skip the Surf part of that. I don't want to see another fish for a while, if you know what I mean. Not that I'm ungrateful or anything. God knows I've a lot to be thankful for where our finny friends are concerned."

"Probably more than you know, Josh. I'll brief you on your new economic status over a glass of expensive champagne. You, uh, didn't forget my oranges did you?"

"No. As a matter of fact, I was just thinking of them. See you next week. Say hi to the dogs and Slats for me, will you?"

"The dogs and Slats, hmm? Some priorities you have there, Mister Jackson. Oh well, I'll do that for you. Hurry home, I . . . I miss you."

"Thanks. I'll be there as soon as I can. 'Bye."

Now that's more like it! the animals sang to her in harmony.

"Yeah, it is!" she agreed, then bounced off to her bedroom to finish sticking the paper Joshes to her wall like so many pinned butterflies in a box.

23

Josh was still grinning long after he had hung up the phone. A lazy bottlefly buzzed past on its way to the outdoor market where butchered animals of all descriptions, along with some which defied any, hung in the open air. Nearby the sound of chopping cut through the warm air, sounding almost as out of place. Josh reasoned that wood being chopped would sound right at home most anywhere else, but here in the blessed warmth where no one even had heat in their homes? It was definitely alien.

He paused to watch the men manhandle the mesquite bushes over to the chopping block after trimming off the upper branches and most of the foliage. In no time they could hack a small tree into short chunks then feed those through a shredder until the whole was reduced to no more than finger-length chips. Each burlap sack of chips, he learned through Canebrake who could speak a smattering of Tex-Mex, would bring less than a quarter in U.S. currency. It was a measure of these people's exploitation that a mere pound of the chips would be resold in the states for nearly three dollars.

Reynosa is a sleepy little border town that boasts a bull ring, a monastery of sorts, and numerous shops and liquor stores to service the tourist trade. It also has two reasonable hotels, one of which they'd found themselves lodged in once they deter-

197

mined no other rooms were available in south Texas. The spring feed grain harvest was underway, along with early pickings of tomatoes and other vegetables. So the entire area was saturated with itinerant workers and their foremen.

This they had learned from Don Juan Peres, the owner/operator of Texican Air. On arrival at Corpus Christi International Airport Don Juan was a rotund man with a brilliant smile containing two gold teeth. He dressed in loose-fitting clothes that gave him the overall appearance of an unmade waterbed with sunglasses. Don Juan had agreed to fly them over Lake Guerrero en route to Reynosa and to use his "good offices" to secure them transportation back to the lake the next day. He also claimed to be available to fly anywhere, at any time of day or night, for any reason, by either helicopter or fixed-wing craft. Without specifically mentioning it, Don Juan gave Josh the feeling that he would probably fly in or out any cargo, licit or otherwise.

At noon a Dodge Powerwagon truck pulled up in front of their hotel, its horn blaring brazenly until the manager came running out shouting obscenities and asking questions. The young driver joined in the melee, their voices blending together, rising and falling in total confusion until the conversation sounded like an old Fats Domino record being played backward at 78 r.p.m. After much rapid Spanish with English phrases used for punctuation, the manager came into the cantina where Josh, Canebrake, and a few people of the photography crews were lounging over margaritas and Dos Equis beers. This four-wheel drive dinosaur was their transport to the lake.

The trip to the lake was dusty, hot, and thoroughly enjoyable for Josh. Once past the stalls featuring velvet paintings of Elvis, Jesus, or both; past the silent ranks of tin suits of armor and rose trellises; outside the hubbub and honking that was a work-a-day border town, the road opened up on a panorama that inspired Josh as much as it had the early Spaniards and Texans.

The low mesquite and greaseberry bushes provided a flat canopy that undulated up and down slopes that seemed to go on forever. Here and there stands of hardy wildflowers added bright splashes of color to the foreground while tiny puffs of white cloud hung suspended like dollops of bird dung in the fountain that was the sky.

The nearer to the lake they got, the more lush the vegetation became until right at its banks there was a near jungle of wide-leafed plants, ferns, and mosses. The truck slid to a halt amid a cloud of brick-hued dust at the foot of a hill. The driver smiled happily and checked his knock-off Bulova watch to see how he'd done.

"Seven minutes off my last time, *Señor!* The truck is old, but once she gets moving, yaaah-eee!" Then he sat down on his horn again, which seemed to be the way folks announced their arrival in this part of the world.

"You drive out here a lot do you, Miguel?" Josh asked.

"Two, three times a week. We are cutting the mesquite on the other side of that hill, and I come to pick it up for shredding in town," he answered, indicating with one coffee-brown finger the rise above them.

Josh followed the finger and saw a large hacienda perched majestically atop the hill, though there appeared to be no road leading up to it. It seemed unoccupied.

"What's that place up there?"

"That, *Señor,* is the old ranch house. It's boarded up now, and there are probably snakes there. The company that cuts the mesquite caught the workers sneaking up there to take their *siestas,* so they closed it up. It was one of the first buildings in this part of Mexico, *Señor,* built over two hundred years ago by the Jesuits, The Society of Jesus?" he paused and crossed himself at the mention of these religious pioneers. "And later given as part of a grant to the Garza family by the Emperor Maximilian.

"The Garzas moved on to Mexico City after the bad times in the '30s, so they say, but they used to come here for a few weeks each spring to see the orchards in bloom across the lake. Last year when the peso fell so badly, they gave it to the brothers at the mission and moved back to Mexico City for good. The brothers cannot keep up such a grand house. In fact, they must now sell off the mesquite just to keep electricity in their own buildings and the school. It is a shame, but that is our heritage, no?"

Josh nodded, still eyeing the noble adobe-and-red-tiled building that sat upon the crest like an eagle in its nest, surrounded by whitewashed walls and grown up gardens. By standing on tip-toe, he could just make out a crease in the foliage that might be a narrow drive leading up to it. At the foot of the hill stood another house, smaller but nicely maintained, and a collection of boulders around which the greenish waters of the lake lapped like friendly puppies.

A boy of about twelve years stood atop one of these rocks holding a beer can in one hand and whirling the other hand around as though about to throw a lasso. One of the overweight cameramen waddled up wiping a combination of reddish dust and perspiration from his face. He looked liked he was bleeding to death.

"Three hours of light left, Mister Jackson, maybe four. If you're gonna have any chance of getting a fish caught on camera today, we'd better get after it," he said through a parched throat.

"Right. Miguel, I understand we can lease a boat around here. Is that right?"

"Sure, if you think you need one, *Señor*. The lake is so full of fish that most people don't bother with boats, but there's one here for the people that work . . . that need to get to the other side of the lake sometimes. I'll get it for you."

Miguel pierced the air with a shrill whistle that brought hands to ears and nearly caused one fat man to toss his camera into the bushes in surprise. The boy on the boulder waved in response and shinnied down to wade ashore. Along with his can he carried a stringer so full of one- and two-pound bass that from a distance it looked like a stalk of bananas.

A large woman materialized from the shadows near the water's edge, took the fish from the boy, and hustled them back into the shade of the low greaseberries. The boy pulled an aluminum boat from the treeline and launched it, then carried a small outboard motor to it and mounted it on the transom. Fetching a gallon Purex jug that served as a gas tank, he shoved the rig off and set about rowing the hundred yards to where Josh stood and the rest struggled to inflate the lone craft they'd brought with them, a ten-foot Zodiac with a five-horse motor.

Josh couldn't believe it, and neither could the camera crew. Within two hours he had boated over two dozen bass, some of which had fought spectacularly for their size. The camera crews were so spoiled they began unloading along the banks to get reverse-angle shots of fish being caught right in front of where they stood. Some of the close-ups of the line hitting the water, followed by an obliging bass striking the lure, would net them awards they were certain.

Soon the cameras were spread out around the near bank and cries of "Catch one over here! Wait, wait. Now! Go ahead, catch one here!" rang up and down the lake as they juggled for even more exotic angles and took the fish for granted. Though they tended to be smallish, averaging no more than a pound and a half, the fish did seem to be everywhere and cooperative. But why were they so small? Josh asked Canebrake, who had been contemplating this very question himself.

"Dey ain't no covers down deep's why, I t'ink. Don't see no stumps, no. Ain't no big rocks down deep nuther, or I'd have felt 'em wit' my lure. I'd say dese here are shallows fish and don't get no bigger 'cause dey got to chase down dey food, dat's why. If'n dey had good cover down deep, dey'd stay dare an' git big an' fat. 'Course it might be dey don't get no bigger 'cause dey jes' don't, too. Shame, huh?"

"Yeah it is. Well, there's certainly plenty of them! I don't think I've ever been anywhere that the bass bit quite like this. Reckon it's because they're not used to these fancy lures of ours?"

"No, *Senor!*" the boy said from his seat by the motor. "They like this all the time. I catch fifty or a hundred most days, only fish once a week now."

"Fifty to a hundred? How? What do you use?" Josh asked, then noted the merriment dancing in Canebrake's eyes.

"This!" the boy declared, flourishing a sixteen-ounce beer can around which was wound clear monofilament line with a beer can pop-top and a set of treble hooks tied to its end.

"That? You catch fish with that?"

"Sí! Watch."

The boy took the line in hand two feet behind the ersatz lure and began to twirl it like a watch fob. When he had ginned up the requisite speed, he turned the line loose on the upswing and merely pointed the can in the same direction as the lure's flight. The line ran off the can smoothly and the pop-top lure rose in a gentle arc toward the bank, landing with a muffled plop.

He began rewinding the line onto the can while alternately jerking the line and allowing it to sink back. When he'd retrieved less than half the line it suddenly straightened and pulled his arm out at length as the fish sounded. Both men were cheering the boy on as he fought the spirited bass with both hands, pulling the line in with one and winding the slack onto the can with the other until the fish was lifted into the boat.

Josh had to pause in thought. Here he was fishing with a rod and reel combination that cost roughly the same as a small computer, while this boy was easily matching his efforts using gear available at any dumpster! Warily he looked around to see if any of the cameramen had caught the kid in action. None had. They had exhausted the supplies of film they'd brought with them and had retired to the shade.

"Okay, enough fishing for me today, *amigo*. How about we get the deluxe tour of this place."

"Sí! I like to run the motor, but it catches on fire sometimes, so stand by with that can of water, okay?"

"Sure," Josh agreed, then dipped a coffee can full from the warm lake. Then he looked over to Canebrake and asked, "I take it you knew about the native fishing habits, huh?"

"Yeah, I done seen 'em done dat before. T'ought it might make ya a good beer commercial, if'n you's a-mind to borry that boy's can."

"It might at that!" Josh agreed, then settled back to enjoy the scenery.

* * *

Lake Guerrero was an impounded bend in the Rio Grande that reached a depth of thirty feet in its channel even during the dry season. As Canebrake had noticed, there were few natural breaks in the bottom where a fish might hide, and the food supply appeared to be limited to small minnows that flitted around in schools and would not be sufficient to support larger fish. The minnows, too, were stunted due to lack of proper cover and the protection it would afford them while they matured.

On the back side of the hill was a large bald spot where the mesquite had been systematically removed. Workers sat or lay in small groups nearby, taking their afternoon siestas while a pile of treetops stood smoldering in the middle of the clearing sending an angry white finger of smoke into the sky like an exclamation point. It seemed such a waste. A light wind was blowing off the water, and no hint of wood smoke smell made it out onto the lake. Another smell, however, rode the freshening breeze over from the Texas side.

At first Josh thought it must be aftershave lotion, then considered who else was in the boat. Standing downwind of Canebrake could be an experience at times, but rarely due to his aftershave. Then he recognized it as the same scent he'd first smelled in Reynosa, only much stronger. The hundreds of acres of grapefruit, tangerine, and orange trees in the area combined to give off the heady perfume he now drank into his lungs in deep, lingering breaths.

The smell drove bees crazy as soon as the blossoms opened and tempted them into making some of the sweetest honey in the world. The smell was narcotic and aphrodisiac rolled into one, and he knew now why Pam had been so keen on it. He also wondered if she would be affected in the same way, especially the aphrodisiac part.

"You awake in dare?" Canebrake wondered.

"Huh? Yeah, I was just . . . just smelling this air. Ain't that nice?"

"Yeah, dat's nice awright. Dat ole sun's what I like mostest, though. Make dem rheumatiz go right away, don't you know.

Make de Canebrake's hips an' back feel like a kid's. Ain't like no swamp, done tole you dat!"

"Tell me something, 'Brake. If you was to add some cover to this lake, how would you go about it?"

"Well, we take some ole Christmas trees back home an' sink 'em out in de bayou so's de *sac au lait* come 'round 'em, see? Might could do dat here, but you'd need a whole lot of Christmas trees, I reckon."

"That's about what I thought. How'd you like to stay down here a while? I'd like for you to check on some things for me. Might be a nice place to have a fishing lodge, don't you think? Feller could get rich acting as a guide on this lake, huh?"

"Man'd starve to death, most likely. What kinda one-eyed fool would need a guide out here? But yeah, I could stay here some time. Jest 'til t'ings cool down a mite back home, mind. You t'ink you can get along wit'out me for a while?"

"Well, I'm doing much better since Major Mike decided not to join us down here, and I think I might survive without you for a while. Especially since I won't be doing much fishing. I think the boys'll want another session out here tomorrow, then I plan to hit Don Juan up for a lift back to civilization and back home for a while. I think Major Mike has some local stuff to do up there until we start hitting the major tournaments and TV shows next month. Looks like a long hot summer ahead, huh?"

"Dat kinda heat I can stand. Maybe I get Pedro here ta teach me how ta use dat beer can, an' maybe I jest stay here an' drink him up some more 'quipment!"

"And your 'rheumatiz' will get better all the time, right?"

"Yep, bet I'll be better off dan my ole uncle Claude done made his rheumatics. He go see dis doctor, see. Tell dat doc he say, 'Mon, I done need me some rheumatics medicine, yah.'

"De doctor he say, 'Claude, how long you done had dem rheumatics, son?'

"Claude say, 'I ain't got none yet, but I t'ink maybe it time I start on dem medicines, 'cause medicine take its own time 'bout woikin' on me, don't you know.'

"Doc say, 'An' what make you t'ink dat way about dem

medicines, boy? Hell, you ain't old enough to be havin' no rheumatics, yet!' Dat doctor talk a whole lot like my uncle Claude, don't he?

"Well, Claude he told him, 'Shit-fire mon, I done been in dat army durin' Worl' Wah Two, an' dey give us all dat saltpeter, right? Hey, dat's been over t'irty-five year ago, an' it's only jes' now startin' to woik on me, so I figger I better get a leg up on dem rheumatics while I still got time!'"

"You're full of shit, Canebrake. You know that?"

"Yeah, I know dat. T'ink maybe it run in de fam'ly."

*　　*　　*

Big Un didn't know what to expect next, but would have almost welcomed death. His rude transfer from the spacious tank at the university to the tiny portable tank with its myriad of bubbling hoses had come as abruptly as his initial capture. His sophisticated lateral-line system had registered the vibrations of the men's voices as they'd argued about it, but in the end he was summarily corralled and deposited in the tiny tank where he scarcely had room to extend the opercula of his gills to breathe.

He was taken aboard an airplane and suffered the strain on his hardened swim bladder as it strove to expand with the decrease in pressure when the plane climbed. Within hours after his arrival, he was transferred into another tank, a somewhat larger one this time, and left alone in the dark.

When the lights came on the next morning, he found himself staring out into the large and startled eyes of several people. The faces changed throughout the day, but their looks of incredulity remained the same. He was the largest bass they'd ever seen, and the people who attended the Sports Products Trade Fair in Dallas were accustomed to seeing large bass.

When again the lights went out and his tank covered for the night—the cage around it securely locked—over four thousand people had pressed their noses against the glass and stared at him. Each had paid up to three dollars for the privilege. Major Mike was ecstatic. Big Un was just hungry.

24

When Josh arrived at the Nashville airport, his truck's engine turned over but an extra half-dozen times before coughing to life, a tribute to its manufacturer and maintainer since over a month had passed since it was last strated. He wondered if he should tell Major Mike about it. There might be a battery company out there that would be interested in a commercial.

The thought brought him up short as he considered his mental processes that had changed to look for profit from the most insignificant of sources. Was that how he was to be in the future? It unsettled him and made the prospect of getting back to quiet, unassuming Dilbert's Forge all the more desirable. First, though, he had decided to stop by the Japanese auto factory to tell them why he had not reported for work and to thank them for the opportunity anyway.

An Asian man sat in the personnel waiting room when Josh arrived. Though probably in his mid-thirties, he appeared to carry the ages of several men in his eyes and on his face. There was a grim set to his jaw as though he were perpetually expecting a sucker punch, and the eyes behind their single-fold slits were constantly on the move. Josh felt his presence from across the room and felt awkward, as though he should apologize for being there.

"Good morning. Are you here to interview for a job?" Josh

asked at length, reasoning that anything said would be preferable to the fat silence.

"I come to speak of work, yes. And yourself, sir? Are you here for work also?" the man returned in a soft, unsure tone.

"Well, I guess you could say that. What time is your appointment?"

"I have none. I merely come here as always in hopes of being hired, but my presence is of little consequence if you, too, are after the same job, sir."

Josh's eyebrows rose in curiosity at this, then gathered in confusion.

"And why is that? I mean, I don't really know anyone connected with this place."

"You need not. You are American. I am Vietnamese. You will have precedence over myself. That is the way they work here to avoid showing favoritism to other Asians."

"I see. Vietnamese, eh? Did you come over before the war ended or . . . ."

"Or am I *Boat People*?" he interrupted, then smiled a tired smile made humorless by the obvious disdain he held for the term. "Yes, I am *Boat People,* sir. I was a major with the Army of South Vietnam fighting in the Delta when Saigon fell and was unable to get my family out in time. After three years in a reeducation camp, we were united on a collective farm near Ben Hoa. At night I stole and sold things on the black market until I had enough monies to buy passage on a small boat to Thailand. It was not a pleasant trip, sir. There were pirates and bad storms along the way and many refugees ahead of us in Thailand, many with more marketable skills than my own. America, it seems, has enough farmers, so I must try here."

"I live on a small farm myself, and I didn't mean anything bad about being *Boat People,* sir, I assure you. I didn't serve in Vietnam, but I was in the army for a time and met many of your countrymen. In fact, I'm here to give back a job, not to take one. I'll mention that you're out here and interested, if you like."

"Thank you. I doubt they will take much notice, but everything helps. My name is Tan, sir. Nguyen Van Tan."

"Josh Jackson, Nug . . . Mister Tan. I'm sure something will turn up, have you tried elsewhere?"

He knew better than to ask, but it seemed like something to say at the time. Tan's expression again molded itself into a smile, only this time there was a trace of humor there.

"Oh yes. I clean floors at night for a sausage factory, and my wife works at one of the hospitals doing such things as they require, but I will continue coming here until I am employed, Mister Jackson. That is one thing all Asians understand and the one thing you Americans had so hard a time learning in my country: patience. They will one day tire of me sitting out here waiting and will put me to work. This I know. And when they do, I will make them sad they allowed me to sit so long, for I will be their best worker! As an Asian, I must work twice as hard to be thought half as good, but fortunately this is no problem."

"I'll just bet it isn't! What kind of work do you hope to get?"

"Just work. As a farmer in my own country, I learned to love being outside all the time, working in the soil, making things grow where and when I would have them. It is a life I long to return to one day, and in America, Mister Jackson, this will be possible. Then, once again, I can hold my head up and be proud. Until such a time, I will work for these men who only last generation invaded my homeland as they are now invading your own. There are differences, of course, but I think in time you will see what I mean."

"Mister Jackson? Mister Tanaka will see you now," a prim secretary spoke from the door to an inner office. "Good morning to you, Mister Tan."

"And a very nice morning to you, Miss Kowalski. You look lovely today as usual," Tan spoke amid two quick bows as she disappeared into the office.

"Good luck to you, and I'll be sure to mention your name to Mister . . . to whoever it is I'm supposed to see. Maybe this will be your lucky day," Josh said as he rose to leave.

"To use one of your country's saying, 'From your mouth to God's ear!' Mister Jackson. And health and happiness to you and your family."

"Thanks."

The brief interview was interrupted by a company photographer arriving to make a photo of Josh and Tanaka shaking hands. Tanaka was an avid fisherman and recognized Josh from his many advertisements. Josh felt this was an opportune moment to mention Tan's plight and promptly did so. Tanaka's expression never changed when he cited Tan's lack of education as the prime reason he had not been hired, but he also cited the man's determination as just reason to hire him eventually.

"You must understand, Mister Jackson, that life here would be extremely hard on Mister Tan until such a time as he acquired enough seniority to rise above his difficulties. The Vietnamese are viewed as an old enemy in this country now, much as, regrettably I must mention, we Japanese were viewed not so long ago. As such, he would face many slurs on his heritage and possibly even harassment at the hands of your countrymen were he to start at a sufficiently low station that would justify our hiring him over other applicants.

"This would cause bitterness on both sides and bitter employees are not efficient! Do not concern yourself with his welfare further, Mister Jackson, he has the patience of water. And water will eventually go where it would go, is that not correct?"

"I suppose so. Well, I'll be driving one of your new Comanchero four-wheel drive jobs, it seems. Doing some ads for your outfit in the near future, I understand."

"Ah yes! I supervised its delivery myself. You'll find it waiting at your home, Mister Jackson. Your . . . uh . . . house lady, told us the color you'd prefer and so forth. I hope it meets with your approval."

"I'm certain it will, Mister Tanaka. Thank you and good day."

They bowed to each other a few times until Miss Kowalski opened the door for Josh to leave. Tanaka sat back at his desk and admired the fresh Polaroid photos of himself and the bass champion and secretly envied him his luck. Mister Tan rose and offered a bow as Josh came through the door, the merest

209

spark of optimism in his dark eyes. Josh felt awful about not having any encouragement to offer, but bowed back before walking the few steps to shake hands. The Vietnamese had an iron grip for his small stature, causing Josh to comment.

"Did you milk cows on your farm in Vietnam, Mister Tan?"

"Eh? Cows? Yes, but we only had cow, never more than one. Mostly we grew rice and other vegetables, not so much meat as here. Good luck to you."

"And to yourself, Mister Tan. Perhaps we will meet again."

"Perhaps so, Mister Jackson."

Had he not known where Dilbert's Forge was, Josh would have been hard-pressed to get directions from anyone farther than thirty miles away. Now, however, Dilbert's Forge was beginning to rival Rock City and Ruby Falls for roadside advertisements. The nearer he got, the more commercials marred his view of the countryside until he was frankly disgusted with the whole thing. Hand-lettered signs offering bait and guide services littered the crossroads, lending an Election Day air to the still day. Cars and trucks, most with a boat in tow, crowded along the narrow road, slowing his progress until he came to his turn-off and darted down the gravel road to home.

The house had its own share of revelations waiting. For one thing, the grass needed mowing, but this chore would require a lot more effort than it had. Four assorted vehicles were parked in the yard along with six boats, two self-contained campers and a pop-up affair, and a shiny new TechnoTrek trailer. The dogs sprang from their hiding places among the vehicles to give chase, grateful for the opportunity. At the last second Josh saw the chains strung from vehicle to vehicle and stretched across the road, just in time to slam on his brakes and skid to a halt.

Two muted thumps came from under the truck as a pair of beagles failed to anticipate Josh's sudden stop. The dogs didn't want to stop barking at the first honk, but gave in reluctantly after the second. They retired to the ersatz parking lot and began lifting their legs over each wheel of trailer and truck until, happy and thoroughly drained, they wagged their ways under the house for a nap. After leafing through a stack of mail, Josh decided to emulate the hounds and take a nap himself. He stopped in the bathroom and found Pam's note penned on the mirror in a white smear of his jockey rash medicine.

"Why can't she just use lipstick like everyone else?" he wondered aloud, then toddled off to bed. The note said she'd call later.

As is the wont of an old bed that hasn't felt the weight of a human for some time, Josh's virtually swallowed him up as soon as he was horizontal. After the weeks of motels and hotels, it felt so good to be back in his own rack that he cozied up and fell out like flipping a switch. This comparison came to him as he awoke to the sound of someone flipping a switch.

A light tread upon the kitchen floor sounded through the walls, followed by the rustle of a dogfood bag. Josh began to grin in anticipation, then a pulse from his bladder bade him get on with business. He arose silently, slid into a pair of worn and comfortable jeans (a brand he didn't have a contract with, he was pleased to note), and padded barefoot to the bathroom. Rather than announce his presence with a flush, he shouted a greeting.

"Hello you good-lookin' devil you!" he said.

"Hello yourself!" a gruff voice came back.

"Slats?"

"Yep. Thanks for the compliment, though. Pamalou's off somewhere doin' somethin' and don't expect you until later on. She asked me to feed these hounds and check on the place. Saw yer truck and figgered you might be restin', so I's tryin' to keep hushed."

"No problem. I needed to get up anyway. How's the bugspit coming?"

"It's comin'. I been cruisin' the country lookin' for pigweed patches. You know how hard that shit is to find when you're a-lookin' for it? Anyhow, you got a patch right here on your place, if you'll part with it."

"Take it away. How soon until you . . . we . . . can go into production?" Josh yelled above the sound of running water in the sink. The yell was made easier as the flushing commode took away most of the cold water, leaving him to wash his hands in near-scalding liquid.

"Depends. Lawyer says we should have a "pending" status pretty quick, and we can go with that. I went ahead and filed for incorporation with the state, got us a sales tax account set up, a federal tax number for withholding, and a wholesaler's license. Managed to locate a old baby food outfit what's gone outa business due to lawsuits . . . chipped bottles or somethin' . . . and I'm tryin' to buy their bottlin' and labelin' machinery. I reckon we could be goin' in a month or so. You still interested, ain't you?"

"Damned right! You wouldn't believe the crap they're selling out there, Slats. The crap *I'm* sellin', I should say. Bugspit seems downright legitimate compared to much of that shit, and I don't see why we shouldn't cash in on it. What has happened around here, by the way? On the way here I saw more signs along the road than there was the last time a Clement ran for governor!"

Slats finished pouring the dog food into a broad pan and restowed the bag before answering. Josh stood in the doorway rubbing the sleep from his eyes.

"Whole place has gone to shit, that's what. You won't like much of it, I'll bet. The Ba-Da's raised their prices, and you have to wait forever to git a seat anymore. Gas has gone high as a cat's back, and it takes forever to git from one end of town to t'other 'cause of the traffic. Klotz and his bunch are rezonin' the whole place as people apply for licenses to set up bait stands and the like. The boys down to the feed mill and barber shop are tryin' to git somebody to run against Klotz next time, but ain't havin' much luck. Most folks are too busy hirin' out as fishin' guides or diggin' worms to git into politics."

"You doing any of that?"

"Naw, I been too busy gittin' things set up for business."

"Sounds like you've gone about it the right way, too. I didn't know you knew all that about licenses and stuff."

"I didn't. I got most of it from the library, but your lady and Mavis helped out a lot, too."

"Pam?"

"Yep. There's more than big old Jersey cow eyes and teeth in that head, Jackson. She's got herself a good edgi-ca-shun, for all that she works there with ole Klotz. Knows all about this shit."

"That's good to hear. Has she . . . uh . . . has she asked . . . ."

"About you? Not much more'n twice a day. Don't know how she'd figger I'd hear from you before she would. Hell, I didn't even have a phone when you left."

"You got one now?"

Slats set the pan of dogfood down on the kitchen table, tucked his thumbs under his belt, and rocked back on his heels with pride.

"Yep. An' I got me one of them fancy answerin' deals, too. Just like yores!"

"Well, well. How're you fixed for bucks?"

Slats drew on a somber face at this, tempted to tell how he'd been put on hold by Klotz until he'd accepted a lesser amount than he wanted, at a higher interest rate, and for only ninety days. Pride kept him from doing this, however.

"I'm doin' awright, I guess. Might could use a little help when we start gettin' the machinery together, though. If you can spare it."

"See Pam if you need anything. I'll set up an account we can both draft off of with her."

"You still bankin' with Klotz?"

"Yeah, now that you mention it. Don't know why I bother, though. God knows I don't owe that sonofabitch anything. Guess it's handy, though. I mean, Pam will look after everything there for me."

"If you say so," Slats agreed grudgingly while hefting the dogfood from the table and starting out the door. "Still pisses me off, though, to have to go see him hat in hand to borrow your money and pay *him* interest on it!"

"How much did you borrow?"

"Not much, a few thousand."

"What did you have to put up for collateral?"

"Oh, a few things. Won't matter though, not once this stuff starts sellin'."

It didn't occur to Josh that 'a few things' encompassed everything Spivey owned.

"Yeah, that's probably right. Well, if you need anything, like I say, you can just write it yourself. We'll need to set up books, too, so I'll fill Pam in on things this afternoon and get everything taken care of."

"You don't mean you're gonna tell her about the . . . stuff?" Slats asked from the doorway.

"Not directly, no. I'll just say you're looking after some business for me and might be coming in for a draft from time to time. Speaking of that, I'd better get a shower and see if I can find her. Did she say what time she'd be home?"

"Gettin' a mite antsy, are you? Son, you seem struck! Can't say as I blame you, but ain't this kinda quick? I mean, have you even got shed of Thelma yet?"

"Next week, unless she decides to sue for something, which wouldn't surprise me at all. Have you seen her?"

"Oh, yeah. Everybody's seen her! She's doin' shows all over, and they do a tune or two to open and close Brother Whats-his-ass's show on Sundays. Them shows are all reruns, I reckon. I mean he's a-talkin' about Thanksgivin' and such, but the parts Thelma Jean's in are new. She's lost some weight, looks like. Looks real good, in fact. Word is she and that preacher are . . . well . . . keepin' house, I guess you'd say."

"More power to her, both of 'em! All I want is out, Slats. There's a big world out there, and I intend to see me some of it, partner."

"Yeah, I figgered as much," Slats said while eyeing Josh's faded jeans and bare feet. "Good to see you ain't changed, Jackson. I's expectin' you come back wearin' them shirts with the little rep-tiles on 'em, snortin' cocaine, an' doin' them *manage a twats* every night."

"Ha! I spent most of my time lounging around in swamps feeding the mosquitos. This isn't the type of show-biz you're thinking of, Slats. But I'll get myself some of them shirts for our commercials, if you like. Yeah, we'll call it *Designer*

Bugspit: The slime of choice for discerning fishermen! You slay me, you know that?" Josh punched Spivey on the shoulder, delighting in the yellowish grin he saw on his face.

Then he caught a whiff of something out of place. He took another sniff in disbelief, a chance he'd never have taken with the Slats Spivey of old who, in the winter months, regarded showers with the same attitude most people reserve for root canals. Not today, however.

"Is that cologne I smell, Slats?"

Spivey reddened and stepped away, busying himself in gnawing a chaw from a twist of tobacco.

"It is! What's going on, Spivey? You and Mavis getting . . . ?"

"Ain't nothin' goin' on! I jes' figgered I ought to look and act more businesslike, that's all. I gotta feed them hounds now, so 'scuse me. I'll be over to the Bide-A-Wee afterwhile, if you feel like sluggin' down a couple."

"Might do that. Thanks for takin' care of the dogs, by the way. I'd have asked you first, but I figured you'd be pretty busy."

"That's awright. I come over here the first time Pamalou came by to feed 'em to show her how to shut 'em up. You forgot to tell her 'bout that, now didn't ya?"

"Yeah, I did. Thanks again."

"Nothin' to it. She took that mangy cat home with her, by the way. Whatcha gonna do with all them boats and stuff, Jackson? I roped 'em up with chains so they wouldn't git stole or nothin'."

"Noticed that. Much obliged. I don't know. I won't have time to use them myself, it don't look like, and after this fishin' season is over I doubt I'll want to look at one for a while. Feel free to use whatever you like. See ya."

The dogs gathered around Spivey, barking insanely, so Josh had a hard time hearing his reply.

"Right. Don't go gettin' none on ya!", Spivey said, a golden smile fighting its way through a light film of tobacco juice.

It was Josh's turn to blush.

"Beats stayin' out here and smelling the shit, doesn't it?"

Slats just looked off and started whistling while he filled the dogs bowls.

"What do you know about Plato?" Pam asked as they sipped at a before-dinner cup of coffee with Grand Marinier.

"It's a bitch to get out of carpets," Josh observed.

"Not Play-Doh, Plato! With a T."

"He's dead. What else do I need to know about him, hmmm?"

"You're not the ancient type, are you."

It wasn't a question and brought a little pout to her lips.

"I'm more ancient than you are, now that you mention it. But I don't see what that has to do with anything. All right, I've read some of Plato's stuff, but that was a long time ago and I found most of it pretty dry. Don't tell me you read it regularly? If you do, you really ought to get to know Slats Spivey better. He reads a lot of classic stuff."

"Spivey can read? I wouldn't have thought it. By the way, how's your partner on the road?"

"Canebrake? He's a dandy! He's a lot like Slats, by the way—seldom right, but never in doubt."

"I was referring to the fish, but Mister Canebrake sounds interesting."

"You wouldn't believe how interesting. Ever wonder why dogs hike their legs when . . . ."

"Later, Jackson. Right now I need to put on the sauce for the spaghetti. You want to slice some mushrooms?"

"Love to. Did I tell you Slats once tried to make mushroom-flavored ice cream? He thought it would appeal to the hoity-toities or something."

"Yuk! What did it taste like?"

"The floorboard of a taxi."

"Hope he's not roping you into any of his wild schemes. Sprinkle oregano over them once they're sliced. I like to add the two together so it'll let the flavor soak into the 'shrooms."

"Well, he's looking after some things for me while I'm gone, now that you mention it. I need to set up a separate account that he can draft against, too. Is that too much trouble?"

She was in the act of teasing a single strand of spaghetti loose from the rest and flicking it against the wall above the stove. It stuck there briefly, then slowly started to come unglued. She intercepted it before it could slither off the wall and flicked it into a nearby garbage can.

"I'd think about that one real hard, put in limits and so forth, but no, it's no trouble at all. Are you still going to leave your accounts open at our bank, by the way?"

"So now it's *our* bank, is it? Hmmm? Don't tell me Klotz has brought you in as a partner!"

"Perish the thought! Perish any other thoughts you might have had or are having concerning Rolly Klotz and me. I'm not his type, anyway."

"Oh? And what exactly is his type?"

"I'm not sure. But I think it would have scales or maybe a long hairless tail."

"Speaking of scales, the fish is doing just fine and languishing down in Florida, the University of."

"I'll try not to be jealous. At least you did bring my oranges. In honor of their arrival from Suntan Land, I'll make us a whiskey sour so we can use one for garnish. Okay with you?"

"Fine, but they're from Texas, not Florida."

"Texas? Never thought of Texas as an orangy kind of place. Where in Texas?"

"Right on the border near McAllen. I called you from there, remember? Anyway, it's a pretty spot near an old ranch they're stripping of mesquite so suburbanites like ourselves can flavor our barbecues."

"Something else to feel guilty about, huh? It's not like I club baby seals or anything, is it?"

"Not yet," he said while attemping to finger test the sauce. Pam intercepted his finger with a wooden spoon across the knuckle causing him to put it in his mouth dry. It tasted like Spivey's ice cream. "Just a matter of time I'd say, until the hillside is denuded and all the soil runs off into the lake. That'll mess up two nice things."

"All right, I'll stop buying mesquite. Slice the mushrooms a little thicker, dear. I like them with a little fight left in, and you could read a newspaper through those after they're cooked."

"Bitch, bitch, bitch!" he said playfully, registering her "dear" and liking it.

"Yes? Yes? Yes?" she said in return, then drug a finger through the sauce and lifted it sensuously into her mouth to taste.

Josh stepped forward, encircled her with his arms, and pulled her to him. After burying his face in her hair and breathing in the smell of her, mingled as it was with that of spaghetti sauce, he nipped her on an earlobe and whispered huskily, "I hope you're saving a few of those 'yeses' for later."

"Perhaps," she said in an equally hoarse whisper, thereby ensuring she didn't waste another.

"I'd hoped you'd save at least one," he said with a smile, then picked her bodily from the floor and started out of the kitchen.

She had just enough time to reach back and turn off the stove as they went out and to wink at the cat who licked his lips in anticipation. His master did likewise. As she was about to lay her head upon his shoulder, he stopped.

"Which of these is . . . uh . . . yours?" he asked, nodding down the hallway leading to the bedrooms.

"You'll recognize it when you see it," she said, then wondered if one's photo staring down on him from the walls would be the same psychologically as using mirrors.

The thoughts of mirrors suggested a mild degree of kinkiness, which she had always thought humorous. She'd pictured them together in her mind often enough that she wondered how accurate her images were. She could have satisfied her curiosity a short while later by merely looking at their reflection in the shoe-button eyes of the panda, but by then she had no inclination to keep her eyes open.

25

Foo-Foo knocked again on Brother Ray-Bob's door and again was greeted with silence. Behind the thin veneer door, in the upper right-hand drawer of the corner desk, lay the keys he'd come after and without them he would have to face Thelma's rage and/or disappointment. He checked both ways and, discovering no one near, took a credit card from his wallet and easily tripped the fragile lock on the door.

He was certain Brother Ray-Bob would approve of his actions, would laud his initiative in getting the key to the supply van and replenishing the depleted stock of *Heaven Calling*, their new album that was selling like lotto tickets everywhere they went. Foo-Foo and Mellow Man got in some vicious licks on the album, too, and were both tickled to be back in a studio again. Thelma was ecstatic! Even now she was stationed outside the souvenir tent autographing albums, tickets, and even the funeral home fans that many of the congregation carried clutched in their sweaty little hands.

In his haste he very nearly overlooked the small pink pill on the lamp table that seemed to be left out for him like cookies for Santa. He popped the tiny orb into his mouth, swallowed it dry, then departed for the supply van fully expecting the speed to kick in and add some spring to his step. He was disappointed. Upon reflection, he decided that ripping-off Brother

Ray-Bob's Godspeed was a pretty silly thing to do, especially since he had but another few weeks to go on his good-guy work until he could get back into the hard rock scene. Taking a hint from one of Ray-Bob's services, he decided to repay the good minister with two of his own pink pills and left them where he'd found the other when he returned the keys.

Thelma stood in her usual place during Ray-Bob's sermon that night exuding warmth and goodwill. It was his second night presentation, and she knew each of his sermons by heart, knew when his voice would rise and his fist fall on the pulpit to emphasize a point. Silently, she lip synched the words along with him and watched the crowd.

"But was Samson a-scared? NO-SIR-EE-BOB! For he ha-yud the FORCE of GOD ALMIGHTY behind him! So verily, he TOOK the JAWBONE of an ASS *(uh!)* . . . and he SLEW THREE HUNDRED! Glory," Ray-Bob intoned, sweat forming a sheen on his forehead and upper lip.

Subtle changes in lighting from below and behind the elevated pulpit underscored the mood he was trying to achieve and isolated him above the rest. In time the lighting was all focused upon him and the lower lights extinguished, so he appeared to be suspended in midair. He was working up a point about giving, about how blessed it was to give and further the cause of righteousness, and how every gift given in God's name tended to be returned to the giver in strength, as was the case with Samson and, specifically, if given immediately and to Reverend Ray-Bob Thomas! She knew he would be successful and knew further that, should the offering total a goodly sum, he would expect her to do some giving of her own after the meeting had closed.

This thought caused her to remember her birth control pill, the one she was almost certain she'd left on the table in Ray-Bob's room on the bus. She resolved to use her own key and retrieve the pill between numbers because she knew he'd be pissed if he found it, particularly so when he saw what color it was, and she didn't want him upset with her. Not now. Not now that the album was doing so well that there was talk of putting it in general distribution through one of the major labels. Not now that there was further talk of using the Hallelujah Choir on more television shows and (the very thought made her weak in the knees) perhaps even giving them *their own show* as a lead-in to Ray-Bob's!

So many good things were happening now that she barely noted the brief pain that had come with her divorce. *What a farce,* she thought. The actual session was nothing compared to what she'd always thought it would be, what the television shows suggested them to be. No name-calling, no "he did/she did," just a simple reading of the decree and a couple of signatures, then they were no more. Josh looked well, perhaps even more handsome than she'd remembered with his deep tan and rugged good looks. A pity. She'd not asked for a thing from him. In fact, she was tempted to offer some restitution now that it seemed she would be coming into some major money of her own. Brother Ray-Bob had nixed that idea as soon as she'd mentioned it, though, citing the need to leave Josh with his dignity even though he *was* an acknowledged heathen.

The nearest thing to a cross word between them had been Josh's reference to Ray-Bob as her "hypocrit buddy." She'd countered by asking him what he thought he was, posing as a world authority on fishing just because he lucked into one big one. He'd had to agree with that. In fact, he was far more agreeable in general than she'd remembered.

Oh well, she thought, *that's all past now, and there's nothing but blue skies ahead for me and Ray-Bob.* Idly, she wondered when he'd ask her to marry him. Nothing was barring the way now, and he did seem to hint at it from time to time. They'd make a couple, all right. The darling pair of the circuit, stars of sound and screen, worshiped by millions, envied by many more.

Better yet, next week they would make the turn of mid-season and start back over their route. That meant she'd be able to return triumphantly to Dilbert's Forge and again be the apple of its citizens' eyes. *Life is good,* Brother Ray-Bob had just said. Thelma agreed wholeheartedly and felt a warm tingle of contentment flow through her. ᵗ

Foo-Foo stood near her, a headset on his ears, silently tuning and setting up his new Korg synthesizer for their next number. She started to reach out for his hand, to share some of her good feeling with this semi-wild man who had taught her so much about the music industry and never asked anything in return. At the last instant, she remembered the tiny microphone clipped to the neckline of her gown and what would happen if she touched him while he had his hands on the keyboard. That much warmth neither of them needed!

Ray-Bob closed his spiel with an appeal for funds, after which the girls rushed bouncing and swishing among the throng to collect. The band whipped into a beatific soft rock tempo number that featured the rich tones of the Korg doubling and tripling themselves until it sounded like a full orchestra instead of a lone hophead with a flare for electronics. Ray-Bob launched into the next portion of his service, laying on of hands and healing, that was so popular wherever they went, while the girls hustled the collection plates backstage. Brother Ray-Bob's voice went up in volume and pitch, followed by the crowd gasping in unison. Without looking around the curtains, Thelma knew her man had just done something wonderful. Then another voice came over the speakers and shattered her illusion.

"This dog ain't white!" the voice cried plaintively.

"This DAWG *(uh')* . . . ain't . . . WHITE! Hallelujah!" Brother Ray-Bob echoed sweetly.

"Drape some diapers over the bushes off camera and flip the mirror over to bright. I want some more light on the raccoon, and someone take the shine off Josh's nose!" the director shouted over his bull horn.

In response, the lighting men began unfolding white cloths that, while not actually diapers, did seem strange to Josh. The effect sharpened the scene through the camera's lens as light reflected off the white sheets to brighten the background. A withered make-up woman in her fifties strolled up, an unfiltered cigarette dangling from one corner of her mouth, and smacked Josh in the face with an oversized powder puff.

The raccoon seemed oblivious to everything and kept splashing around at the water's edge chasing minnows and crawdads. Josh particularly liked the raccoon, a lively specimen of some twenty-five pounds named Rachet.

"Okay, people, let's make a commercial here!" the director implored. "Give me quiet! Camera, up to speed?"

The cameraman, another two hundred-plus pounder, nodded without taking his eye from the viewfinder. A cue girl held a stack of cue cards under her pert bosom and looked bored. Josh lifted the rod and felt it bow, it was intentionally hung on a stump out in the lake but would look like it had a fish on it on film. He licked his lips and focused on the little red light above the camera lens. The director pointed a finger at him to get ready, and a crewman began fanning him with an extra cue card off camera to get the "gentle breeze in the hair" effect.

"Annnnd action!"

"The good folks at the Tennessee Fish and Game Commission have asked me to say a few words about the great outdoors of the Volunteer State. How about Musky, Smallmouth, and Largemouth? How about world records in each? Tennessee has a wealth of open water and hungry lunkers just waiting for you, and southern hospitality to boot! This year why not make plans to spend a fishing vacation down here with us? Serious anglers keep coming back year after year and some . . . stay on forever!"

At his pause the camera panned over to where the raccoon was busily splashing. They waited for a full minute and were rewarded for their patience when the raccoon slapped a fat bullfrog tadpole up onto the bank then bounced out of the water to eat it. The camera zoomed in as Rachet shook the water from her coat and waddled off with the tadpole in her mouth.

"Outstanding! Did you get that, John?" the director asked, smiling.

The cameraman nodded again.

"Okay, keep rolling. Back to Josh now for the close."

Josh waited until he got the nod from the camerman, then jerked up on the rod sending the reel to screaming against its drag.

"Come on down! The water's fine!" he said happily, pretending to fight the fish.

"Annnnd cut! That's it folks. Next setup. Somebody get our little fuzzy friend a can of sardines, will ya? He was just great! You were, too, Josh. Take ten and we'll be ready for the next shot," the director said in his rapid-fire, never-enough-time-or-budget, way of talking.

"How long you had him?" Josh asked a skinny man who was busily toweling off the raccoon.

"Oh, about a year and a half I reckon, and he's a she."

"Cute. Are they much trouble to keep as pets?"

"Bet your ass! They're like barracudas, anything that shines they'll go for in a heartbeat. I'll bet I've gone through two dozen sets of car keys. Don't know where she puts 'em, but somewhere around the house she has about fifty dollars worth of quarters, five pounds of keys, and every piece of tinfoil that's been in the house the past year. They can get into anything, too. Look at these feet. See how much like hands they are? Well-sir, she can open doors, drawers, boxes, you name it."

"Must keep you busy, huh?"

"Yeah, she does."

"Are they expensive?"

"You mean to buy? Not really. About thirty bucks at weaning time, then a couple of dollars for a permit. They eat catfood and use a litter box, so that's not much bother. Where they do get expensive is their mischief. Rachet learned how to flush the commode and ran my water bill up to nearly fifty bucks one month, didn't you girl?"

The raccoon let go a chittering sound that was a cross between a purr and a growl as the man roughly toweled off her head.

"Permit?"

"Yeah, you gotta have a permit to keep any wild animal as a pet, though I don't think that's enforced much. A game warden told me he started to give a guy a ticket once for keeping a pet groundhog, but the guy got all pissed off and threatened to kill and eat it if he did. All kinds of crazies out there, but possession is still nine-tenths of the law, so if you caught it you can keep it or eat it. I got the permit so she could be used in commercials and films. That's how these guys located me, by the way, through Fish and Game's computer."

"Sounds like you might have something there. Does she work much?"

"Lots! You'd be amazed how many fairs and wildlife shows we get booked into. The South's big on 'coon huntin,' you know. By the end of the year we'll have worked about fifty shows of one sort or another. Not as many as your fish, of course, but a pretty good hunk of change."

"My fish?"

"Yeah, Big Un! We were at a show together down in Mobile last week, and poor little Rachet couldn't take her eyes off that big bass. Don't worry. I kept her at a safe distance."

"Yeah . . . I . . . uh . . . appreciate that. How did the fish look, by the way? I haven't seen him in a while."

"Huge! I'll bet you could stick a basketball in his mouth. What a fish!"

"Yeah, he's a dandy all right," Josh agreed, still wondering about Big Un's being on display, but reasoning that Mobile was fairly close to the university. So it was probably nothing to worry about.

Pam was in her back yard digging in a flower bed when Josh arrived from his session in Nashville. Nearby, FrankenKat was torturing a crippled cicada, the insect buzzing loudly. Josh paused in the kitchen to open a beer, then watched out the window. Pam had her hair pushed up under an old ballcap, the bill of which pointed off at an improbable angle, and she wore cut-offs with one of his old T-shirts, sans bra. This last fact was made evident by the delicious way her breasts swayed as she scratched in the soft earth. He felt himself getting aroused and decided to go out to her. She looked up as he approached, and the look on her face caused him to stop short.

"What's the matter?" he asked.

"We need to talk, Josh," she said softly, her voice tinged with dread.

"Oh shit. Are you . . . uh . . . pregnant or something?"

"No, thank you. I've just been thinking, that's all."

Josh joined her in dreading whatever was coming next. Having lived with one woman for several years, he knew that when a woman says she's "been thinking," it was rarely about anything good. Try as he might, though, he couldn't see what could be wrong. Things had progressed exceptionally well for them the past ten days, at least to his notion. They'd made love often, and it had been wonderful. There was the divorce, of course. A generic sort of thing, that. In fact, it was so cut and dried he wondered why he had to be there at all. Surely she wasn't hung up on that. If anything she should be happy about it now that they were more-or-less keeping house together. If it wasn't sex, and it didn't seem to be a lack of affection, then what else could it be? What else indeed! What was left?

"It's money, isn't it?" he asked, realizing what was left.

"Yes, I suppose so. It's just that, well, if we'd gotten together before you came into all that, there'd be no problem."

"We did, sorta."

She smiled in a sweet-sad way and shook her head.

"Not really, Josh. Do you even know how much you have on deposit? It's over a million dollars now. That's a hell of an attraction, you know? I just can't be sure what I feel for you isn't somehow driven by that."

"Don't tell me you're beginning to think you're a gold digger, Pam. I don't think that at all. What are you suggesting?"

"I just don't think I can carry on this relationship, Josh. Not while all that cash lays there taunting me every day, making me question my own motives."

"Then quit! Or I'll transfer it out to another bank or something."

"Then what? Go to work for you I suppose, right? Don't you see? Then I'd just be another 'kept woman,' and I don't want that. I want to know I love you for you, Josh. I guess

226

that's what it all boils down to, I *do* want to love you. Just you, not all the niceties that would go with it."

"Look, Pam," he said, taking her into his arms and feeling the warmth of her against him, wondering if it were for the last time. "I don't know what to do about this. What happened to the gal who had to be chauffeured around in a red Porsche?"

"She grew up, I guess. I don't know what to do either. I can't ask you to just give it all away. You'd be a fool to do it for starters, and I don't know how I'd feel about you if you did. You'd never forget or forgive me for it, either."

"Is that what it would take to, uh, prove I love you?"

"I don't know. I'm just a little messed up in the mind, I suppose. Somehow I'd always thought someone would just drift into town and sweep me off my feet and there'd be no second guessing."

"More knights on white chargers, huh? I don't think it ever quite works that way in real life, Pam. I'll have to think about this and, in the meantime, I guess it'd be best if I moved back to my own place."

"I suppose so. I'm sorry, Josh. Maybe once you're gone, I'll realize I don't need that kind of commitment and my mind will clear up."

"Yeah, maybe so. I hope so. You'll keep the cat for me?"

"Sure. I'll feed the dogs, too. When do you go back on the road?"

"Tomorrow. I was going to put it off for a few days, but under the circumstances I think it'd be best to get on with it. I'll . . . I'll miss you."

They kissed, the bitterness of the occasion seasoned by the salt of her tears. The cicada gave a final buzz before dying, and FrankenKat padded off to find more challenging victims. Josh left Pam sitting in the flower bed while he packed his things.

He phoned the airport in Nashville and, as an afterthought, rang up Slats Spivey. Spivey was out putting the finishing touches on his new bottling plant in an old building that had in the past served as a basketball gym, American Legion hall, and skating rink. Josh left a message on Slats' machine, then started to go back out and say good-bye. Pam was holding FrankenKat, stroking his fur while dripping hot tears onto it.

He fought back an urge to run to her, take her again into his arms, and swear to divest himself of every penny he had if it would set her mind at ease. Instead, he walked resolutely out to the pickup, slung his suitcase into the bed, slapped the hood, and left. He resolved to stop in Nashville to visit someone on the way to the airport, some business he felt needed to be taken care of, and a plan began to form at the back of his mind.

Pam heard his hand come down on the hood, which brought forth another flood of tears. *How very stupid all this is,* she thought. *The fickleness of the mind preying on the heart.* She hoped that he'd call her so she could recant everything, knowing that she probably wouldn't, couldn't. She felt empty, hollow, and the feeling was even more wretched for being self-inflicted.

Major Mike was unaware of the personal problems his prime performer was going through, and even had he been aware it is unlikely he would have paid more than a moment's notice to them, for he had problems of his own. The fish was now scheduled to appear at a sportsman's conference in San Jose in two weeks and Seattle the following week. The problem was, Josh would be doing a credit card commercial in Carmel, just a few miles away, and it would be difficult to keep him from seeing ads and flyers touting the fish's appearance. There had to be questions. He went down to the basement of his newly leased home to feed the fish and there saw a sight that sent adrenaline coursing through his veins. His previous problems were moot: the fish was lying on its side, its immense mouth working ever so slowly.

26

Josh returned to another anonymous hotel room following yet another hot day in front of cameras and lights, his tenth straight including two television fishing shows. Today it had been a line of baits, a line of tackle boxes, and a line of lines. He was getting sick of it already. Idly, he reflected on the truth versus the lie. The truth was, he'd gone out fishing with a slightly eccentric friend to test a bizarre fish bait. While there, they'd happened upon a small fish that was, in turn, eaten by a big fish. A *very* big fish! There the truth ended.

Now, according to the series of endorsements he'd done, the public was led to believe that he sprung from bed at the crack of dawn, assisted by his Big Ben alarm clock, donned his L.L. Bean longhandles and flannel shirt, pulled on his Levi jeans, laced up his Red Wing boots, put on his BassMaster's hat, took a dip of Skoal *and* a chew of Levy-Garrett, then sat down to an equally name brand breakfast. Following breakfast he'd hooked one of his several trucks up to any of a half-dozen boats, filled the thing with Blue Ribbon Beer, Ugly Stick rods, Daiwa reels, Stren line, Tom Mann and Hoosier HawgHunter baits, Eagle Claw swivels, Coleman lanterns and coolers, and enough electronic detection gear to find the Titanic, then headed out to do battle with monstrous fish, presumably at the behest of the governor himself!

The lie was blatant, but it was extremely profitable. *Far better,* he thought, *if we had just put the bugspit on the market directly and made a few dollars that way.* Thelma's question as to who was the biggest hypocrite rang truer every day.

The clock on the wall was missing its hour hand, but it was twenty after something. Josh sat on his bed and watched himself and Bill Dance fishing on the television. Dance was a lot of fun, a true Southerner who wore a University of Tennessee cap and spoke with a soft Memphis drawl. Dance was now enumerating the merits of a new pH monitor, and Josh let go a hearty laugh when he said, "It's a fine piece of equipment, once you know how to use it. A real addition to your overall bass fishing system!" At twenty after something else, the phone rang.

"Jackson," he answered.

The voice on the other end was melodious, though somewhat masked by the static on the line.

"One point two? Fine 'Brake. Give me their address, and I'll forward it today. You keep doing what we talked about, and I'll join you at the end of the week. I'll need to get everything taken care of quick 'cause I've got something to do next week. Oh yeah, check with the bank in McAllen and make sure Major Mike's office is forwarding my pay to them now, okay?"

After he'd hung up, he laid back in the bed and smiled, wondering what Pam would think when she knew. A flick of the channel selector next to the bed and a canned porn movie popped onto the screen. It was another film with nymphomaniac young females. It didn't interest him much, but did make him think more about Pam.

With a scowl splitting his features, he jabbed the remote control again and a grizzled man wearing what appeared to be a hand-me-down band uniform from Michael Jackson appeared on the screen. At first Josh thought the man must be hustling John Phillips Sousa records for K-Tel ("and for the first two million customers, a copy of every record ever made, by the original artists, as a bonus, along with half a dozen Ghin-zoo steak knives!"). When the man mentioned *God* and

Money, however, he recognized the truth. Even California had its versions of Brother Ray-Bob Thomas.

The man went on to cite a couple of young programmers at Cal-Tech who had come up with the ultimate in Godly gadgetry, a software matrix for sin! As it was explained, these guys had reduced the Old and New Testaments into digital representations of everything expressly forbidden in the texts and "weighted" each sin with a numerical value. Coveting one's neighbor's wife, for instance, might net one a negative, or Sin-Score, of five points. Killing a dormitory full of orphans with an axe, on the other hand, put the miscreant right up there in the Doomed range: do not pass Go, do not collect two hundred dollars, go straight to hell.

Using this matrix, the viewer/Christian could tote up his sins at the end of the day and compare them to a predetermined "Mean" (RAM-Accessed and adjusted for age/sex/denomination) and get some idea of how he was tracking. The true beauty of the system, though, was the Contrition Feed-Back Option. The CFBO would assess the damage wrought on the DOS operator's soul, in less than eight microseconds and offer options on atoning for at least a portion of the numeric sum. The option was how much in funds and/or "good acts" would bring the person back into the HeavenBound range or how much to wipe the slate completely clean.

On the average, one point of SinScore equated to half an American dollar, bringing your garden variety ogling of your neighbor's wife in somewhere under minimum wage. The name of the program? The Wages of Sin!

In total disgust now, Josh again jabbed the remote, ridding himself of the watery-eyed minister and his alpha-numeric attitude toward righteousness. A dubbed version of Jap-Slap Theater came on in its stead. He marveled at the way the actor would say "No!" and then continue to move his lips for an additional ten seconds, and the fact that the star could kill off the entire population of Kowloon between commercials without attracting the attention of police, ambulances, or even bystanders. Compared to what had been on before, however, Jap-Slap Theater seemed intellectually stimulating.

* * *

Major Mike took his tongue-lashing in stride. The professors had unleased several creative phrases when he'd walked in carrying the fish in its case. In particular, they had been upset at the green slime on the glass of the case and the fact that the pH had not been maintained as directed. The fish had lost nearly five pounds and was now just a very large fish, not a record. They placed him in the large pool and turned up the aeration. The fish swam unsteadily from one end to the other, then just stopped next to one of the bubbling air vents.

"He'll take some time, if he makes it," the head professor said. "You can check back with us next week or phone if you like."

"I'll do that. You'll let me know if there's any change, hmmm?"

The prof nodded affirmatively, and Major Mike departed. On his way back to the airport, he stopped and phoned his office. By noon the next day he'd had letters sent to every major taxidermist in the United States, offering the highest bidder the honor of stuffing the fish when its demise came about. He'd also wondered again if maybe he should speed that day along since a stuffed fish would be so much easier to transport and would probably still be very much in demand.

Slats walked proudly through the tangle of blue plastic drums, pausing here and there to lift the lid off one and check the progress of its fermentation. The place stank to high heaven, blotting out the offensive odor of the sewage refinement plant in the distance. Another week, he figured, and the first big batch of bugspit would be ready for bottling. Lunker Liquor, he'd decided to call it, and he made certain no mention of contents made it onto the label.

It had been tempting to name it Spivey's Lunker Liquor, but Mavis had talked him out of it. The labels should arrive sometime this week, and he was anxious to see them. Now if Josh would just get his butt back here to do some commercials, they could get started. Hopefully, they could sell fifty or sixty thousand bottles this year and, even at two dollars a bottle, they would still realize nearly seventy thousand in profit. *Then,* thought Slats, *once the major outlets start stocking it, we can up production and be well-off forever.*

Only a few weeks remained on his loan now, and each day brought new headaches as he strove to tie up all the loose ends in starting up production. Mavis had been a lot of help. He had begun to wonder what he had ever done without her. A frown pushed a parade of lines across Slats's face as he thought of how things were going. Josh had all the money, so far, but something was wrong there.

He had met up with the Swift girl over at Jackson's place when she'd come to feed the hounds, and there was a distant look in her eyes, a sadness. At first he'd thought maybe it was just because Josh was on the road, but the more he thought about it the more certain he was that they'd had a disagreement of some sort. *Jackson's been awful lucky in getting fine-looking women,* he thought, *but damned if he can seem to hold on to one!* Maybe he should have a talk with the boy, 'cause it was obvious Pamalou thought the world of him.

"This shit would gag a maggot, Spivey," Mavis observed from behind him.

"Not so, honeybun," Slats countered. "It smells like money!"

"I'll bet that's what Rolly Klotz said about his little plant up yonder, too."

The mention of the banker's name brought the frown back again. *Women!* he thought, *How can you explain anything to someone who'll go down on you one minute then raise holy hell for using her toothbrush the next?* Had he been able to read the thoughts going through Pam's mind a scant three miles away, he'd have had an even better reason to feel this way and more reason to frown.

"Shit!" she cried aloud, causing an elderly woman at the wall desk to look up and lose count of the pennies she was patiently rolling.

Rolly Klotz made the sharp turn out his door on one leg, wondering what on earth was so alarming as to make Miss

233

Swift say such a thing. He nodded an apology to the older woman, who had dropped her coin rolls and was now clutching her chest, then knitted his brows in a frown that caused all his chins to bunch up like a Shar-pié puppy's. Pam eyed him briefly, then burst out laughing.

Rolly alone looked funny enough to provoke such a reaction. Today he was dressed in a chartreuse jacket, paisley tie, blue striped shirt, and Purina-checked pants. *If he's making a fashion statement,* she thought, *he's saying "I am retarded and colorblind!"* Between peals of laughter she handed him the slip of paper that had started it all.

Klotz felt his heart leap into his throat, and his already high blood pressure inch up to dizzying heights as he read it. It said *Doom.* It said *Ruin.* It said "Pay to the order of The Society of Jesus, Punta Verda District . . . $1,200,000!" It was signed by Josh Jackson and, to Klotz's calculating little mind, virtually depleted his entire account! Worse yet, it would mean pulling all that money out of his Federal Reserve account and halting the new load for the water treatment plant.

Rolly felt his legs about to give out under the strain. Pam's laughter found its way through the roaring in his ears.

"You think this is so damned funny, Miss Swift, you can go share your humor with those who will appreciate it! Go on over to the court house and sign up for unemployment, bitch, 'cause you're fired!"

"Really?" she asked, wide-eyed, noting with pleasure the string of spittle that had escaped one corner of Klotz's mouth and how it made him look even more like a pig. "Great! I was about to ask for a leave of absence anyway, to go out west for a time. Since you've never seen fit to provide *paid* vacations, it looks like you're doing me a real favor. Choke on that for a while!"

"You'll never work around here again, Missy. I can assure you of that! By the time I get through with your reference letter . . . ."

The phone ringing in his office, along with the startled look on the elderly woman's face, caused him to momentarily stop mid-sentence.

234

"Pack up your stuff and be out of here before lunch," he hissed. "You and your 'Mister Macho' boyfriend deserve each other, you know that? He just pissed away a fortune, so I don't see what you have to laugh about. I'll have his place, you know, as surely as I'll have yours bulldozed when we widen the road! And his slimy little friend's, too!"

Abruptly he wheeled and departed, clutching the check in one hand and balling the other hand into a fist. Pam began zeroing out her transactions of the day and wondering what she would say to Josh now that he'd apparently taken her at her word and donated everything he had. *Why did I even say those things?* she wondered. Then she saw Klotz through his office window and understood.

Her only other associations with wealthy men had been this porcine putz and the Blalocks. Somehow she'd equated money with personality as a cause-and-effect type of thing. *What a time to realize that!* she thought. Now she owed Josh a huge apology and wondered if he'd even want her after she'd caused him to do such a thing. Why a Catholic church? Was he Catholic? She'd never asked. Apparently there was some reason he would choose such an outfit to receive all his funds, but she couldn't for the life of her figure out why. She wondered if she'd managed to alienate him with her wishy-washy behavior. The thought took some of her glee away and caused her to look deeply inside to see if she was actually getting what she wanted. Then she realized she really didn't know what that would be or why.

"I know why!" Klotz said irritably in response to his caller's question. "You want another friggin' percentage hike, that's why!"

"Rolly, Rolly, Rolly! Let's calm down here. Did I catch you at a bad time?" Ray-Bob wondered in his most soothing voice.

"Damned right, you did! That painted bitch of yours' ex-husband just jerked the rug out from under my ass, and now I'll have to put up some of my own funds to cover loans outstanding."

"Ah! Then I called at just the *right* time, friend! You need cash, right? Well, we'll be back in town Saturday and I'd be happy to . . . let's say . . . leave some offerings on deposit with you? In return, you can just give ole Ray-Bob an extra point and a half on our usual deal. What say?"

"That, that's mighty nice of you. I could use a little help right now, and you could help my soul some by ditching that bitch you're with right where you found her!"

"Odd you should mention that, Rolly. I've had similar thoughts myself. She's gettin' a mite too prominent here lately, if you know what I mean. Would it ease things if I sent her home to her folks for a while, then perhaps forget to come back for her?"

Rolly knew what he meant; Thelma was beginning to become a household word throughout the South in the same way certain hostesses on game shows tended to rise above their male counterparts, though their roles were largely decorative. Ray-Bob was not one to share the limelight with anyone, though he would share his profits to a degree in return for a favor or two.

"Fine, fine. I take it your tour's going well?"

"Well? We're up nearly fifty percent over last year's take, and on an acceleration that should carry us to the end of the season! My producers from the TV show? They'll be in the crowd there in Dilbert's Forge, and I think a good showing will fatten my contract with them, so I want you to touch base with the Blalock boys and have them cut everybody loose for the services and maybe hold payday until Thursday this time— give folks a chance to buy groceries and have a little something left to jingle in their jeans, if you know what I mean."

"I think I've got you, Brother Ray-Bob. That's quite an operation you've got there, boy. The same folks just keep coming back for more, huh?"

"You got it, Rolly. Why do you think the Lord *Himself* referred to them as *sheep*?" Ray-Bob asked, then laughed heartily.

Rolly joined in the laughter, feeling far better now, then rang off the line and stared at Pam as she tidied up her teller's window and made ready to leave. It was tempting to try to stop her, particularly now that he'd have to get someone to take her place. Someone whose salary would come out of his own pocket instead of the trust fund Pam's aunt had left in his care to dispense as he felt she needed it!

Silly women, all of them! he thought and was again thankful he'd never married one. Pam's trust fund had another couple of years to go before he absolutely had to surrender it, and since she had no idea it even existed, there was no reason he should enlighten her yet. Despite Jackson's sudden craziness, the day seemed to have some merit to it after all. Who would have thought Jackson would give all that money to a church anyway? He knew the answer.

"The IRS!" he said aloud. "The same people who believe I do the same thing when I buy Brother Ray-Bob's nightly offerings from him, then produce the canceled checks at the end of the year as a deduction!"

27

Brother Ray-Bob awoke in the middle of the night, cold sweat soaking his sheets and pillows. He flicked on a lamp and studied himself in the door mirror, not liking what he saw.

You look like someone who's losing his mind, Raymond. You know that?

"You wouldn't do that to me. Like you said before, then you'd have no place to live."

In your mind, Raymond. I'm just your conscience. Madness wouldn't bother me one little whit. Heck, I might just enjoy it! Be nice to have a little change of scenery.

"What's this about, the girl?"

Oh, she's hardly a girl, Raymond, and far from innocent, too. She's got her own little thing going, and right now you're a part of it. Maybe she's playing you to your Brother Clay! Ever consider that?

"No."

I see we're drinking again. You forget about the ulcer?

"It's well now. Besides, this is just a little something for my throat."

Oh yeah. Nothing serious. Not like last time, at all.

"No, it's not. That was . . . ."

Therapeutic! That's right. Now let's see, how did that begin?

238

"You know damned well how it began! Didn't we just go through this the other night?"

I did. I'd kinda like to hear your version, though. You always manage to inject so much emotion into it!

"And you'll taunt me until I do, is that it?"

Raymond! I'm crushed! I only do what you tell me to, and I'd swear I heard you mouth something tonight to the effect that an honest confession was good for the soul. Really, you ought to stay away from such dog-eared phrases, Raymond. You're better than that."

"Shepherd's Acres: A Home For The Homeless. It was a good idea. I saved and prayed and begged for two seasons on the road to build it. Even wintered over in Georgia instead of Florida to make sure there was enough money left to break ground in spring, remember?"

I remember, Raymond. Go on.

"I paid cash on the barrelhead, $57,000. Nothing fancy, just a shotgun building with four family units and a little park. Nice."

And free! Don't forget free.

"And free to the tenants. They paid their light bills, we provided a good well of sweet water. Nice."

But not very businesslike, was it? Don't leave out the lawyers, Raymond.

"No, it wasn't very businesslike. They said I could have used the money better, could have paid a quarter of the cost down and had two units just like it built. Then put the balance in some sort of high-yield bonds that would have handled both the mortgage payments *and* the folks' light bills."

And that's what you did two years later, huh?

"Yes. Only I took it a step further and decided to build a little better where I could get in for fifteen percent down, build eight units, and rent half of them out at reduced rates. It was still a good deal for all concerned, an honest deal."

And then?

"And then the lawyers came again. Set us up as a nonprofit corporation with accountants and cash flow and all that. We went out for bids and built some more."

And the units were even cheaper this time, weren't they Raymond?

"Yes! Dammit. They were dirt cheap, so we built lots more and rented all of them out this time, to keep cash flow up and get funds to build the church and expand the park, and get a proper sewage line installed. I don't want to go on with this tonight."

You're almost to the important part, Raymond! Surely you don't want to leave me hanging. I'll only have to make you go back to the beginning again.

"The codes."

Speak up, Raymond. There's no one here but us.

"The building codes! The reason the last units were so cheap was that the contractor used substandard materials, bribed the inspectors, and . . . ."

And?

"And the wiring wouldn't handle two lousy little space heaters, and a family of three . . . ."

Burned! They burned, *Raymond! Then the lawyers were on the phone again. More bribes had to be paid to hush it up, and you've been running from it ever since. Admit it Raymond.*

"Yes, they burned."

And now you're worried that you'll *burn, too . . . eventually. Aren't you Raymond?*

"Yes."

Go ahead and cry. I'll leave you for now and let your heart keep you company for a spell. I don't like doing this to you, you know.

"Like hell you don't."

No, really I don't. It's just my job, Raymond. We all have to do what we have to do. You know what it'll take to hush me up, don't you?

"You've said so often enough."

Well, when the time comes, Raymond. I've always hoped it would be a time of your choosing, but that might be His job. G'night, Raymond.

28

"Who?" Thelma asked, the confusion and feeling of *déjà vu* heavy in her voice.

"Cindy, I think. Or maybe it was Sandy. Or Wendy. It was one of those cheerleader type names. Anyway, she'll be checking in with you this evening, and you'll need to get her fixed up with a gown and a place to stand on stage. You sure Ray-Bob didn't mention this to you?" Carla, the soloist stated in her crystal-sharp voice.

"No, uh, I don't think so. *This* evening, huh?"

"That's what he said. If I were you I'd take it up with him. I mean, if you're supposed to be leading us, it would seem natural that you have a say in who gets hired and all. Hell, she might not even have a voice at all, she might just be another . . . ."

Carla let it drop there, her eyes widened in disbelief that she'd actually mouthed the words—the same words she'd heard from another when Thelma had been hired a few months before. Thelma knew well what the rest of the passage would have been without hearing it. Knew, too, that it would have been largely true. Hot tears of shame, hurt, and disgust welled up in her eyes, threatening to send a stream of mascara cascading down her cheeks. Briefly, she wished she still had Josh to run to for comfort and advice. Carla excused herself mid-blush and hurried back to the main tent where roadies were busily setting up equipment. Hurt turned to rage in Thelma's heart, then slowly burned down to hurt again.

"Why now?" she asked the rain-cleansed skies. "Why wait until I'm back in my own back yard?"

The skies didn't answer. Neither did the puffy clouds that rode an invisible breeze at a smart clip that brought them between Thelma's glistening eyes and the summer sun. The day was thrown into a gray funk as the sun went behind the clouds, a color that etched itself onto her heart and brought forth an earnest heave of her chest and an audible sob. She held herself as much in check as possible, then marched off behind the souvenir tent feeling the moist wood chips and sawdust give under her heels without protest.

Foo-Foo watched her walk past, enjoying the way her buttocks tightened with each sinking footstep and the way her hair swung in counterrhythm to her hips. Only as she turned to dart behind the smaller tent did he notice the peculiar hunch of her shoulders and the telltale smear of make-up that told him she was crying. He started to leave his keyboard and follow, then thought better of it as he saw her continue past the souvenir tent and around the back of the Silver Eagle. He'd give her a few minutes to compose herself, he thought, then go to her.

Thelma leaned her forearm against the bus's polished aluminum side and her head upon her forearm, then gave herself to her hurt. The dying sun was playing peek-a-boo with smaller clouds now, alternately brightening and dimming. Having grown accustomed to mood lighting over the past few months, she found it hard to concentrate on her feelings under the rapidly changing conditions and soon gave up the tears. Her chest was still tight, however, and a lump too large to swallow had risen into her throat.

It could all be a mistake, she thought, trying to rationalize the thing in her mind. *Ray-Bob could, in fact, have lured an accomplished vocalist away from any of a number of prominent gospel groups to enhance our act and give us an even better shot at impressing the network people who in just a couple of hours would be in the audience. He could have done that very thing and was just saving it as a surprise. Sort of a Homecoming present to herself! Yeah, that's it! He'll laugh at my foolishness,* she thought and welcomed his laughter.

Her reflection in the shiny aluminum looked awful. Her eyes were raccooned with make-up and the person staring back at her from behind the E of Eagle looked more like Alice Cooper than Thelma Lewis Jackson. Hurriedly, she prowled through her purse in search of a Kleenex and her make-up pouch. She found a wadded tissue hiding in one deep corner and plucked it like a cotton ball with her long nails.

Beneath the tissue, sitting there like a minuscule clutch of bird eggs, were the two pink pills she'd fetched from Ray-Bob's lamp table and promptly forgotten. *What the hell,* she figured, *once this thing is settled and he puts my mind at ease, we'll probably have some making up to do. Might as well finish off this cycle.* She downed the two pills dry, cringed a bit at their bitterness, then moved to the more mirrorlike chrome around one tail light to repair her make-up. This done, she straightened her skirt, patted her hair into place, and walked around the bus and up its steps.

She had her hand drawn back to knock on his door when his voice rose in its fire-and-satin manner, and she overheard his words. She didn't need to inquire as to whom he was saying them . . . or why.

"I say-uh, THOSE who GOD . . . hasjoinedtogether, Bambi! GOD! Not some nig-nog elected flunky, honey. GOD!" he said.

Bambi!! her mind screamed to her. She could see this interloper too clearly—tallish, twentyish, blonde hair falling loosely around her bronzed shoulders and framing an equally tanned face within which was set a large set of blue eyes. All Bambis on earth were in their twenties, highly tanned, blue-eyed, and blonde. *And,* had monstrous tits! It was almost a law of nature that they had to have huge boobs, though how parents knew they would when they named them as infants she couldn't imagine.

It was enough, though. Enough to make her clench her fists

in such tight balls that her nails dug into her palms and made little crescents of blood bead up around each. Enough to set fire to the lump in her throat, which in turn set her eyes ablaze with an intensity that dried up all her remaining tears. Enough to send her stalking back out of the bus with hate dancing the Virginia Reel behind her pupils.

The lighting was appropriate this time. The last of the clouds had fled on the wind, leaving a midnight blue summer sky overhead, and Thelma was seeing red. The combination of the two came out purple, as in rage. Brother Ray-Bob would have time to learn about women scorned. He'd rather have played leapfrog with a unicorn than make an enemy of Thelma, but he didn't know it at the time.

The crowd was already gathering, and it promised to be a dandy. Thelma reflected on this while signing her two hundredth album of the evening outside the big tent. She was amazed at how much easier it was getting to sign and make small talk, partly because she knew many of the congregation but mostly for a reason she didn't as yet fully appreciate. Her pen flew across the album covers, and she never stopped talking. It should have dawned on her that the sudden burst of energy was more than just a reserve of adrenaline she was storing up for Brother Ray-Bob, though that was a considerable boost in itself.

Bambi had reported for duty and was everything Thelma had imagined a Bambi would be, with the exception of the eyes, which were the reddish brown of Hershey's chocolate. Thelma had received her warmly and had even chatted with her while they attempted to find a gown that would house her boobs without cutting off her breath completely.

The network people arrived and introduced themselves. One was a thin-lipped man in his early sixties who could have won the Mr. Adam's-Apple contest going away and looked for the world like the Walt Disney version of Ichabod Crane. The blue-haired lady accompanying him also had a puritanic cast to her mouth, but the yellowish nicotine stains on her fingers bespoke a somewhat more liberal outlook than her escort.

After meeting them, Thelma revised her plan of revenge against Brother Ray-Bob. She might still have a shot at the TV show if they were really good. After all, why jeopardize that just to even the score with that two-timing four-flusher? She'd have her revenge, all right, but it would be on her own terms. She didn't know that Brother Ray-Bob planned to cut her loose following that night's show. If she had, it's doubtful the chemicals racing around in her system would have allowed her to do anything differently.

"Do you have something really kick-ass that you could play tonight, Foo?" she asked in a voice that was punctuated with little spurious sparks of energy.

"What? You want something upbeat? Yeah, we got some licks for sure, but Bre'r Ray-Bob'd shit a goose if we split from his standard set, wouldn't he?" Foo answered, then took a slug of Wild Turkey from a paper cup before passing it to Mellow Man.

"We've got the network people in the audience tonight, you know. . . ." she began.

"And His Nibs wants to send them outta here snappin' they fingers an' hummin' a tune, right Angel?" Mellow Man finished for her.

"Right! That's exactly what he said! Something stout, with some drive to it. Make the crowd butt walk right up onto the stage! That's what he wants," she lied.

"Say no more. We got what you need. You want something you can sing to, of course," Foo-Foo rejoined.

"Not necessarily, though that would be nice. How about you just take off from something we have going, then improvise? Could you do that? I mean, once the crowd gets behind it, just carry them along."

"Yeah, dig it! We can do that, for sure. Which number?"

"I'll let you know with a hand signal or something. Oh yeah, plan on maybe doing an encore or two tonight. I've got a feeling it's going to be one to remember. Can I, uh, have a drink of that?"

"Sure," Foo-Foo volunteered, then produced a bottle from a

245

small door in the back of one of his amps and refilled the cup. "You're sure?"

"Hell, yes! In fact, I think that we'll all need whatever we can get to get through this one. Take that for whatever you will, boys," she said with a pretty smile and wink that sent Foo-Foo into full flush. Then she doffed the Turkey in one gulp and walked off swaying her good parts to some internal rhythm.

"Gal marches to the beat of a different drum, Foo," Mellow Man observed while staring at the bottom of the empty cup.

"Or a broken one," Foo-Foo McCool muttered as much to himself as aloud.

"Your time's up here, ain't it?"

"About. I figured I'd hang on until we get into Nashville next week and then see what happens."

"You feel like giving a farewell performance tonight? Your gal there seems to think one's in order."

"She's not my gal, but she could be if she wanted to. Yeah, I feel like kickin' some ass my damned self, now that you mention it. Not sure I can get my head in the right place, though. Think I'll drop a couple of pinks to ease me on down the road. Want some?"

"Maybe one. You know how I get between speed and Turkey, man."

"Yeah, well you'll need a couple of these little shits, my man. I took one the other night, and it didn't do diddly squat except make me sweat! Nice of Preach to provide 'em, but he needs to check into a new connection. Get some consistency."

"Well pass 'em aroun' and let's *get down!*" Mellow Man said with a smile, looking forward to a good session.

And a good session it was. After the usual opening number by the organist, which was about the gospel equivalent of elevator muzak, the Hallelujah Choir opened up in earnest. Their newest member stood at one end of the bottom row mouthing the words inexpertly and struggling to breathe without exposing herself completely. Thelma was feeling the full impact of her accidental dose of speed, augmented by the catalyst Wild Turkey.

She attempted, successfully, some of the most impressive baton tosses, twirls, flourishes, and gyrations ever witnessed by human eyes. The crowd began to interrupt the choir with its *ooohs!* and *aaahs!* at her antics. Her heart was beating like a trip hammer. Sparks seemed to fly between her fingertips and crackle like static in her ears. She had such an elated feeling she was honestly smiling and glowing with enthusiasm . . . too much enthusiasm.

When the choir hit the final note and held it for the lead in of Foo-Foo's synthesizer, she felt an invisible hand push her forward and out toward the audience for her usual part of the intro. Instead, she picked up the cue of the music and moved forward with it.

Brother Ray-Bob was just putting the finishing touches on his ledger at the time, well aware that his intro music had run through its obligatory eight bars in escalating fashion. He was also aware that the band would do an additional eight bars when his sound engineer gave them the sign that he wasn't yet ready. The extra wait would add emphasis to his entrance, probably tack another thirty seconds onto his ovation and maybe even bring the collection of bumpkins and clods to their feet! He smiled smugly at the thought, drew an extra line under Rolly Klotz's name, then rose to go greet his adoring audience.

He paused in front of the full-length mirror on his door long enough to insure that his hair and tie were just so and to reflect upon the afternoon's frolic with his new groupie, Bambi. *She was perfect,* he thought. *Just the right amount of body and soul, particularly body, and not brain one. Perfect.* He cleared his throat and started to say his opening line, just to prepare himself. As his lips began to move, however, he heard it in two-part harmony—the up-scale voice coming to him via the main PA system!

"GOD, has a message . . . FOR YOU!" Brother Ray-Bob and Thelma said in unison.

His brow furrowed into a deeply knit frown, and the hairs at the back of his neck pressed against his shirt collar like quills on a pissed-off porcupine. His mouth dropped open in shock, then slammed shut with a moist *plop!* In panic now, he slammed through his door and raced out into the gathering darkness.

". . . HE is your SAL-VA-SHUN! HE is your GLO-RY! Through HIM, we ALL canfindabetterlife," Thelma spoke huskily into a hand-held microphone, uttering the words with eyes closed and in perfect mimicry of Brother Ray-Bob.

The crowd *Amened, Hallelujahed,* and *Gloryed* with enthusiasm at each passage. At first they didn't know what to think of her, and neither did the choir or the band. The sound engineer sat on the sidelines slack-jawed, his eyes fixed somewhere between the top of the tent and Jupiter. The lighting engineer, however, recognized each syllable and translated it into shifts of color and intensity. The lights, he noticed, played wonderfully off a light film of perspiration on Thelma's heaving chest and reflected up onto her face to form the halo-like aura he'd been trying to achieve with Ray-Bob for the past four years.

Brother Ray-Bob screeched to a sawdust scattering halt at the rear of the tent, started to mount his forklift up to the pulpit, then decided against it.

Foo-Foo and Mellow Man got caught up in Thelma's performance. The words sounded so much more believable coming out of her mouth than they had the first ten or so times they'd heard them. The lights had all been shifted to center stage now, so they didn't see Brother Ray-Bob arrive in the wings. Didn't see the animal fury in his darting eyes or the collection of spittle at each corner of his mouth, which now worked in silent curses.

She was usurping his words, all right, and she was putting them out in a much faster pace than he would have, was putting the argument out there, citing the scriptures, but not playing the audience! She'd run through it in half-time, but she wasn't lingering on the passages that tended to loosen the congregation's purse strings as well as its heart.

He foresaw a dismal collection on the second pass of the plates and, foremost, he foresaw trouble with the network people. In horror he noted that they were in attendance, right where he'd ordered them seated in the center of the audience among a dozen professional "fans" he'd sprinkled in the audience to hype response, and . . . horror of all horrors! . . . they were hanging on her every word. My *every word!* his mind screamed. *Damn that bitch anyway!*

With relief he heard the closing words of this segment and knew that the music would soon start, and the girls would trot out the collection baskets and pass among the audience. He waved at the lighting engineer until he caught his attention, scowled at the pleasure written on the man's face, then pointed to the overhead lights while drawing his other forefinger across his throat in the classic "cut" signal. The lights faded over Thelma until just a blue spotlight played on her lower chin and bosom, just enough to retain the halo effect the lighting man was so reluctant to kill entirely.

Thelma turned to the band, smiled happily, exhilaration in her every motion, and yelled, "Hit it!"

Foo-Foo's synthesizer droned out a note just below the range of the human ear and slowly rose to a growl and then a mellow bass note that could only be called sweet. Mellow Man's thumb caressed the *G* string of his guitar while his foot rose gently, allowing the pedal of his distortion unit to rise with the pitch of the note. The drummer punctuated the marriage of the two sounds at their apogee with a series of rifts that brought the scalps of everyone in the audience to the tautness of his snare drum.

Lights came up backstage, and the Hallelujah Choir opened their throats and gave forth their best rendition to date of the stirring hymn. The blue spotlight faded reluctantly, leaving Thelma and the lower stage in darkness. She began to walk toward the band feeling full of life and truly happy. Brother Ray-Bob chose this moment of relative darkness to dash across the stage.

Thelma looked radiant as she held her arms out to her sides and curtsied toward Foo-Foo and Mellow Man. Foo acknowledged her with a grin and a nod, Mellow Man by tilting the neck of his guitar toward her like it was a rifle then running a high string down the neck in a descending lick that highlighted the voices. The audience could see the honest joy on all their faces as they weaved in time to the music under the soft glow of the red monitor lights on the amplifiers.

The audience felt the joy in their own hearts, too, felt a part of what was going on on stage, felt a part of the human race in an honest, clean, fashion that all hellfire-and-brimstone preachers fear. They felt like giving of themselves, in terms of brotherly love rather than the filthy lucre. Then they felt confused and shocked as Thelma disappeared abruptly from the red glow.

"Give me *that,* you *bitch*!" Ray-Bob hissed after he'd snatched her back into the relative darkness of the stage, then wrung the microphone from her hand.

"What . . . ?"

"What? *What?* That's what I'd like to know!" he all but shouted into her face, spraying her with a fine mist of saliva. "What the hell do you think you're doing?"

The answer crystallized in her mind and zipped at the speed of light in overdrive to her tongue.

"I'm doing my farewell performance, you sanctimonious COCKSUCKER!" she retorted, the last word coming out as a shout.

Brother Ray-Bob cringed at the shriek of her voice, knowing well it had carried for at least the first two rows. He instinctively clenched his hands, yet didn't feel the flush-mounted power switch on the microphone in his sweaty hand as it slid the quarter inch from death to life.

"You damned *right,* you are! That, sugarpuss, was preordained! I can do quite well without your prissy ass, you know. You've got *too big for your britches,* missy, and around here there's only room enough for *one* star, and you know *damned well* who that's going to be, now don't you? Bet your sweet

250

ass! And speaking of your ass, I hope you noticed your replacement up there tonight."

The voices of the Hallelujah Choir faltered briefly, confused at the new voice joining their own and barely able to make out the words over the sound of the band. Folks sitting nearest the speakers heard it all in clarity and uttered little choking sounds. The network lady thought perhaps she had hallucinated the word *Cocksucker,* but knew damned well she'd heard *damned well*!

Ray-Bob still had a grip on Thelma's arm and was beginning to twist it to emphasize his words. Thelma uttered a little mewling sound that the microphone picked up and dutifully transmitted to the headset Foo-Foo was wearing to monitor the overall sound of the number. He turned to see what was the matter. Brother Ray-Bob's face was a mask of hate and frustration, Thelma's one of fear and loathing.

Whatever was going down, Foo didn't like it. He willed her to look his way, and the mental energy jumped between them immediately. Instead of crying out in pain or for help, she summoned all her fury as the voices of the choir faded to a finish. "Kick that mule!" she yelled.

Foo-Foo dialed up his volume, softened back his attack, pressed down on a pedal and took over the very atmosphere of the tent. The synthesizer sent up such a wail that even Ray-Bob was stunned. He released his grip on Thelma's arm and pressed his hands to his ears in an effort to block out the sound that rose uniformly for a second before starting to stutter and warble its way up the scale.

Mellow Man Marshall pulled a string out a half an inch from the neck of his guitar then released it; a colossal explosion rocked the peak of the tent, followed by a multi-octave rift that rose to greet the synthesizer's note like an antimissile missile. Together the notes played there for a moment in quivering counterpoint, then jelled into one note and softened down so quickly the audience could hear each other releasing the breaths they'd been unconsciously holding. The drummer broke in along with the rest, and they picked up the theme of the hymn in cut-time.

The audience caught on and began to clap and repeat the chorus of the tune. Some of the Hallelujah Choir fell from their trances in time to grab their collection baskets and hie down the aisles, smacking themselves on thigh and tush like they were tambourines. Brother Ray-Bob could stand no more. He fairly leaped the distance between himself and Foo-Foo, clenched his hand tight around the microphone to bash in the musician's face, then grabbed Foo by the arm to spin him around. Then . . . .

A soft rain was falling as the sun struggled, unsuccessfully, to make its existence known to the denizens of Memphis the next morning. Foo-Foo held an old army field jacket over both their heads to stave off the rain and marveled again at how good she looked now, even without makeup and her hair plastered down into strands. She still wore her gown of the night before, though now one could easily have wrung a gallon of rainwater from it. *She needs,* he thought, *to get out of those wet things before she catches a summer cold.*

"You want to go somewhere and warm up?"

"No," she said. "It won't be much longer now. You go, though, if you feel like you need to."

"Believe me, I welcome the cold right now!" he said, and they joined in brief laughter.

It was true, though. When Brother Ray-Bob had grabbed Foo's arm, he was just hitting a nice minor chord on the Korg while dialing up some *white noise* with his other hand. Ray-Bob should have known better than to do that while holding a live mike in his hand. The resultant shock had flowed through Foo-Foo warming the very cockles of his heart, but that was nothing compared to what Brother Ray-Bob received! The minister had time to shriek one loud "fuck!" which reverberated off the tent walls and out into the night before he flew backward and into a coma.

He'd live, of course, but he wouldn't be shaking a whole lot of hands for a while. In fact, he'd find himself answering a lot of questions once he woke up, for the police and ambulance that had come to fetch him insisted upon searching his quarters in case he was taking heart medication. The "medications" they found were hardly what one would think of as heart remedies, but they'd taken them along anyway.

"You're still sure you want to do this? I mean, he's in enough shit already, what with the booze and the pills and his little tirade and all."

"As ye sow, so shall ye reap!" Thelma said, then stuck out her chin. "I intend to see that he reaps plenty, too."

"Whatever you say. Might be a good way to start off your new show . . . ."

"*Our* new show!" she said, then smiled happily and cozied up next to Foo, seeking shelter under the coat. The book she clutched to her was being sheltered by her bosom. She held it in the fashion she imagined Moses held the Commandments.

"Right, *our* new show. Anyway, it might be a nice gesture to open up by forgiving Brother Ray-Bob. Be good press, you know. Besides, it'd go a long way in explaining why you . . . we . . . are in his time slot."

"I might do that, Foo. But first I'm gonna nail his ass to the wall! That way *he'll* have something to forgive, too."

"Sounds fair."

Further discussion was precluded by the arrival of a sickly green car that splashed its way up to the curb and discharged a scrawny accountant-type man who greeted them both hesitantly before unlocking the door and letting them in. A stylized eagle was emblazoned upon the door of the car and upon the glass door to the building. Above the eagle on each were the letters *IRS*.

29

For reasons only commercial producers would know, Josh was forced to wear hip waders for the credit card spot. It seemed idiotic to him, but the pay was good and this particular producer enjoyed a reputation as an ad genius. Josh realized fully that the main difference between genius and stupidity in this business was that genius had limits. Still, he had to seriously consider who of the viewing public would really believe he'd wear hip waders while fishing at the beach! This beach in particular.

He was standing ankle deep in the Pacific where it nipped in for a brief visit at the foot of the long hill that was Carmel, California. The beach consisted of a sandy crescent not more than two hundred yards long and was surrounded by scantily clad young lovelies who were waiting patiently for them to finish so they might get back to doing nothing in the sun. Doing nothing is an art form of its own in Carmel-By-The-Sea. The scenery (which probably included more than a few card-carrying Bambis) was marvelous, but the hot sun caused Josh's foot powder to run like gravy in the waders. He felt like he was walking on bologna slices.

"Take it away, Josh! Up, zoom! Go long on my signal and . . . action!"

"Hi there! Do you know me? I've probably made more out

of one fish than any man since Jonah, except maybe Steven Spielberg, of course. Still, people don't always recognize me when I'm on the road so I carry my American Express Card. With it I never have to worry about transportation, lodging, or whether or not I can catch my next meal. Do yourself a favor. Apply for an American Express Card today, and *don't leave home without it!* And don't feel too badly if you can't think of my name. Most folks don't remember who caught King Kong, either!"

In the background a crewman drew back and slapped a rubber swim fin against the placid water, then did a belly flop. The resultant sound was an ad man's idea of what a truly large fish would sound like jumping. Josh raised his eyebrows for the camera in a display of surprise or anticipation, then smiled a toothy smile that looked all the brighter against his deepening tan.

"Cut! We'll add card close-up graphics and the whale footage later. Let's do one more as a safety and call it a day, people. Josh, let's see some more teeth and crowsfeet around the eyes when you say 'King Kong,' okay sweets? And this time, just for luck, how about you toss your fishing thing toward the sound after you do your take into the camera, got it?" the producer said with true genius, leaving Josh to decipher what his "fishing thing" might be. The rod and reel he was holding had no line on it.

Following the session, they did some dry runs for other commercials to be shot the following week. The term *dry runs* seemed odd, too, like they would be simulating a bout of diarrhea or something. Notable among these, however, was a promo for a sportsman's confab being held just north in San Jose the next weekend, and Big Un was slated to be there! He reasoned that he really should stop by and pay his respects to his finny partner in all this and made a mental note to do so. Then he went to Sadi's pub and sat in the shade drinking Corona beer until the sun rode down the steep hill to sizzle out behind the watery horizon. The scene had a solemn beauty to it, a loneliness, and he knew well why.

He thought about phoning Pam, then he thought better of it.

It was already past eleven in the evening back in Dilbert's Forge and . . . .

Yes? And? a small voice with foul breath and sharp teeth asked from the recesses of his mind, then proceeded to answer its own questions. *And what if she's not at home? Hmmm? What then Mister Piscator? What if she's out making nice-nice with one of Dilbert Forge's leading eligibles? What then, sport?*

"Who?" he asked aloud, causing a waitress nearby to look his way only briefly before chalking it up to experience.

There's some strange people in this old world, her glance seemed to say, and working here I think I've met most of them.

Okay, I'll give you that one. the voice conceded. *But there's always Nashville and Clarksville, you know. Might be someone there with the right combination of abject poverty and shining future, not to mention a yen for fun in the sun! What about that, hmmm?*

Josh made a sour face. He didn't particularly like the sound of the voice, thinking perhaps it sounded a bit too much like Major Mike. Yet there *was* something to what it said. What if she was out with someone else, would he care? He didn't exactly stick around to debate her confusion over the money issue, did he?

No! You didn't! She did say she wanted to love you, you know. Is that what you're afraid of? When are you going to call her?

"Sort of soon, I think," he said aloud again, eliciting not so much as a flinch from anyone nearby but startling himself. He looked around sheepishly, then decided he'd have to do more than mumble to himself to draw attention in California.

Well, what about her? Gonna forget her and take up with one of the mush-minded models you've been working with? All depends on you, my boy. If you don't know what you want, then maybe you should consider that maybe Pam doesn't either!

"Shut up! I'll do something . . . soon. There's just a few things I need to finish first, and then I'll . . . well . . . I'll know when the time comes. A gesture of some sort, give her a chance to react. I don't know."

You're right, you don't. You also probably don't have a lot of time left. You know the old adage, my boy, "for want of a horse. . . ." But if you fart around and lose her and then discover that she means a lot to you, well, don't come running to me!

"You're going somewhere? Without me?"

Seems to be the popular thing to do, doesn't it? Look around, my boy. Thelma's off somewhere doing TV, records, and saving souls with Brother Hoo-Ha's Goodtime Hour, Pam's probably contemplating fleeing to the Sun Belt, Canebrake's down in Old Mexico baking his bones, and even the friggin' fish has an itinerary of his own.

"What about Slats?"

The erstwhile Mister Spivey's sitting back home until you stop gallivanting around the countryside and get back there to give him a little boost. It'll work, you know.

"What will?"

That little germ of an idea that's been growing in your pastoral little brain, that's what. Give yourself in to it. Roll with the flow! You've spent all your money, so what else do you have to lose?

"My mind?"

You're sitting here talking to yourself, my boy. There's them as would consider that tantamount to having lost it already. No, I think there's something else. Have you ever wondered what it would be like to be happy? I mean no shit, down-home, grinnin' like a mule eatin' sawbriars happy? Well, if you want that, you've got to do some happy-making of your own, and I think you know where to start, don't you?

"No."

You start where you are, here. Buy these good folks a beer, tell them you were just running some lines for tomorrow's session. Once they find out you're an actor of sorts (and face it, that's what you've become!) there's nothing weird enough you could do that would seem out of place. Make 'em happy. Then, tomorrow . . . .

"Yes?"
Yes!
"Bartender? A round for everyone, on me!"

Major Mike was faced with a decision. Big Un was responding well to treatment. He actually had begun to eat on his own now and moved across the big pool with majestic sweeps of his broad tail. The professors resented Mike's presence and scowled openly. The fish was back up to twenty pounds again, a mere matter of dehydration they said, though how an animal that lives under water could become dehydrated was beyond Major Mike's ken. No, the fish definitely looked like he was up to traveling, and he told them so.

They told him a number of things, most of them uncomplimentary, and finished by swearing the fish would be dead within a week if confined to the claustrophobic display case. This caused Major Mike to pause and do some quick arithmetic.

Ten thousand dollars minimum for Big Un's appearance in San Jose, plus another five thousand for an ad layout there at the same time, then another ten grand for his appearance in Seattle. If he lived that long. If not, why there was the twenty thousand bid by the taxidermist in Minneapolis for the honor of embalming him! These trips back and forth to Florida were getting to be a nuisance anyway, not to mention the expense, so the decision was quick in coming: they were leaving. The profs protested, of course, to which Major Mike merely fanned the Tennessee permit for keeping the animal. Even they knew the law was the law.

Brother Ray-Bob Thomas awoke to the sound of voices. They filtered in from the hallway and mentioned him by name from time to time. The gist of their conversation was that he'd not be fit for travel for at least three days, which came as no surprise to him. Then someone addressed one of the speakers as Sheriff and his interest sharpened. The events of the previous night slowly came flooding back on little spiked feet, and he wondered what he was going to do.

What are you going to DO? the voice asked with a snicker. *Why, I suggest you go back to doing what got you into all this mess.*

"What?" Ray-Bob croaked weakly.

Remember what Hattie and Gert always said?

"You mean . . . that I can sing?"

Yeah, sing. Do it.

"Okay," he said, then fell into his first peaceful sleep in years.

30

Pam pulled her last load from the dryer and sat on the edge of her bed folding the items that would be packed or stored. The other items, curtains mostly, she set aside to be dealt with later. *Might as well rent the place out,* she reasoned. Her aunt had been frugal, so the house had been free and clear since before the depression and there was really no reason not to keep it inhabited in her absence. She wondered how it was that a house like this could remain watertight and tidy while people lived in it, yet houses of the same or later vintage tended to just fall in within a few years if abandoned. It seemed as though the structure and its inhabitants enjoyed a symbiotic relationship that was crucial to the building's very existence.

Her great aunt's photo watched her from atop her chest of drawers. The photo was the last she had taken before retiring from nearly fifty years of teaching. It had *Schoolday Friends* emblazoned across the bottom, though the "strictly business" countenance depicted didn't really look all that friendly.

FrankenKat gamboled across the back yard in hot pursuit of a purple martin whose shadow slid lazily across the ground ahead of him. The bird was a good hundred feet up, but to the feline's lone eye it could have been just four. The chase was cut short by a tomato cage that happened to be in the cat's way. FrankenKat bounced off, shook himself back into some semblance of order, then stalked off indignantly. Pam smiled at this and wondered again if she should take the cat with her. Above her aunt other pictures smiled back at her, causing her own smile to fade into a kewpie doll pout that most would have found attractive; it looked nothing at all like a dog's rectum, chapped or otherwise.

She was saving the photos, a pinking-sheared collection of slick magazine ads, for last. Whether she should pack them, store them, or just consign them to the trash was a matter she wanted to give some more thought. The pout degraded into a frown as she asked herself questions she knew had no immediate answers. Perhaps Josh would hunt her up in Nevada, would ask her to explain and point out the huge donation he'd made largely at her suggestion.

Perhaps he'd be angry at her for ruining his life, or perhaps he'd be hurt and walk out of *her* life. Of the two possibilities, she found his anger the more palatable.

All the demands for red Porsches had merely been a ruse, a prodding in hope that someone would finally have courage enough to tell her to get stuffed, someone with enough backbone to demand something of her, to force his will upon her own. She had honestly felt Josh Jackson would be that someone until his check came through demonstrating that he, too, would bow to her every whim. The disappointment had been a shock, one that caused her to actually laugh out loud, costing her her job at the bank and making the offer in Vegas seem almost fated. The thing with Josh had come on too strong and too quick to be real anyway. Still . . . .

"Face it, kid," she said to the mirror. "What you were really looking for was a father figure, huh?"

Her image nodded slowly.

"Do all orphans go through this? Did Josh?" she wondered. Realizing she would probably never know, she uttered a sigh so deep it threatened to end in a sob, then went back to packing and folding.

Across town, which encompassed a distance that could easily be covered afoot while holding one's breath, Rolly Klotz was busily toting up his pre-lunch transactions and cursing. The temporary help he'd been forced to take on was costing him plenty and was inefficient in every regard. Her handwriting was near illegible, and she had yet to arrive before opening time. The tinny jingle of the bell on the main door told him something else: she hadn't locked up when she left for lunch. A frown pressed his chins into accordion folds as he rose and marched resolutely around the corner of his office to shoo-off the latecomer.

His mouth fell open when he saw the group assembled outside the teller's cage. He recognized one of them as the bank inspector who had done his biannual check the week after Easter. The others looked equally bookish yet had a grim set to their faces that said *authority*. One of these stepped forward and reached into his hip pocket to produce a flip wallet. Rolly expected a badge to be flipped out at him and was ready to panic. Instead the wallet contained a laminated ID card with an eagle logo emblazoned across its background. He panicked anyway.

"Mister Klotz? I'm Gerald Blassingame of the IRS. We got a few questions we'd like to ask you, sir. I believe you already know John here. He'll need to go over your books."

"What in the name of God is this all about?" Klotz answered, his voice rising to a pitch.

"An interesting choice of words, Mister Klotz," Blassingame said with a smile the color of skim milk. "In fact, that's exactly what this is all about!"

The phone in his office jingled twice while Klotz gasped to catch his breath. His eyes wallowed in their sockets, and his blood pressure rose to new heights, causing a shrill roar in his ears.

"You might want to answer that. If it just happens to be your lawyer, I suggest you get him on over here," Blassingame said matter-of-factly.

Klotz nodded slowly, turned, and walked back into his office. The phone rang again while he watched it. The sound sent a shudder up his spine as he considered what might be on the other end. Brother Ray-Bob perhaps, calling to warn him belatedly that he'd spilled the beans while under general anesthesia or something. The ringing held all the dread of a rattlesnake singing in the night and was as insistent. Taking a deep breath, he snatched the phone from its cradle and grunted a greeting. Transcontinental static filled the earpiece.

"Hello? I'd like to speak with Miss Swift, please," came Josh Jackson's voice over the line.

Klotz grimaced at the voice, recognizing it instantly. It also led him to a conclusion that, while inaccurate, seemed only too logical at the moment: somehow Pamalou Swift had dropped a dime on him! She had had access to most records and transactions of the bank. Probably he had gotten careless, and she had seen some of his checks to Brother Ray-Bob and made the connection. Maybe she'd gotten wind of her trust fund! Whatever the reason, he felt certain that somehow she was to blame. The men waiting outside the glass-walled office saw Klotz as his face evolved from the twisted mask of terror it had been into something far more ugly.

"She says she doesn't want to speak with you, Mister Jackson," Klotz said after a pause. "In fact, she says she *never* wants to speak to you again! Good day, sir."

A small victory, he thought, and not much considering the battle now at hand, but it gave him a brief glow in his heart. The glow winked out as his eyes fell upon the telephone book, the one covered in a plastic sleeve that bore a graphic depiction of the Blalock Brothers quarry and kilns. *They* were the ones who'd put him onto Brother Ray-Bob Thomas and his scam! *They* were the ones at fault! He'd cooperate with the investigation, throw the brothers and that smug-mouthed preacher to the wolves and probably get off with a fine and probation. Yeah, that's what he'd do. Smiling a far more pleasant smile now, he stepped to the door and nodded to the men waiting there.

"Gentlemen? Let's get started," he said.

A continent away, Josh sat on the edge of his bed and pondered what to do next. A flurry of emotions ran through his mind, starting with shock, progressing to hurt, then settling on anger and fatigue. Today he'd already done some tuna fishing off the coast, a guest shot on "American Sportsman" that he'd had to put off twice due to Major Mike not leaving adequate travel time between gigs. The fishing had been only marginally successful, but the lone yellowfin they'd caught was put back in and boated repeatedly to satisfy the hungry eye of the camera before being retired as steaks, some of which he was forced to take with him.

And next? Nothing for two whole days. There was the San Jose thing to attend, a promotion idea he wanted to get to Slats, and he needed to check on Canebrake. *It's all beginning to come together now,* he thought while watching a pair of malcontents on the television arguing about their upcoming wrestling match with such agitation that physical violence seemed imminent. *Odds are they arrived at the studio in the same cab and will depart the same way,* he thought. Another thought entered his mind then, or perhaps it was the voice again only whispering this time instead of shouting.

For want of a shoe, the horse was lost. For want of a horse . . . .

Josh picked up the phone receiver again and dialed Slats's number. He got the recording, of course, so left a thumbnail sketch of what he planned to do. In retrospect, he was glad he'd gotten the recording because it eliminated any possible arguments or discussion. Sink or swim, it was solely upon his shoulders now, and that was the way he wanted it. If the voice had been right, and he had no reason to doubt it, it was time he struck a blow for himself.

The next couple of steps would be critical. He would possibly anger a bunch of people and could well leave himself even more alone in the world than he already was. Quickly, before he could change his mind, he phoned Major Mike's office in Nashville expecting to end up speaking to yet another recorder. Instead a secretary answered.

"Hi! Is Major Mike in?" he asked pleasantly.

"I'm afraid not. He's out on the coast. May I ask who's calling and take a message?"

"Sure. This is Josh Jackson."

264

"Oh! Hello, Mister Jackson. Mike said he'd try to get in touch with you while you're both out there. He has your tentative schedule for the next few weeks and wants to go over some contracts with you. Let's see now, you're staying at the Parmelia Hotel in Monterey, right?"

"Right."

"Well, I'd be expecting Mike to call sometime tonight or tomorrow morning. He should have gotten there about noon your time, but he'll no doubt want to rest up a bit to acclimate to the time shift. Was there any message in case he should call?"

"Yes, there is."

"Okay, go ahead. I'm ready."

"Good. I think you'll be able to remember this without writing it down. Just say 'You're fired!' Thank you, and goodbye."

Next he phoned the main exchange in Reynosa and left word for Canebrake to call him back. To his surprise, the call came within the hour. Canebrake's voice sang through the wires, losing none of its melodious twang this time. Josh found himself all but laughing at the Cajun's unique brand of Spanish patois.

"*Como está,* you stud."

"I think that's *usted,* 'Brake. You taking up the local tongue, are you?"

"Done been speakin' some kind o' Spanish all my days, Jackson. We Cajuns got to do all dem lang-iges 'cause we done been run outa so many places, don' you know?"

Canebrake pronounced Spanish as something approximating "spinich."

"Well, how's it coming down there today?"

"Done got de phone nailed on de wall, fack here's where I'm a-callin' from rat now! Place look plumb good too, done tole you dat. Got dem ole trees up an' de new trees down. She be ready whenever you are, boss man."

"That might be sooner than I thought, 'Brake. Any trouble with anyone down there?"

"Nope. It's downright amazin' jest how little shit folks give a man what's packin' a choppin' axe on his shoulder, you know dat? You jes' brought yoreself on down here, *mon ami*. We be ready."

"Good. I'll see you real soon."

"By that way, Jackson, are you done sure you want dat sign put up dare? I mean, dem ain't really words you know. Not in no Span-itch lang-ige, dey ain't."

"Yep. Just like I spelled it out for you."

"You got it. *Abiento!* uh . . . *Adiós!*"

"Adios."

No sooner had he hung up than the phone rang again. He was expecting it to be Canebrake with some forgotten item and welcomed it since he'd neglected to ask the new phone number or even what name it was registered under. Instead, it was the hotel chef advising him that his tuna steaks would be ready for consumption at six, unless that was inconvenient. Josh assured the chef that six would be fine and rang off. He showered, dressed, then loaded into his rental car for the short drive up to San Jose.

For want of a horse . . . . the voice chided him on the way, causing him to stop and make yet another series of phone calls. When he was finished, he felt much better.

*   *   *

Big Un was in his portable case awaiting the final load of water being poured into his display case on the rotunda. He didn't like the sterile feel and bland texture of the distilled water. It lacked the body and minerals of honest creek or lake water and didn't support soluble oxygen as well as perhaps it should. This was largely due to it being situated beneath a tent on a sweltering California day, and it remained warm despite the addition of two bags of Igloo Ice Cubes. The truck that brought his water was an electric green with the shimmering Sparklets *sign on the back dancing to the tune of some unfelt breeze.*

Big Un couldn't care less. He was swimming, or actually sitting was more accurate since he'd long since lost the will to swim, at the bottom of the glass slowly fanning his tail. With each sweep, little coils of feces looped-the-loop behind him. The water was foul and iron-tasting, its constant cascade of bubbles rising from all four aerators with a sound he'd come to detest. Hesitant hands came for him, and he lacked the energy to resist. By now he was conditioned to being held by these beings, but this time he was relatively certain it was to be brief, probably just the transfer to the larger tank. He was wrong.

*   *   *

Josh pulled up to the main entrance of the Valley Area Sportsman's Exposition and began casting an eye about for Major Mike. He checked in at the main registration tent and learned that Major Mike was attending an exhibitors' cocktail party in town and would not likely be back until the following day. He also learned that there was a photo session in progress on the back lot and was granted a VIP badge so that he might visit the source of his fame.

In his mind's eye he saw Big Un on his pedestal, the massive jaws working, bringing cries of awe from all who witnessed him. He felt a tinge of something approaching envy for the big fish, coupled with a grain of resentment that Major Mike had not seen fit to advise him of his plans or to include him in the revenues as witnessed by his latest statement from the Nashville office. He planned to take this matter up with Major Mike later and maybe give him a pop in the jaw to boot.

These thoughts occupied Josh's mind so fully that he almost walked right past the scene of the photo session. At first he couldn't fully accredit his eyes, then found himself near blinded with rage. A shapely model wearing cut-off jeans with a scalloped pattern like Daisy Mae's in the comic strips, was hunkered down next to a campfire while a photographer snapped and ground out yards of film around her. In a huge skillet next to the fire, Big Un lay gasping weakly. The photographer, an oily man with a ballcap screwed down over his forty-dollar haircut, the cap's bill pointing incongruously down his back, pressed an eye to one of a video camera and began barking out orders.

"Dry the fish a little more, Roger, sweetheart, we're still

picking up some flare from it. Debbie? This time grab the handle with *both* hands, sugar! Can't have you spilling the damned fish in the fire again, so if you can't manage, we'll just have to get someone stronger. Chaz? I want you to pan the pan, then zoom up and in to cover Debbie as she leans over . . . lots of tits, lots of tits! All right now, people, let's make a . . . *umph!*"

Josh jerked the photographer around so quickly that the bill of his hat maintained its relative position in space and was now pointed the same direction as his face, albeit over his eyes.

"What the . . . ?" he got out before Josh released him roughly and charged toward the campfire.

Debbie took several deep breaths as he approached, the swell of her silicon-enhanced breasts peeking up like Kilroys in the open space below her neck. She uttered a small frightened squeak as he stopped in front of her and bent at the waist as if to grab her. In her hurry to crawl away she burst the seam of her tight cut-offs. Totally without grace now, she scurried off on all fours.

Josh ignored them all and pulled Big Un from the skillet. The eyes, as big as quarters, rolled pathetically and seemed to transmit an accusation at him that he took to heart.

"What the hell do you think you're *doing*?" the oily man screeched. "Someone call security! You! Unhand that fish and get out of here!"

Josh snarled and began gently flicking bits of grass and cinder from Big Un's underside.

"I'm taking him out of here, that's what! Who the hell said you could kill this fish anyway?" Josh spat out at him.

"We're not *killing* the damned thing! Just *shooting* it, that's all. But what is it to you?"

"I'm the one who caught it, that's what."

The man resituated his ballcap, feeling on sturdier ground now that the wild man had identified himself.

"Well! You no doubt know we have a contract then. So if you'll be kind enough to release the fish, we can get on with our work and get him back into his precious water!"

"Forget your contract! You can take that up with Major

Mike. For now, I'm taking this fish with me, and heaven help anyone fool enough to get between me and the gate!"

The director winced and fell silent. The look on Josh's face said murder, though for whom was a matter of speculation. Debbie stood at last, assessed the damage to her wardrobe, and backed up against the fender of a black Jeep they were using as a backdrop. The California sun had been at work on the black metal, though, so when it met with the tender section of her nether regions two of the only six untanned square inches on her whole body tried to seize to the surface. Debbie howled with pain and went dancing around the campfire fanning her fanny. Josh escaped virtually unnoticed, collected Big Un's portable case, and split.

Josh was not in his room when a red-faced Major Mike showed up three hours later and pounded upon the door. Major Mike was more than just upset. He was still tipsy from the cocktail party and more than a little panicked by the threats of legal action the director of the ill-fated cookware commercial had yelled at him in a high falsetto voice. "Breach of contract," he'd screamed. "Mental anguish, not to mention a second-degree burn of the tush, on behalf of Debbie." All charges with substance. He knocked once more, then backed up to charge it in hopes of crashing the door down. Once he'd backed off, however, his eyes fixed upon a sight that turned his ire into anguish. Next to the door sat a silver serving dish, and upon it rested what could only be fish bones . . . very *large* fish bones!

Major Mike was now faced with two certainties. He had lost the fish as a silent partner, and he still had several contracts he would have to break with the resultant loss of income. A quick call to his office confirmed another certainty he'd more-or-less assumed yet still thought he might correct with an eye-to-eye meeting with Jackson. During the next four days, he haunted the hallways of the Parmelia while changing his own lodgings daily to avoid a bevy of summons servers. At last he had to face the facts and do what he'd always done when business deals went awry: he ran off.

269

31

Pam looked at the phone one last time before she left. It wouldn't ring now. It couldn't. She had held off on having it disconnected in hopes Josh would call, which of course he hadn't. Idly, she licked a tear, tasting its bitterness. In the back yard FrankenKat was on the stalk again, a bluejay this time. While she watched, he mounted the scaly bark of a small oak tree and shinnied up to the first branch, the bluejay scolding him solidly every inch of the way before flitting off to a neighboring tree.

Now the cat was at a disadvantage. Her heart leapt into her throat as she saw him crouching as if to jump. Lacking the depth perception afforded by two eyes, the fool would probably leap down and break his neck. She ran to the back door to try and dissuade him.

"Kitty, kitty, kitty?" she yelled in a high voice. "Wait! Jump down onto the fence first, or wait until I can get a ladder! Please?"

FrankenKat eyed her curiously, then uttered a plaintive "Yeeow?"

Pam's heart was thumping loudly. The sky in the east was the color of ashes, in west the color of embers as the summer sun sank slowly into evening. *It'll still be bright in Las Vegas,* she thought, then noticed the thumping sound coming from the greenbelt behind the short fence.

FrankenKat let loose another "Yeoow!" and fixed his monocular gaze on something past the fence. Pam let her eyes leave the stranded puss and follow his eye toward the sound. A small gasp escaped her throat as a flash of white appeared over the fence.

The horse's hooves dug into the soft earth of her garden, sending great gouts of mulch and loam into the air behind it. Josh reeled in the saddle as he reined the beast to a halt beside her. Pam's mouth hung open like a mailbox that had just been cherry-bombed, and FrankenKat's tail stood fuzzed out like a bottle brush. The horse whinnied and rolled one pink-rimmed eye toward her.

"This is as close to a white charger as I could find on short notice, babe!" he laughed happily, then leaned out to lift her easily onto his lap. Josh pulled her to him for a kiss, which she returned with enthusiasm. By the time their lips parted, FrankenKat had relaxed and was studiously scratching his back with one hind leg.

"If you can get packed within the next couple of hours . . ." he began.

"I don't think we'll need two hours to get packed," Pam interrupted. "Where are we going, if I may be so bold?"

"Why, we're going to follow the sun! Lucky for you, I found where it lives year 'round. Now, I'll tie up this beast while you gather your things, quit your job, and trip your little circuit breakers."

"Is this . . . really happening?" she wondered, eyes wide and spilling fresh tears now.

"Just like in the movies. In fact, we can even ride off into the sunset if you like."

"I'd like! But first we need to get that cat out of that tree."

"Bullshit."

"Pardon?"

"Bullshit! When's the last time you saw a cat skeleton up in a tree? Slats can come by for him tomorrow and bring him and the rest of the critters down later. Right now I don't want to think of anything except you and me, got it?"

"If you say so," she purred, then laced her fingers together behind his neck and laid her head upon his shoulder.

The horse, a ten-year-old plow mare he'd rented for the day, chose this tender moment to let go a huge bubble of flatulence that rang like a shotgun blast through the still air. Josh wondered absently if Canebrake could have sniffed and known what size collar the mare wore. They'd meet Canebrake soon enough, and he'd probably have some more explaining to do. As he was letting Pam slide down from his lap he felt the horse stiffen beneath him and discharge a steaming stack of pellets, which were about the size of Brussels sprouts.

"You need anything while I'm inside?" she asked from the doorway.

"Wouldn't happen to have a seven-iron, would you?" he replied.

32

Unlike the land where the sun lives year-round, Dilbert's Forge passed through summer and into fall. School kids decried the fading of summer loud and long as the school bells again sounded, teachers screeched chalk upon blackboards making student bodies cringe, and the high school coach sobered up long enough to select twenty-odd boys who hadn't flunked the previous year and set out to do battle, or martyrship, on the gridiron. The twirling squad this year would be below par, due to their usual mentor being otherwise occupied, but the cheerleaders were buxom and loud and this kept the alumni happy. No one thought to ask if any of the cheerleaders were named Bambi.

There had been, however, many other topics of discussion around town over the past several months. Banker Klotz had pulled the Blalock brothers down with him and, despite their lawyers' impassioned pleas, all had received healthy prison terms. Rolly Klotz was interned in Brushy Mountain State Penitentiary, where he was promptly raped.

The experience had been life changing, and Rolly was now known around the exercise yard as Rollina. He had shed nearly fifty pounds and now affected a wig, fake eyelashes, and a bizarre collection of mismatched frocks. When word filtered back to Dilbert's Forge, no one was really surprised. In fact, several of his former classmates made a point of telling everyone that they'd suspected he was "different" ever since they were in the second grade playing leap-frog. Something about him never jumping high enough.

The bank's charter was picked up by an institution in a neighboring county and operated as a branch for several years until a young black man named Sampson graduated college with a degree in banking and came home to assume its stewardship. The Blalocks spent their time in the prison at Only, Tennessee, and Brother Ray-Bob Thomas, by virtue of his crimes in many states and felonious behavior where the government was concerned, went to a Federal Prison in Georgia.

There he set up a prison ministry and wrote a best-selling book, about just how his halo had slipped down until it became a noose, entitled *Let Us Prey*. The legitimate clergy was pleased, but no fewer than twenty television ministers and several hundred jack-leg evangelists rallied to pan the book or accuse Brother Ray-Bob of being the AntiChrist, thereby assuring a sellout of *Let Us Prey*'s first printing and keen interest in the movie rights. Next to being banned in Boston, having a work damned by television ministers is the best thing that can happen to a publisher, and Brother Ray-Bob's was no exception. His royalty account zoomed to over six figures in less than six months, proving that crime pays every bit as well as virtue, or feigned virtue anyway.

But a change had come over Brother Ray-Bob. During the trials he sang like a mockingbird, naming names, dates, places, and severely depleting some smaller towns of their business men and officialdom. In his book he chronicled his life on the evangelistic circuit from his early days with Reverend Clay, which included a candid, if sordid, tale of sexual abuse at the old man's hands, right up to his "seeing the light" his last night on stage.

He cited a quirk of fate as his genesis in the healing business. Shortly after the unmourned passing of Reverend Clay, the old converted Bluebird school bus the troop traveled in managed to twist a gear cluster in its rear end while fording a stream en route to a brush arbor that was to be their last engagement before breaking up. Their paucity of funds found its remedy in the eyes of their bus driver, Thurlow Beddows. Thurlow kept folks entertained with his impressions of Ben Turpin, the silent movie star who actually had his eyes insured with Lloyd's of London . . . against their ever coming *uncrossed*! Thurlow could cross one at a time, or both, and hold that pose for minutes at a time.

Following the service that fateful night, Ray-Bob called forth any who would have him pray for their special cases, and Thurlow was third in line. It was dramatic. When the hat was passed following an altar call, the congregation coughed up a lordly sum and a junk yard operator donated a new rear end for the bus. Not only that, but the brush arbor was extended for three more nights and grew in attendance and offerings each night.

After the first time, it was only too easy for the healing bit to get out of hand. Each member of the troop developed, and divested themselves of, a wide range of maladies to the delight of crowds. In addition, real members of the audience came forward with real problems, some of which they left at the altar as so much psychosomatic baggage. Then, in Mobile, at the last scheduled show of both the season and his planned career, an old woman staggered forward so stooped that bystanders often offered to help her find whatever it was they thought she'd dropped. Ray-Bob honestly tried reaching out to this, his last, petitioner. And it *worked!* He felt the sweet heat as it flowed down through his arms and hands and into the old woman. He heard her bones creak as she rose to her former height and stood before him, her eyes afire with elation. And he was hooked.

Once he'd allowed himself to be pulled back onto the road, he had to do whatever it took to keep going. If another tent preacher had cured a game knee, he healed polio. If whoever went before allowed the lame to walk, he made the paralyzed dance. All the while he hungered for the feeling, but soon he was feeling only his ego. He began to feel something akin to the raw chicken-eating geek in a sideshow, yet realized that people threw money at that geek and that his hours were pretty much his own. To ease his conscience, he built the housing project for the poor, then ran into Satan incarnate in the form of some lawyers who took even more shortcuts than he did. The rest followed as inexplicably as water down a hill.

Now he was wealthy again, despite all he'd done. No, because of it! How easy it would have been to resume his old ways; but he didn't. He plowed his royalty checks into The Shepherd's Acres and even had a small chapel built on its grounds. He received hundreds of letters from people whose lives had changed for the better after attending his services and came to feel the fullfilment that had been missing while he herded the bloated juggernaut that had been his road show. The best, though, was a letter he received from the old woman in Mobile; she was still getting around just fine and mentioned him prominently in her prayers each evening. He even sent back the check she'd enclosed.

Thelma took up with Foo-Foo, and together they merged the Hallelujah Choir with his old band to form something called the Holy Rock'n'Rolly Gut Bucket. The Bucket featured Mellow Man Marshall playing a highly synthesized guitar in the shape of a cross, Foo-Foo on keyboards, and a collection of other rock notables all scrubbed, sequined, and sanctified. Foo-Foo did new arrangements to old standards, laying in a strong bass line and some lively licks in place of the chorus from time to time, and Thelma put out the Word between numbers in her airy, little-girl voice.

Soon they had a youth following second only to pizza, and their television show, in Brother Ray-Bob's old time slot but expanded to a whole hour, routinely drew a thirty share. To the producers a thirty share was as clear a sign of divine intervention as a burning bush might be to others. Thelma was awarded the Golden Pulpit Award in the Best Newcomer category and finally got to stand before a large group of adoring people and give the speech she'd memorized for the Catfish Festival many years before.

With all these subjects to occupy the minds and tongues of Dilbert's Forgians, it is only natural that on this particular December day, a scant two days before Christmas, the topic of discussion at Carl's Barbershop, Bar, and Grill was . . .

"Dogs!" Amory Johnson averred in response to Carl's question about which was the smartest animal. "Dogs by a damned sight!"

Carl slackened his grip on his customer's head and stared off into space to consider Johnson's opinion. Then he reached back with his clipper hand and lifted a semi-cold Budweiser to his lips, drained the remainder of the can in one long adam's apple-jogging swallow, then crushed the can in one hand and the customer's neck in the other.

Carl was proud of having the first wet barbershop in the state since prohibition days, but then most anywhere from the feed store to the funeral parlor could get a liquor license now that the new mayor was in office. In fact, it was nearly mandatory! The hue and cry that would normally have gone up from the more fundamentalist local churches was never heard due to their unwillingness to come forward so soon after their favorite son, Brother Ray-Bob, was carted off to the hoosegow.

This arrangement wasn't without its disadvantages, of course. As witness to this, the current customer—indeed everyone in the room at present—looked like he'd had his hair cut with a Weedeater.

"How come dogs, Amory?" Carl slurred out while reaching as far as he could to fetch another Bud from a distant cooler, nearly dragging his customer out of the chair while doing so.

"'Cause dogs can overcome damned near anything. Why I had an old dog once, half beagle and half Walker he was, an' he up an' got into a steel trap down by the crick and had to gnaw off one leg to git out! An' you know somethin'? Ole Tripod there, he was still one of the finest squirrel dogs ever to bark up a hick'ry in these parts!"

A round of agreeing grunts and belches went up from those seated nearby, followed by a couple of throats being cleared.

"I'm inclined to believe that one, Amory," Jim Polson allowed in a voice somewhat muffled since it was strained through a huge cud of Rough Country Twist tobacco. "And you might just be old enough to remember my pappy's old rabbit dog, Sooner. You 'member him?"

"Can't say as I do, Jim," Johnson countered, a tad miffed at being called as witness to something that had to have occurred before he was even born.

"Well, anyhow, old Sooner was one hell of a rabbit dog. A Mississippi Beagle he was. Had ears so long he could roll over twice and look like a Roi-Tan cigar! Sooner got into a muskrat trap, too. Didn't slow him down a bit, no-sir! He'd still jump more rabbits than any dog in the country for the next couple of years and then, damned if he didn't up and get into *another* trap and lose t'other leg . . . on the same side! Well sir, pappy figured sure that'd be it for that dog and was downright thankful he'd got a couple of pups by Sooner out of an old bitch we had at the time. But you know what?"

No one knew, though several might have guessed.

"Once them young dogs commenced to huntin', ole Sooner just joined right in! Yessir, he'd lope along on the trail kinda leanin' to one side as he went and chase them rabbits like he always did. Only difference was he'd hafta lean up ag'in a tree to catch his breath now and then and he had one helluva time learnin' to balance on one leg while he took a piss."

The room was quiet. Even the customer forgot about his mangled hair, which by now looked something like the first tee at a very popular golf course, and stared off into space trying to picture Sooner on one leg—the force of the dog's urine no doubt causing him to pirouette like the ballerina on a music box. Several men took slugs from their beers, and the one seated in "amen" corner on the nail keg rose to rub circulation back into his thighs. Then he cleared his throat in such a harsh manner the others instinctively ducked.

"That there's one helluva dog, awright. Won't see many like that in a lifetime, an' that's a fact!" the keg sitter said in a solemn voice, made less sinister by the *S* his false teeth amply whistled.

The men nodded agreement with Mister Peevey's judgment and were about to dismiss the subject when he continued.

"We had one a whole lot like him when I's a boy, though.

278

Yessir, we shorely did. Dog was so nearsighted he'd back off into the livin' room to beg from the table! Poor little bastard, he shore did love to chase them rabbits, though. I recollect as how I damned nearly cried my eyes out the day it happened to him, 'course I's just a kid of a boy at the time, mind ye."

"What happened to him, Mister Peevey?" Carl asked while lowering his clippers to the scalp of his customer.

The customer tilted his head back to take a slug of his beer and deprived himself of a wide patch of hair above his right ear.

"Well-sir. 'Tweren't so much different from what happened to them other dogs, I don't reckon. 'Cept this'n came a-chasin' a swamp rabbit across a field Pa was a-mowin' and ran right under that blade mower before my pa could get it shut off! Clipped ever damned one of his legs off right smooth with his belly."

A symphony of sighs and clucking tongues went up around the room followed by heads wagging sadly back and forth. Amory Johnson broke the silence created when Mister Peevey paused for a drink.

"Bet that made yore daddy feel like shit, havin' to put that little dog down, huh?"

"Yeah, he felt poorly about it awright, but he didn't put him down. Ya see, we hadn't had a chance to breed this-here dog yet, and it seemed a right shame to let him ease out of the world without no pups to carry on his blood line. Pa, he got off'n the tractor in time to take some bailin' wire and tie off the dog's stumps and afore you know it, that dog was feelin' pretty good! We figured to breed him soon as one of our bitches came into season, an' until then I'd put him up in a wheelbarrow and push him around the place so he could feel like he was still more-or-less whole.

"He liked it so much he'd even wag his tail as we went along and bark at the other dogs and such. Even got to where I knew when he had to go and could lean that wheelbarrow up on one side so he could squirt through a knot hole."

Eyebrows went up all around the room, all except Carl's

customer who'd managed to lose his when he lowered his head from taking another drink.

"Mister Peevey . . . uh," Amory Johnson began, unsure of his ground but fairly certain at least some qualifiers were in order. "You ain't gonna tell us you held that dog up to a bitch and let him breed . . . are you?"

"Nope. I'm afraid we never could do that, and it's a damned pity, too, 'cause that dog was just born to hunt!"

Some sighs of relief escaped into beer cans up and down the long bench, then Mister Peevey took a good grip on his teeth and finished.

"Little dog liked to hunt so much that one day while I was out pushin' him around behind the barn we scared up a rabbit, and he damned near run *my* legs off a-chasin' it!"

Carl shrugged, removing the remains of the customer's side-burns, and realized that the first liar just didn't stand a chance. Johnson was about to challenge the old man when an unusual combination of vehicles pulled up outside, drawing the men's attention away from crippled dogs. It was the new mayor.

"Afternoon, Slats!" Carl slurred. "That's a fancy rig you got there."

"Howdy, Mayor," the customer managed while weakly, and cautiously, raising one hand to wave a hello.

His honor James Obadiah "Slats" Spivey, naturalist, scientist, inventor, entrepreneur, and half-owner of Dilbert's Forge's newest and most prosperous business, squinted and stared at the customer for several seconds before recognizing him in his current state.

"Oscar? That you, son?" Slats asked, then nodded back and lifted a hand to his hat as a greeting to the rest. "Howdy. An' the rig ain't mine, Carl. You know I'm too country for something like that. Why puttin' me in that thing'd be like puttin' earrings on a hawg."

"Mavis seems to like it jest fine, judgin' by the way she's out there rubbin' on the 'holstery and all," Mister Peevey observed, sending a spray of spittle flying as he pushed "hol-stery" through his store-bought teeth.

"Yeah, well it's a gift for Jackson. Christmas time, you know, and we had us a pretty good year."

This was an understatement of near criminal proportions. Lunker Liquor had come on the market at the first of August and was still selling faster than it could be made. Its very scarcity jacked the price of a bottle into a range enjoyed by only the finest perfumes. It wasn't the smell or rarity that made it go; it was a little coupon enclosed with each bottle. Following the next fishing season, some lucky fellow would have his coupon drawn out of a hamper on the Bill Dance Show and would win a chance to be rich and famous himself, maybe.

"What can I do for you, Slats? A trim?" Carl asked, the slur in his voice more pronounced following his most recent, and tenth, beer of the day.

Slats eyed Carl's present victim, shuddered, and then demurred.

"No, thanks. Me an' the wife are drivin' that mess out there down south, and I figure we'll need some road sodas along the way. Gimme a couple of six-packs, cold."

Carl released the customer who lumbered from the chair, surveyed what used to be his hair, then bolted for the door. When Carl returned with the beer, he opened a stray and handed it to the mayor, then popped one of his own and raised it in a toast.

"You give our best to Josh Jackson and that fine lookin' Pamalou when you see 'em, Slats. Luckiest man to ever live in these parts, if you ask me," Carl offered.

Slats raised his own brew to clink it against Carl's, which took several attempts due to the unsteady nature of his target. In the interim, others in the room muttered their heartfelt "Here-here's," "Amen," and "I'll drink to that." While Slats was turning his can up to his lips and drawing down a belt of the cold amber liquid, Mister Peevey made a toast of his own.

"And to the ab-so-lute purtiest female ever to grace this-here county, bar-none! I'd give a pretty to know how Jackson managed to steal her away from here."

Slats finished his long pull and lowered the can with obvious

281

reverence. He smacked his lips, let fly a small burp, then uttered the lone word he felt described the brew.

"Elixir!" he said.

Mister Peevey looked off for a second's contemplation then said, "Yeah, that would explain it awright."

The barber shop crew gathered at the window and watched as Slats and Mavis pulled away from the sidewalk in what had to be one of the more unusual tandems ever witnessed: a Porsche the color of a bloody nose dragging a TechnoTrek trailer on which rode Josh's truck and half a dozen barking beagles, all pointed aft.

Epilogue

Ahead of Slats and Mavis lay a drive of some fifteen hundred miles, and they chose the hour before sunset to begin it. Driving nearly as far south as one can go in the United States, one comes to the Texas town of McAllen and from there across the border to Reynosa. Past the open air markets, past the stalls selling velvet paintings of Elvis and bulldogs in derbies playing poker, past the souvenir stands offering inflated toads shooting billiards, and past a sleazy bar advertising "Juicy Lucy and Her Trained Gila Monster" (Three Shows A Night!), one comes to a road. Not a highway, mind you, though the good padres did intervene and have the road oiled and graveled recently. But a respectable road.

There's one house at the end of this road, two if you count the converted boat house currently occupied by an expatriot Cajun and a female acquaintance he's taken in to teach him Spanish. Separating the road from the driveway is a pair of stone pillars over which is suspended a wrought iron arch with words that exclaim the name of this million-dollar estate of some seven thousand acres: *Los Tres Assjoles*.

Past the arch the drive rambles and bends up a hillside overlooking a lake. It is a scenic drive now, for most of the tangled mesquite bushes have been taken out and a young orchard of citrus put down in their stead. Most of the trees are decorated for the season with multicolored fruits that *could* be taken for glass ornaments if viewed from a distance. The house at the crest of the hill is immense, yet cozied into a surrounding courtyard like an especially large egg in its nest. Bougainvillea climbs in a riot of colors over the walls of the courtyard, contrasting with the white adobé while blending in harmony with the peach-colored tones of the gathering sunset.

Josh Jackson (*Sēnor* Jackson to the locals who all but genuflect when they say his name) leans idly against the short wall of one of three rooftop sun porches and stares off across the placid waters of the lake. He is thinking about getting older. He is also thinking about the diamond ring in the pocket of his cut-off jeans, a gift he's hard pressed not to give a couple of days before Christmas since it implies something more permanent than one yule season. It is for this reason—this modicum of uncertainty—that he is thinking about getting older.

Pam is laying buck naked upon a multicolored serape behind him, gathering in the last rays of the day and feeling the cooler breeze flow up from the water. The light wind robs ten degrees from the air surrounding her breasts, causing her nipples to tighten into hard pebbles. She moans lightly, momentarily distracting Josh's attention from his thoughts then emphasizing them even more when he glances at her. *What,* he wonders, *will happen when I get older and cabbage fever sets in?*

Is there such a thing as cabbage fever? Canebrake seems to think so; said it was common in men once they got older. It drew its name from a similar disorder in that noble vegetable, a condition common to both wherein the stalk would no longer support the head. What then? Would she leave him? Throw rocks at him?

No, he thought, *she'll be older, too. And those marvelous breasts will begin to sag a bit and then what? They'd lay together all flaccid and have to take care not to roll over in their sleep lest one mash some part of the other. But she would still be beautiful. Yes, indeed, when she stood up of a morning and those tits fell—their weight jerking the wrinkles out of her face and neck—why she would still be bee-oo-tiful!* He stifled a giggle at the thought, feeling younger all the time.

After all, getting older was merely part of the great plan. Some irrefutable law of nature cited perhaps as, "As one ages, things shall get larger, hairier, and closer to the ground." A chortle got completely away this time, drawing an unconscious yet beatific smile from Pam and a one-eyed glare from FrankenKat who was busily stalking about a hundred crickets. The insects were gathered under a mercury-vapor security light that was just beginning to blink to life. The wide dispersion of the crickets made even a one-eyed cat's pounce consistently lethal.

"Josh?" Pam called, batting her lashes to adjust to the reduced light. "What are you doing?"

"Just thinking of you, babe."

"Oh?"

"Yeah. You're beautiful, you know that?" he said, then chuckled under his breath.

"There was a bit of the devil in that laugh, Hoss. You wanna explain it?" she said in a husky tone that implied he'd not gotten away with anything.

"Actually, I was just thinking about what'll happen when we get older."

"Having regrets? We're still young, you know. Not even middle aged. Plenty of time left to do or be anything you want to . . . except be a gigolo, of course."

"I thought about giving that a try once upon a time, but I don't think my jiggle's low enough."

"As the doctors say, bring it over here and I'll give you a second opinion," she purred, then curled onto her side with a grace that made FrankenKat's stalking seem gawky in comparison.

*　*　*

Three hundred feet down the hill, thence five hundred feet out across the lake and thirty feet beneath it, Big Un slid from beneath a giant evergreen tree, feeling the tickle of a leftover foil icicle drag over his massive head. The tree was last year's, as brown as the surrounding water and anchored among a forest of similar concrete-footed trees, most of which were mesquite tops. A hapless crawdad scooted and skittered along the bottom before darting into the shadows of the big tree in time to be vacuumed up in Big Un's mouth. Nearby were other bass and schools of minnows, each weaving its way among the tangle of boughs in quest of cover and most succeeding.

Soon the female bass would be wallowing little depressions at the bases of these trees and laying their eggs. Big Un would then fertilize some of these and augment the gene pool of the lake to such a point it would become known far and wide for its scaly denizens. It was unlikely that he would personally contribute to its legend beyond stud service, however, for he had learned a hard lesson about acting on instinct alone.

His experiences along the sawdust trail of fairs, conventions, and sportsmen's do's had taught him well, though he was still confused as to why the first human he'd met turned him loose when the truck stalled. He was even more at a loss to explain why the last one had loaded him onto a series of planes and helicopters and brought him here in the dead of night. He would, however, be afforded an opportunity to prove he'd learned his lesson in about a year. A year and two days, to be exact.

*　　*　　*

Even now, back in the small town where the two transplanted Floridians had first met and made history, people were working late nights bottling and labeling a foul-smelling liquid that, if used as directed, was guaranteed to catch fish. The directions provided with each bottle proclaimed it to be ". . . essence of grasshopper and other selected natural baits," and that it should be applied to the bait then deposited where any right thinking fish would expect a grasshopper to be. Since this meant the user should toss his bait among natural cover, more fish could logically be expected to be caught.

In addition to the directions, each bottle came with a coupon the buyer could fill out and mail back. On Christmas Eve next, Josh would draw out one name on national television, and that lucky individual would be the first to know where Big Un had been released and would be afforded exclusive rights to fish there—all expenses paid, of course—for one week.

As an advertising campaign, it was without peer. In the first month alone they had sold out of supplies on hand and had to scrounge up more pigweed. The farmers of Dilbert's Forge began receiving fat finder's fees for the noxious plant, and some had even started to cultivate it. Among these weed farmers was the Tan family, who had accepted Josh's offer of a lease-purchase agreement on his place.

Josh no longer needed the house since they'd elected to keep Pam's and live in Dilbert's Forge during the summer months. It was, after all, home, and Josh was amazed to find how much he missed his friends there. Now Nguyen Tan rose each morning before daybreak to breathe in the air of freedom and independence. It often smelled like the sewage refinement plant, but that was all right by him. It smelled like his homeland at planting time.